Carol Spearman began writing in high school but had little time to do so during a career in social work, community development, business consulting, and teaching, while going to law school and raising a family. She has self-published four novels. The first, *Firewall of the Mind*, is a thriller related to today's white nationalist political agenda, as is *One Tap Too Many*, written with her grandson. A second, *The Lie Beyond*, was inspired by her work in Europe trying to stop the trafficking of children. Her current novel, *Gospatric – The Forgotten Earl,* is a historical sequel to *A Half Forgotten Dream*, a story of grief, family history, DNA memory and reincarnation. Carol has worked and lived in the US and the UK, where her novels are often set.

This book is dedicated to the thousands of descendants of this forgotten earl. Gospatric somehow survived losing his uncle, father and grandfather in the struggle against Macbeth of Shakespeare fame. He lived to fight against William the Conqueror and participate in three attempts to take back the English throne for the designated heir, Edgar the Atheling. His story has been lost in time and I feel I was meant to write it and share his story with people across the world with names of Dundas, Dunbar, Hume, Ormiston, Hamilton, and many more in their family trees. At times, he seemed to speak to me in my dreams, filling in his feelings about his losses, his love of his family and his soul-searching journey of faith.

Carol Spearman

GOSPATRIC – THE FORGOTTEN EARL

AUSTIN MACAULEY PUBLISHERS™
LONDON * CAMBRIDGE * NEW YORK * SHARJAH

Copyright © Carol Spearman 2024

The right of Carol Spearman to be identified as author of this work has been asserted by the author in accordance with sections 77 and 78 of the Copyright, Designs and Patents Act 1988.

All rights reserved. No part of this publication may be reproduced, stored in a retrieval system, or transmitted in any form or by any means, electronic, mechanical, photocopying, recording, or otherwise, without the prior permission of the publishers.

Any person who commits any unauthorised act in relation to this publication may be liable to criminal prosecution and civil claims for damages.

This is a work of fiction. Names, characters, businesses, places, events, locales, and incidents are either the products of the author's imagination or used in a fictitious manner. Any resemblance to actual persons, living or dead, or actual events is purely coincidental.

A CIP catalogue record for this title is available from the British Library.

ISBN 9781398499027 (Paperback)
ISBN 9781398499034 (ePub e-book)

www.austinmacauley.co.uk

First Published 2024
Austin Macauley Publishers Ltd®
1 Canada Square
Canary Wharf
London
E14 5AA

I would like to acknowledge Helen Robertson, a distant Gospatric relative. We met at Dalmeny Church in South Queensferry, Scotland, quite by accident or was it fate? Months later we began to collaborate on research about Gospatric's life, meeting occasionally in the UK. Helen has also been the editor for historical data. I would also like to thank Carol Masters, Nancy Hughes, Sallee Spearman, long term friend Judy Vrdoljak and my husband Rowland Joiner for their patient reading and suggested edits to the manuscript. I am grateful to my deceased friend, Lady Jane Stewart-Clark, for her kindness to me and my family during our stays at Dundas Castle, over a period of years, when I was writing *A Half-Forgotten Dream*, the prequel to this book.

Table of Contents

Prologue	13
Minneapolis – November 2016	15
Northern Ireland – November 2016	19
Allerdale – The Year 1045	27
Northern Ireland – November 2016	31
Dublin – November 2016	33
Minneapolis – February 2017	36
South Queensferry, Scotland – February 2017	38
Edinburgh, Scotland – February 2017	40
South Queensferry, Scotland – February 2017	44
Bamburgh Castle, Northumbria – The Year 1054	50
Edinburgh, Scotland – February 2017	52
York – The Year 1055	67
Edinburgh, Scotland – March 2017	70
Northumbria – The Year 1055	76
Edinburgh, Scotland – March 2017	79
Northumbria, England – The Year 1055	91
Aspatria, Cumbria – The Year 1055	94
Edinburgh, Scotland – March 2017	102
Cumbria – The Year 1056	107

Edinburgh, Scotland – March 2017	110
Cumbria – The Year 1061	117
Rome – The Year 1061	122
Edinburgh, Scotland – March 2017	125
Aspatria, Cumbria – The Years 1064–1066	135
South Queensferry, Scotland – March 2017	141
England – The Years 1066 and 1067	159
South Queensferry, Scotland – March 2017	166
England – The Year 1067	169
Bamburgh Castle – The Year 1068	180
South Queensferry, Scotland – April 2017	183
England – The Year 1068	186
Edinburgh, Scotland – April 2017	190
Northumbria – The Year 1069	193
Edinburgh, Scotland – April 2017	196
England – December 1069	199
Edinburgh, Scotland – April 2017	201
Northumbria – The Year 1070	205
Edinburgh, Scotland – April 2017	208
Bamburgh Castle, Northumbria – The Year 1070	210
East Lothian, Scotland – April 2017	215
Northumbria – The Years 1071 and 1072	219
South Queensferry, Scotland – May 2017	223
Northumbria – The Year 1072	226
South Queensferry, Scotland – May 2017	240
Flanders – The Year 1073	244
Edinburgh, Scotland – June 2017	250

The Border Lands, Scotland – The Year 1074	257
Cumbria and Lothian – The Year 1076	263
Lothian, Scotland – June 2017	266
Cumbria – The Year 1076	274
Allerdale, Cumbria – June 2017	280
Cumbria and Northumbria – The Years 1080–1085	288
Allerdale, Cumbria – July 2017	292
Lothian and Cumbria – The Year 1087	297
Edinburgh, Scotland – July 2017	301
Lothian – The Years 1088–1093	308
Durham Cathedral – July 2017	315
The Tower, Ercildoune – The Year 1108	321
Epilogue	325
Appendix	338

Prologue

Dunkeld, Scotland

The Year 1045

The early morning mist was rising from the flowing river beside the battlefield, revealing the carnage across the land. The stench of death was overwhelming and there were bodies strewn as far as the eye could see. In the heat of the battle, there was no way to tell who had survived and who had fallen. The eerie silence was broken by one of Siward's men calling out to him that he had found Maldred.

Crinan was lying at his son's feet. Siward joined his men, and they surrounded the body. Maldred knelt over his father with a heavy heart and wept. The plan to avenge his brother's murder by Macbeth might still be possible, but at what price? He had now lost his brother and his father. Siward was speaking of Maldred as King of Scots, but that title seemed far away from this moment of grief. Maldred's mother had begged Crinan and him to give up their plans to attack Macbeth's forces. Maldred's wife had pleaded with him to stay in Allerdale with her and their two small sons, Gospatric and young Maldred, and not join Siward's men. He had not listened to either of them. The need for revenge was powerful. His brother, King Duncan, had been slain five years earlier when he went north to call on his cousin. Macbeth killed his king and took his place.

Some said there was a battle and others, including MacDuff, said it was a pre-meditated killing of king and kinsman. They might never know the truth, but he and his father planned to take back the country, with help from his uncle Siward, the Earl of Northumbria. Their joint army had attacked and forced Macbeth's forces to retreat north. Their next offensive might result in the retaking of all of Scotland. Then Siward could talk of Maldred being king, with the support of the English and Northumbria. As Lord of Allerdale Maldred had maintained the areas of Cumbria and Strathclyde, even when Macbeth had taken over the land north of the Forth.

Maldred wiped his tears and stood, indicating to the men to carry Crinan to the burial area by the Abbey. Leaving Siward to secure their position, Maldred rode beside his father's body towards the place where his mother had been buried. They were all unaware of the remnant of Macbeth's men, who were waiting for an opportunity to attack once more.

The story unfolds on the following pages, as modern-day descendants search for the hidden story of Gospatric's life, his relationship with the King of Scotland and his struggles against William the Conqueror.

Minneapolis
November 2016

Helen stared at the offer on the screen. Too good to be true! She thought for a minute about the implications, the rationalisations that would be convincing and then picked up the phone. Kit answered on the first ring.

"Just about to call you. I was in too big of a shock yesterday to talk about it," Kit said, having seen her sister's name on her phone.

"I don't even want to think about the implications of the election. That's why I looked at an email from Aer Lingus. Kit, there's a super deal to fly to Dublin during Thanksgiving week. We can book flights out of Chicago, a car, and a couple of nights in Dublin. We could rent a cottage and do that trip to Northern Ireland that we have always talked about…"

"Wait a minute. Are you crazy? Thanksgiving week?"

"Why not? We both have the holiday and Friday off, so we only need to take three days of vacation and we can be gone for two weekends."

"Why not? Because it is Thanksgiving, and you and I always make dinner and have the family here."

"That's exactly the point. Why should we? Why doesn't Susan do it this year?"

"Because we always do it. It's tradition," Kit exclaimed.

"Get serious. We do all the preparation. They watch football, barely get to the table long enough to eat during half-time and then they are back watching television, while we clean up and get dessert ready."

"What about John? I can't just tell him to have his sister cook Thanksgiving dinner, because we're going to Ireland for a week, can I?"

"You can. You know he'll be okay with it. It's an opportunity to search for our ancestors, just the two of us for ten days of sister-time in Ireland, where we have always said we would go and never have."

"All right; try it."

"I'm on it. Bye."

Helen was two years older than her sister Kathryn, always called Kit, and both were named after their grandmothers. Their parents had retired to Mesa, Arizona and came back to a cabin in northern Minnesota during the heat of summer in the Southwest. Kit and Helen usually spent a few days with them in January on their way to some beach location.

They had talked about a trip to Ireland since learning about the family history in their twenties. By the time Helen and Kit finished university, two years apart, they were both involved in relationships that led to marriage and children. Helen had been divorced for four years from Jim, who had just recently married an old classmate from their college days, and he was putting pressure on Helen to sell the house and give him his share of the proceeds.

Kit had married John shortly after finishing her degree in nursing. John was older than her and a university lecturer. He was an easy-going type of person, intellectual but with a sense of humour that was dry and quick.

Helen booked the flight to Dublin for Saturday night and early morning train tickets to Chicago on Friday. All the pieces were fitting together. They would land on Sunday and pick up the car at the airport to drive straight north. She started looking for a cottage, confident that the season of the year should provide plenty of options at reasonable prices. She was not wrong. There was a perfect one just south of Enniskillen, the main town in County Fermanagh. As she picked up the phone to call Kit, it rang.

"John says, go for it," Kit exclaimed, as Helen answered. "What have you found out? Can we go?"

"Yes, train on Friday morning, a night and day in Chicago and a flight on Saturday evening arriving early Sunday. We drive to a cottage outside of Enniskillen, with six days there, turn in the car and have an afternoon and evening in Dublin before our flight back on Sunday."

"Sounds wonderful, but John has one condition…"

"What's that?" Helen was surprised that John would make anything conditional.

"You need to tell Susan that she is making Thanksgiving dinner!"

"Brilliant, I'm on it. Should I call her right now?"

"She's coming over tomorrow night for dinner. Why not join us? John wants to see her face when you tell her."

"Tell him that's a little sadistic!"

"She says you're a little sadistic, John," Kit shouted back to her husband. "I am so excited. We need to look at that family history information. Do you know where it is?"

"I think so. I'll check tonight and bring it along tomorrow. It will divert the conversation from the election."

"I think that's what John has in mind. Be prepared to occupy the dinner hour with tales of Ireland."

Helen put down the phone and smiled. What a difference this trip could mean for her. She had a lot of decisions to make in the coming months, not only about where to live. She was the head librarian at a large library, but this was never a conscious choice of career. She had majored in English and had intended to get a master's degree and a doctorate, and then teach at university level. Marriage and children had changed that plan. Now it was decision time. She really didn't know what she wanted to do with the rest of her life. She felt that whatever happened on this trip would be the beginning of something new.

With only a short amount of time to prepare, packing and organising took precedence. Now, Helen and Kit sat waiting to board their flight. The anxiety of getting to the airport was behind them, they had easily negotiated their check-in procedure and security had been reasonably quick.

"I can't believe we are really doing this," Kit stated, chuckling to herself. "I can still see Susan's face when you told her we were not going to cook Thanksgiving dinner."

"I loved the look on John's face when I said he had agreed to help her make dinner!"

"Poor John! That would have been a disaster. He would have ended up doing it all."

"I was sure it wouldn't happen. I just wanted to get back at him for not being brave enough to tell Susan himself. I knew she'd leap at my suggestion to have the dinner catered by that new business."

"She practically ripped the paper out of your hand," Kit said, laughing out loud.

"It looks like they're starting the boarding process. I'm going to hit the restroom one more time. You?"

"You go and I'll stay with our things, then I'll go. We have plenty of time," Helen assured her.

"Can you make sure we have that family history stuff out so we can look at it?"

"Already thought of it. It's right here on the top of my carry-on."

Northern Ireland
November 2016

They hadn't gone over the family papers on the plane, falling asleep instead while watching a movie. When they woke it was light outside and breakfast was being served. When the plane broke through the clouds, as they started their descent to the airport, they looked at each other with excitement. Below them there was the sea and then a plush green landscape they hadn't seen in Minnesota since late September.

"I want to know why they left. How could they?" Kit questioned, feeling an unexpected identification with the people who had lived here on this beautiful green island.

"The simple answer is for a better life, but let's read about it tonight so we know where to start."

Helen and Kit were in the rental car, trying to understand the instructions to exit the Dublin airport.

"It looks pretty simple after we get on the motorway," Kit said.

"Let's just go. The signs should tell us which way to turn. Just keep looking for the road numbers and tell me what to do, and I'll watch the traffic."

A couple of hours later they were approaching a small town and needing a break. After turning off the main road they noticed a pub that had a sign saying off-license.

"We could buy a bottle of Irish whiskey, if it means what I think it does," Kit suggested.

"It won't hurt to ask. I need a toilet, anyway."

They weren't used to the Irish accent yet and found themselves struggling to translate the comments of the bartender into American English. They found the 'loo,' bought the whiskey, and got directions to a meat market and small grocery store. In the next fifteen minutes they had enough supplies to make dinner and breakfast, and some snacks to keep them going to their destination. Dusk was threatening, and they wanted to be tucked away in their cottage with a wood fire burning before darkness fell.

It was only four o'clock when Helen made a call to the place she had rented. The owner's wife said her husband was waiting for them to arrive, and a few minutes later he was waving them into a driveway. He showed them how to operate the heating and locking systems and left. Within minutes of their settling in his wife came by with fresh scones, still hot from the oven.

Examining the family tree material, after their dinner of lamb chops, potatoes, and carrots, they found they were too tired to do much. They could see that their great, great, great grandmother Mary had arrived in Canada with her parents and brothers and sisters in 1822, when she was nine or ten. Her father, John Dundas, had been the Steward of the Marquis of Ely until 1818. It said that the family had been prosperous before illness and crop failures began in Northern Ireland.

It was a slow start the next morning, with jet lag settling in and the dawn coming late, hidden by a foggy mist across the fields. After breakfast they gazed once more at the information about the family, reading sections aloud when they found something interesting.

Helen read, "Ten-year old Joseph Spearman arrived with his father James and mother Mary Moore, and an older brother and sister, Benjamin and Susanna. Joseph Spearman and Mary Dundas met in Lower Canada, married in 1835, and left the area for Upper Canada after the birth of their first child. The Dundas and Spearman families may have known each other in Ireland, where both John Dundas and James Spearman were serving in the military. Joseph's siblings stayed in Hemingford, in Lower Canada, and were buried there, along with their children. Their father James had a Crown Grant of lands which were issued to ex-members of the military. He farmed his land for 15 years and then joined Joseph in 1837 in Upper Canada. He was buried in the Pioneer Cemetery in Banner, Ontario, close to where his son lived."

"There is no mention of his wife, so maybe she died before he left to be with Joseph, who had a lot of kids by then," Kit said. "It doesn't really explain why the family left Ireland, but I suppose they had an opportunity in a new country and a grant of land would have enticed them."

"Well, here is an explanation," Helen read. "The Dundas family had left the difficulties in Ireland behind to join other Irish families, many of them farmers who had been ruined by the fall in prices of their produce and the failure of their crops. The great hope in the new world lay in their ability to be granted or purchase land. There would be no more rent to powerful landlords, fewer taxes to be paid, and no gamekeepers to prevent their killing deer or catching fish." Kit shut off any more reading.

"Let's just drive around and see if we can find this Ely Lodge."

Kit and Helen drove into the estate that had been the property where John Dundas, their ancestor, was Steward to the Marquis of Ely. Now they were looking at an impressive hotel, set on the shore of a glistening blue lake.

"Why don't we go in for a coffee?" Kit asked.

"It will probably be expensive at a place like this, but you're right. Let's check it out."

They wandered through the entrance following the signs to the restrooms and then found that the bar was serving lunch. It was an open room with a fireplace burning on one side and floor to ceiling windows on the other, with views out over Lough Erne. It had a classic feel to the furniture and the carved wooden bar was elegant. Kit looked at the lunch menu the waiter had given her.

"The prices aren't that bad, but I'm not ready for lunch after that breakfast we had."

"I'm not either, but tea with a scone is perfect."

They ordered and sat back with satisfaction, just enjoying the day.

"I still can't believe we're here. I don't really care if we find out anything. I'm just excited to be doing this with you."

"We don't often get this kind of time alone anymore."

"No and I need this. I love John and he's a lot of fun, most of the time, but he's not like a sister!"

"Well, I would hope not!"

"You know what I mean. Do you miss being married?"

"Sometimes I miss the idea of it, of having someone to share things with at the end of the day, but if you mean missing being married to Jim, then no, I really don't. I like not having to check out my decisions with anyone."

"It doesn't seem like he is going to let you make the decision about selling your house."

"It's what we negotiated in the divorce agreement, so I can't complain. The kids are out on their own, so I have no need for a four-bedroom house. I just wish

I knew what I want to do, because once it's on the market it will sell fast. I'm hoping this trip will help clarify some things for me."

"You can always live with us while you're making up your mind."

"I wouldn't want to do that, Kit. I'm ready for a serious change, but if it comes to needing a place for a short time, I can always store things and sleep in your guest room for a few weeks."

"You know it will take a while to find a place and close on it. You can't expect that to happen unless you start looking as soon as we get back."

"I won't be buying another place, not now anyway." Helen looked away, not wanting to say more.

"Okay, but don't even think of moving away! How about going back to Enniskillen to check on the family history centre?"

"Let's do that and then we'll know if they have anything useful," Helen agreed. "We can get some lunch in town and find a grocery store."

The rest of the day passed quickly. They discovered they needed to make an appointment to see a volunteer at the family history centre, so they spent a couple of hours after lunch exploring the shops and getting groceries. By then, it seemed best to head back to the cottage before five o'clock and spend the evening in the warmth by the fire. Still on jet lag, they had another early night.

The following morning was another slow start when they found their car covered in frost. Helen started the engine and put the defrosters on full blast, while they attempted to scrape the windows without any equipment.

The appointment with the volunteer was fun but proved to offer little in the way of information they could use. Some of the data about the English and Scottish owners, who were given land in the 1600s, was only in the records in Belfast. They did understand now that Northern Ireland had been treated as a colony, just like other places around the world. Queen Elizabeth I, followed by James I of England, both thought they could suppress the Irish by settling people loyal to the Crown and the Protestant faith in Ireland. The wealthy landowners needed soldiers for protection and farm families to work the land. Often the landlords spent little time in Ireland, but reaped the rewards, while those who served them faced the hostility of the local Irish. Kit and Helen knew that this colonisation was the beginning of the terrible history of Catholics being displaced by Protestant settlers.

After the appointment, Kit and Helen sat in a local cafe having another delicious scone and tea, not knowing where to go next.

"I think I sympathise more with why they left Ireland for Canada now. It must have been difficult to live in such a hostile environment," Helen said.

"And to realise your placement in Northern Ireland was the reason for the anger," Kit added.

"Maybe we should try the library to find out more about that period when they left Ireland. I wish I knew more history," Helen said in frustration.

"They didn't exactly cover British history in school."

"And I hated history. I just couldn't identify with Minnesota or American history, but some people love it. I wonder what that's about?"

"Don't dump that past life rationalisation on me again," Kit said, laughing.

"Well, think about it. If I had never lived in the US in another life, I wouldn't care about its history, but if I had fought and died in the Civil War, I might be fascinated by it."

Helen and Kit walked the short distance down the hill to the library and found there was a family history section. Helen went up to the young man at the desk.

"Excuse me, can you tell me the best place to start looking for the Scots-Irish plantation history?"

"Yes, and is there anything specific you are interested in?" Sean, the family history staff member, was always happy to help people who were searching for Irish roots.

"Well, the family is Dundas, and they came to this area of Enniskillen in the 1600s and later our ancestor served the Marquis of Ely," Helen answered.

"What did you say the family name was?" Sean asked, looking at Helen with a strange expression she couldn't interpret.

"Dundas was our ancestor's name and he left here in 1822." Helen waited to see what he was going to say next.

Without any explanation, he indicated that they should go to the research room on the upper floor. When they arrived at the second floor, he used a key to let them into a space which had a couple of tables and numerous stacks of books spreading back across the entire floor. Kit and Helen looked at each other with a questioning expression when he told them that a few years earlier a John Dundas had donated his personal collection to the library.

"These are the items from his library," Sean said, as he pointed to a ten-foot wall with books from floor to ceiling. "You can start here, and I will see what I can find about the Marquis of Ely and any other references to the Dundas family."

As he walked away, Helen and Kit stared at the hundreds of books available to them, wondering where to start.

"How should we do this?" Kit asked.

"Let's start on this middle shelf, you from the right side and I'll start from here. Check the table of contents and then look for Dundas in the back to see if there are any pages listed. If there are, take them to the table and make notes, or maybe we might be able to make photocopies of the most important information."

By the time they needed food and coffee a couple of hours later, they had found a family history that was done in Canada, and a book called *Dundas of Dundas*, tracing the family back to a castle in Scotland. Sean had also set several documents on the table.

"I need to eat before I can do anymore," Kit moaned. "Let's ask Sean if we can leave and come back after lunch."

"I hope so because I'm not putting these books back until I go through them. What a find!"

Sean was amenable to them leaving for lunch and finding him when they returned. Helen could hardly eat her sandwich fast enough. She just wanted to get back to spend the time reading what they had discovered.

Back at the library Kit found their grandfather's name in the Canadian book, which was primarily tracking descendants of the family that had emigrated to Canada. They agreed they could contact the people in Canada who published the book and purchase their own copy. A couple of pictures on Kit's phone was all they needed. The other book, tracing the family that built Dundas Castle, was amazing. There were copies of letters to the Laird of Dundas Castle from King James and Mary Queen of Scots, with printed copies of the handwritten text in old English that was difficult to read.

"Listen to this, Helen," Kit whispered. "It's an invitation to the baptism of the son of King James VI at Holyrood House on 6 December 1600, and asks that they send venison, capons and other items."

"It sounds like a pot-luck weekend, doesn't it? Come to the baptism celebration but bring food to share and drinks! Open that parchment at the back and we can find our ancestor. The rest of the family is only related to us at a distance."

They found the Walter Dundas who was listed as the progenitor of the family that went to Ireland; Kit took pictures of the names on the chart and of the pages describing the line of inheritance to the Dundas Castle. Helen asked Sean if they could make copies of a few of the most important pages and he agreed to do it for them. The book was very old but still in good condition. They could see that there were only 119 copies printed in 1897. Next, they both settled down to read as much material as they could from other books with references to the Dundas family. Their ancestor Walter Dundas was listed as Walter of the Magdalens but there was no explanation for what Magdalens meant. They found another reference to James Dundas from the Magdalens, who was accused of treason for sending messages to Cromwell. Neither Kit nor Helen knew much about this period of history, but their instincts were negative about Cromwell because of all the damage he did in Scotland and Ireland.

"That first page we copied from the Dundas of Dundas book talked about Crinan and Bethoc, the father and mother of King Duncan and Maldred, who was the ancestor of our line. Apparently, Maldred had two sons named Gospatric and Maldred. This other page has some information about Dunbar and Gospatric. He was the Earl of Northumbria, before being granted Dunbar and lands in Lothian. I'm going to have Sean make me copies of this and a couple of other items. Then I think we better call it a day and get home before it's totally dark," Helen said, as she rose to search for Sean.

"I'm stiff from sitting here and in need of some Irish whiskey. I'll take photos of this document I'm reading, and we can see if it is important. We can always come back tomorrow," Kit said, rubbing the back of her neck.

A few minutes later Sean was back with the copies, as they were packing up to leave.

"Sorry to ask this, but could I have a photo of the two of you, in front of the Dundas Collection, for our Facebook page," Sean said, in an apologetic tone.

"No problem," they said simultaneously. "Just give us the Facebook page name, so we can send it to our friends," Kit added.

An hour later they were back at the cottage and Kit was trying to get the fire started when Helen brought in some cheese and crackers and poured the whiskey. The fire died to a little red ember.

"You try it. I'm tired of trying to start it," Kit said, in frustration. "In fact, I'm just tired. This research work isn't much fun and it's exhausting."

"The fun is the gems in the puzzle pieces you put together, but it's not for everyone. Let's just leave the fire tonight. I'm ready to relax too." She sensed there would be no time at the library the next day, and maybe not again during the remainder of the week. She knew Kit well enough to understand her need to do something more active in the next few days.

After dinner Helen suggested that Kit plan out a route to explore the area the next day, instead of returning to the library. Helen wanted to look at her emails since Wi-Fi was available.

A plan was formulating in Helen's mind, as she confirmed that Jim was fine with her contacting their friend Mary to get the house on the market. After sending a message to Mary, she mindlessly looked at the rest of the emails, deleting many without reading them.

"I said, how about this for tomorrow?"

Helen closed the computer and directed her attention to the map that Kit was holding in front of her. She agreed to the plan. It didn't matter anymore. She had decided on a path to the next step of her life.

Allerdale
The Year 1045

The small child rose and listened to the sounds that had awakened him. He was right…it was horses thundering into the castle grounds. He heard shouting and he shivered, not so much from the cold but from the knowledge that the sounds were not what was expected. His father had said goodbye to them a few days earlier. His mother had cried, and little Maldred had clung to their father, while Gospatric tried to be brave. Maldred, asleep now at his side, was only five and too young to understand what was happening. Gospatric knew their father was going away to help Grandfather Crinan, in Dunkeld, and that he might not be back for a long time. Had he returned now in the middle of the night? Gospatric rose quietly and tiptoed across the floor of the loft. It creaked as he crossed the landing, and started down the ladder, far enough to see the men talking below. He could not see his father, only some of the men who rode with him, and then his uncle Siward strode in.

"We must get the children to safety. We will leave for Bamburgh yet this night. Wake them and dress them warmly, for it will be a long time before we see the sun," he ordered, addressing the old woman who had come from the kitchen with food and ale. Gospatric saw his mother come forward and collapse into Siward's arms. He slipped back up the ladder, and into bed next to his brother, knowing that something terrible had happened.

The men below talked quietly as they fortified themselves with mutton and bread, drowned in the brown ale. Macbeth might come here to claim this territory now that Maldred was dead. Maldred's men who survived the battle would help shut down the castle and pack belongings for the journey. They would bring the children's mother to Bamburgh Castle, as soon as she was able to travel.

Gospatric's mother Ealdgyth had grown up at Bamburgh, just a babe when her father Uchtred was killed. Her mother Elgiva was the half-sister of Ealdred, who took over as Earl of Northumbria. Ealdred's daughters grew up with Ealdgyth, as sisters. Siward had married one of the sisters, Elfleda, and had negotiated Ealdgyth's marriage to Maldred. When his brother Duncan became King of Scots, Maldred was made Regent of Strathclyde. When they married, Ealdgyth had left Bamburgh for Allerdale to join Maldred.

They made ready to leave, tying the small boys in front of them, Earl Siward taking Gospatric and Robert, his steward, taking Maldred. Siward knew that Gospatric was wise beyond his years and that he comprehended that there was danger. He could not yet tell him what had happened at Dunkeld. They had achieved much, pushing back Macbeth's forces, but Gospatric's grandfather Crinan had been killed in the fighting. Siward himself had declared Maldred King of Scots and made plans to reach Scone to crown him. As Maldred's men prepared for his father's burial, reinforcements of Macbeth's men surprised them on the sacred Abbey grounds. They pushed back the siege once more but found Maldred dead at his father's grave. The survivors buried him with his father and that day, more than nine times twenty good men died with Crinan and Maldred. Siward vowed that he would avenge these deaths if it took the rest of his life.

Five years earlier Siward's young nephews Malcolm and Donald were in danger from Macbeth, just like the children he was bringing to the safety of Bamburgh Castle now. Siward had taken Malcolm to his home when Macbeth had killed his father. Siward's sister, King Duncan's wife, had travelled to Iona to bury her husband, and she insisted on keeping Donald with her.

Elfleda was caring for their new-born son Waltheof and the older boys, Osbjorn and Malcolm, and now she would have two more to care for with the help of Ealdgyth.

A few soldiers would remain to help the servants secure the castle. Some of Maldred's men and their families would come to Northumbria in the following days and the rest would return to their homes with the livestock and anything they could carry. They had no other choice until they knew what territory Macbeth might invade.

The small group with Siward and the boys made their way quickly at first, but the horses were tired from the hard ride from Dunkeld, and it was difficult to keep going at a fast pace. They stopped to rest and lifted the children from the horses, placing them close beside them in a sheltered area. At dawn they resumed their journey and by afternoon could see the green fields leading down to the sea. Gospatric awoke and gazed at the sun sparkling on the water.

"My father is dead, isn't he?" Gospatric asked, turning around to look at Siward.

"Yes, child. He died bravely as a king should. He was burying your grandfather when we were attacked a second time."

"And grandfather is dead." Gospatric tried to push away the tears. His grandmother Bethoc had died in the winter. They had let him go into the room where she was lying in bed. She wanted to say goodbye. She kept crying and trying to hold him, but she was too weak. Then in the spring his mother had a tiny baby and they told him it was dead. He ran from the room and found a corner to hide in where he could cry. His grandfather Uchtred and his grandmother Elgiva had died before Gospatric was born. Now his grandfather Crinan and his father were gone.

"Your aunt and I will care for you and your family," the big man assured him, with tears in his own eyes. "Your mother will follow, as soon as she can travel." Gospatric had always been a little afraid of his uncle. He was so tall and powerful. His voice would boom through the castle when he came to visit them with Auntie Elfleda, who was quiet, small, and so much like his mother. He liked her, and now she and Uncle Siward would be his family. He leaned back again into the safety of his uncle's arms and fell back asleep, with his tears drying on his face.

Gospatric woke again as they galloped into the castle grounds. As they dismounted, people surrounded them eager to hear of Siward's attempt to take back the Scottish throne from Macbeth. Siward and Robert strode through them, carrying the boys into the castle where Elfleda was waiting. She was nursing a small baby and she wept as Siward knelt in front of her to tell her why Ealdgyth's sons were with him. She motioned to the boys to come forward and she touched their faces with gentleness.

"This is now your little brother, your cousin Waltheof. He will be happy to have you here to play with when he grows a little bigger," she whispered, fighting back her tears. "Osbjorn," she called to Siward's son, "please take the children to the table and have Matilda bring them porridge."

A young boy, tall and red-haired like his father, came forward and guided them to a long wooden table. The cook quickly brought bowls of warm porridge for the three boys. Siward and the other men came to the table, next to the roaring fire, and more food was placed before them. Gospatric felt small and forgotten in the conversation that went on, and Maldred snuggled against him and started crying. Elfleda settled the baby in a cradle close to the fire, then came to take the boys. She picked up Maldred and carried him, directing Gospatric to follow.

Northern Ireland
November 2016

After making their plans for the next day, Kit turned on the television and they watched some mindless programs until they were too sleepy to stay up any longer. Helen was relieved to have a diversion from the thoughts that were coming through faster than she could process them. She had considered walking out of her job without notice, then rejected that idea as totally irresponsible. She needed to give at least a month's advance notice, which would be the end of December. When Kit went to bed, Helen quickly checked her emails again. She saw that Jim had suggested a price that would satisfy him. Mary had written that she was picking up the keys to their house from John at five o'clock.

Helen and Kit had another slow start after a leisurely breakfast. They found it was best to wait for the sun to warm the car windows. They set out to drive around Lough Erne, stopping at any sites that may have been related to their family history. They had lunch at the famous Belleek China factory but were disappointed that it was not possible to visit the little islands, where there were often ancient stone circles and Celtic crosses. Mary Dundas was supposedly born on the island of Inishmacsaint. It was more likely that she was born in that parish, and they found a couple of Dundas memorials in the graveyard of the parish church.

On the way back they needed a break and decided to stop at a hotel that must have been one of the manor houses of the English Protestant families who took over Northern Ireland. They were led into a lovely sitting room, with large paintings of rural scenes. The walls were covered in richly textured wallpaper in pastel rose tones. The furniture was elegant and eighteenth century. Helen doubled the price of a cup of tea in her mind. They ordered a pot of tea and scones that were as good as those delivered to them the first day at the cottage.

Helen had not said a word about her emails to Jim and Mary. She was concerned that Kit would find out that John had given the keys to her house to Mary, but she had avoided the subject during lunch. Now it was time to tell her and face the reaction.

"Kit, this trip is already clarifying things for me, and I need to explain. I told Jim I would contact our real estate friend and start the process to sell the house. Mary will get the keys from John and do the work-up for pricing to get it on the market right away." Helen was dreading what was coming.

"You're joking! You did that last night, and you didn't tell me."

"I'm telling you now. I'm seriously thinking about a leave of absence and having some time to travel."

"Travel, where? For how long?"

"Scotland for sure and then I don't know." Helen expected Kit to explode, and she was not even sharing her real dreams for the future. Just then, a couple came into the room. Helen took a deep breath and sighed.

"Let's move on. I'll pay the bill."

Dublin
November 2016

Kit and Helen had been walking around the central section of Dublin since arriving at their boutique hotel in late morning. They had started by looking for a good place to eat lunch and had ended up at a quaint French restaurant. Kit had been distant since Helen had shared her news about the sale of the house. Mary had written that she wanted an exclusive listing agreement and would then present an exceptionally good offer for the house from a couple she had been working with for a few months. This information had put Kit over the edge, and Helen had spent the remaining days in the library while Kit shopped, buying presents for everyone. As they finished lunch, there was still tension between them.

"I'm exhausted and we still have to walk back to the hotel and to that pub tonight," Kit whined.

"What about just picking something up in that lovely supermarket we saw and getting a bottle of wine?"

"Great idea. They had a salad bar and a deli and it's on the way back."

Helen was relieved. It seemed like the first thing they had agreed on for several days.

Back in their pleasant room, with its two comfortable chairs and a coffee table, they set out their elegant snacks and poured the wine.

"I'm glad we did this trip, in spite of the fact that it made you decide to take a leave of absence to travel."

"I was going in that direction anyway. You know that, right?" Helen asked, glad that Kit was finally broaching the subject that had been off the table for days.

"I know, but it's still a shock. I keep thinking of the implications and I don't like them."

"Where is that magazine that was on the table? I thought it said something about Karma and Macbeth," Helen said, ready to change the subject.

"It's on the windowsill behind you."

"Little did we know when we read Macbeth at school that he had killed a relative of ours! I want to read the play again now." Helen commented, as she picked up the magazine. "Here it is, Macbeth's Karma by Vishvapani. The author studied English literature at Cambridge and often explores the relationship between Buddhism and literature."

"What's the name of the magazine? I didn't think I had ever heard of it," Kit asked.

"URTHONA, issue 29. We will have to look that up. We never explored Buddhism in my English literature classes. Listen to this:

As the Buddha continually insisted, actions have consequences, always and everywhere, that comprise a form of judgement. Here Macbeth realises that by killing Duncan he will:

>*Teach Bloody instructions, which, being taught, return*
>*To plague the inventor: this even-handed justice*
>*Commends the ingredients of our poisoned chalice*
>*To our own lips*

This even-handed justice is what the Buddha called the law of karma: a subtle process operating on numerous levels."

"Well, did that happen? Was Macbeth killed by someone else who wanted to be king?" Kit asked, now fascinated by the fact that their ancestral uncle was murdered by Macbeth of Shakespeare fame.

"Not sure. Here's where my lack of historical knowledge is a real deficit. I'm sure there is some distortion in the play anyway, but I have forgotten how powerful Shakespeare's language is."

"Wait a minute. I can check it on my phone since we have internet service."

As she put in the question, Helen read on in the article.

"I found it, Helen. Macbeth did kill Duncan to become king, and most sources believe it was murder, although some say it could have been in a battle.

Next there was a King Lulach for a brief time, and then Duncan's son Malcolm took the throne."

"Wow, what drama! Reading more of this article, I am blown away both by Shakespeare's writing and this analysis. I'm going to see if the owner will copy this article for me in the morning."

"Speaking of the morning, I think we should get to bed. We have an early start if we are going to fully appreciate that full Irish breakfast before our taxi comes."

Minneapolis
February 2017

Helen studied the documents in front of her, trying to take in the information. She was living with Kit, sleeping in the guest room, and eager to be on her way to Scotland on Thursday. With Kit and John at work during the day, she finally had time to get prepared for the journey and all that it might bring. Her negotiations with the library board had been successful and she had a six-month leave of absence, with her assistant filling in for her. The closing on the house had proceeded without much drama. She had a ticket just short of six months, and had booked an apartment in South Queensferry, close to the airport and Dundas Castle, for just a week.

Now, she was trying to plot the locations she was reading about on her map, so she could take the best advantage of the time when she arrived in Scotland. She had photocopies from a document called "Dunbar, Earl of Dunbar" and it said the family was of Celtic origin and were descendants of Gospatric. Crinan, the grandfather of Gospatric, was the lay abbot of Dunkeld, as well as holding land in Dull. She found Dunbar on the coast east of Edinburgh but had to look up Dunkeld and Dull on the internet to get some idea where they were located. She chuckled as she read that Dull was twinned with Boring, Oregon. It was possible to reach all three places from South Queensferry.

Things began to connect as she read that around 1005 Crinan married Bethoc, daughter of Malcolm II, King of the Scots. They had two children. The older was King Duncan, who was killed by Macbeth in 1040. The other son of Crinan and Bethoc was Maldred. He was Regent of Strathclyde when his brother became king in 1034. It was thought that he died along with his father in 1045, having been declared king by Siward, before he was killed in a battle with Macbeth's forces. He was the father of Gospatric and a younger son named Maldred. Helen was amazed that there was any information at all from the eleventh century. She imagined the little boys; their uncle the king is murdered, and the future of the family completely changed, leaving them in danger from Macbeth. Then, they lose their father and grandfather five years later. Somehow the boys survived, but where, and how had Gospatric managed to become the Earl of Northumbria and Dunbar? Something deep inside her was stirring as she read about her ancestors. She was feeling like they were coming alive, like she was seeing them, and sensing their pain.

South Queensferry, Scotland
February 2017

The taxi sped down the hill towards the water, with Helen trying to take in the landscape slipping quickly by. As they reached the foot of the hill, she stared at the huge rail bridge above to her right. The driver quickly turned left into a driveway and Helen could see that they had arrived at the place she recognised from the picture on the internet. The taxi driver hauled out her heavy suitcases and carried them up the outside staircase to the door of the large Tudor building. Normally she would have travelled light but, with six months and two seasons of clothing, she had packed larger cases than usual. The communication she had with the owner said the apartment would be open and the key inside, so she climbed the long staircase with only her backpack and her purse. When she opened the door, she was impressed by the living area, open to a modern kitchen, all with large windows over-looking a bay called the Firth of Forth. After dragging her suitcases up the stairs, she knew that she could not move around like this more than once. She needed a home base, preferably with no steps or with an elevator. Now aware of how hungry she was, Helen left to explore the town, hoping to find a place to buy some groceries. As she started down the street, with a sweeping view of 'the Forth' on her right, she found a place for a quick bacon and cheese baguette and a coffee. The server was friendly and gave her directions to a grocery store. The narrow cobble-stone street along the water led to a steep road going up to the store.

As she started to leave with her groceries, she saw a notice board. There were two flats for rent, and she wrote down the numbers and addresses listed. Helen called the number from one of the notices. The owner answered and was reluctant to show her the flat because he wanted a long-term renter. When Helen said she would sign a lease for six months, and pay the deposit and the first month's rent, the owner was willing to meet her.

The flat was clean and the bedroom and living areas were quite large. The small kitchen had all the equipment she needed for cooking, but there was no table and chairs for eating and no room for one in the kitchen.

"I'm not sure how I can get a table and chairs for the living room. There is plenty of space, but I have no car to move furniture. Would you have any ideas about that, because otherwise it would work for me?"

"I have a gate-leg table I can bring over with a couple of chairs if that is acceptable. It doesn't take much space, but it will open if needed."

"That's perfect. Could I transfer the deposit and the first month's rent and move in next week? I have a place to stay until then."

"Of course. Once you have paid the deposit and signed the lease, you are free to move in."

Helen left the flat with Mr Roberts, arranging to meet him to sign the lease and transfer the money the next day. She walked back feeling excited that her plans were made, and she could start her research with no delays.

Edinburgh, Scotland
February 2017

Helen had decided to take the bus into Edinburgh and ended up at the bus station. She had to check the map to see how to get to George IV Bridge, where the library was located.

She wound up the steep street towards the Royal Mile, with the distant sonorous sound of the pipers stirring something inside of her. Rather than taking the George IV Bridge, she turned right and continued uphill to Edinburgh Castle. She had no intention of taking a tour, but the view from the ramparts was spectacular.

Later, as she found the Scottish Room at the library, she noticed a book on Macbeth and took it to a table to review it. It clearly made him out as a great king, even if he had murdered Duncan I, and she found that irritating. It did contain a lot of history and she wrote down the name and author so she could buy a copy later. Going through the card catalogue produced little that was on the shelves. She realised that much of what she wanted to see had been removed to the remote regions of the library. She was trying to check some of the sources given in the material she had copied from the Dundas collection in Ireland. She took the names up to the librarian at the desk.

"I'm afraid you would be better served at the National Library. They have a reading room and reference material, but you must be registered to use the service," she explained with an apologetic tone that indicated that Helen might not qualify for such an honour.

"Thank you. Can you give me directions?"

"Just cross the street. You will see it and they will give you instructions about the registration process," she answered, still sounding like she wanted to add 'good luck with that.'

When Helen found the registration area, she realised what the woman was talking about. She needed to present her passport but also evidence of where she lived. The clerk was about to reject her for not having a utility bill or something else with her address, when she remembered she had a copy of her lease. She convinced him that she really needed to proceed with the application right away and he finally took her picture and issued her a card. Next, she found she could take only a pencil and her research papers upstairs to the reading room, so she needed a locker for all other items. She finally arrived at the reading room desk to ask for one of the documents she wanted, only to find that requests were only dealt with on the hour and that meant three o'clock. By then, it would be time to go home. She decided to wait for another day and asked about other references. The woman sent her across to another desk, suggesting she ask the librarian to help her search for items that might be more accessible. The librarian, with a name listed as Andrew Ramsay, smiled at her, and seemed grateful to have someone to help. The others had been moderately unpleasant, with the subtle attitude of—here is another silly American searching for their connection to royalty. Andrew, on the other hand, took her list and began searching through his computer.

"We have this one," he said, as he pulled his display around so she could see it.

"Since it is getting late, perhaps I should just look at it and make some copies."

"Let me see. Sorry, but you can only look at it on microfiche and then you could print copies from there," he explained.

"Oh, I hate looking at things that way. Is it possible for you to help me get started?"

"Yes, of course. Just find a place in the room through the door and I will set it up for you."

A nice man, Helen thought, as she sat down. He was also quite attractive, about her age with dark wavy hair and green eyes, slender and not terribly tall, yet substantial looking. She decided he was probably gay, and she was not here to prospect for men. A minute later Andrew was beside her installing the microfiche tape in the machine. As she watched, she noticed there was no wedding ring on his slim hands, with fingers that would do well playing the piano. He left her too soon and she struggled to work the equipment. Finally, she got to the section she wanted to read and was sure she should make a copy for further use. She read on to identify the number of the pages she needed, hoping it was possible to print all eleven at once on some super machine. When she returned to Andrew's desk, he was helping someone else. She observed him while she waited, and she felt that he was aware of her. When the young man left the desk, he spoke.

"Need some help?"

"I have the numbers for the pages I would like to print," she said, as she handed him the slip of paper.

"I'm sorry, but it is not that simple. With the microfiche system, you will have to choose and print each page." Helen's look of dismay caused him to add, "I'll come with you and show you the process. It only takes six steps for each page."

Helen looked at him and realised, from the twinkle in his eye and his smile, that he was making a statement about the idiocy of the system. He patiently showed her the process to print a page and Helen wrote down the steps, trying to grasp the process.

"Libraries are the last to modernise, especially this one," Andrew commented, still sitting beside her.

"I'm a librarian on a leave-of-absence from my position in Minnesota, so I understand. Have you been here long?"

"Probably too long. I used to work across the street, and this was a promotion, but it is incredibly quiet. It becomes interesting when you can help someone who has in-depth research to accomplish, as I suspect you do."

"I want to look at some of the primary sources listed as references in our family's history. We are related to some important characters and events, but I don't want to report them if someone fabricated the information. There seems to be some discrepancies about our ancestor. Anyway, I'm sorry to bother you. I should try to print these pages before I must leave."

"It's no bother. It is part of my job description. If you want me to look at some material while you are printing, I can probably give you some advice about sources that are listed and how reliable they are."

"Here's some of my initial material. I got it from a collection in a library in Ireland, and it's about my family," Helen responded with excitement, as she handed him what she had brought with her.

Helen struggled through the printing process focusing on not missing a step and having to start over on a page. It was a mindless task, but her thoughts were elsewhere. It would be great to have another librarian, one who knew about these ancient British sources, help her look for the right materials. He might even become a friend and she realised that would be welcomed. Much as she wanted to be off on her own, she was used to talking with Kit most days, and having a group of friends at work to do things with on weekends. She returned to the desk to collect and pay for her printing.

"I've made some notes for you on the references. Whenever you are reading the *Anglo-Saxon Chronicles* you need to realise that they wrote everything from the English point of view. It's always a good thing if an event is recorded in more than one source, but sometimes it sounds different because of interpretation." He handed her the notes and went to get her printed pages. When he had collected the money for her printing, he continued. "Will you be back? I think I could help with this research. I'm somewhat familiar with part of the family you are studying…"

"Yes, I plan to be here quite a bit. Do you work most days or on weekends?"

"Usually I work Monday through Friday, unless I'm covering a vacation for someone else."

"Thank you. I'll see you again then, in the next day or two. My name is Helen," she added as she shook his hand.

"Andrew, Andrew Ramsay, as you can see," indicating the nametag. "I'll look up a few things before you return."

South Queensferry, Scotland
February 2017

It was midnight, and Helen was sharing her experiences with Kit on FaceTime. Kir was putting the final touches on dinner as they talked.

"So, tell me what you learned?"

"That the library system is very complicated, that ancient documents are very difficult to find and when you do, you may not be able to make copies of them."

"Is it that white glove thing where they turn into dust in your fingers," Kit joked.

"I think so, but I didn't get that far. I am now the proud owner of a card for the National Library of Scotland. I did make some copies of a few pages that I couldn't look at except on that blooming microfiche. And I think I'm falling in love," Helen added, getting the expected effect.

"What? Tell me all about him!"

"Well, he's a very impressive man. He seems to have survived a bad family situation and grown up to engender a lot of respect. He's a real leader of the people, even though he has royalty in his background and he's a fighter against injustice…"

"Who did you meet? A political leader in just a few days? That would only happen to you. I thought you were at the library."

"I was, and I was reading about Gospatric, and I think I'm falling in love with him."

"Damn you. I thought you were serious."

"I did meet someone, however, a real person. He's a librarian and he was helping me find some of the primary references in the material we found in the Dundas library in Ireland."

"And?"

"There are enough sources to verify that Gospatric was the son of Maldred, that he had Gaelic ancestry through his grandfather, and Northumbrian connections through his mother, who was a granddaughter of King Ethelred of England, but there's more. In some way he was related to Siward, Earl of Northumbria, and…"

"Wait a minute," Kit interrupted. "I can't take any of that into my brain. But what I wanted to know was about the librarian."

"I was trying to get your attention. He's a librarian, my dear, probably gay, and terribly nice. Not my type, although I do imagine Gospatric a bit like him."

"Enough about Gospatric! On another subject…you said you found a place to stay and will be there by Friday. Is it safe? What's it like?"

"Perfectly safe and ordinary. I was hoping to get a little bigger place so you could visit, but we can travel if you come over. I'll be in this village close to the castle and on the bus line to Edinburgh. I've rented it for the whole six months, so any other exploration will be from here."

"John just came in the door. Do you want to say hello?"

"Skip it this time. I need to get to bed. Talk to you in a couple of days."

Helen signed off before Kit could argue. She didn't want to talk to John or to Kit about mundane things.

Helen slept later than she expected but got ready quickly. She had decided to take the train and headed towards the staircase that led up the hill to the station. When she reached the path and saw the steps looming above her, with woods on the edge, she wondered if she had made a mistake. The stairs were endless and led to a path that levelled off and then turned upwards again. She was relieved that she would be heading downwards on the return journey, but this could be a challenge in the dark. She vowed to leave in time to make it back while there was still some light.

Andrew was not at his desk when she arrived, so she put in a couple of requests for documents at the main desk and was given a time to pick them up. She wandered into the reading room and looked at the different section titles, occasionally pulling out a book and checking the back index for names—Gospatric, Maldred, Siward, Crinan. She still had some time to wait and found a book by William Kapelle, called *The Norman Conquest of the North*, where all four names were mentioned. When she looked up Maldred, she found that the author believed that Siward had declared him king before he was killed by Macbeth's forces, along with his father Crinan.

It was time to pick up her documents, which were in a small case. She was given gloves to wear, and the entire process was quite intimidating. Helen remembered Kit's words about the paper turning into dust, as she carefully took the document out. The gloves may have protected some part of it, but it didn't help the feeling that the parchment might disappear as she unfolded it. Dismayed, Helen stared at the illegible handwriting, and then she realised she was looking at Latin. She opened the second box, finding a similar piece of parchment with no hope of comprehension. Then it occurred to her to look towards the end, and she found a word—*testibus*—that indicated witnesses. She tried to read the names she found. It was strange, but some things became clear—*filio* was son of—she thought and *fratibus* was brother. There were other references she understood like *regis* meaning king, but some would require Latin to English translation later. She copied the names and identifiers on her paper. She searched for dates and found none, but she could see that the identification of a king might help with dating a document—also the title was a hint. She added these to her notes and decided that Andrew would be able to tell her if it was necessary to verify items referenced in an article or a book. When she turned her documents back in, she could see that Andrew was now at his desk and alone. She thanked the clerk and went across to the other side of the library.

"Were you successful with some documents?" Andrew asked without hesitation.

"If you call it success to realise that my lack of Latin is going to be a barrier in doing this work. I did copy down some witnesses hoping that might help with dates, but I don't think I'll keep trying to read those old writs and charters, until I know more."

"I have some general reading for you that might give you some perspective," he said, seeming eager to be helpful.

"Whatever you have. I must start somewhere."

"Since Gospatric is from a royal line back to Crinan, I thought we should start there."

"I've also found characters named Siward and Uchtred. Are they important?"

"Yes, let's look at those as well. How much time do you have today?"

"I brought a sandwich, so I can spend the rest of the day. I'd need to get the train to Queensferry before it's too late, but there's always tomorrow."

"I'll just tell the main desk staff that I'll be away from my station and meet you in the reading room. Won't be a minute."

Helen thought how lucky she was to have the personal attention of a librarian, but she knew that it was satisfying to help someone with research, and Andrew was the right person to work with her. She found an empty table towards the back of the reading room and saw Andrew striding towards her with a stack of books. He obviously had selected them in the morning, so perhaps he had seen her enter the library.

"I think it would be best for you to start making a chart of the people you have identified," Andrew whispered. "It's easy to lose sight of the relationships if you don't have a visual of the family trees. I'll show you some family trees in a couple of books, one for Uchtred that includes Siward and one that includes Crinan, Maldred and Gospatric. It takes a lot of work to understand the relationship between the characters, and many historians have made errors because they haven't spent the time to see the connections."

"And you? Have you spent the time?"

"I have to confess that the reason I've spent some time on this is because I'm also related to this family."

"Seriously! How lucky is that for me?"

"Let's look first at Crinan and Bethoc, parents of Maldred and King Duncan. Maldred was the father of this Gospatric who later becomes the earl of Northumbria and then Dunbar."

"I read that King Duncan was murdered by Macbeth, right?"

"Yes, and although there are some distortions in the story, there is a lot of truth in Shakespeare's play, and he was known to be a student of history. Local lore fits with the story that Duncan and Macbeth were related, and that Macbeth plotted his death. Some revisionists would like to characterise the murder as the way things were done, but there is certainly evidence of betrayal of loyalty. You must understand that I am a bit prejudiced on the subject. The next scenario is that both Duncan's father Crinan and his brother Maldred are killed by Macbeth's forces five years later, when they try to avenge Duncan's death. This is where Siward enters the picture. You will read that he brings his Northumbrian forces north to join Crinan and Maldred, at Dunkeld. Some sources say that he declares Maldred—King of Scots. Either Siward leaves with his men, and Maldred is overcome by a new show of force, or there is a pause in the battle and then reinforcements approach and they kill Maldred. In either scenario, Siward escapes and returns to Northumbria. Following so far?"

"And why does Siward get involved in this Scottish struggle? Isn't he English?"

"He's a Dane, but he married into an Anglo-Saxon family and became the Earl of Northumbria through that connection, probably after killing another family member. What is not acknowledged by many historians is that Siward's sister was married to King Duncan. When Duncan was killed, she fled to Iona with her son Donald Bane. Siward took his sister's elder son, Malcolm, to the safety of Bamburgh Castle in Northumbria."

"How old would the children have been?"

"Probably about seven and nine when Duncan was killed."

"So, they lose their father, they are separated, and then five years later they lose their uncle and their grandfather. What about their mother and grandmother?"

"I've read that their mother died on Iona shortly after she buried her husband, but I can't verify that or a date for Bethoc's death. The battle where Crinan and Maldred died took place at Dunkeld, where Crinan was the lay abbot. If that is so, they were buried or left on the field. Bethoc may have been buried there as well. It's a beautiful place today, but I always feel an overwhelming sense of sadness when I'm there. Here's another chart for Uchtred that includes Siward," Andrew went on, not giving her a chance to comment on his sentiment about Dunkeld.

"Can I make some photocopies of these pages, or should I copy them?"

"I'll do some copies for you, but I would start making a large chart yourself that shows the links, and one where you can fill in more information. Let me explain this chart, and then leave you to read about the events and the people. Some things may contradict, and often it is because the readers are confusing the numerous Malcolms, Maldreds and Gospatrics. Uchtred had married three times, and there were at least four Gospatrics in his family, although two were descended from a second marriage of his first wife, and not biologically related to him. His third wife, Elgiva or Algitha, was the daughter of King Ethelred II, and they had a daughter, Edith, who had married Maldred, the father of our Gospatric. You may see her name spelled EALDGYTH. This connects all our characters. I'll make copies of these charts for you and have them ready for you with anything else I might find." He turned and left the reading room, and she was sure those around her were grateful there was no longer whispering coming from her table. She stared at the remaining books and wondered where to begin.

She looked up Crinan and started there. She hardly noticed Andrew, as the two books with the charts were slipped back on the table."

She had a bite of her sandwich and continued eating surreptitiously while reading about Crinan. He was not only the lay abbot of Dunkeld, but the Abthane of Dull, and the Lord of the Isles. He must have been part of some royal family to qualify to marry Bethoc, the daughter of a king, she thought. She read on, finding that when King Malcolm II died, he had no son to take over. He named his grandson Duncan, as the designated heir to the Scottish throne. There was some information about his history with long charts going back to Kenneth MacAlpin, and earlier. That meant that her ancestors were from an ancient Irish family that had settled on the west coast of Scotland. They were a part of the early Christian Church, which was Celtic and related to St Columba.

When she got to the desk, Andrew was waiting for her with several photocopies. She asked him about the cost and got out the four pounds to pay him. She knew that what she was about to say was inappropriate, but she was going to do it anyway.

"Andrew, could I ask you something…librarian to librarian?"

"Of course," he answered, leaning closer to her.

"I was afraid that we were disturbing people in the reading room, and I wonder if there is a way to meet and talk about our common family history outside of the library?" Helen looked down as soon as she blurted out the sentence, afraid to meet his gaze.

"I wanted to suggest that myself but was afraid you would think me presumptuous. I know you want to get home tonight, but could we have lunch or dinner tomorrow night perhaps?"

"If I take the bus tomorrow, I won't mind getting back later. Let's say dinner and it's on me!"

"We will talk about that. I'm finished at half five tomorrow. Is that all right?"

"That's five-thirty, right? That's perfect, and if you know a good place nearby that would be great. I'll see you tomorrow, probably in the afternoon." Helen looked around to see if anyone was paying attention to their conversation, but they all seemed oblivious and busy.

"I'll bring some of my own research," Andrew added, with a sense of excitement.

Bamburgh Castle, Northumbria
The Year 1054

Gospatric was filled with dread. It was happening again, and it brought back the memories he had buried in the nine years they had lived with his uncle Siward and Aunt Elfleda. His little brother Maldred was too young when it all happened, and he had never asked any questions about their real father. He was fourteen now and Waltheof, Siward's son, was nine. That was older than he and Maldred were on the horrible night when Siward and the others came to take them to Bamburgh, because their father and grandfather had been killed by Macbeth's forces. Now Siward had gone north, taking his older son Osbjorn with him, into another battle with Macbeth. Gospatric's cousin Malcolm had come from the English court with soldiers, and they left the next day. They were leaving only a few men to protect the castle and Uncle Siward had told Gospatric that he needed him to be very brave, to be a soldier and to protect the women and children. Gospatric's father had said many of the same things when he left for Dunkeld to avenge the murder of his brother. His father was the Lord of Allerdale then. When he was killed, Gospatric lost not only his father, but the land and the title. Gospatric hated King Macbeth for what he had done to their family, for taking away the throne, first from his uncle Duncan and then from his father, but he didn't think they should fight him.

It was Malcolm who they wanted to be king now. He was the son of King Duncan and Siward's sister. Siward had first fought to put Gospatric's father on the throne, because Malcolm was too young to be king. Now Malcolm was a young man and had been protected and trained for this day at the court of King Edward in England. Gospatric feared that it would all end in the same way. The soldiers would be killed and those left behind would be helpless. They had been waiting for several days to hear if there had been a battle, but so far there was no news.

Maldred and Waltheof were playing together in the courtyard, pretending they were fighting with the soldiers. They thought it was all exciting. They had begged Siward to take them along, but it should have been Gospatric who had asked to join the warring party. At sixteen he was old enough to fight and he had been trained well for this day. Gospatric had overheard his mother, Aunt Elfleda and Siward arguing about it. The women did not want Siward to take him, and they didn't want Osbjorn to go. They must have won the argument, for Gospatric was not included and he was relieved. He watched his two brothers, for Waltheof was as much of a brother as Maldred, sparring below him and prayed they would not die in battle.

Looking into the distance, he could see riders along the coast. As they got closer, he recognised Siward at the front of the soldiers riding hard towards the castle. He could not see Osbjorn or Malcolm beside him, as they had been when they left. Gospatric ran from the ramparts, down the spiral stone staircase to alert those who had not seen the soldiers.

Now, he was standing with Aunt Elfleda, his mother and his brothers, waiting for Siward to ride into the courtyard. He barely heard the words Siward said to Elfleda, that Malcolm was alive and holding the territory north of the Forth, but Osbjorn had been killed in the battle. Siward did not acknowledge Gospatric, Maldred or Waltheof, as he led Elfleda away in tears. Gospatric knew that his aunt had loved Osbjorn, even though he was not her child. That was why she had begged Siward not to take him along, and now he was dead. Gospatric wondered if she would forgive his uncle for his decision. Unlike Gospatric, Osbjorn wanted to go. He was ready to die in battle, he said, but did he really think that he would be killed? Gospatric knew that it was only a matter of time before he would be forced into battle. His cousin Malcolm would have to fight Macbeth for the rest of Scotland, and he would be by his side. The little boys holding onto him now, wanting to know what happened, would be there as well. The only way to escape the danger of war might be to enter the Church. He did not think that would work for him and Maldred, but Waltheof could become a priest. He was already showing signs of conformance to the Church's teaching, often admonishing Gospatric and Maldred for the slightest transgression. He knew the ten commandments and the creeds by heart. Gospatric thought that Elfleda encouraged this. She hoped that Waltheof could go to Crowland Abbey to be trained by the monks, instead of by her husband's soldiers.

Edinburgh, Scotland
February 2017

Helen arrived at the library in the early afternoon, after having lunch at home and catching the bus into Edinburgh. Andrew was busy when she came in, but he acknowledged her as she came through the automatic gate, as if he had been watching for her. She went through the second set of doors to the stacks and located a book she had glanced at the day before. She had the charts Andrew had given her and a large piece of paper to begin her own chart as Andrew had suggested. She started with Crinan and Bethoc at the top of the chart but left a little room above their names to add a link to each of their family trees. From that point, she listed their known children, King Duncan on one side and Maldred, Lord of Allerdale and Regent of Strathclyde on the other. Duncan had two sons with Suthen, Malcolm and Donald, as Andrew had said. Now it made sense that Siward had taken Malcolm to England when Duncan was murdered, first to Bamburgh Castle and later to the court of Edward the Confessor. He was Siward's nephew.

 She filled in the other side with Maldred and Edith, the daughter of Uchtred and Elgiva. She pondered again how their two sons, Gospatric and Maldred, survived when their father and grandfather were killed by Macbeth's forces. As she began filling in Maldred and Gospatric's names, it occurred to her that if Siward had protected his nephew, Malcolm, and had supported Maldred and Crinan in their attempt to take back the throne, then he would have also protected Maldred's children. She determined to see if she could find any proof of that connection. Any child who was a potential heir would have been a threat to Macbeth. She would ask Andrew about it over dinner. She took out a separate piece of paper and started a list of questions to discuss when they met.

 Helen's neck was sore, and her shoulders ached when she left the reading room and headed downstairs to the lockers where her coat and other items were stored. Andrew had placed a note for her to meet him at the pub on the corner, back on the Royal Mile. As she walked in that direction, he caught up with her.

"I didn't know how fast I would get out, but I was able to leave immediately. Do you like Indian food?" he asked, as they reached the street crossing.

"Yes, but I'm never sure where it is authentic when I'm in a foreign city," she answered, noticing his arm lightly guiding her across as the lights changed.

"There's a very nice Indian restaurant on the way down to the train station and it's quiet," he said, as he let go of her arm when they reached the other side of the street.

When they had placed their orders, Helen told Andrew about her supposition that Siward may have protected Maldred's children.

"Have you encountered any evidence of where they were after their father's death?" Helen asked.

"There is little known about Gospatric and Maldred until much later, but…let me look up something I have here." He shuffled through some files, that looked well organised.

"Yes, here's what I'm looking for. I went to Aspatria, in Cumbria, because there is some connection with Gospatric in that area. In one of the documents Gospatric is listed as Siward's son, and I don't find this anywhere else. If Siward took Gospatric and Maldred to Northumbria with him, he would have raised the boys from the time they were quite young, so perhaps they were known in the area as his children. I don't think we can verify that, but it makes sense to me. We can watch for any other clues that might contribute to that theory."

"Well, this Cumbria connection is new, and I have never heard of Aspatria."

"I hadn't either, until I stumbled on a doctoral thesis that contained information about Gospatric's children. It quoted documents of land transfers, all in Cumbria. There's not a lot of information about Strathclyde, Allerdale or Cumbria in the history books, but if you look closely enough you can find it. Perhaps we can make a trip to the area sometime and I can show you what I found first-hand."

"I'd like that," Helen answered without thinking about whether there was a deeper meaning in Andrew's offer. Perhaps he was a little embarrassed by his bold offer because he changed the subject.

"I wanted you to see my family tree so you can understand how we link together. Someone else prepared it and I'm working to verify their conclusions. I made a copy so you can refer to it when we dig deeper into the history of the

Dundas family. Sometimes you must know where other members were and who they married, and particularly the names of their children, to differentiate the lines." She stared at the family tree but had a challenging time following what Andrew was pointing out. The food arrived and they set the papers aside for a while.

After the dishes before them were identified, they began to eat in silence for a few minutes. Helen was feeling a little uncomfortable with the silence when Andrew began to speak.

"Helen, there's a man I know who has a tremendous amount of information about the history of your family and I wonder if you want to meet him. I'm not sure if he would be prepared to do this, so I want to know if you are willing before I approach him."

"Tell me more…why my family and not yours? Is he related to me?"

"It's a complicated story. He came to the library to find out more about the Dundas family. I think his ancestor had married into the Dundas Clan. Since I'm not a Dundas, but another branch, he isn't related to me. We became friends as we worked together on the earlier history…the people we have been looking at and some further back."

Helen sensed something strange about the way Andrew was relaying his connection with this person and wondered if he would now reveal that he was in a relationship with this man.

"What's his name? Do you see him often?" She was hoping to get a different story.

"Alexander Robert Hamilton, the third. He uses the name Robert, and he is wealthy and unmarried. The source of his interest was a woman, an American woman."

"Is that why you are unsure of his willingness to meet…because I'm an American?" Helen asked, now more curious than ever.

"Not exactly. It happened a long time ago, but he kept doing the research over the years. I got the impression, although he didn't admit it, that he thought the American woman held a key to a secret of some kind. He invited me to his home a couple of times to thank me for my work and to look at what he had found out."

"A bit eccentric, perhaps? How old is he?" Helen's interest was growing by the minute.

"I would guess he's about seventy, but he doesn't appear that old. I wouldn't label him eccentric, but there is a secretiveness about him. Perhaps he would be more open with you."

"Why would that be?" Helen asked, now satisfied that Andrew was not involved with this Hamilton character.

"He has this attraction for American women. I have only heard rumours, but…"

"Well, I am willing to meet him. In fact, now I will be disappointed if he refuses. Where does he live?"

"He has a house, or should I say an estate, between Queensferry and Edinburgh. He used to sail out of the marina at South Queensferry, but I am not sure if he does any longer. I haven't seen him for a year or so, but I could call him, I suppose."

"I sense you're not sure if you should do it now or are you wondering if it's really a promising idea?" Helen was confused by the offer and the hesitation she felt in Andrew.

"I'm not sure I want you to be swept off your feet by him…you know…the perfect fantasy of meeting a rich Scot with a manor house," Andrew said, as he looked into her eyes.

"As opposed to a poor librarian, you mean?" She was referring to Andrew and taken aback by his response.

"I didn't mean to imply that you are a gold-digger or whatever that expression is," he said with a defensive tone, clearly missing her reference to him and not herself.

"Never mind," Helen interrupted, as she looked away. She was relieved when the waiter appeared, taking their plates, and asking about dessert.

"I think I should try to call in the morning and perhaps plan some time to get together on the weekend. Would you be available if Robert is amenable?"

"Certainly, but how would I get there, or do you think we would meet somewhere else?"

"Let me check with him. He might be travelling, or ill, or even dead, although I think I might have heard about his death."

"Does he have family? Children? Do you know?" Helen asked, still finding herself curious about him.

"No, I remember that his parents were killed in a car crash, and his uncle had already died when that happened. He has never been married, so no children…well, I haven't ever heard of any."

"So, is it necessary to be legitimate to inherit in this country?"

"A child could be named in a will, but I'm not sure about the law if someone hasn't made a provision for them. Speaking of that, let me show you this information about Gospatric's children. I think you will be particularly interested in the way his daughters were treated."

"Am I going to like this? Gospatric's become quite a hero in my mind. In fact, I told my sister I had fallen in love with him," Helen confided, hoping to also get a certain message across to Andrew.

"Well, look at this chart…first child is Dolphin, and that name is still a mystery because it is probably a Brittonic name. He becomes the Lord of Carlisle and has that title until 1092. Some records say that some of Gospatric's children were illegitimate. I have read that this myth was started much later to prevent a Dunbar from being a contender for the throne. I would think the idea came earlier and may have been because there wasn't a record of a church marriage. We can't find a record of his wife or wives, but only speculation. On the other hand, we have a name for his mother and for his grandmother."

Helen was following now and trying to put notes on her own chart to make sure she had them later.

"Some records have Octreda born next. That is likely to be more accurate than listing the men first and then the females as an afterthought. Her brother Waltheof granted her land in Cumbria when she married a son of Gilmyn, also named Waltheof. Later he gave his sister Matilda land when she married Dolphin, the son of Aylward. This continues with Gunhild getting land when she married Orm, son of Ketel. The land always went to the men, but it resulted in Gospatric's children being landowners across Cumbria. Another sister Ethelreda was married to Duncan, the son of King Malcolm and his first wife. It took some serious sorting to get this far, because Waltheof also has daughters named Octreda and Gunhild who get land from their brother Alan, when they marry. I found all this in the *Chronicon Cumbriae*."

"I was keeping up at first, but now it is too confusing. Where does this next Gospatric come in?" Helen asked as she erased and replaced name after name.

"He was the third brother, perhaps the youngest, but his descendants ended up with Dunbar on the east coast, and land known as Lothian, and that brings us to the next generation. That's where we connect, but you will not find that in the records. Our ancestors were younger sons, so they were less important than the men who would inherit. I have a copy of this for you and you can digest it on your own, fill it into your chart and then ask me questions. Will you be coming in tomorrow?"

"No, I think I will stay in Queensferry and try to get this straight in my mind. I also need to wash clothes and buy groceries. It's all a little difficult without a car, but I don't want to rent one until I can make effective use of it."

"That's wise. We can start a list of locations to visit, not because there is information, but to just feel what it is like to be in places where they lived," Andrew said, as he began to pack up his materials. "Best to get you on a bus."

Helen felt dismissed but had to agree that she wasn't certain how late the buses ran, and whether there were long gaps in the schedule. Andrew said he would take her to the bus station, but she declined. She was ready to be alone with her thoughts. She liked him, but she didn't have that instantaneous feeling of connection she wanted to experience. That was a silly notion, a romanticised one. When she reached the station, her bus had just pulled in and was leaving for South Queensferry in a matter of minutes.

The next morning Andrew called Robert Hamilton and was glad to find him at home; Robert was also pleased to hear from him.

"You say she is an American…another one looking for her royal past in a week?" Robert spoke with a sarcastic tone.

"No, she's a librarian, very interested in research, and she has taken a six-month leave of absence from her position," Andrew countered.

"Well, if she's serious about this, that's different. I have been thinking of a trip to Dalmeny, a drive through the Dundas estate and a meal in South Queensferry. Would you be available to introduce us at lunch tomorrow?"

"I checked with her before I called you and we are both available. Where and what time?"

"I'll make a reservation and call you back."

After the return call from Robert came within minutes, Andrew called Helen to explain the plan.

"He wanted to know if you had seen the Dalmeny Church and the Dundas Castle, so I think you can count on an invitation to visit those places after lunch," Andrew said, with a sense of reluctance.

"Seriously! That would be wonderful. I can't thank you enough. I know exactly where that restaurant is located."

Helen was on her way out the door when the call had come from Andrew. Now, she picked up her backpack and hardly noticed the long walk to the grocery store.

By the time Helen went to bed, she had memorised the connections from Crinan to her ancestor Helias who was the first to take the name Dundas. Somewhere she had read that Robert the Bruce, tired of repetitive names that couldn't be differentiated on documents, decided that surnames were necessary, and most came from land ownership. She had read about Dundas Castle, when it was sold to another family, and what part her ancestors had in building the old keep, an early strategic tower. They had left for Ireland long before the modern manor was built in the early 1800s. Dalmeny Church was also built by her ancestors, and she hoped that Robert would invite her to go with him to the church and the castle. She tossed and turned with thoughts about the next day and worries about whether she would make the right impression on Alexander Robert Hamilton, the third. As she drifted into sleep, she entered a confusing dream where Gospatric and Robert were merged into one elusive figure.

Helen woke with the morning light streaming into the bedroom. At first, she was unaware of where she was. Normally she awoke in the night, often several times, sometimes getting up to use the bathroom. She had no memory of being awake; rather, she felt as if she had spent the entire night in another time. As she opened her eyes, the realisation that she was meeting Andrew and Robert for lunch struck her. After making a cup of coffee, Helen climbed back into bed and tried to remember the dreams of the night. She had an image of Robert from her dreams, and she wondered how close to her picture he would be. It bothered her that she was so concerned about making a good impression, about choosing the right clothes for the day, and not appearing as a 'silly' American. She thought that meditating might be a good idea. She didn't do it often. She preferred to do something active to settle her anxieties, but today it was not possible. The phone rang and suddenly Helen felt as if she had slammed back into her body. She was dizzy, as she tried to get out of bed to reach the phone in the living room.

"Did I wake you?" Andrew asked, apologising for calling. "I thought you would be up. I'm sorry."

"I am up, now. I was meditating and I must have fallen back to sleep."

Helen walked into the entry of the restaurant and glanced to the back where the large windows overlooked the Forth. She saw Andrew immediately and slowly made her way towards him, looking into the eyes of the man gazing at her with intensity.

"Helen, this is Robert Hamilton," Andrew said, knowing he need not have spoken. The two just stared at each other as they held hands, in what was supposed to be a handshake. Robert wasn't tall but had stature. His hair was dark, but turning grey, and his eyes were penetrating as if they were searching for her soul.

"I apologise for staring," Robert whispered, as he let go of her hand and pulled out the chair for her. As he sat down beside her, he continued. "Have we met somewhere before?"

"Only in dreams or a previous life," Helen answered, even surprising herself and startling Andrew. "I'm sorry. I didn't mean to be flippant, but I dreamt about you last night."

Andrew watched with dismay, seeing his unexpressed fear was a reality. Helen was falling under the Hamilton spell. The waiter came to take their drink orders, easing the uncomfortable situation.

When the drinks were ordered, the three of them turned their attention to the menus. Helen was trying to recover from her remark and wondering what to say next. She was relieved when Robert commented on what she had said, without dismissing her feelings.

"I think I would rather go with the theory that we have related DNA, and we somehow recognise each other…all three of us," he said, now including Andrew in the conversation.

"And do we have common DNA? I wasn't sure that you were related to our ancestor Gospatric," Helen commented, hoping her question wouldn't antagonise him.

"Later perhaps than Gospatric, but because I know so much about him, I think I must have an earlier connection with the family. I just haven't found it."

"Helen is curious about Earl Siward, Robert. I couldn't remember everything you told me about him."

"He's an interesting man and a powerful one. Historians believe he came from Denmark to England following King Cnut's takeover and received land to rule under the king. He held some of that territory as early as 1019 and he died of dysentery in 1055, a very distressing event for a warrior-type. His relationship to our story is particularly important, and for that I need to tell you about Uchtred the Bold. Uchtred held Bamburgh Castle and was an Earl of Northumbria. The image of him is not unlike that of Siward—both being large men, with considerable strength and fearless in battle. Uchtred had three wives and how he got them is of interest, but I will not bore you with that now. He set aside his first wife who proceeded to marry another man and produce a couple of Gospatrics to confuse us all. She had produced a son, Ealdred, and he had only daughters. Siward married one of these named Aelfflaed or Elfleda. Siward's sister, Suthen, had married Duncan, who was the King of Scots from 1034, until he was killed by Macbeth in 1040. Siward protected Duncan's son Malcolm in 1040 and later took him to the English Court." When no one spoke, Robert continued.

"Historians still question Siward's motivation for invading Scotland in 1045 and again in 1054. Some of them are even confused about whether there were two dates. They simply have not taken the time to look at the available information. Siward takes Duncan's son to England, then attempts to take Scotland back from Macbeth. He supports an attack by Duncan's father Crinan and brother Maldred. Later he attacks Macbeth again with Malcolm at his side and succeeds in taking back part of Scotland. Siward loses his older son Osbjorn in that battle and his friend Thorfinn also loses his son Dolphin. Sound familiar?" Robert asked, taking a deep breath.

"I think so. I've read about this part. Following the deaths of Crinan and Maldred, I've been wondering how Maldred's children survive, and is their mother alive? I'm also wondering about that second battle, where Malcolm does regain part of Scotland," Helen commented, trying to sound knowledgeable. The food was set before them, and the conversation stopped for a few minutes as they began to eat their meals.

"I've had a theory about how the attempts to take the throne back happened and Robert agrees with me that it fits with later information." Andrew spoke with an authority Helen had not heard before. He continued, as Helen and Robert listened.

"Malcolm and Gospatric were cousins, their fathers were brothers. They would have known of each other, and they may have been together at Bamburgh Castle before Malcolm left for the English Court. They certainly knew each other as adults. We know Malcolm protected Gospatric later in history. Macbeth's forces kill both Crinan and Maldred, who some sources believe was named King of Scots by Siward, but then was killed before he could be crowned. Now, it was clear that Malcolm was the next potential leader to take on Macbeth, but he was still young. Nine years later, with the support of King Edward of England, Siward invades Scotland with Malcolm at his side and wins a victory in the southern areas. Malcolm takes over but is still not king until he defeats Macbeth in 1057 and Macbeth's stepson Lulach the next year."

"And Siward is ill and dying in 1055, a year after the battle with Macbeth, but he has put a change in kingship in motion that lasts for many years," Robert added. "At the same time, he is about to lose Northumbria, the kingdom he had taken over after Eadulf's death, and had successfully ruled for several years. At one time he ruled much of northern England and when he married the granddaughter of Uchtred, he entered the House of Bamburgh. Uchtred had managed to get rid of wife number two who bore him two sons, Eadulf and a Gospatric. When he was offered Elgiva, the daughter of King Ethelred, he jumped at the chance. All we know of their offspring is that they had a daughter named Ealdgyth who married Gospatric's father Maldred. When Siward died, both Uchtred's son Gospatric and our Gospatric would have had some rights to Northumbria. Siward had lost his elder son Osbjorn, and Waltheof was too young to take over. It was an extremely important strategic area and Siward would have known that the King of England would want a powerful leader to replace him. As it turned out, King Edward's wife was probably responsible for the choice Edward made to put her brother Tostig in that position."

"Do you know what happened to Gospatric's mother, Edith?" Helen asked. "I'm thinking she may have died in childbirth."

Robert answered, "I thought that myself until just recently. I have a book here for you to read, called *Mighty Subjects*. It is about the Dunbar line, but of course it covers the history of the first two Gospatric families that are your ancestors. In the Appendix it describes a charter in the 1070s, where Bishop Walcher grants land to Ealdgyth, or Edith. It is at Thornley, near to Durham. As our story progresses you will see how Durham is connected closely with Siward, Malcolm and the Gospatric family. We need to think more about where Edith was during the troubled times and about what happened to young Maldred. We hear nothing about him or Gospatric when their father dies and where were they when Siward dies? Once we have some ideas about Gospatric, we can go on. But now, let us talk about a trip to Dalmeny and a drive around the Dundas Castle grounds. Would you like to join us, Andrew?"

Andrew wanted to say yes, but he sensed that Robert really wanted to be alone with Helen. "I should be getting back to do a few other things today but thank you. Do you think we should plan another time to discuss our findings next week?"

"Of course. Helen and I will make some plans and let you know what we decide."

Helen was aware of Andrew's reaction to Robert leaving him out of the decision-making. She thought he felt left out.

Her concerns were forgotten as she entered the churchyard at Dalmeny. Robert had picked up the key to the church from a cottage across the road and Helen had been staring at the gravestones around her as she waited.

"What's your first impression?" Robert's question was demanding, but understandable.

"The number of graves with skulls and crossbones. I haven't seen another churchyard like this. What's the explanation?"

"Some say they are just representations of death, others that they represent Masonic connections, which is true, but nothing explains the numbers here at Dalmeny. Before we go in, look at the carvings above the doorway."

"They don't look Christian, but I don't know much about medieval religious symbols."

"We can talk about them later," he said, as he unlocked the wooden door with the old key. "I'll let you go in alone and then come in a few minutes. Just experience the space," he added, again with authority in his tone.

Helen wasn't thinking about Robert as she walked through the door. At some level she was drawn into the past. The church was small, compared to cathedrals she had visited, but it had a similar effect on her. It was one of awe, but also familiarity. She felt drawn to the pews across from the pulpit. She sat in the front one and continued to look around. She knew she should take in the details, because Robert would ask her about them, but she could only absorb the whole. She rose when she heard him near the door and walked to the altar, staring at the gravestones in the floor. Her ancestors would be here, buried beneath these stones, others interred in the graves outside, all without names to identify them. She felt weak and shaky, connecting to something in the past. Robert came up behind her and she wanted to collapse in his arms, but she stepped forward and turned to him. He sensed her distress and took her hand. "We'll come back another day when you have read about the church and what it represents. I will give you a book to read. Let's go to Dundas, before we lose the light."

Helen allowed herself to be led out and stood beside an ancient sarcophagus, as Robert turned the large skeleton key to lock the door. He helped her into the car, and she sat with her eyes closed waiting for him to return the key. They drove in silence on narrow country roads, then entered the castle grounds from a back entrance with a gatehouse. There didn't appear to be anyone around to check their entry, and Robert did not hesitate before driving on. Helen was observing the fallen tree on the side of the lane, and then an imposing grey country house loomed ahead. The whole scene was breath-taking, and she could see that the year 1818 was engraved at the top of a turret.

"My ancestors would have been gone by the time this place was built," Helen commented, speaking for the first time since leaving the church.

"Yes, but the fountain on the right side was commissioned by Walter Dundas," Robert answered, as he slowed the car to a near stop before driving through the courtyard at the far side of the house. "Your ancestors built the old keep here at the back," he continued, as he stopped the car at the top of a slope.

Helen stared at the iron gate across the door and then looked up to the top of the large tower. "Can we go in?" She knew the answer before he spoke.

"Not today; we will try to make an appointment for a later date," he stated, as he started the engine. As he drove slowly down the slope, Helen turned to see the view from the bottom of the hill. This was Dundas Castle, her ancestor's home, she thought. Helen saw that there was a farmhouse on the left side in the distance, and cottages and derelict stone buildings on both sides of the narrow lane. Robert was driving slowly, letting her take in the environment. He pointed out the gamekeeper's cottage as they turned right to drive out another entrance with a gatehouse. He pulled to the side of the road and turned to her.

"It's a lot to take in the first time you see it. I would suggest that we go somewhere for a cup of tea and talk about plans. Is that acceptable?" Robert was looking at her, observing her reactions, as much as waiting for an answer.

Helen's thoughts were whirling in her head. Should she ask him to come to her apartment? Should she say yes, or no? What did he have in mind? "Do you have time?"

"Of course. I thought we might drive across the bridge to North Queensferry. There's a small hotel that should be serving afternoon tea."

"I'd love to cross the bridge. I thought about taking the train across just to have the experience."

"The new bridge will be open soon, so you will have this experience and hopefully still be here when that happens." He drove down the lane and confidently negotiated the roundabouts that took him to the bridge. There was silence once again, as Helen took in the sights and the impact of the suspension bridge crossing the Forth and the exit that led back down to the shore on the other side. Robert parked at the hotel, and he was at her door before she could open it herself. It was an older car, but it felt quite luxurious and appropriate for a man like Robert.

When they were settled in a corner of the hotel bar, next to a log fire, Robert asked her how she was feeling.

"Like I am in a dream. Everything during these last few weeks has been so different from my life in Minnesota. I'm just trying to experience it, without analysing it."

"That's probably wise. You're from Minnesota? Andrew hadn't said."

"Yes, it's central and near Canada…"

"I know where it is," Robert interrupted. "Strangely, I received a letter from a man in Minnesota yesterday, from Minneapolis…"

"Really? That's where I'm from. Maybe I know him, but it is a large city. Why was he contacting you?"

"He has some connection to the Gospatric story, and to Dundas…" Robert seemed to fade away into another place as the tea and cakes were served. After the tea was poured, he was still distant.

"What is the man's name, the one who contacted you?" Helen hoped to jolt Robert back to the present.

"His name? His name is Samuel McCarthy. Do you know him?" There was a slight sense of accusation in his tone.

"No," Helen declared, trying to clear up any suspicion Robert had. She was now curious about who this man from Minnesota might be and why he would contact Robert, rather than the library, about a family history question. "What made him contact you, rather than someone like Andrew?"

"It's a long story. I knew his sister, and he wants to see me about the family tree I gave to her. He's a lecturer at a university and he has some time off soon."

"If you're concerned about him, I could check him out…see if he is legitimate, but there are several universities in Minneapolis and St Paul."

"No, no, I'm not worried about that. It just seems odd that he contacted me just as Andrew called me about you, and you are both descended from the same family."

"And then there is Andrew, as well, and you…"

"Perhaps we are all meeting for a reason at this time." Robert seemed to drift away again with this thought.

"What will you do about his letter? I assume you haven't answered it yet."

"I think I'll invite him to stay with me…yes, stay with me, and then all of us can spend some time together. Now back to the Dalmeny church and Dundas Castle, any other thoughts or things you wish to know?"

"I have many questions, but my head is swimming with information. I think I should read some of the material and make a list of my questions. I'm still wondering about Gospatric and his brother, and their mother. Where did they spend the next years? If you and Andrew are right, they were with Siward—but what happened when Siward died?"

"That is a good question and one we could all work on together. I will have Andrew look for documents about that period. I think he has some things he found on his visit to Cumbria. There is nothing in the historical records about Gospatric until perhaps 1061 and again in 1067, so we may need to use other techniques and some common sense to arrive at an answer. I am thinking that I could host you all for a weekend. With us all looking over documents together, we might make some progress. My housekeeper would be happy to have more people around for a few days, rather than just cooking for me."

Helen tried to not look shocked at the thought of a weekend house party with three men at a mansion on an estate, with a cook serving food, and perhaps a butler. "Should I mention it to Andrew if I talk to him? He may be wondering what we are planning next?" She certainly expected to talk to Andrew about what he thought of a weekend together at Robert's.

"Yes, do, but I will talk with him also and I must find out when this man from Minneapolis is arriving. Now, I should take you home and be on my way."

It was clear to Helen that Robert was used to making decisions and acting on them. It was also very possible that this man, the brother of someone he knew, was related to the rumours that Andrew had shared about Robert's relationship with an American woman. He must be extremely interested in spending time with Samuel McCarthy, to be willing to invite him to stay at his home. As for

Helen, the dream was continuing. She could hardly wait to tell Kit that she might be invited to a weekend house party at a mansion with three men, including one from Minnesota.

York
The Year 1055

There had been a year with no battles to be fought and life was quiet at the castle. Malcolm continued to hold the lands north of Northumbria and his grandfather's land at Dunkeld but not the territory further north. Siward had remained at home, becoming more and more ill. Waltheof was too young to succeed his father, being not yet ten years old.

Siward called for Gospatric, who was now seventeen, to come to his bedside. He needed to talk about what would happen when he died. He was so angry that he would not die in battle, but instead from a disease that was overtaking his body. When Gospatric came to his side, he motioned to him to sit and explained his concerns. He warned Gospatric that the family would lose their home at Bamburgh, as well as York, because there were many who wanted the territory of Northumbria.

"King Edward is going to decide who becomes earl. He will not choose your uncle Gospatric; his wife will see to that. You and Waltheof both have a hereditary claim to this land, but neither you nor Waltheof will be strong enough to keep it. I want Elfleda to take Waltheof to Crowland Abbey now, before it is too late. There he will be safe from those who would wish to eliminate him from his birthright in the future. I believe Edward will choose Tostig, his wife's brother, to succeed me." Siward stopped for a moment, taking a deep breath, and looking intently into Gospatric's eyes.

"If I agree to grant Tostig that right before my death, I can also protect Waltheof, Maldred, and you, as well as saving the lives of my loyal soldiers and servants. I believe he will see value in having you in Cumbria, as Lord of Allerdale, as your father was. You are now old enough to assume that position."

"But Uncle, I don't even know where my home is and how would we survive?" Gospatric interrupted, thinking back to his limited memories of the rambling hall where they had lived.

"If there is any doubt of Tostig's support, you must join your cousin Malcolm in the North and follow his lead about going to Cumbria. We will ask my soldiers and servants if they wish to go with you. My friend Thorfinn MacThore has been making the hall in Allerdale ready, since we secured the South from Macbeth last year. I have sent him a message that you are coming soon, and I have also sent a messenger to Malcolm to tell him of our plans. He will defeat Macbeth, and he will be king. You and your brother are his father's nephews, and he will be obligated to take care of you both, as I was obligated to protect him and his brother, and you and your brother. Malcolm understands family loyalty and he will help you. Remember this, Gospatric—there will be plenty of enemies in your life but protect your family, and they will do the same for your children."

"But wasn't Macbeth also family? Wasn't he related to my uncle Duncan?" Gospatric asked, confused by what Siward was saying, when he knew of so much killing among their kin.

"This is true, my son, but Macbeth chose power over loyalty to his kin. There has been a great deal of sorrow in our family because of the struggle to take power away from one family over another. I did this and I will forever suffer for it, and I lost Osbjorn because I wanted to take back the throne for our family." He took another deep breath and continued.

"There is a time to fight for justice and I was fighting for it because Macbeth murdered my king, my sister's husband, leaving her desolate. I took Malcolm from her to protect him, and she left with her younger son for the Island of Iona, to bury her husband among the other great kings of Scotland. She died from grief. I vowed to avenge Duncan's death, and you know that your father and grandfather died in our struggle to defeat Macbeth."

"Some people say that Macbeth has been a good king," Gospatric blurted out, not wanting to hear about how his father and grandfather had died.

"Yes, some would say that our failure proved that Macbeth is the rightful king, that he has been a successful king and more effective than Duncan ever could be. It is true that he has survived all these years and that he has won battles, but I believe his soul is dead. He has gone to Rome for forgiveness and no doubt paid the Church dearly to escape hell, but he lives in his own private misery. He killed his King, his cousins and many more of his relatives and loyal friends. His wife is no better and led him in that direction, but he will suffer for this, as we all suffer for our sins. Sometimes it is better to run away from conflict, rather than confront it. When your time comes, Gospatric, you will make your own decisions. Try to first protect your family and especially your brother Maldred and my Waltheof."

"When is Waltheof leaving? Shouldn't Maldred and my mother go as well? Wouldn't they be safer?" Gospatric asked, not wanting to have the responsibility to protect his younger brother.

"I will speak with Elfleda, but she is torn between leaving me like this and protecting her son. Your mother is angry about my decision for you to go to Allerdale. I don't have the energy to argue with them. We don't have much time left. You can be sure that Tostig has heard of my distress and is nearing here at this very moment."

"Should I leave now with Maldred and ride north to find King Malcolm?"

"The road will not be safe. Let me first send the bishop to speak with Tostig. I think he won't want senseless killing, for we are both sure to lose good men for nothing. I'm weak. I need to sleep. Wake me when you hear that Tostig's arrival is announced by a rider," Siward answered in a whisper, as he sank back on the bed. Gospatric fought back his tears as he left the room to search for Elfleda.

Edinburgh, Scotland
March 2017

Robert decided to send an email to Samuel McCarthy. He hadn't told either Helen or Andrew the reason he was interested in seeing the man from Minneapolis. It had been more than twenty years since he had seen Samuel's sister Sarah. Samuel had written to say that Sarah was ill, and she had recently given him the copies of the family tree that Robert had prepared for her before she left Scotland. Robert believed that Samuel had more to discuss than genealogy and he wanted to hear what that was. He had hoped that Sarah would have shared his research with her sons and had always believed she would ask for more information. He kept researching, knowing he would be ready to respond, perhaps even to travel to see her. The years had passed, and his continuing research had become the only thread to his distant past with Sarah. Now her brother had made contact. He would welcome Samuel to his home and introduce him to Andrew and Helen. He wrote the message, suggesting the offer for accommodation while Samuel was in the area, and explaining the possibility of friends meeting together to explore the family history. He wanted to sound enthusiastic and encouraging, without being aggressive. He wondered how much he knew about Robert's relationship with Sarah and Samuel's mother. He hit the send button and held his breath for a second, willing an answer to be returned in the affirmative. It was afternoon in Minneapolis, and perhaps Samuel was the type who checked his emails frequently.

Robert reflected on his afternoon with Helen. Was he going to fall for another American woman, with that same pleasing accent? She was nothing like Sarah. She was more relaxed, less concerned about her appearance, more natural. Maybe she was more like Mary, Sarah's mother, intuitive and responsive to the information she was reading, forming theories based on more than the words on paper. He would have to be careful to keep her at a distance. She must be twenty years younger than him. She could be his child if he had ever had one. Also, Andrew seemed quite taken with her. He didn't want to hurt Andrew. He had not ever known him to have a woman in his life, but he didn't think he was otherwise inclined. He just seemed content with life as it was, but there was a story behind his exterior demeanour.

Robert had never shared his personal life with Andrew or anyone else. The society he was a part of knew his circumstances, the death of his beloved uncle and his parents, his failure to produce an heir, but they had no idea how he felt about any of it. They discussed economics, politics, the plight of the planet, not feelings and painful experiences. A ding on the computer brought an end to his reverie; the answer was there. Samuel accepted the offer and would land in Edinburgh on Thursday, staying for the following week. Robert answered with a plan to pick him up at the airport and phone numbers were shared. He closed the computer with a feeling of relief and anticipation. Perhaps he should pick up Helen on the way to the airport, use her to break the ice, a go-between. He could size-up Samuel by observing their interaction. On the other hand, he wanted to discover why Samuel was coming. He would think more about it, but for now it was time to tell Mrs Wakefield they were expecting a house guest and that he also was planning a weekend house gathering to compare research on his topic of interest—the Gospatric family.

It was Monday and Helen had decided to spend the day at home, doing house chores and trying to digest the information she had collected. The phone rang just after ten and she expected it would be Andrew, asking about her plans for the week.

"Helen, it's Robert. I received a confirmation from the man Samuel from Minneapolis. He lands on Thursday and will be with us through to the next weekend, so I have made plans to gather this weekend."

"Have you spoken to Andrew? He seemed a little hesitant when I talked with him yesterday."

"He must be there. He has the most complete information on Cumbria and what happened with Gospatric's children. I wanted to ask you if you would go to the airport with me and then have dinner with Samuel in Queensferry. It would give you an opportunity to get to know him."

"Robert, the man's going to be on jet lag, flying from Minneapolis to London and then on to Edinburgh. What time is he landing?"

"In the afternoon. I thought he might want to see the area before I took him home."

"I think he'll want a shower and a bed. He will have been up all night and then had to stand in line for customs at Heathrow or wherever he is coming from. I wouldn't think you should expect too much from him on Thursday."

"Friday, then. I can drive him to Queensferry so he can see the Dundas Castle and Dalmeny and pick you up. We can eat lunch in Queensferry, and I will drive you to my home for the weekend. We can get an early start."

"What about Andrew?"

"He's quite capable of getting here himself after work," Robert answered, in a tone that indicated there should be no further discussion. "Now what about the plans for Friday?"

"That's fine, Robert. Just let me know what time you want me to be ready. I am looking forward to meeting this Samuel character."

"Let's say half-one for lunch, and if we haven't had a chance to do everything, I'm sure you wouldn't mind riding along, would you?"

"Not at all. I will see you on Friday, then." When Helen hung up, she decided to send a message to Kit. In their last talk Kit had said that under no circumstances should she attend a house party with three men, and then followed that comment with asking for more information. Now she would ask her to find out something about Samuel McCarthy. Armed with some knowledge of him, she wouldn't go into the weekend blind. She didn't even really know Andrew or Robert that well, and she was committing to days together. She had already told Kit about Samuel and she didn't have much to add; all she knew was that he lived in the city and taught at the university. She didn't really know if it was the University of Minnesota or some other university. Andrew did call in the afternoon and wondered about her plans for coming in during the week. Helen was relieved to hear from him, and they chatted a while about what to expect, what to wear, and why the 'American' was coming for this visit.

After the call, she checked her email to see if Kit was willing to do a little research. There was an answer from her, filled with information. "No need for research. I have a friend who used to work with his wife, and she knows all about him. His wife, named Helen, would you believe, was a nurse in the obstetrics section with my friend Peggy. Samuel met her when his sister was having twins and it was a family crisis. Their mother had just disappeared in Scotland and was presumed dead, and it was a difficult birth for his sister. He and Helen were married a few years later, but never had any children. Helen was diagnosed with uterine cancer and died within the year. Peggy lost touch with Samuel, but knows he went back to get a doctorate in history, after Helen died. She thinks he's teaching at one of the private universities. He is very legit, single and, according to Peggy, the nicest kind of guy. He and Helen spent a lot of time with his nephews. Well, that is my sleuthing for the day. I will be waiting to hear what is happening, so please keep me in the loop. Bye for now."

Helen spent the rest of the week trying to comprehend all that she could about the history of the Gospatric family. She made charts with notes, wherever it seemed helpful. The amount of information made her dizzy, but some of it was sinking in. Although they had no absolute proof, it made sense that Siward had taken Maldred's sons to his own home. He had been attempting to put their father on the throne, had witnessed the end of that dream with the death of both Maldred and his father Crinan, and would have known how vulnerable the children would be. Looking at the charts, Helen could see that Siward's wife would have been close to the same age as Maldred's wife, and they may have grown up like sisters.

Now that she knew that Gospatric's mother had not died young, she was curious about what would have happened to her when they all lost the protection of Siward. Thinking as a mother, Siward's wife and Gospatric's mother would have been focused on what would happen to their sons. Helen felt the butterflies in her stomach, that bit of anticipation and anxiety that always warned of things to come, both good and bad. She packed up her charts and any information and books she had, and then went to select some clothes to take to Robert's. Robert had a reservation at another lovely restaurant overlooking the water. Despite her anxiety, Helen was looking forward to meeting Samuel, and to the weekend. Hopefully, the American wasn't a pompous bore, a right-wing religious nut, or a beer-belly sports fanatic with no appreciation of history or culture.

Helen need not have worried. The tall, well-built man with blond, slightly greying hair, gallantly put her in the front seat for their short drive, as Robert took her bags to the 'boot' of the car. As they settled into their table and ordered drinks, Helen asked about Samuel's reaction to Dalmeny and Dundas.

"Dalmeny, so much to take in and think more about…the gravestones, the carving over the door, the dedication to Brigid, Adamnán and Cuthbert, and the stained-glass window dedicated to St Margaret with that incredible blue glass. Dundas was another matter. Its beauty and tranquillity are clouded by some powerful memories. My mother and my sister both stayed there at different times. What about you? I presume you've seen both places."

"Much the same as you about Dalmeny. I need more time there, after I know the history. I'm envious of your mother and sister if they were able to stay at Dundas Castle. I am hoping to have a tour, at least," Helen recognised Robert's observation of their discussion and wondered if he was uncomfortable. He certainly wanted to bring them together. When she drew back and took a sip of wine, Robert entered the conversation.

"Samuel is a lecturer in world history, Helen. I think his knowledge will be helpful to us."

"Not at all sure of that," Samuel stated. "You can imagine there is little depth when you are trying to teach young people about the history of the world. I'm extremely interested, however, in the family history. My sister gave me the Dundas family charts Robert had shared with her many years ago, but I wasn't aware of them until recently. I had some vague notions about Dundas Castle from my mother, but no real sense of the relationship of the family to the Celtic Church and Northumbria. I'm a real novice at this."

"I'm not far behind you. I knew about the Dundas family in Canada and their journey from Ireland, but little more until a few months ago," Helen assured him.

"I think we will make an interesting team," Robert said, just as the server arrived, and they paused to make their choices.

The conversation continued, as the server left, and Robert shared his thoughts. "Helen and Andrew have the skills I lack…research ability and perseverance in the search for obscure threads of information. You will both be amazed about what Andrew has found in Cumbria."

"Unfortunately, Robert, I know almost nothing about history, although I am fascinated by certain periods of time now. How did you get interested in history, Samuel? Or do you like to be called Sam?"

"Either is fine. I wasn't interested when I was in high school, and it was all focused on American history. I was reading novels and seeing films set in Britain, Germany and France and feeling connected to those places. I took a few European history classes and ended up with a double major in English and history. I taught high school English for a few years, enjoying the summers off more than the teaching. When my wife died, I just couldn't face going back to teaching in the fall and I applied for a master's program in history."

"And now, do you enjoy university level teaching more?" Helen asked, realising she was focusing on Samuel, and not at all on Robert.

"I do. I can tailor a lot of my lectures to helping students understand the relationship of history to current issues and that is satisfying, and I have several discussion groups for upper-level classes, which I really enjoy."

"I've always heard there is a lot of pressure to publish, if you teach at a university. Is that true?" Helen asked.

"It's there, but I don't mind. I have a passion for medieval history, particularly for the issues around persecution for beliefs. That leaves a wide field of exploration…Cathars, Templars, the Inquisition. Robert and I have found that it is an interest we share."

Helen was relieved that the comment brought the three of them back into the conversation, although she wanted to know more about Samuel. He was a remarkably interesting person, and very nice. The food arrived and they spent the rest of lunch discussing how they might proceed during the weekend.

Northumbria
The Year 1055

Tostig had come and gone, but he was camped nearby waiting for word of Earl Siward's death. He had agreed to the terms that Siward had offered, a bloodless turn-over of the earldom. A small party of Siward's men would provide safe passage for Elfleda and Ealdgyth and their sons, first to the church to bury Siward's body and then to Crowland Abbey in Lincolnshire. The rest of the soldiers and servants and their families who wished to do so would travel west to Cumbria, taking Gospatric back to the home he had left in the middle of the night ten years earlier. The planning and packing were already in progress, but the castle was quiet despite the activity. They were all waiting for the final hour of Siward's life, with deep sorrow in their hearts. He was one of those giants whose physical size and fighting strength hid a gentle heart and a wise soul. He had asked to be dressed in his soldier's attire and to have his sword and shield at his side in his final hours. His wasting body made him eager for death now that he had done all he could to protect those he cared about from danger and potential death. He trusted Tostig to keep his pledge to allow safe passage to all who wished to leave. Siward received the last rites from the priest and fell asleep for the final time. In the early hours of the morning, with Elfleda, Waltheof and Gospatric at his side, Siward slipped away. Gospatric woke Maldred, who was asleep nearby, and led him to their beds. There were others to take care of the body and prepare for the burial. They would need rest for their separate journeys the next day.

Parting from his aunt and mother was difficult but leaving Maldred and Waltheof had been the painful moment. His brothers didn't understand why they couldn't go with Gospatric, having been his constant companions since childhood. Elfleda promised they would visit Cumbria when everyone was safe, but Waltheof couldn't stop crying as the escort of soldiers led the party out of the castle and headed south, first to the church outside York for the burial of Siward and then onwards to Lincolnshire. As soon as they left, the rest of the large party of soldiers mounted and made their way down the ramparts of the castle with Gospatric in the lead and Siward's most powerful soldiers at his side. Tostig and his men were waiting below and Gospatric sat tall on his horse, trying to appear as confident as he could. He made an obvious nod to Tostig as he passed him, hoping he interpreted it as one warrior to another. He had insisted that the more vulnerable stay farther back surrounded by soldiers just in case there was an attempt to stop them and a need to fight.

Gospatric's heart was pounding as they headed west, with over a hundred men, women and children following with their carts and all the possessions they could carry, as well as food for the journey. As he looked back and saw Tostig's followers moving towards the castle, rather than attacking them from the rear, he sighed with relief. He was finally able to consider what it meant to be returning to the land where his father had been the leader. Some called him Lord of Allerdale, but that was too much to contemplate this day. What he really needed to think about was how to be a leader of seasoned men, men who had followed his uncle Siward.

Gospatric had learned to physically handle himself in a battle, but how do you know if you can lead men into potential danger? He tried to think about what had made Siward such a powerful person and felt small in comparison, not just in stature but maturity. Siward had said that he should look to Thorfinn for advice, and he would do that. He just hoped they would all safely make the journey without any problems and have a chance to settle in Allerdale. The thought gave him his first insight into leadership. He needed to be concerned about every person who had chosen to come with him. They had made their decision because of loyalty to Siward, and because they thought they had a better chance of surviving with Gospatric, rather than serving Tostig or making their own way. Gospatric knew then what he must do. It was his responsibility to protect each person in his service and thank them for choosing to come with him. He needed to assure them that he was worthy of their trust by taking charge. He turned to the soldier on his right and gave him orders to send two scouts forward to ensure that the trail they were following was secure and then he asked the soldier on his left to keep leading the party while he turned back with two other men to check on those families who were the farthest back along the road. When they stopped for food and to rest the horses later, he would talk with every one of them and acknowledge that he was aware of their difficult choice in leaving Northumbria, after calling it home for many years.

Edinburgh, Scotland
March 2017

Helen settled her things in her lovely bedroom. She thought it might be the grandest in the house, but she didn't intend to find out what the other bedrooms looked like. Hers had soft cream-coloured walls with lush green draperies and accents. The large bed was covered in a cream duvet cover with a beautiful lace pattern.

Robert had outlined the plan for them. The group would be having drinks in the drawing room before dinner. They had already placed all their reference materials in the library, where they would be working for the weekend. Tonight, there would be general discussion, but they would begin to review their findings after breakfast. Helen changed into her skirt and top, tying her elegant scarf around her neck. She looked in the mirror and approved of what she saw. The excitement seemed to have added a glow to her complexion and she was enjoying the butterflies, because she knew it was about the expectation of a fantastic weekend.

The drinks were poured, and they had a toast to the weekend. Both Samuel and Helen had turned down sherry in favour of white wine. They were waiting now for Robert to initiate any conversation.

"Although I don't want us to work too long tonight, I'd like to establish a few 'knowns' that are not in dispute. We may have historians who disagree with some of our conclusions, but they are always challenging each other. It is quite clear that we have covered a lot of material in detail, searching deeply for information. Most historians are not able to do this on selected topics as we have done."

"They have also not looked at women in many cases, and we have found that much of their confusion or lack of clarity is due to that," Helen stated, without thinking about interrupting Robert.

"Right, Helen, and that is particularly true of understanding Siward's motivation for challenging Macbeth. His family ties and his protection of Duncan's son and Maldred's children fits in that category," Robert said, making Helen feel comfortable with sharing what she knew. "Anything else, that anyone feels strongly about?"

Andrew entered the conversation. "We know that Maldred, Gospatric's father, was the Lord of Allerdale with other titles in Cumbria and Strathclyde. I will show you the data tomorrow, but I am sure that Gospatric was in Aspatria as an adult, and the only time that makes sense is that he went there after Siward died and before he became the Earl of Northumbria in late 1067."

"Agreed, and we will review that information this weekend so we can all follow the thinking of Andrew. Any thoughts, Samuel?"

"Since I've been looking at various sources, as well as what you gave me, I have seen at least five potential years for Gospatric's death. I feel certain that he didn't die in 1074, although I did see some record of his wife dying then and being buried at Norham, but it was on an ancestry site."

"Yes, we know there is a lot of inaccurate information that individuals have put on sites, but sometimes it might provide a clue. Does everyone agree that we have enough verified information to accept the death of Gospatric in 1074 as false?"

"We're not ruling out a possibility that he did want William the Conqueror to think he was dead, are we?" Andrew asked, as they were all nodding their heads in agreement.

"The first novel I read by Nigel Tranter had Gospatric faking his death, putting on a monk's habit and spying for King Malcolm," Helen shared.

"I support the idea that he outwitted William, but we will get to that possibility as we progress," Robert stated.

"I can't be of much help, being new to this research, but I know quite a bit about the period and the Conqueror. William often thought he had more support than he did, not unlike some current leaders. If Gospatric was as popular in Northumbria as he appears to be, he wouldn't have needed to fool everyone. Most of the noble families would have helped him."

A knock on the door announced that dinner was served, and they all finished the drinks in their hands and proceeded to follow Robert to the dining room.

After a lively conversation about their own lives and relationship to Gospatric, they had after-dinner drinks back in the drawing room. Samuel was the first to declare that jet lag was catching up to him and announced he needed to get some rest. Andrew and Helen left the room at the same time, both unwilling to be the last to stay with Robert.

Helen felt that she would never fall asleep, but she drifted away quickly. Her night was filled with scenes from the distant past. It was almost as if there were characters in her dreams trying to tell her something.

Breakfast was a lively affair with all four of them in good humour and feeling excited about getting started. Robert suggested that Andrew begin. "Andrew has some solid information about Cumbria, and I think it will provide us with the foundation we need. Andrew…"

"I'll start with an overview and then we can look at all the documentation together. We know that Gospatric's father, Maldred, held titles in Cumbria from the time that his brother Duncan became king in 1034, and perhaps earlier. Then we have records of Gospatric's children in the area: Dolphin is Lord of Carlisle, and a second son Waltheof is Lord of Allerdale. Waltheof is granting land to his own children, Alan, Octreda and Gunhild, and an illegitimate son with the name Gospatric. Waltheof also grants land in Cumbria to his sisters, as they marry Cumbrians. They take the names of their husbands and their connection to Gospatric is lost over time. One of the sisters, Ethelreda, becomes the wife of Duncan II, King Malcolm's oldest son. Their son William later has land in Cumbria. I've been over the lands they were granted, and it begins to cover the entire area. What connects the time of Maldred, ending with his death in 1045, and the time of Gospatric's children taking over Cumbria in the late seventies and eighties, is Gospatric's assumption of the title of Lord of Allerdale that was his right upon his father's death. In other words, there was a continual line of ownership as a part of the Dunkeld royal family."

"Andrew, we should check that everyone is familiar with Gospatric's Writ, which has caused a lot of controversy," Robert interrupted. "Helen and Samuel, have you read about this?"

"I recently read about the original findings and the arguments about which Gospatric wrote it and when," Helen stated. "I found no definitive answer."

"I'd say the same," Samuel added. "I am hoping we can apply some logic to arrive at our conclusions."

"I think that is what Andrew has done and we need to see if it also makes sense with everything we know," Robert said, as he turned back to Andrew. "Sorry, Andrew, please continue."

Andrew smiled at Helen. "Knowing the confusion, I did look at the possibility that Gospatric, the son of Uchtred by his second wife and born about 1010, was the writer of the Writ. His position in Northumbria was changed when Siward killed Gospatric's older brother, and married one of the daughters of Ealdred, Uchtred's oldest son. Uchtred's family held the area around Bamburgh Castle, not Cumbria. There could be many reasons why Gospatric accepted Siward as earl…fear, his own lack of support, the sheer power of Siward, who held York. Later, following Siward's death, Tostig held Bamburgh and the Gospatric who was the son of Uchtred held a position under him but made some moves that resulted in his death in 1064 at the hands of Tostig's sister. Therefore, I see no reason to associate him with Allerdale and the Writ."

"When you lay out the information," Robert agreed, "it is difficult to see why it isn't quite clear."

"Some historians have simply mixed up the two men and confused the issue. I know how difficult it is to follow this." Andrew admitted.

"I definitely need to see this on paper," Helen was now completely confused. Sam nodded in agreement.

"I will write it out for you. Regarding the date, I found that records in Cumbria say the Writ was written in 1050, but a date closer to Siward's death in 1055 would make more sense. If Siward wanted Maldred's son Gospatric to return to his father's lands and title, he would have shown his support for that action. Thorfinn MacThore who is mentioned in the Writ was a supporter of Siward in the battle in 1054 against Macbeth. Both men lost their sons in that battle. Thorfinn was a powerful leader in Strathclyde and our Gospatric was still young…seventeen when Siward died…he would need Thorfinn's help and guidance. The other option I think possible is that the Writ was not prepared before Siward's death but written to give power to Thorfinn when Gospatric left to become the Earl of Northumbria in late 1067. Reactions?"

"How did you find all of this information?" Samuel asked. "It certainly isn't in the books that I have been looking at in Robert's library."

"It took a lot of digging and reading of obtuse papers, old documents, and multiple sources, but the most significant confirmation was from Aspatria's library. A fellow librarian was extremely helpful."

"I'd love to read all of this information you brought with you," Helen interjected with eagerness. "I'm fascinated by the brother granting land to Gospatric's daughters…taking care of them. It feels like something a father would do to ensure their safety and security, but does it imply that Gospatric was dead?"

"I don't think so. He could have been in hiding," Robert commented. "Let's have a cup of tea and a short walk and then regroup."

The four of them could not stop talking over tea and as they strolled around the estate. They were excited to return to the library, spending the rest of the morning reading the documents that Andrew had brought and making a large chart showing the relationship of the characters. Just before lunch, Samuel asked a question. "Where is Malcolm in all of this? He hasn't completely defeated Macbeth, his supporter Siward is dying, and his father's nephew is returning to Allerdale."

"I think Malcolm was busy, occupied with regaining his father's territory, but still aware and approving the plans to put Gospatric in Allerdale," Andrew answered.

"That would make sense from what we know happens later," Robert added. "Let's have lunch and then Helen can share what she has found about Gospatric's brother Maldred."

When they gathered again in the library, they were ready to hear Helen's information. There had been some discussion about how important it was to have different perceptions of the facts they were reading, and the significance of a woman's perspective. Helen felt comfortable sharing her data and a possible scenario from her reading.

"First, I am looking at what happened when Siward died, from the perspective of Gospatric's and Maldred's mother Edith. Gospatric is older and prepared to take on a new role in Allerdale but the outcome is unknown. Although Malcolm has taken over part of Scotland, Macbeth is still king. Edith is aware of how quickly fortunes can change with the death of a leader. Also, she grew up with Siward's wife and I think both women would want to take their children to a safe place. We are almost certain that Waltheof went to Crowland Abbey with his mother, and I am posing the likelihood that Edith took Maldred there as well."

Andrew chimed in. "That makes sense to me, because we never hear about him being involved with the planning against William in the North. What did you find about where he was later that could support the theory?"

"Well, the best evidence I found is the Doomesday Book. In 1086, Maldred had property called Altor's manor at Wilton. Both his manor and those of the

Lords of Lazenby were in Langberg, Cleveland. It's now known as Redcar, on the coast northeast of Middlesbrough. Another thane named Ligulf had property in that area. There is evidence that Maldred married the widow of Ligulf, when he died in 1080. It was a second marriage because Maldred had children born in the 1060s." Robert interrupted her.

"His descendants have married into prominent families. They maintained their position as one of the most powerful families in England after the conquest, by their connections to the Stutevilles, Middletons and then the Neville families. Once the males started taking the names of the wives, they were lost to most historians as relatives of Gospatric. Sorry, Helen, go on."

"There is a reference that the descendants of Maldred made a bid for the throne and claimed the connection to Crinan and Bethoc but failed to prove it. I found this in the family history section of the library in Edinburgh, and it's in the documents I copied for us. As a mother, I believe that Edith made sure her son and his children were provided for, and you can imagine her arranging strategic marriages. We have the evidence that Edith had property at Thornley, east of Durham. This was confirmed by Bishop Walcher in 1071, but I suspect that she had land in the area much earlier. She could not do much to protect Gospatric from his own dangerous alliances with Malcolm and Edgar Atheling, but she could ensure the survival of Maldred's family. Later, he has land west of Wilton at Staindrop and is known as Maldred of Winlaton. His descendant becomes Lord Raby. His first marriage may have been to a sister of Morcar, but his sons are named Robert, Uctred and Ulkil. It is likely that he was married to someone with the names Robert and Ulkil in their heritage, as only the name Uctred is in Maldred's family. I want to keep digging, but there may not be much more that I can find. It makes the War of the Roses and the involvement of the powerful Neville family more interesting to me."

"Let's all go over this information that Helen has presented, and I will pull out a few books from my library that may add to our knowledge. Dinner will be at seven, so feel free to walk the grounds or rest when you've had enough. There will be drinks in the library. Please help yourself."

They worked silently for a while, but it was difficult to concentrate. When they were working together, their group energy kept them alert and devoted to whatever text they focused on, but now the weariness set in. Andrew withdrew first, with a sign that he was going to take a nap. Samuel looked at Helen, and quickly spoke.

"Helen, I need some help, some advice from a woman. Could we go for a walk?"

"I'd love to. I'm tired of reading endless documents and sometimes feeling more confused than when I started." They left their open books and papers and headed for the front door together. Both were silent for a brief time, until they reached a small garden area, with two comfortable chairs. It seemed natural to sit in them.

"You said advice…from a woman. What it is, Samuel?"

"It's very complicated. You have probably surmised that it is no accident that I'm here. I did come about family history, as I told Robert, but my assignment from my sister Sarah was very specific. I don't know if I should be sharing it with you, but it's so strange that you are here and that you're from home and you…"

"And I am a woman. What does your sister want you to do?"

"She wants me to decide about Robert—find out if he's trustworthy. She met him for a short time, under strange circumstances. Let me just blurt it out. My sister came here to find out about my mother's death. My mother drowned off the coast of St Abbs and there was a strong possibility that it was suicide. It was awful—Sarah was pregnant with twins and the shock put her into an early labour. Her husband Will and I thought we would lose her and the twins. They all survived, but Sarah was never the same again. When the boys were six, she seemed to be doing better and then Will convinced her to come to Scotland to deal with our mother's death."

Helen leaned forward observing Samuel's face as he talked, and she saw the pain drawn in lines that she hadn't noticed before. She thought she should relieve him by asking a couple of questions.

"She had twin boys, then?"

"Yes, Jake and Matt, grown-up now, and she has a daughter Juliana, who was born after she came here. I might as well tell you. My sister got involved with Robert, but she told no one. She came back happy and found out she was pregnant a couple of months later. She had been afraid to have another child, but she was like her old self. No one questioned her. She came here to resolve her feelings about how our mom had died and she seemed to have achieved it."

"But—I'm assuming there is a but…"

"She's dying now, of cancer, and she told me three weeks ago that Juliana is Robert's daughter. She wants me to decide if I should give him a letter from her."

"How does she know this? Surely, she hasn't been able to compare Robert's DNA with your niece's."

"Will died a few years ago, also of cancer, and she decided to send samples of his DNA and Juliana's for testing. Will was not a match, and the only other conclusion was that Robert is her father."

"How will Juliana take that news?" Helen asked, starting to feel the drama of the situation that was facing Samuel.

"If I had to guess, I'd say badly. She was close to her dad, to Will. She was his little girl and he doted on her, as did I. Both Will and I spent a lot of time caring for the boys, when Sarah was recovering. When Juliana came along, they were ready to be more independent, so we transferred our energy to her."

"You didn't have any children?"

"My wife got ill, not long after we married. She had radiation and chemotherapy and having a child seemed impossible. We even talked about adoption, but it became clear that she wasn't going to win the fight," Samuel ended with a whisper and Helen could feel the loss inside of her.

"You lost your mother, then your wife and brother-in-law, and now your sister…all three to cancer. How do you cope with that kind of loss, Samuel?"

"When my mother died, I wondered if I was just pushing the pain away. I had just met Helen, at the hospital. Will and I were trying to care for Sarah and two little babies. I was experiencing the loss of our mother differently, somehow understanding what happened to her in Scotland."

"Were you close to your mother?"

"Very close, closer than Sarah—they clashed, but Sarah was counting on her to be there to help with the twins. The possibility that she had chosen to take her own life was devastating to her."

"And not to you? Did you believe it?"

"It's a long story, Helen, and one for another time. We need to get back and I just don't know what to do about the letter I am carrying."

"What's your gut feeling?"

"That he deserves to know he has a daughter. He may be angry when he finds out that Sarah is dying and has known the truth for some time. She is afraid to tell Juliana. If she does tell her, Juliana might not want to meet Robert."

"We can't control all those reactions, can we? So, if you want my advice, I think you should tell him, knowing you will have to help him deal with the information. What's next if you give him the letter?"

"I gather my sister will then tell the boys. She wants their permission to leave a greater share of her assets to Juliana."

"Why? It doesn't follow, or does it make sense to you?"

"Maybe, guilt. She wants to leave her the house and some money to travel to Scotland. The boys are well-established. When do you think I should tell him? I will have so little time if I wait until this weekend is over."

"That's a good question. My sense is that Robert has few friends and Andrew would probably agree. Although this is a very private matter, he might want to share the knowledge with us. It'll be a shock. He has lost his family and has no one, as far as Andrew knows."

"Is it all right if I tell him that I talked with you about this? I'd like to be honest with him, about how I was feeling and why I needed some advice."

"I think it's a good idea. You will also see how he reacts to someone else knowing he has a daughter. What happens if your sister dies without telling your niece? Will it fall on you?"

"I haven't thought that far ahead. This all happened so quickly. It was a shock to me, but I suppose I would feel obligated to tell Juliana. We'd better go back, and I need to decide if I should approach Robert tonight or wait."

"How about leaving it up to him? Tell him you have an important message from Sarah to discuss with him but are unsure about when the best time would be. Let him decide."

"Good plan. Now you see why I needed a woman's advice," he said, with a twinkling in his eyes that pleased Helen.

As Helen went up the stairs to her room, she overheard Samuel asking Robert if he had a minute. Robert would either agree to talk immediately or would postpone the discussion. She was betting on his decision to talk to Samuel. He had welcomed Samuel into his home because he was curious about Sarah, perhaps still in love with her. Helen decided to take a shower and dress for dinner. Later she would go to the library to see if Robert and Samuel were there.

Samuel and Robert sat in the library, next to the fire. Robert invited Samuel to proceed.

"I think you knew when I contacted you, that there was more to my visit than just learning about the family tree."

"Yes, after more than twenty years of silence, I did suspect that Sarah was choosing to make contact. When you said she was ill, I was afraid you were coming to tell me of her imminent death and perhaps to bring a message. I'm not sure how much you know about our relationship."

"Until a few weeks ago, I knew nothing about your friendship or about the family tree you had given her. I am sorry to tell you that my sister is dying. She may have only a few months, at best. She asked me to see you and left it to me to decide if I should give you a letter from her."

"Do I presume that I have passed some kind of test and you have decided to give me the letter?"

"It was a difficult decision, and I must tell you that I discussed it with Helen," Samuel added, waiting to see the response.

"For a second opinion or for moral support?" Robert seemed curious, not angry.

"Both, but at the time I just felt the need for a woman's perspective. The decision has implications for several people. I was also unsure about the timing, given our work together this weekend. I must confess that at times I wanted to burn the letter to spare future grief, but Helen supported my better instincts to not play God."

"I don't understand. I assumed this was about a sick woman putting her life in order. Now I believe it is more than that." Robert spoke softly and his arm was shaking as he reached out to accept the letter Samuel was handing him.

Samuel sat quietly, as Robert opened the envelope and read the short paragraph that was typed and signed. He knew it lacked any personal quality and was devoid of emotion.

"Do you know what this says?" Robert asked, now in a voice barely loud enough to hear.

"Yes, I do. I apologise for my sister's legalistic writing. At this point she is obsessed with settling her affairs and getting her will completed," Samuel answered, realising that the use of the word affair was unfortunate. "I believe she wanted to assure you that there is no question about you being my niece's father, but you could ask for a DNA test."

"That might be required for reasons I am not at liberty to discuss, but at this moment I am more concerned about her final comment that her daughter may not want to meet me." Robert had tears in his eyes and Samuel stayed silent, letting him go with his thoughts.

"You must know her well. What do you think? Who is she? What is she interested in? Does she know?" Robert's questions spilled out, not waiting for answers.

"She doesn't know or suspect. No one has ever questioned her heritage. You and Will had similar colouring. She has dark auburn hair and green eyes. She's quite tall and slender. She adored her father and was devastated by his death four years ago, as we all were. If I determined that I should not give you the letter, then no one else would ever know. Now, depending on your decision, Juliana's brothers will be told."

"On my decision?" Robert questioned.

"Yes. If you don't wish to have the opportunity to meet Juliana, there will be no further discussion. That is my sister's plan, and I will honour it."

"Wait, what if she dies before you return or before she has the opportunity to execute her plan?" Robert asked with panic in his voice. "Do I have no recourse, now that I know?"

"If you want to proceed, then I now feel obligated to take the responsibility to tell the family, if my sister dies before she gets the chance. I must tell you, that she is so afraid of Juliana's reaction, her anger about the lies, that she doesn't plan to tell her until her dying hour."

"That seems quite cowardly, but then I don't know Juliana. It was the name of the second Gospatric's daughter," he mused. Then quietly repeated, "Juliana."

Just then, the library door opened, and Helen walked in, then stopped by the door.

"Should I come back later?"

"No, no. Come in. I presume you know what we have been talking about," Robert said, as he rose to greet her and escort her to a chair by the fire. "What would you like to drink? Scotch on ice?"

"Yes. How are you feeling?"

"I'll get the drinks," Samuel said, as he jumped up. "The usual, Robert?"

"Make it a double. I think I will need it. You asked how I am feeling, Helen, and I can't really say. Like I just gave birth, like I have just been given a gift that I may never see. I don't know whether to laugh or cry or both."

"I gather that means you are interested in knowing your daughter, if she is willing to meet you."

Andrew entered the library and Robert immediately turned to welcome him. "Andrew, welcome and you have come at exactly the right time. Samuel has brought me news that I have a daughter, his niece, and her name is Juliana. Isn't that extraordinary? We will tell you the details, but I was about to answer Helen's question, about how I am feeling. Let's just say that we must all have a drink in our hands and toast to my new status as a father, a title that has escaped me for all these years."

Samuel filled in Andrew about his task, including his need for support from Helen earlier in the day. He apologised for the diversion from the weekend's task, but they all agreed it was an interesting twist of events. Robert shared more about his own family, in a way he never had before. He told them stories about his uncle and his parents setting him up with suitable marriage prospects and his resistance. All he said about Sarah was cloaked in a comment that the only two women he had loved were unavailable to him.

At dinner, they all needed relief from the questions they were left carrying inside their minds. They enjoyed the roast lamb and drank lots of wine. When they retired to the drawing room where a warm fire awaited, the after-dinner drinks mellowed them even further. They decided to have an early night and begin the process of research anew in the morning.

Northumbria, England
The Year 1055

Gospatric continued to send soldiers ahead to ensure that the passage was safe. They had made only one stop to rest the horses and distribute food. Gospatric took two of his closest compatriots with him, riding back to thank the travellers for their decision to come with him. He saw the changes in their faces when he greeted the men and women with that message. The children stopped hiding when they saw him riding up. The nature of the entire procession changed, as they rode on again turning north. Within the hour, the advancing soldiers brought back a message from Malcolm, addressed to Gospatric, my cousin, the 'Lord of Allerdale'. Malcolm was sending a party south to Aspatria and they were bringing provisions and livestock. Several soldiers with families would be joining them, as well as masons who could help with building. Macbeth was still occupying the territory north of Atholl and parts of the Highlands, although loyalty to him was waning. This group of volunteers had chosen to re-locate to Cumbria, as Malcolm would strengthen his hold on the area, with Gospatric as the lord.

The party rode on, now confident of assistance when they reached their destination. Siward was right, Gospatric thought to himself. Malcolm was loyal to his family, and he would always be loyal to him as kin and king. A lump formed in his throat, and he pushed the tears away, as he thought of Siward, the father he remembered most.

Since heading north and west into the forest, their progress had slowed. The trail was rougher and more difficult for those walking. Gospatric wondered if they should stop before reaching Westmorland on the River Eden, where they hoped to find water and food for their horses and themselves. Then the scouts returned and announced that Thorfinn's soldiers were camped about an hour's ride ahead and preparing food for their arrival. Gospatric sent two soldiers back to announce the need to keep going for another hour before they stopped for the night. He choked back his grateful tears and thanked God for this news. He took a few soldiers and rode ahead to meet the welcoming party.

When they entered the camp, they saw a tent set up and several fires burning with meat on a spit and pots boiling. The tiny bit of anxiety he had felt disappeared. He swore he would, from that day forward, be faithful to all those who had helped on this journey, supporting and fighting for them if necessary. As he dismounted, a young man came forward to greet him. He was dressed in ordinary clothes, but he carried himself like a soldier. Gospatric could hardly look at him. His attention was captured by the fair-haired woman at his side. Gospatric pulled his gaze from the green eyes that met his and greeted the impressive man who was about his age and size.

"I am Osulf, sent by Thorfinn to greet you and provide safe passage, Gospatric," he announced, as he put out his hand with a welcoming smile. "This is Gunhilda, Thorfinn's daughter." Gospatric felt strange, as he shyly nodded to this young woman, who he feared was connected to Osulf.

"We have been sent to assist you. We have prepared a tent for you to rest in while we bring you food and drink," Gunhilda said quietly.

Still bewitched by the beautiful girl beside Osulf, Gospatric spoke, hoping his voice would sound confident and bold.

"We thank you for your generosity, but we will sit among your people and mine, in order to acquaint ourselves with each other."

"Avail yourself of the water to wash then, Sir, and join us at our make-shift table. I see the others are arriving and we will help them to join our families while we care for the horses. Gunhilda, please show them to the tent to wash and then to our table."

"Please follow me," she said as she opened the tent flap and disappeared. Gospatric was entranced with her voice, as he followed behind her.

Well-fed and in high spirits, the enlarged party moved on in the morning towards the coastal area east of the sea. Osulf and Gunhilda rode with Gospatric at the front of the party with both Siward's and Thorfinn's soldiers spread throughout the procession, to ensure that no one was hurt or left behind. Gospatric could hardly focus close to Gunhilda, therefore he placed himself on the far side of Osulf. He wanted to find out more about Malcolm, who had left Bamburgh for the English court while Gospatric was still young. Osulf talked freely of his lord, whom he admired and feared.

"I believe he will be king of a Scotland that will include all of Cumbria and perhaps even Northumbria. That is certainly his intention and most of the nobles are behind him. His nature is fierce, and it is best not to anger him. Some do not trust him because he spent so much time with the English, but I say to them that he is truly one of us. His grandfather Crinan, and yours as well, was a descendant of the clan of Columba, and Malcolm supports the Celtic way. He is loyal, as you have seen, to those he considers kin and to his supporters. But for those who stand against him, he will have no mercy."

Gospatric wanted to ask Osulf about Gunhilda but there was no opportunity. If she were his wife, he would have said this when he introduced her. He looked across at her, meeting her eyes. She did not turn away but smiled at him in a knowing way. He wondered if it was possible that Thorfinn wanted Gospatric to meet her like this, because he had plans for the two of them. Remembering his title as Lord of Allerdale, he straightened up and held his head high. He was young, but he was ready to assume his father's title, and he would need a wife by his side. Gunhilda might be only fifteen or sixteen, but she seemed older. She had fair hair, plaited under her hood. He remembered how intense her eyes were, when he had looked at her across the table when they were eating. She would have beautiful children. They could be his children and their alliance would cement Thorfinn's support. He had felt certain that he did not want someone arranging a marriage for him, but if this was the choice of Siward and Malcolm, he was more than willing to accept. He wondered how he should approach Thorfinn but first he had to find out if she was already promised to Osulf.

Aspatria, Cumbria
The Year 1055

Gospatric was eager to make it to the coast. The group was in high spirits after the food and camaraderie with the Cumbrians and he felt they could make it by evening. He was now riding beside Gunhilda and finding her even more enchanting than at their first encounter. Osulf often left them at the front of the party, either riding ahead to ensure that the path was clear or checking out the end of the march, to see if everyone was handling the trip all right. He would report his findings to Gospatric and then move on. There did not seem to be any energy flowing between him and Gunhilda, and Gospatric was becoming more convinced that she was feeling comfortable with him. She spoke of the sadness of the past year, when the soldiers returned, bringing her brother Dolphin's body back with them for a quick burial. Her mother had died when Gunhilda was born, and the remaining family had become very close. Gunhilda had begged her father not to take Dolphin with him, but of course her brother wanted to go. After Dolphin's death, his wife had returned to her family with their child. Now Gunhilda and her father were the only ones left. Gospatric confided his feelings of loss for Siward and for leaving his family. She knew that Siward had also lost a son and a nephew in the battle at Dunkeld, but did not know about his younger son, Waltheof.

"Osbjorn's mother died and Waltheof is the son of Siward's second wife, Elfleda. My mother and Elfleda were raised like sisters at Bamburgh. My mother was the only child of Uchtred's third marriage. He died shortly after my mother was born and Elfleda was a granddaughter from his first marriage," Gospatric explained.

"I heard that Uchtred had a way of setting aside his wives and getting offered a new one. Were you named after his son?"

"I think so. He was my mother's half-brother, and they were probably growing up together at Bamburgh. My mother chose my name, but my brother Maldred is named after my father."

"No religious names, then, in your family?"

"Not biblical, but my father came from an old Celtic family, one that goes back to Saint Columba. You know that my grandfather was the lay abbot at Dunkeld, and the Abthane of Dull?"

"Yea, I have heard of this, and my father says that he was also the Lord of the Isles. My father was close to your father and hoped he would be king if they succeeded in overcoming Macbeth."

"Siward told me that he had named him king, but they were overcome by another wave of Macbeth's forces when they were burying my grandfather. So many people in my family have died because of wanting to have the throne of Scotland. It almost makes me afraid of being the Lord of Allerdale."

"You won't have to fight for the throne, now. Malcolm is strong and he will be a good king."

"But what if he is killed? Who is next? He has no children, and he is older than I am. I am hoping I can be a good leader here and help him."

"He has the support of the King of England and that means peace for all of us," Gunhilda said softly.

"Yes, Malcolm stayed with Siward when his father was murdered by Macbeth and then was at the court of King Edward. Siward knew he might be killed by Macbeth. Donald is a brother of Malcolm's, and he could be king if something happens to Malcolm, but we know little of him. Siward told me that his sister took Donald with her to Iona to bury King Duncan, and he has not returned."

"I have heard of him, but I don't know where he is now…one of the islands I believe."

"Siward's sister died on Iona. It made him very angry, and he wanted to bring Donald back to Bamburgh, but it never happened. I think Siward was busy trying to raise an army and the support of the English, and it took him five years to attack Macbeth and avenge my uncle's death. I don't remember much about those years, except that moment when my father left for Dunkeld with his men, and then Uncle Siward coming back without my father. My mother was not able to take care of us for a while, and I grew up closer to my aunt Elfleda. She had her own new baby, Waltheof, but she kept Maldred and me close to her."

"Siward's son Osbjorn was killed in the battle, like my brother, wasn't he?"

"Yes, I wonder if they knew each other. Osbjorn wanted to go but I didn't. I was afraid that I would die like my grandfather and father. My mother and my aunt wouldn't let Siward take me, and I was glad. Do you think I was a coward?"

"No, not at all. I think sometimes the most important thing is to stay alive."

"To fight another day or perhaps not to fight at all? I want to have children, but I don't want them to grow up without a father. What do you think about having children? Are you afraid? Your mother died having you…" Gospatric stumbled through his words, immediately sorry he was so personal.

"I suppose I am a little afraid. It would hurt so much to look at your babe and know you couldn't be there to hold him and help him grow up."

Gospatric loved her from that moment, watching her expression as she thought about leaving a babe behind with no mother. He wanted to ask her right then if she would be his wife, but he knew he shouldn't. Instead, he decided he could tease her a bit.

"How many children should we have then?"

"You and me? Well, I must name my first son Dolphin and my first girl after my mother."

"What about my mother, she'll want me to name my first girl after her and I will want to name my first son after Waltheof. He is like my little brother."

"That's four already and your mother will want you to have children named after her parents."

"And I must have a Gospatric, mustn't I?"

"I think that now makes seven, so what shall we do about this?" Gunhilda continued to tease him.

"I could ask your father for you in marriage, but I haven't even met him. He might not like me. He might not approve of our plan."

"Oh, my father will approve, but you will have to ask the king because you are an important lord now." Gunhilda laughed as she said it and smiled at him. He smiled back, feeling something inside him that he had never felt before.

"I will do that then, send a message to the king, but only if your father approves."

"What about me? Will you ask me if I want to marry you?" Gospatric blushed. He felt flustered. He had started this as a joke and then proceeded as if it was real.

"I'm sorry, I didn't mean to presume…"

"Don't worry. I will say yes if you ask me."

Osulf rode up to them just then, delivering the message that he had seen the coast from his ride ahead and it would not be long before they reached the settlement at Aspatria. He remained with the two of them for the rest of the journey as they headed southwest towards the sea.

There was much to do when they arrived. There was activity all around them when they rode into the hamlet surrounding the crest of a hill. Gospatric had some vague memory of this place from his childhood. Thorfinn was there to greet them, and he took Gospatric with him to meet the settlers who had been sent by Malcolm, and to see the buildings they were erecting. They surveyed the livestock and talked about planting grains and vegetables as soon as possible. Gospatric's head was filled with things he had never had to think about. How could he be the lord of these people who knew so much more than he did? He wanted to see Gunhilda, to talk with her about his fears and his hopes, but she was nowhere in sight. Finally, Thorfinn said it was time to see his new home. He apologised that not all the repairs were finished, and that the hall was much smaller than the great Bamburgh Castle. He invited Gospatric and his companions to follow him, riding west towards a wide path winding up the hill. As Gospatric entered the courtyard at the top of the incline, he felt a lump tightening in his throat. He remembered something, more a feeling of despair than of surroundings. They entered the hall, where a large welcoming fire was burning. He felt like he was in a dream, as servants came to place food on the table for all of them. Eating a hearty meal of fish and venison, and drinking the mead, he hardly heard the voice of Thorfinn asking them to raise their glasses to the Lord of Allerdale and to Malcolm, the rightful King of Scots.

Gospatric woke in the early dawn, unable to understand where he was. Gradually his thoughts went back to the previous night, the celebration, and the drinking of too much mead. After relieving himself, he crawled back onto the primitive platform covered in straw. Thorfinn was right. It was not Bamburgh, but it was in a high position overlooking the sea. Much smaller than the fortress where he had lived for the past ten years, it felt right to be here, to return to the home he had been taken from in the middle of the night. He slept again, waking much later feeling very hungry. When he reached the hall where there was a warm fire burning, a bowl of hot porridge was placed before him. Now that his basic needs were satisfied, he needed to find Thorfinn, and he wanted to see Gunhilda. He wanted to know if she was just a dream, her willingness to marry him a fantasy. With her at his side, he was sure that he would be able to be a competent and caring Lord of Allerdale. If Malcolm was crowned King of Scots, and if Edward remained King of England, they might be able to have a peaceful life. Without constant war, it would be a world to bring children into without the fear that they would be starved, abused, or killed. As Gospatric mused about the future, Thorfinn strode in as if on demand.

"You are finally awake, my son, refreshed from the journey and ready to meet more of your subjects?"

"Yes, I am, and ready to learn all I can to be a just and able lord to them. I have but a question. I have not seen Osulf and Gunhilda since we arrived. Have they gone somewhere else?"

"Yea, lad, they have returned to my home north of here, since I am needed here until you are established and comfortable."

"How shall I call you, sir?" Gospatric asked, unsure of how to give deference to the man who was so welcoming to him.

"Thorfinn is suitable. It is you that I should address properly, as you are now the lord of this land."

"How shall we tell your people of this?" Gospatric asked, unsure about how things would be done to best integrate his followers from Bamburgh, mostly Saxons, with the Gaelic settlers sent by Malcolm, and with the Cumbrians and Nordic people living in the area.

"I think we jointly prepare a feast, inviting all the leaders who could cause you trouble and together we can announce our alliance with one another."

"How soon should we do this then?"

"There is one other thing that should happen at that event to solidify your position with people here."

"What is that? I am willing to do anything that will bring harmony to the area."

"My daughter says she is pleased with you, and she believes that you feel the same for her. I would not force a marriage on either of you, but the alliance of our families will go far to unite our new settlers from the North and your followers with our people. If we can announce your marriage, it would be a joyous occasion." Gospatric was unable to speak, hardly believing that his fantasies could become reality. "You are silent on this subject? It is not pleasing to you?"

"Yes, I would be pleased, but Gunhilda implied that I would not only need your permission, but that of Malcolm."

"My son, this was a suggestion made by Earl Siward to King Malcolm and to me, as we celebrated our success against Macbeth. We had heavy hearts burying our loved ones, and the thought that we might unite our families and solidify our position against Macbeth gave us hope for a better future. I made no promises, knowing only what Siward said about you. He loved you as his own son, and Malcolm and Siward had great plans for you."

"Forgive me, what kind of plans?"

"Malcolm has ambition. He wishes to bring all of Scotland and England under his control. He sees that you have both Saxon and Celtic ancestry and the potential to be a leader of men."

"Does this mean fighting and killing for power? I have seen too much of this already."

"Malcolm would achieve his goals by alliances of power, not by bloodshed, if possible. I believe he would go to war, if necessary, but he knows the power of the English. I support him because he wants to bring peace to our troubled kingdoms and unite us. It is for this reason I am willing for my daughter to be wed to you, but I sent her to meet you that she might make her own choice and now I offer you the same…a choice."

"I gladly accept your approval of our alliance, but I would like to have an opportunity to see Gunhilda and ask her to be my wife."

"Certainly, and we shall set a day for the feast a few days hence. Now shall we be about the business of seeing your territory and inviting our countrymen to the celebration? We can begin by riding north to my home. There you can make your proposal and determine the day for the betrothal."

Disoriented from the last few minutes of conversation, and still spinning from the changes since Siward's death only a few days earlier, Gospatric followed Thorfinn in a daze. In a few minutes he mounted a fresh stallion waiting for him. They started out with a small party representing Scots, Saxons, Cumbrians and Nordic peoples, a group already strategically selected by Thorfinn. Gospatric could understand how wise Siward was to select this man to be his support as Lord of Allerdale. He had much to learn about the land and the people, but more importantly about thinking carefully and cautiously about how he presented himself. He could see that he needed to show no favouritism to one group over another but ensure that he was the protector of all.

When they rode into Thorfinn's manor a few hours later, Gunhilda was not in sight. They entered the hall and Gospatric was introduced to all the servants and families living close to Thorfinn. Food was set out, and many joined them at the large table and others sat around the fire. Gospatric tried to be present, taking in names and faces and hoping he could remember them. He kept watching for Gunhilda and he saw that Thorfinn was observing his growing agitation. Was she avoiding him? Had she changed her mind? Was she only pretending to want to marry him? A person came to the table and said something privately to Thorfinn. Thorfinn directed him to Gospatric, with a signal to follow him. The servant led him to a garden, where Gunhilda was waiting for him on a bench. He found that he was unable to speak or to move towards her. She was dressed in a lovely gown that was the same colour as her eyes. He felt again as if he was in a dream, and that she might disappear when he tried to reach her. Then she smiled at him, with laughter in her bright eyes, and the spell was broken. He moved forward and took her hands to pull her to him. She melted into his body and for a few minutes they remained in their embrace. Then he released her so he might see her face, and looking into her soft green eyes, he asked the question.

"Gunhilda, will you consent to be my wife, making me the most fortunate man in all the land?"

"I most certainly will, my lord, and I think we should not wait for long," she teased, as she reached up for a quick kiss.

"At the feast, then, we will announce our alliance."

"And marry the next day, my lord, while all are still about the land."

The feast was five days later, and in the ensuing days Gospatric had travelled across Cumbria, meeting as many of the landowners as possible and inviting them to Aspatria.

After the feast, there was a simple hand-fasting ceremony in the garden overlooking the water. Gunhilda wore a fine, simple garment the colour of the sea and had a garland of fresh flowers in her long flowing hair. Gospatric had only a white woven shirt over his leggings for the temperature was unseasonably warm with little breeze. Many of the guests from some distance left, but Thorfinn's men and their families and those of Gospatric and Malcolm enjoyed another banquet before leading the wedding couple to their sleeping space, now decorated with flowers. Gospatric shut the large wooden door on all of them and slid the heavy block bolt across, leaving him alone with Gunhilda at long last. Siward's son Osbjorn had taught Gospatric some important things about his body and how to please a lass, but Gospatric had never done more than steal a kiss and fondle a servant girl. He wanted this young woman in front of him with his whole heart and body. He did not hesitate to take her in his arms and begin to undress her. Gunhilda was not shy, and he found her to be a willing participant, leading him to the bed strewn with soft coverings. The first time was a little awkward, but during the night the two of them found their bodies entwined over and over with pleasure spilling from their lips, as they could not get enough of one another. When Gospatric woke in the late morning, Gunhilda was smiling at him. He put his arm out and she snuggled beside him.

"We shall surely have a bairn in the springtime," she whispered.

"And Malcolm will be king and there will be peace in our land for our children."

Edinburgh, Scotland
March 2017

"How are you feeling today, Robert, about the news that you are a father?" Helen asked, as they settled in at the breakfast table. Robert remained quiet for a moment, contemplating the question. All eyes turned to him, as he spoke with a voice that quivered a bit.

"I spent much of the night awake, so I hope you will forgive me if I can't concentrate this morning. The reality of what this means is very powerful. Not knowing how the information will be received by Juliana is now my greatest concern. I understand that I will have to wait weeks, or even months, before she even knows that I exist and then she may reject any contact. I just don't know how I will handle that possibility." He paused, leaving the group silent. Finally, Helen spoke, directing her question to Samuel.

"I know there is no way to predict what she will decide, but is there any way to change your sister's mind about not telling her until her last hours, Samuel?"

"I can try but knowing my sister I think it will be a futile effort. She has been thinking about this for years and the plan she's devised is methodical. She made me swear I would follow her directions before she even shared her story. I think we should count on her sticking to her decision. I know how difficult this must be for you, Robert."

"There are other considerations that I'm not at liberty to share with you. I can say only that I am a part of a group that holds responsibility for certain information handed down from one family member to the next for many generations. Regarding my family line, there has been no heir to accept the responsibility. With Juliana, I should inform the group that I now have a child who is entitled to have access to the information. If she refuses to see me, she still has the right to have the information passed on to her. I can't say more about this." Everyone started a question at once, and Robert stopped them.

"I truly cannot confide any details. I have already said more than I should, so please respect my privacy on this! I only shared what I did to say that there are more complications than you could contemplate."

Finally, Andrew filled the silence, which they all accepted with relief.

"I'd suggest that we summarise our assumptions of Gospatric's childhood until his return to Allerdale and then move on to the years ahead—1055 to 1067. What happens to him in those twelve years, and how does he become the Earl of Northumbria?"

All four gathered in the library, still feeling the tension of the breakfast announcement by Robert. Andrew, Helen and particularly Samuel had questions racing through their minds. Andrew, again, took a leading role in structuring their conversation.

"We have all agreed that it is likely that Gospatric, his brother Maldred, and his mother Edith stayed under the protection of Siward, after the death of Crinan and Maldred at the hands of Macbeth's forces. We know that Siward's son and nephew were killed in the same battle and that Thorfinn MacThore's son Dolphin also died. When Siward died, we have documentation that Tostig was named Earl of Northumbria by Edward the Confessor, who was married to Tostig's sister." Andrew had set up a flip chart and had a marker in his hand. "I'll write down the facts we know from the records about Tostig, Gospatric, Malcolm and other characters who enter the period, then we can speculate about the likely scenarios in that twelve-year period. Agreed?" They all nodded, and Andrew continued.

"It is essential to establish that Gospatric returned to his father's land and title, as Lord of Allerdale. From the work I did in Cumbria and the records we have found, we know that Gospatric held that territory. We know that he was at Bamburgh by the end of 1067 and working with Malcolm and others as they plotted against the Conqueror. He was given Dunbar Castle and the large territory of Lothian, after his return from Flanders in 1072, so logically the only time he could have been in Allerdale was from 1055 to 1067."

"Yes," Robert interrupted, "and there is the Writ that shows the connections between Gospatric, Siward and Thorfinn MacThore. Whenever it was written, 1050, as it said in the Aspatria information or prior to Siward's death in 1055, or later, it does show they were connected."

"What about the conflicting opinions about it being Gospatric, Uchtred's son, who wrote the Writ? I know it is not the majority opinion, but is there enough evidence to claim our certainty?" Samuel asked, hoping he did not sound argumentative.

"The best evidence for me is that Gospatric, the son of Uchtred, had rights to Bamburgh and therefore a reason to oppose Tostig. He did not have a connection to Maldred, the Lord of Allerdale," Robert emphasised. "Our Gospatric obviously did have a hereditary claim to the title. I think the researchers who take the opposing view haven't studied the relationships deeply enough."

"Thank you," Samuel said. "I apologise for my limited knowledge. I am very curious about Malcolm's and Tostig's journey to meet with Edward the Confessor in 1059, not long after he was crowned king. Is it too early to put that on the board?"

"No, I think it is the most significant event in this period," Robert acknowledged.

"Then, there is the passage in Edward the Confessor's records that Gospatric accompanied Tostig to Rome in 1061, or was with him upon the return, and supposedly saved his life. Fact or fiction?" Helen asked.

"Let's put it up, because it certainly was recorded and it seems unlikely that it was another Gospatric, although there were plenty of them around at the time. I keep trying to keep the ages of them in mind, but it can still be confusing," Robert confirmed, as Andrew wrote it on the sheet. "I think we may need to divert now to some speculation before William the Conqueror enters the picture. Helen, what do you think is happening to Gospatric in Aspatria?"

"Well, he is a virile, young man with a title and a territory, apparently favoured by Malcolm and supported by Thorfinn. We know he has a son named Dolphin, sometime soon after getting to Allerdale. Since we don't have any name for his wife or wives, I think he may have married Thorfinn's daughter and that they named their first child after her brother who was killed in 1054. That's speculation."

"Sounds logical to me. We can keep looking for that gem that confirms a name for his wife, but so far nothing I have found is documented," Robert said. "We have that one later reference that his wife had a brother named Edmund, who seems to have holdings in Edlingham."

"So, what do we make of the trip to Edward the Confessor with Tostig and the Bishop of Durham along?" Andrew asked. "I see Malcolm and Tostig joining forces to ask Edward to approve a marriage proposal by Malcolm, King of Scots, to Margaret, sister of Edgar Atheling, the logical heir to the English throne.

Tostig's part is that he gets to rule Northumbria and he keeps his brother Harold from becoming king, by supporting the idea that Edgar will be King Edward's heir."

"I think there is some evidence that this is true, but I can't remember where I read that King Edward believes that Margaret is too young, being about thirteen," Robert commented.

"Remember the power of the king's wife, Edith," Helen interjected. "She probably had something to do with his decision. She would have been pushing for her brother Harold to be named the successor to the king and emphasising the youth and weakness of Edgar Atheling."

"If we are right, then Malcolm's marriage to Ingibiorg is not just strategic in keeping Orkney happy, but he needs a wife and he needs to have some sons to keep his line going," Andrew conjectured. "If they failed to get the king's permission for Malcolm to marry Margaret, he may have been forced into another plan. Do we think that Tostig's trip to Rome fits into this scenario? Did he go to lobby the Pope on behalf of Edgar Atheling, as the rightful heir? If that failed, is this when he decides to support Harald Hardrada as a successor? Someone look up who the current Pope was and find out which way he was leaning regarding England."

"I'll do it," Samuel chimed in. And we should check on Hardrada, as well. "Where was he, and what title did he have at that time?"

"Is there anything else we should look up?" Robert asked. "I think we should take a break anyway. If Samuel works on the Pope, and Andrew, if you take Harald Hardrada, I think I should check on the visit when Tostig arranges to take Malcolm and others to court to meet with King Edward."

"And I'll look for that reference to Gospatric marrying the daughter of Thorfinn and why it's thought to be another Gospatric," Helen sighed and added, "if I can find it in all of this material."

"Let's regroup at eleven and have a couple of hours before lunch. If we can move into the next phase of Gospatric's life this afternoon we will have covered a lot of territory. Let's plan on quitting by five so we can all rest or walk before dinner."

As they started to go their separate ways, Samuel touched Helen's arm to get her attention. "Could we have a walk again this afternoon? There is something I want to talk to you about my staying on with Robert for my last couple of days or doing something else."

"Of course." Helen wondered what he had in mind. She had to admit that she was tempted to ask him to come to Queensferry and perhaps rent a car with her for a couple of days.

Cumbria
The Year 1056

As the snow melted, giving way to primroses and new buds, Gunhilda and Gospatric felt very grateful. They were welcomed wherever they went in the land that was Allerdale, and in Strathclyde, where they often visited her father. Thorfinn had married a widow with two young boys, and they were pleased for him. Gospatric had sent a message to his mother and his aunt telling them of his marriage, hoping they would bring Waltheof and Maldred for a visit in the spring. When the response arrived, he was sorry to read the note from his mother. She wrote of her disappointment that he should take a decision to marry without her counsel, aligning himself with the Nordic Cumbrians, rather than waiting for a strategic marriage with a powerful Anglo-Saxon family, which she would have arranged in the next few years. She cited his young age, lack of maturity and experience, the influence of powerful men in the North, and the fact that he would live to regret his mistake. Although saddened by her lack of trust in his judgement, he knew that he had made the right decision. He had faith in the wisdom of Siward, Thorfinn and Malcolm, but he also trusted his own instincts about marrying Gunhilda. His mother leaned more to the Roman Church, and she would see this marriage as a closer alignment with the Culdee priests, who practiced the old Celtic ways of his father's family. He did not tell anyone of the content of the letter, simply saying the family would try to come in the spring. He had burned it in the fire so that no one would know of his mother's feelings. He was sure that she would change her mind when she met her first grandchild.

As her time approached, Gunhilda was convinced that the babe was a boy and she asked Gospatric if they might name him Dolphin after her brother.

"Of course, my love," he answered, "but if it is a girl, it shall be Gunhilda."

"That will be confusing, and I don't wish her to be Hilda. In any event, it is a boy. Father will be pleased."

Although he had sent messages to his mother, suggesting he would bring Gunhilda to meet the family, there had been no response. Although Maldred and Waltheof had both been taught to read and write, as he was, there were no letters from them. He sent one more message telling them that his child would soon be born and asking them to plan a trip for the baptism. He pleaded with them to commit to a time in May when they could travel and insisted that the messenger wait for an answer. He returned with a brief note in his mother's handwriting saying, 'We will not be travelling to see you.' The messenger said that Waltheof had run after him. He wanted him to tell Gospatric how much he and Maldred missed him. He decided that he would take Gunhilda and their son to see them as soon as they were able to travel. If his mother refused to see her own grandchild, there was nothing more that he could do. He made a vow to never shut his children out of his life, no matter what they did. He wondered if his mother's heart had hardened when his father had gone to Dunkeld against her wishes. Perhaps she had a premonition that he would not return. She fought with Siward about Gospatric going off with him to fight for Malcolm's right to the throne. She won that battle, and he was relieved, but he had gone against her wishes by returning to Allerdale, and by marrying Gunhilda. Did she know something he didn't? Did she have the 'second sight' or was she just a controlling woman who wanted her own way? Maybe the truth was somewhere else. She just wanted to protect those she loved. That was the most likely option, but he felt a quiver go through his body.

It was only days later that Gunhilda's time came, and he sent at once for the midwife. He left his wife in her capable hands and those of their loyal servants and busied himself with the horses. When he returned for his evening meal, there was no news, and he began to worry. What seemed like hours later, he heard the cry of a babe and ran up the stairs to the room they had set up for the birth. The midwife stopped him at the door. "She is very tired, my lord, very tired. It was a difficult birth, but you have a son."

"I must see them," Gospatric said, wanting to push the woman out of his way.

"We need a moment to prepare." She shut the door and he saw that there was nothing to do but wait until he was summoned.

Entering the room a few minutes later in the flickering candlelight he saw the women removing bloodied sheets and clothing from the room. His stomach turned, as he looked at the pale face of his beloved. Tears were flowing from her half-shut eyes, as she looked down at the swaddled bundle in her arms. He was unsure of what to do. She looked too fragile to hold, too desperate to comfort. All he could do was say her name, as he knelt beside her and heard her whisper, "He'll not have a mother, my poor little bairn…" Her voice faded away and her eyes closed. He saw her let go of the babe and he moved to hold it for her, torn between looking at his son and his wife's dying moments. The midwife came to his side, taking the babe from him and he fell onto the bed to hold Gunhilda's lifeless body. He heard a voice screaming: "No, no!" and realised it was his own. He remembered little of that night and the following day. Some of his men took him away from his love, forced him to drink spirits, and put him in his bed. When he awoke, it was minutes before he realised where he was. Thorfinn was there weeping at his side. He turned away and couldn't speak. It couldn't be true. She was not dead. She was not dead, he kept saying it in his head, but he had seen the last breath taken, as she released their son into his arms.

Gospatric didn't speak or eat that day, or the next, as they went through the motions of burying Gunhilda. Thorfinn's wife was with him now and she held the tiny babe through to the end of the ceremony. They stayed by Gospatric as the others left. Thorfinn spoke quietly to him.

"We can take him home with us, Gospatric."

"No, he is my son. He is all I have left. I will care for him," he said, as he reached for Dolphin.

Edinburgh, Scotland
March 2017

Gathering back at eleven, the group shared the information they had found. Robert started with a summary once more.

"We are looking at 1055, when Siward dies and Tostig takes over Northumbria. We have concluded that Gospatric has now returned to assume his father's title as Lord of Allerdale. This would clearly be approved by Malcolm, who still has his own problems with the thanes in Moray in the North. He is busy taking on first Macbeth and then Lulach. Meanwhile, we think it possible that Gospatric married or had a relationship with someone. We know he had a son named Dolphin, as early as 1056 and certainly by 1058. We also know that his other children came later, so perhaps there was a death, in childbirth, of his first partner. We can assume that he ruled in what was known as Allerdale or Cumberland and that he was supported by Thorfinn in Strathclyde. It would seem to be a relatively quiet time, which might indicate that Gospatric was successfully integrating the newcomers with the Cumbrians, who were themselves diverse."

"Helen, did you find anything about the marriage of Gospatric to Thorfinn's daughter?"

"Nothing definitive, although the claim is that one of the other Gospatrics married a daughter of Dolphin, son of Thorfinn. This could have been a later generation, based around Appleby, where those names get repeated. There is a Gospatric, son of Arkill, who took to wife a daughter of Dolfin de Bradley, son of a Thorfin and they had a son named Gospatric. In any event, the fact that our Thorfinn's son Dolphin was killed in 1054, therefore a young man the same age as Gospatric or a bit older, makes it possible that he was married and had a daughter, who married a later Gospatric. We do know that Gospatric had a son named Dolphin, while in Allerdale. From the information Andrew has from

Carlisle Cathedral we know that someone trained Dolphin to read and write in Runes. We can't prove it, but I think his mother was of the same Nordic background as Thorfinn."

"Let's proceed on that basis, knowing we can't definitively prove anything about Dolphin's mother. The next we know in history is that by 1058 Malcolm has defeated Macbeth and Lulach, Macbeth's stepson, and has been inaugurated as King of the Scots. Now he has the northern territory in his hands and Gospatric and Thorfinn securing his Cumbrian border. Tostig is in Northumbria and Edward the Confessor, who supports him, is King of England. The next thing we know is that Tostig and Malcolm visit the court together in 1059," Robert said, as he picked up a book from the table.

"Now listen to this, from *Lords of Alba*, by Ian Walker. 'In 1059, a late Durham source reports that King Malcolm, escorted by a great body of men led by Tostig, Earl of Northumbria, Cynesige, Archbishop of Canterbury; and Aethelwine, Archbishop of Durham, visited King Edward in England probably in recognition of his military and political support.' It poses reasons for this event, including a possible meeting with Margaret, for which there is no evidence. I think from our perspective on the future, we can glean that there may have been a pleading for a peaceful future by asking King Edward to name Edgar Atheling his successor and to align his sister Margaret to Malcolm. With Scotland and Northumbria supporting this plan, as a route to stability between the two nations and Bishops agreeing, there was a strong argument to place before the Confessor. There is some scant evidence that Malcolm had been promised Margaret as his Queen much earlier and there is, again, some evidence that Agatha, Margaret's mother, thought she was too young. She may have been protecting her innocent and pious fourteen-year-old daughter from a known warring and uncultured king twice her age, or she might have been waiting for a better prospect. Whatever the purpose of the visit, we suspect that this was the beginning of an alliance between Tostig and Malcolm, as they became sworn blood brothers the following year."

Robert continued, "Also, we know that Malcolm needs a wife and heirs, and he chooses another strategic alliance to protect his northern border, by marrying Ingibiorg, probably because of a refusal of an alliance with Margaret. Let's go on to the documentation that a young man named Gospatric, travelling back from Rome with Earl Tostig, saved his life. We need to explore why Tostig would go to Rome, not an easy journey, and why Gospatric would be with him. Any information on the Pope, Samuel?"

"Too much information and we can't explore it all. It was an explosive time in the history of the Popes, and one of those times that makes you wonder how the Roman Church has been able to justify this holier than thou and continuous male supremacy back to St Peter. Anyway, it was Pope Nicholas II, from the 24th of January 1059, to when he died in July 1061. He was a reformer and wanted to get rid of simony and forbade clerical marriage and concubinage. Married priests with wives or mistresses were to be boycotted. That's a subject in itself," Sam emphasised. "The story is that Tostig, probably with his wife Judith and Gospatric along, was taking three priests to have them receive the pallium for their positions, a form of official approval by Rome. The Pope refused to grant Bishop Ealdred the pallium for York because he already held two other positions. There was a rule against having more than one bishopric that had been ignored in the past, so the Pope was justified in his refusal. The other two bishops got their palliums. Tostig was angry and stayed in Rome, sending others back to England. He was hoping for another audience with the Pope. When no audience was given his small party left, including Gospatric and Bishop Ealdred. They were set upon by robbers on their way out of Rome, and one of the robbers was recognised as a person well known to the Pope. Tostig rode back to Rome, demanded an audience, probably accused the Pope of arranging to get the gold they brought for him by another means. Supposedly Gospatric pretended to be the earl, and when he later told the robbers he was not Tostig, they let him go. No one knows what fact or fiction is. Some sources say they stayed in Rome until the heat of August. Well, I don't think so. The Pope died in July 1061, and another was not selected until October, when more fun began with two popes appointed and fighting for legitimacy."

"Thanks for that refresher of the facts or fantasy," Robert commented and went on. "Ealdred did finally get his pallium, by promising to give up his other lucrative positions. Let's suppose that the trip by Tostig was in aid of two things…the Pope's support for naming Edgar Atheling as successor to the throne and not Harold, the brother of King Edward's wife. Harold Godwinson's children were with his mistress, therefore illegitimate. Knowing that Pope Nicholas would be concerned about legitimate heirs to the throne might have led Tostig and Malcolm to think that he would support Edgar Atheling and look favourably on a marriage between Margaret, a professed Catholic, and Malcolm, a wayward soul."

"I guess we won't ever know why Tostig was the one chosen to accompany the priests to Rome and whether it was our Gospatric who travelled with them, although most sources agree that it was," Samuel added. "If Gospatric did go, was it because Tostig didn't trust him and wanted him out of Cumbria or was he along to represent Malcolm?"

"It has made me wonder about one thing in particular," Helen stated. "Could the Writ have been written after Siward died, which many researchers think is possible, and could it have been written in 1061? If Gospatric was going to Rome with Tostig, perhaps at the request of King Malcolm, Gospatric needed to make it clear that Thorfinn was in full charge while he was gone."

"That is an interesting point," Andrew commented. "I'd like to hold that possibility in my mind, as we sort out the rest of the scenarios. We know that Malcolm has married Ingibiorg, either the daughter or widow of Thorfinn, the Mighty, and now has young sons and wouldn't want to leave Scotland open to invasion, although he supposedly plundered Northumberland in 1061 when Tostig was gone."

"When I read that and then about Gospatric's raid on Cumbria, neither made sense," Samuel commented. "I was hoping that you have some explanation."

Robert answered. "It bothers me as well, and the only way to think about it is that he was keeping a watchful eye on the area while Tostig was in Rome— perhaps on his behalf. What seems reasonable is that Malcolm heard of a move to take over the territory or a problem at Lindisfarne. Perhaps he invaded to make it clear that Tostig, his blood brother, was not going to be deposed. If Tostig, Gospatric, and Malcolm had a grand scheme, they could not afford to let one of them lose control. I think Gospatric's invasion into Cumbria was the same…making sure he maintained control for Malcolm. Saying that the raid was against Malcolm seems like a complete misinterpretation of their family and strategic relationships. Both cases talk about taking back booty, but that could have been from any of the insurgents who were making a move for power. Remember that Tostig has two local men killed in late 1063, Ulf and Gamel, in his own chamber in York, and may have arranged for Gospatric, son of Uchtred, to be eliminated at the hands of his sister at the Christmas court in 1064."

"That makes much more sense to me," Samuel reflected, "but how much can we depart from the historians who are writing their conclusions?"

Robert addressed him. "Samuel, we often find a historian that has the same doubts that we do and who acknowledges that he or she is simply repeating information they cannot verify. I think the three of us concluded something before you arrived. We know more than most historians about this period and these characters because no-one has studied the records from so many angles except us. The other thing is that many historians have failed to look at the impact of women on what happens in history. Over and over, in our research, the women have defined relationships that explain the actions of men. Some historians don't understand why Siward is involved with Crinan and Maldred against Macbeth, or why he later fights to put Malcolm on the throne of Scotland. They have no idea that his sister was married to King Duncan."

"Going back to the Rome trip, if Tostig and Gospatric were going to Rome to lobby the Pope about the succession after the death of Edward the Confessor, did they still want Edgar the Atheling to be named?" Andrew posed.

"I would think they did, and they may have also been asking for the Pope's support for a marriage between Margaret and Malcolm," Robert interjected.

"But Malcolm now had a wife and possibly two young sons," Helen countered.

"Think how easily Uchtred got away with setting two wives aside…no problem. If Ingibiorg was a widow when she married Malcolm, she may also have been quite old and not likely to survive another pregnancy," Robert responded. "There was also the fact that the Roman Church did not honour marriages that were not consecrated in the Church, so Malcolm wasn't married in the eyes of Rome."

"It may be the reason that we don't have a record of Gospatric's marriage or marriages. He most likely married in a Nordic or Celtic ceremony called hand-fasting," Helen said. "There's a lack of specificity about the date of Malcolm's marriage to Margaret. Once Margaret was made a saint, any rumour of inappropriateness would have to be squashed. The Roman Church could designate someone a bastard if their parents weren't married in the Church."

"I read somewhere that Malcolm was a bastard. Perhaps that was also the reason, because Duncan and Suthen were likely married in a Nordic or Celtic ceremony," Andrew added.

"Back to the visit to the Pope in 1061. If Tostig and Gospatric were trying to induce the Pope to support Edgar Atheling, what happened?" Robert asked and then began to answer his own question. "When King Edward dies, it is probably his wife Edith who manages to get her brother Harold selected by the Witan, the group that voted on the successor or confirmed the choice of the previous monarch."

"He was a logical choice because he was running the country for King Edward." Sam entered the conversation, now confident of this part of history. "By this time Tostig had been replaced as Earl of Northumbria and banished. He decided to support Hardrada against his brother Harold, and both he and Hardrada were killed at the battle at Stamford Bridge. His widow Judith was probably at her brother Baldwin's court in Flanders. We don't know where Malcolm and Gospatric were in that story, but presumably out of the fray. Harold had to march his exhausted and depleted army south to face the advance of William the Conqueror. When Harold is killed, the Witan chooses Edgar Atheling as the rightful king, but William ignores this and marches north to take over London." When Sam hesitated, Helen entered the conversation.

"Gospatric wasn't involved, or William wouldn't have appointed him the Earl of Northumbria. He did that at the end of 1067, after the death of Copsig, who had taken over Northumbria for William. I'm still wondering how all of this is affecting Gospatric's family. We know he has Dolphin and more children before the Conqueror invaded, but was he back in Aspatria waiting for the Confessor to die to execute the plan? The older Edgar was, the better chance for placing him on the throne. Margaret would have been about twenty, and still unmarried, when the crisis of replacing King Edward begins."

"I think I read that Edgar was taken back to Normandy by William after his coronation, along with Waltheof and others who might cause William problems," Sam chimed in. "Christina and Margaret, and their mother, would have been in the convent, probably wanting to take holy vows which Christina did later."

Robert took over again. "Yes, we have evidence that Edgar was taken to Normandy when King William left in the spring of 1067, along with other nobles who might act against him in his absence. When the Conqueror comes back to England in the late autumn of 1067, Edgar Atheling asks to return to Hungary with his family. I could see Waltheof, Morcar, Edwin and Edgar taking the opportunity to plan their next moves while in Normandy. Think of this possibility, that Malcolm spurs Gospatric on to ask for the earldom of Northumbria. He has a right through his mother, who is the daughter of Uchtred. William needs money, and Malcolm pays the hefty price sought. Edgar and his family leave on a ship heading for Hungary, but end up on the Northumbrian coast, met by Gospatric. Now the planning to take back the throne begins, with Waltheof in the South plotting with Morcar and his brother Edwin, and Gospatric and Malcolm working in the North. With that in our thoughts, we must break for lunch," Robert announced.

Cumbria
The Year 1061

Gospatric had been called to Scotland to meet with Tostig and King Malcolm. He left Dolphin with his many 'mothers' at the castle. Not knowing anything different, his son flourished with the attention of the women who surrounded him, and with his father's devotion. In addition to the cooks and servants, several of the unmarried young women from Aspatria spent time with Dolphin, in the hope that his father would notice them. Gospatric was not interested in their attention. Since Gunhilda's death he had spent his time ruling Allerdale, frequently travelling with Dolphin riding in front of him on his white stallion. The people of Cumbria and Strathclyde all knew their lord and his young son. Gospatric visited frequently with Thorfinn and his family, and Dolphin was learning to read and write in Runes from his grandfather.

The years had been peaceful after Malcolm won the battle against Macbeth, and then against his stepson Lulach a few months later. Gospatric had been at the inauguration of Malcolm as King of Scots three years earlier. It was at this time that Malcolm had taken him aside and told him of his vision: he would go to King Edward in England, who had supported him against Macbeth. With Tostig and the Bishop of York at his side, he would ask to have Edgar Atheling's sister Margaret as his wife. This marriage would unite the whole of England and Scotland and bring long-term peace. He complimented Gospatric on his leadership as Lord of Allerdale and proposed a place for Dolphin as Lord of Carlisle, when he was old enough to assume that position. He encouraged Gospatric to marry again, to produce sons who could occupy the lands of Cumbria. Tostig would remain as Earl of Northumbria, but he reminded Gospatric that he, through his mother's family, and Siward's son Waltheof, both had a claim to that title. Gospatric said little. He knew that his uncle Gospatric, his mother's half-brother, had a greater claim than he and Waltheof, a claim that was denied him when Siward took over the earldom.

Gospatric also knew that his mother was arranging for Waltheof and Maldred to have positions of importance in King Edward's court. She was negotiating strategic marriages to ensure their success before the Confessor died and a new king was crowned. Gospatric had learned this in a visit to Crowland Abbey the year before. Coping with Gunhilda's death and the care of his young son, as well as his duties to his subjects, had taken all his energy in those first years. He had made the long journey when Dolphin was four and able to understand that Maldred was his uncle, and that Waltheof was also an uncle, because he was like a brother to Gospatric. His mother warmed a bit, with Dolphin's charm and expectation that every woman would pay attention to him. Elfleda had aged, but she welcomed him and Dolphin with an open heart. He could also see that she was depending on Ealdgyth a great deal, although his mother was the younger of the two. Ealdgyth, the daughter of a King of England, had more power than Elfleda, a granddaughter of Uchtred.

Waltheof was resisting any thoughts of marriage and wanted to take holy vows, but his wishes were being ignored. Maldred, on the other hand, seemed willing to bend to their mother's demands, seeing the benefit for himself. When Gospatric suggested that Malcolm would find a place for him, Maldred had little interest. He had never been in Scotland and had no attachment to his cousin. Malcolm was older and was already preparing to be a king when Gospatric and Maldred were children.

Now there was a new strategy being discussed, with Malcolm and Tostig. King Edward had been hesitant to commit Margaret to marriage at fourteen because her mother was against the plan. Agatha was expecting both her daughters to take the veil at Wilton Abbey, after completing their education. It had also become clear that Edward might not name Edgar Atheling as his successor. Tostig suspected that his sister, Edward's wife, was promoting their brother Harold as the future monarch. Ealdred, the bishop of Worcester, and a favourite of Edward, had been appointed the Archbishop of York and had to travel to Rome to receive the pallium from the Pope. Tostig was to accompany Ealdred. While seeing the Pope, the new plan was for Tostig to plead with the Pope to support their original plan of the marriage of Margaret to Malcolm and the naming of Edgar Atheling as successor to the English throne, since Edward had no children. Two difficulties were discussed. Malcolm had already married the widow of Thorfinn from the Orkneys, to bring peace to the northern part of the kingdom. It had been a ceremony officiated by a Celtic monk, but Pope Nicholas might still consider the marriage a barrier, even though it was not sanctioned by the Church. The other problem was that Edgar Atheling was young, and there was competition. Tostig wanted to make a case that his brother Harold was never married in the Roman Church and had no legitimate heirs. Gospatric was not sure why Tostig was so opposed to his own brother or what this had to do with him, until Malcolm spoke.

"Gospatric, I must continue to be present in all corners of the land. So, I would like you to go with Tostig as my representative, with my full authority." Gospatric wanted to protest, to say he could not leave his young son, but he had learned enough of Malcolm's nature to know it would be a serious mistake. He had promised to serve his cousin in gratefulness for his support and so he was silent about his concerns.

"I would be honoured, Sire. When are we to leave, for I must prepare my people for my absence?"

"As soon as you are able. Tostig will return to York and meet you there to sail across the sea. You need only take one or two of your soldiers as companions. We will send a messenger immediately to ask for an audience with Pope Nicholas and we will expect you to reach Rome before Easter and return before summer."

"This leaves both our territories vulnerable to raiding and a possible move by my enemies," Tostig stated.

"I will ensure that does not happen in your absence, Tostig, and I assume that you can trust Thorfinn to keep your lands in line, Gospatric!"

"With my life, and with the protection of Dolphin, as well."

"How is that young lad? We need him to grow up fast."

"He does just that, Sire. He reads and writes both Norse and English, at only five."

"Skills needed in times of peace, but he must also know how to fight."

"Thorfinn will make sure of that, Sire."

Gospatric left soon after, trying to grasp the position he had been given and his responsibility to Malcolm and Tostig. They wanted him to be known by the English. Tostig saw himself returning to a prominent position at court, in support of either Edgar Atheling or Harald Hardrada, and that would leave Northumbria open for Gospatric to become earl. He would be a more acceptable leader. Tostig was an outsider, but Gospatric was remembered, and many knew of his heritage and of Siward's love for him.

The road to Carlisle was almost directly south, and his horse needed little prompting from him. Gospatric's companions left him to his thoughts, and there were many. He knew Dolphin would be content to stay with his grandfather, where Hilda's boys would be happy to entertain him, but being apart from him for months rekindled his loss of Gunhilda. He would not know if there was an illness, a fall perhaps, some change in Thorfinn's health. There was no point in worrying, but since the loss of his dreams about his life, he often thought of the negative possibilities rather than the positive ones. He should have been pleased that Malcolm had honoured him by asking him to represent his king on this journey to Rome, but it only reminded Gospatric of the intrigue ahead before peace was possible. He could not imagine what it would be like to travel with the Archbishop of York, to have an audience with the Pope, and to see Rome. He had heard stories of those who had travelled there, but he had no desire to do so. Whatever spark of faith he held in God was suffocated with Gunhilda's final breath and wouldn't be rekindled by seeing the wealth of Rome or by kissing the ring of a Pope. If he had any attachment to religion, it would be to the simple life of the monks. He had been told that his grandfather Crinan was part of the ancient family of Columba from Iona. He hoped someday to visit that tiny green island, where his uncle and other ancestors were buried.

They reached Thorfinn's manor while there was still some light in the sky, but Dolphin had been riding with the boys and had fallen asleep early. Gospatric gazed at his precious son, looking like a cherub in his sleep. He thought about Dolphin trying to keep up with the older children while he was gone and felt another cause for worry rising from inside him. Growing up at Bamburgh, next to the unpredictable sea, had created a healthy respect for all it could bring—fish and sea creatures, shells and rocks, stillness and rage, life and death. He knew the risk-taking of children and as he kissed his son's forehead he prayed, to any God that would listen, for protection for himself and his child. He stumbled down the spiral stone stairs, exhausted from the journey and the weight of Malcolm's demands. His life was no longer his own to plan and control. He had to depend on Thorfinn and his friends to keep his son and his inheritance safe, while he was gone for months. He sat at Thorfinn's table, where food was laid out and drinks poured for the travellers and shared his difficult news.

When Gospatric and his companions Donald and Owen reached York, the party with Ealdred and two other bishops had already left to meet Tostig. They proceeded to the seacoast and found the ship, and then went together with Tostig's soldiers to a drinking establishment by the wharf before their journey across the water to the Flanders coast. Judith, Tostig's wife, was travelling with them and they would spend their first night on the continent with her family in Ghent. Gospatric knew two of the eight men with Tostig, and they all seemed to know of him. As the representative of King Malcolm, he received immediate respect and he hoped he could live up to their expectations.

There was work to be done aboard ship, but the weather was quite mild and the seas calm, giving all of them time for camaraderie and much laughter. Gospatric was grateful for the company of friends, something he had missed since leaving Bamburgh Castle. When they were at sea late that night, he sat alone on the deck and all the losses of his life folded in on him. He wept, not for those who had passed on, but for himself…for the little boy who lost an uncle, then a father and grandfather, for his teenage years when Osbjorn and another cousin were killed in battle, then as a young man when he lost his other father Siward. He no longer had the support of his mother and Elfleda and the companionship of Maldred and Waltheof. Then the greatest loss of his life was to find Gunhilda and lose her so soon. He wept until no more tears came and vowed to weep no more…to stop feeling sorry for himself. He had Dolphin and Thorfinn's family, he had all the people in the land of Allerdale who cared for him and now new companions to share in this experience. Perhaps there could be another love someday, not to take Gunhilda's place, but different, and more children. Life was like this journey…there was preparation, different experiences, new friends, fierce storms and calm days, cloudy weather and brilliant sunshine, cold winds and gentle breezes. He had believed that life would be perfect when he found his true love, but he had been unrealistic. He would face his future with a new perspective, with less doubt about his ability to weather the storms, embrace all the experiences and survive the journey, anticipating whatever was coming next. Gospatric fell asleep on the deck, waking in the morning light to see the shore of Flanders ahead. Little did it occur to him that he would make this trip to Flanders again under very different circumstances.

Rome
The Year 1061

The trip after they left Baldwin's court was arduous at times. It was a relief to stop after the day's travel and enjoy the food and drink offered in the company of the group. Judith, Tostig's wife, was a welcome addition to the solemnity of the bishops travelling with them. Only Bishop Ealdred would remain for part of the evening, going over the trials and tribulations of the day. Finally, they entered Rome after more than six weeks of travel, amazed by the scale of the structures around them. They proceeded to the Vatican, expecting a royal welcome. Servants showed them to their living quarters, but there was no pomp and circumstance, which disturbed Tostig. It was an indication of things to come. It only took a few days to realise there would be no chance to discuss the alliance with Edgar Atheling's family with Pope Nicholas. The other bishops received their pallium, but the Pope refused to consecrate Ealdred as Archbishop of York. Because he currently held two lucrative positions, his bishopric of Worcester was taken from him. This was a direct attack on the Godwinson family, and Tostig was devastated. He sent Judith back to Flanders with the main party and he remained in Rome with Ealdred, Gospatric and a small party of men. Tostig attempted to get another audience with Pope Nicholas, and failing, the group left Rome in an angry scene. Tostig was in a foul mood, as they reached the outskirts of the city, feeling he had failed in his primary mission. As they entered a dense forest, they were surrounded by robbers. At that point, Gospatric was at the front of the party and Tostig was at the rear speaking with Ealdred. The robbers mistook Gospatric for Tostig and he allowed them to believe it to be so. It was clear they wanted treasure and, after taking the gold that had been brought for the Pope but not given to him, they left without inflicting any harm.

Gospatric suggested that the robbers seemed to know that Tostig's group was on the road at that time carrying gold. This further angered Tostig, who then suspected the Pope of orchestrating the event. Gospatric had overheard the name Gerard, who was the Count of Galleria and well known to the Pope. Tostig led the party back to Rome and stormed into the Vatican. Gospatric watched as Tostig cleverly turned their unpleasant situation into a winning one, by his accusation of complicity of the Pope. Nicholas acted against Gerard, demanding the money be returned to him, to prove he was not involved. He granted the pallium to Ealdred, with the stipulation that he would find a replacement for Worcester.

Gospatric was relieved to be setting out again, now in the hope that they would reach England in a few weeks, and he could return to his son. When they were getting close to Flanders, Tostig sent a man ahead to alert Baldwin that they were close by and needing food and drink. Soon they arrived and were welcomed with open arms by Judith and cheered for having accomplished the impossible. Gospatric felt that he had failed to achieve his task, but Tostig assured him that Malcolm would understand when they relayed the story to him. They would have to wait for another opportunity to promote Edgar Atheling and the betrothal of Margaret to Malcolm. They could only hope that King Edward would survive a little longer.

Landing once again, they were all grateful to be back on English soil. The sea had been wild shortly after leaving, with the wind knocking them back and tearing the sails. They had managed to find a safe harbour on the Flanders coast to ride out the storm. Gospatric's leadership and humour helped them through the hours of repair work and bargaining for supplies needed to complete their journey across the sea. They reached shore in June, hardly aware of the date. As they delivered Bishop Ealdred back to York, Tostig asked Gospatric to come to Bamburgh for a few days. Although he wanted to get home to Dolphin, he was also eager to enjoy a few more hours with his friends, who had been through a challenging time with him. They continued their journey to the castle, where Tostig's family honoured Gospatric for his courage. Tostig's sister and Judith introduced him to Athelreda and placed him next to her at the banquet table. She and her brother Edmund had come north with the English forces when Malcolm continued the struggle to take the throne. Their father had been killed in one of the battles in Scotland and they had remained at Bamburgh with their mother, who had recently died. Athelreda was a beautiful young woman, with golden braids and blue eyes, characteristic of her Saxon heritage. After spending the evening next to her, with her very amenable brother on his other side, Gospatric began to suspect that this was a deliberate plan to get them acquainted. It may have been Malcolm, as well as Tostig, who felt the need to push him into another relationship. With the rich food and the flowing wine, he was not feeling opposed to the possibility.

Edinburgh, Scotland
March 2017

After lunch Helen began, knowing that her contribution to the group was to ensure that the perspective of women was included in their thinking. "We must discuss the children of Gospatric. We know that Dolphin was older. We have 1058 for his birth, but I would suggest that it was even earlier. There was one reference that Malcolm appointed Dolphin as Lord of Carlisle in 1070. If we believe the other children were born from 1060 forward, was there a second wife, an Anglo-Saxon, accounting for the change in names? Andrew, you know more about how the children were handled in terms of the lands and manors they were granted, right?"

"Yes, to clarify that, we see that Waltheof oversaw the granting of land in Cumbria to his sisters. He was Lord of Allerdale, and that title went to his son, Alan. Dolphin was already the Lord of Carlisle at that time, so I am thinking that Dolphin covered the territory north of Carlisle. As Malcolm is trying to solidify more territory for Scotland, he is placing Gospatric's children in strategic locations. I believe Waltheof is the oldest of the next set of children, but it is difficult to do anything but guess that the rest are born about two years apart with a different mother, perhaps."

"Since Ethelreda is later wed to Malcolm's son Duncan, I think she might have been the oldest girl," Robert interjected. "I think we should look at the probable birth dates of Margaret and Malcolm's children, and Malcolm's sons from his first marriage to Ingibiorg, and compare it to births of Gospatric's family to give us some clues about what was happening."

"I have some information on that, and I made copies for all of you," Helen offered, as she passed around a paper with the dates of Malcolm's children with Ingibiorg and then his six sons and two daughters with Margaret. Another line showed the potential birth years of Gospatric's three sons and four daughters. "If we look at the end of 1067 when Gospatric is given the earldom of Northumbria and then the summer of 1068, when he is plotting against the Conqueror, and has the earldom taken away, we must wonder where his children and his wife are...would they be with him at Bamburgh, in Aspatria or in Dunfermline with Margaret?"

"Good questions," Robert stated, "go on."

"By 1070, Ingibiorg is dead or set aside, Margaret and Malcolm are surely married and have one child, plus Duncan and Donald, who are about ten and nine. Gospatric has Dolphin, aged about fourteen and his other children are from two to eight years old. I have read that Margaret was surrounded by children in several of the biographies about her, and in one of Tranter's novels he places the Gospatric family with Malcolm and Margaret. I am making a guess here, but I think that Margaret and Gospatric's wife may have been caring for all these children at Dunfermline in the difficult times. Gospatric is risking his life in rebellion against William, to put Margaret's brother on the throne of England. Wouldn't Malcolm and Margaret be willing to grant protection to his wife and children? It may be that the promise to wed Gospatric's daughter to Malcolm's oldest son Duncan, was decided when they were young and growing up together."

"It's a lot of supposition, but only a few historians have understood the close link between Gospatric and Malcolm and therefore with Edgar Atheling's struggle for the throne of England," Robert commented.

"Even fewer know the connection of Siward's son, Waltheof, with all three of them," Samuel said. "I keep reading to catch up with you and perhaps it is a good thing, because I see how the writers fail to link the characters with each other, even as they fight together against William the Conqueror. Someone should make a movie about this period. If just one of their attempts had succeeded, history would have been vastly different."

"The drama of those years of 1067 to 1076 are unbelievable," Robert stated, "but let us leave that for our final discussion after dinner. I have some phone calls to make to arrange a meeting this week, so I hope you can excuse me. It is getting close to four anyway, so perhaps it is time to leave Gospatric for a couple of hours. Drinks at six?"

Helen looked across at Samuel and he nodded. Andrew was reading some material, so they both left quietly and met outside the door to the library. "I just need to pick up a jacket and I'll meet you in the garden in five minutes." Helen was eager to hear what Samuel had in mind. She had to admit she wanted to spend more time with him, and she wasn't sure if it was curiosity about his family, or how his connection to Dundas related to hers, or something more.

Samuel suggested a short walk outside of the grounds, wanting more privacy to talk about Robert. They found a small pub about a half mile away, both ordering a half pint of Guinness and then laughing at their mutual decision. "It must be the years in Ireland in our DNA," Helen noted.

"Maybe even that early Irish ancestry that came to Scotland."

"What did you want to discuss, Samuel?"

"Well, Robert has been so kind to me, inviting me into his home, and including me in this experience. I feel that I have brought him welcome news, but a demanding situation for him to cope with. He needs to talk to this mysterious group about Juliana and I will be a burden this coming week."

"You could assure him that you can do your own thing, although he does have some needs for control."

"I have a reservation that I can cancel by tonight, but I want to know if you would join me in some exploration, if I rent a car."

"Absolutely. I would share in the cost, because I was planning to do that myself before these plans to get together came up. What do you have in mind?"

"First let me say that I rented a cottage on the road along the Forth in South Queensferry, from tomorrow until Saturday morning when I leave." Samuel paused, waiting for a reaction. When Helen just looked at him without any apparent reaction, he went on.

"I'd like to return to the Dalmeny Church and drive into Dundas Castle again and Queensferry seemed a good place to stay, since it is so close to the airport…" He felt like he was trying to justify his decision and he wanted Helen to say something.

"It's perfect. We could pick up the car tomorrow and stay in the area, because we wouldn't have much time to drive a distance. We could also get some groceries. I've been walking to the grocery store, and it is quite far to carry much. Does the cottage have a kitchen?"

"Yes, and I thought I could get some breakfast items and some basics and then might eat out if I—we were out in the countryside somewhere…"

"We could come back and make dinner together, although there are some great restaurants in Queensferry. I try to cook to save money, since I am on a leave-of-absence and not getting paid."

"Tell me about that. What prompted you to come here for six months?"

"I got interested in the Gospatric story when my sister and I made a trip to Ireland in search of information about the Dundas family. I didn't know about all this history, until we found a collection of books donated by John Dundas to the Enniskillen Library."

"I hope I can go there, but it still must have been a big decision. I think about a sabbatical sometimes and then I find too many reasons why I shouldn't take one."

"I'm afraid I made a rash decision, or that's what my sister thinks, but the idea was percolating for a long time. I had been through a mundane divorce in that it wasn't painful or emotional. We needed to sell the house to split the assets, and I had been in the same job for a long time. I just needed to take the opportunity to do something entirely different, and the decision to travel to Scotland and research the family tree was just an excuse to make a change in my life. I don't really know what's next. The house is sold, the few things I kept are in storage, and I am free to consider all options when I return to Minnesota. I've considered doing a master's degree, but I don't feel any passion around that idea right now."

"How about writing? There certainly could be a novel of Gospatric's life. I haven't seen much written about Malcolm and Margaret and there is a lot of drama in their story."

"Yes, and do you think we should go to Dunfermline to see where they were buried and married, for that matter?" Helen wanted to focus on their plans and not on her future. For now, she was enjoying living in the moment.

"I think so. It's not far. There is something else I would like to do. When I was looking for places to rent, I found cottages on the Arniston Estate. The owners are from the Arniston line of the Dundas family. The place is expensive, but they do tours on Tuesdays and Wednesdays. I thought I might like to meet them, and it is also close to Rosslyn Chapel, of *Da Vinci Code* fame, and a place called Temple. They both interest me because they are Knights Templar sites. Maybe that wouldn't interest you."

"I admit that I don't know much about the Templars, but I found an old legal document about a Dundas trying to get back some land that had been given to the Templars. I'd love to know more. I think we might find it all connects."

"That's great, we could make a reservation to go to Arniston on Tuesday or Wednesday afternoon and see the other places on the way."

"Also, I think we should go to Dunkeld, where Crinan was the lay abbot, and it is the probable site of death for Gospatric's father and grandfather."

"Where is it? I haven't seen it."

"I can show you on the map when we get back, but it is not that far. We cross the Queensferry bridge and drive past Perth. It's a major road and shouldn't take too long. We might be able to go the same day as Dunfermline."

"I'm so relieved that you are willing to do this. I didn't want to drive alone, trying to find my way on these roads, and then have no one to talk to about what I was seeing. Now, how do I handle Robert?"

"I just think you can be very straightforward with him. Acknowledge that he has been a gracious host, but that he has a lot to think about now, and you would like to explore the area by car."

"Should I tell him we are doing this together?"

"That does pose an interesting question. I don't think we can avoid that. Andrew will be asking if I'll be in the library this week. We usually get together a couple of times a week and Robert—he might ask what I'm planning…"

"I don't mean to pry, but…" Sam hesitated, but she grasped what he wanted to know.

"No, there's nothing going on. Robert is twenty years older than me, and very charming, as your mother and sister found out. He's well-off. He is the perfect fantasy…handsome Scot with an estate and a sailboat. The only thing better than that would be a castle and a title, but I am not interested. As I said, he's quite controlling, and I've done that, been there. He's also very secretive, although he has been more open since you brought the message for him."

"And Andrew?" Helen was a little taken aback by Samuel's direct approach and wasn't sure she wanted to commit to an answer.

"Are you asking if I'm interested in Andrew or if he fancies me?"

"I'm sorry. It isn't any of my business. I'm out of practice about these things."

"What things are you talking about?" She was teasing him now, and he knew it.

"Talking with women who are about my age and single. Checking out whether they like men at all, whether they are ever going to be in a relationship again, that sort of thing. Just before I left for Scotland, I was trying to get back into the dating thing, at the insistence of some of my friends. I haven't had a committed relationship since my wife died." Helen was sorry then that she had pushed him to answer her.

"I'm sorry, I didn't mean to be flippant. I've not been in the dating game at all and can't quite imagine how it works. Let's just agree to be open and honest and see where it goes."

"Agreed, but we still have to decide how to approach Robert and Andrew…"

"I'll think about that, but now we should go back."

When they reached the estate gate, Helen had a suggestion. "When you tell Robert that we are going to continue our research by renting a car and going out to some of the sites, let him know that we want to take him out for dinner in Queensferry, before you leave, and ask him for a date. That will make him feel included. I'll do the same with Andrew. I'll see what night he is able to come to Queensferry after work, to join us for dinner. Okay?"

"Right, fellow conspirator. I'm on it."

By the time they had dinner, plans were in place for Andrew and Robert to join them on Thursday evening. Helen would make a reservation for them at the restaurant with a large outdoor sitting area overlooking the Forth. Their energy for going much further with their research had waned. Robert and Andrew had shared their reactions to Dunfermline and Dunkeld, with some suggestions for driving, parking, and restaurants. Helen's strategy appeared successful—they seemed involved in the plans for Helen and Samuel to spend the next few days seeing more of the sites related to their research. When they got to the drawing room, settled around the warm fire with a glass of scotch in their hands, there was a final toast by Robert, added to by the others.

"To the four of us and to Gospatric, an extraordinary man!"

"To continuing research and sharing," chimed in Andrew.

"To a wonderful team," Helen added.

"To Robert for his hospitality and amazing whisky," Samuel concluded and then continued. "Robert, since Helen and I will be going to Roslin and Temple, could you share a bit about the Templars?"

"You know as much as I do, Samuel, but I have long suspected that the Dundas family had some significant involvement with the Order. It is certain that my Dundas connection through Elizabeth Hamilton was related to the Hospitallers, who inherited the property of the Templars when they were disbanded. There was a hospital in the Magdalens where they owned property, and that connects to the court case information that Helen found in the library. I think you all know a little about the history of the Knights Templar, but we haven't talked much about King David welcoming them to Scotland. Since he became king in 1124, we know that Gospatric's children would have been intertwined with them as well. When the Templars in France were rounded up on the thirteenth of October 1307, some of their ships left La Rochelle. It has been concluded that there was some foreknowledge of the pending arrest and that part of the treasury had been moved to the ships. Do you have anything to add to that Samuel?"

"Some researchers say there were thirteen ships and there is much speculation about why they were never found…lost at sea, travelled to the new world, became pirates…split up. My thinking is all the theories are true. If they had any common sense, they would have split the resources and travelled in different directions. Not knowing the outcome of the trials and imprisonment of their fellow knights, the ships would have tried to get as far away as they could while awaiting news. They have found Templar artifacts in Gotland and on the west coast of Scotland. The islands would have provided a natural hiding place, with sparse population and many harbours. They may have burned their ships in some locations. Without their banners, it would have been possible to sail far afield and not be identified. Since Scotland was remote and they had property in the area, why not go there? It was well-known that Robert the Bruce was in trouble with the Pope and not likely to follow any orders to arrest Templars. As it plays out over the next few years, England finally conforms to orders to arrest Templars and confiscate their property, but the numbers don't add up. It would be naive to think that the men in the Order were not clever enough to go underground, hide among the clergy and transform their lives."

"I was thinking about that," Helen commented. "What loyalty would you feel to your vows when the pope and the king were torturing your fellow Templars, accusing the Order of unbelievable acts, and taking all their resources? None, I would hope. If they wanted to stay in the Church, they could change their hair style and pass as monks; or they could become soldiers of fortune fighting for some other leader, like Robert the Bruce. They could settle on the lands they were given, marry and fit in. Many of them spoke more than one language, they had joint wealth they had contributed to a central body, so why not divide it up and let each person decide their own path?"

"I think that is particularly true as time progressed and it was clear that the Knights Templar were finished," Samuel said.

"I do believe a ship could have come up the Forth, as well as to the west coast, with the Roslin and Sinclair connection to the Templars," Robert continued. "The other thing I have always suspected is that when a Dundas went to France to bring back a group of Cistercian monks to South Queensferry, he was really getting some Templars out of France."

"How could we ever prove that?" Helen asked.

Samuel spoke first. "I might be wrong, but I think my mother had something in her diary about a tunnel from the Cistercian monastery to the Dundas Castle grounds."

"Why have a tunnel unless there was some danger? Is that what you are thinking?" Helen responded.

"What do you think, Robert?" Samuel asked.

"I think we have another time period to investigate. If we spend as much time on the years going forward from Gospatric, we will uncover another mystery," he said, dismissing the question. "It's getting late, and we are all planning on an early breakfast at seven tomorrow. I need to say one more thing before we formally break up this evening." All three turned to him with expectation. Would he say more about the secret organisation? He went back to the Dundas family.

"I told your sister something, Samuel, that I doubt she shared with you. There are some ancient Scottish families that have passed down oral history for many generations. Andrew, I haven't told you this. Gospatric's family would have been one of these, going back to early Christianity in Ireland. All three of you are descendants, but no one from the Ormiston or Dundas line has come forward to suggest this is true."

"What about the Dunbar descendants? They would have been the ones to carry it on, I would think," Helen suggested.

"I am not at liberty to talk about them. There is some strong feeling that there is some hidden documentation, but so far no one has found a clue to where it might be or whether it exists. I told Sarah that I believed that her mother, your mother Samuel, had tapped into some other time, perhaps even into the mind and emotions of another person from the twelfth century."

They all stared at Robert, trying to take in what he was telling them. They continued to listen intently, as he went on.

"If that is true, then it is possible that Juliana might have the same capacity. Sarah may have had it, but she was never going to let it surface."

Helen broke the silence.

"What about Samuel? If his mother was psychic, why not Samuel?"

"I am not suggesting it is not possible, but men are much less likely to acknowledge and explore concepts related to the supernatural." He looked at Samuel and asked a direct question.

"Samuel, have you had any unique experiences or any extraordinary perception indications, as your mother did?"

"Vague premonitions, I suppose, but my sister did. I remember a story that Sarah kept insisting one day, when she was about five, that our mother's sister had broken her leg. It turned out that she had been in a car accident at that time and her leg was injured, not broken."

"Close enough," Robert declared. "What your mother was experiencing was beyond most of us, in terms of its intensity and repetitive nature. It was as if the past was pushing into her present, not by invitation but by demand. Does Juliana demonstrate any tendencies in this arena? You've known her from her earliest days."

"I haven't thought of it in that way, but her primary interest has been research of extrasensory abilities. She uses her journalistic talent to interview individuals and produce material for blogs, radio shows and articles in magazines. Let me add that she knows nothing about her grandmother's history. She has never seen the diary that was sent back from Scotland and has only limited knowledge about that time."

"That seems strange. I would think she would be curious about her grandparents," Helen said, with a questioning look.

"You must understand that my sister made it clear that we were not to talk about my mother with her children. She told me that the diary had been destroyed, that she didn't want to dwell on her death anymore, and since none of her children knew our mother there was no need to bring it up."

"But kids are curious. If their friends have grandmothers, they would have asked about your mother," Helen protested.

"She simply said, 'she died before any of you were born,' and Sarah has a way of shutting off communication, of making it clear that the subject is not to be brought up again."

"That wasn't fair to you. Was there anyone you could talk to about her?" Helen persisted.

"My wife never met her, but she would listen to me. My mother's sister and her husband were embarrassed about the suicide verdict, so they had the same response my sister did. I tried to respect Sarah's wishes. The last thing I wanted was for her to fall back into depression. It was a shock when my sister told me about Juliana's biological father, not only because I didn't have an inkling, but because it opened the door to my mother's story."

"Will Juliana be drawn to the story, and won't that spark her curiosity about Robert?" Andrew asked, speaking for the first time since the subject started.

"They are separate issues. I think after years of silence, she just might want to know about her mysterious grandmother, and she is going to look to me to tell her. I expect some hostility about not sharing any of this with her since she has been an adult. Having an unknown biological father will go straight to the heart. Her loyalty towards Will is going to be paramount. She may feel that seeing Robert would somehow test that loyalty. I'm sorry, Robert," Samuel stated, looking again at his grim expression, and feeling it deeply. "I will try my best to allay her fears. She knows how close I was to Will and how deeply his death affected me." It was quiet for a moment and the heaviness of sorrow for both Robert and Samuel was palpable.

Helen broke the difficult silence. "Samuel, you said that you had vague premonitions. Did you have any about your mother's death?"

"I remember the day she left, that we had this last moment when our eyes met. Sarah was being Sarah—not able to keep from making a nasty comment about Mom enjoying herself while she was dealing with a summer pregnancy. I just looked back at my mom, wanting to convey a message to forget the comment and have a wonderful time. I just saw something painful in her last look, and then forgot about it, or suppressed it until I read her diary entry about leaving. Also, when we got the diagnosis about my wife's cancer, I had this momentary glimpse of the future, even though the doctors were talking about the positive outcomes of treatment. I must say I felt something strange when I got your invitation to stay with you, Robert, and gather for this weekend. It was a sensation of an open door that would change the course of my life…"

Robert rose from his chair. The fire had died down to coals. He looked at each of them in turn and then spoke in a faint voice, barely controlling his emotions. "I believe this time with the three of you has already changed my life for the better. I will leave you now, until breakfast. Good night."

No one spoke as he left the room. Each of them picked up their personal items and walked out of the drawing room and up the stairs, nodding to one another as they entered their respective rooms on the landing.

Aspatria, Cumbria
The Years 1064–1066

The years since meeting Athelreda had been peaceful for Gospatric. After seeing the positive reception of Dolphin and Thorfinn's family to her, the couple married that autumn. The following June Athelreda went into labour. Waiting for the birth, with thoughts of what had happened with Gunhilda, was frightening for Gospatric. He paced the halls of the castle, filled with anxiety, but in just a few hours a healthy boy had arrived with no complications. Dolphin was thrilled to have a little brother, and Gospatric asked to have him named after Siward's son Waltheof, who was like a younger brother to him. There was a healthy girl born in the following year, named Ethelreda after her mother and now Athelreda was pregnant and due soon.

Gospatric was called to Scotland to meet Malcolm once again. There was serious trouble in Northumbria with Tostig's rule under question. He had raised taxes to pay for the extra men he needed to maintain safe passage in the territory. Tostig was often at court or off somewhere with his brother Harold. He left the North alone and the thanes were increasingly feeling they had no representation for their complaints. Two prominent thanes, Gamel, son of Orm, and Ulf, son of Dolfin, had been murdered after being given safe passage to meet with Tostig. Malcolm did not believe that Tostig would openly have his opposers assassinated without thinking of the consequences. Malcolm's plans were now in jeopardy. Gospatric's uncle was the most outspoken challenger to Tostig, threatening to take over Northumbria by force. Malcolm wanted Gospatric to meet with his uncle and find a compromise that would benefit Scotland. Although named for his mother's half-brother, Gospatric had never been close to his uncle. When his mother married his father Maldred, she had moved away to Allerdale and there had been no contact in the family. Gospatric's uncle refused an invitation to come to Scotland to meet with his nephew and Malcolm.

Before he left, Malcolm told Gospatric that they must look for the next opportunity to have him named as Earl of Northumbria. When Gospatric objected, Malcolm pointed out that, if anything happened to his uncle, he was the logical heir as the grandson of Uchtred raised by Earl Siward, and with connections to the Scottish throne. Gospatric suggested Waltheof as a more logical heir, but Malcolm dismissed this, with assurance that Waltheof would be well integrated into the English court through his mother.

Gospatric was relieved to leave Malcolm and return to his family, making it back to Aspatria before the birth of his fourth child. Another girl was born shortly after his return. Once again, it had been an easy birth and Gospatric was grateful to welcome another healthy babe to the family. Gospatric asked that she be named Gunhild, and Athelreda agreed without hesitation.

Peacefulness ended in the new year when Gospatric learned that his uncle was killed while at the Christmas court of King Edward. There were rumours that Edward's wife, Tostig's sister Edith, had orchestrated the murder. Now Gospatric knew he would be unable to stay out of the conflict, and he expected to get a summons from Malcolm within a fortnight. He tried to enjoy the rest of the holiday with Athelreda, his children and Thorfinn's family, but the uneasiness of the brewing situation in Northumbria was ever on his mind.

Unrest continued, but Gospatric heard only rumours during the winter and spring. Malcolm was occupied with danger from the Orkneys despite his union with Ingibiorg. Gospatric had managed to avoid the conflicts in Northumbria and was happy to be in Allerdale with his growing family. Another girl was born in the fall, and they named her Octreda, the female derivation of Uchtred, Gospatric's grandfather.

Gospatric was called to a meeting with Malcolm in October and learned that while Tostig was in the South with Harold, the thanes in Northumbria took advantage of his absence and organised a rebellion. This time they were not going to be stopped. They demanded that King Edward banish Tostig and appoint Morcar as earl. Edward called on Harold to solve the problem and Tostig was sure that Harold would support him and raise an army to suppress the rebellion. Harold attempted to negotiate with a powerful group gathered at York. He told King Edward that, for the good of the country, it was best to agree to the demands to banish Tostig and appoint Morcar earl. Harold claimed that Tostig could return and be granted other lands when things settled down.

"Tostig has left for Flanders to stay with Judith's family," Malcolm added, as he finished his news.

"He must be extremely angry at Harold. He was quite clear about not wanting him to be king when Edward dies and now Harold has so much power."

"He has written of his anger and his support for anyone but Harold as king. The positive news is that Harold insisted on detaching Northampton and Huntington from Northumbria, before turning it over to Morcar and designated Waltheof as earl. Waltheof could have been a logical choice to replace Tostig, but the thanes were already determined to have Morcar in that position. Waltheof is still not powerful enough to take on all of Northumbria. Osulf, the son of Earl Eadulf was not acceptable to the Yorkshire thanes. As part of the negotiations with Morcar and Edwin, Harold agreed to marry their sister and set aside his mistress. The next king will need heirs in a marriage approved by the Church."

"What do you wish from me now, Sire?"

"We wait. We can do little until we see an opportunity to move, with or without Tostig."

When the king died in January, the news reached Gospatric that Harold Godwinson had been named his successor by the Witan. It seemed that all of Malcolm's plans would now be abandoned; Tostig was banished, Edgar Atheling was passed over in favour of Harold Godwinson, and Malcolm was still married to Ingibiorg, who had just had their second son.

Then in early spring, Malcolm called Gospatric to a meeting to share the news and the changes in his plans. Although the snow had subsided, it was still a bitter trip on horseback. Gospatric always felt apprehensive when Malcom summoned him. He understood that power had changed in Northumbria and, with Harold as king, past hopes were no longer possible. He learned quickly that Malcolm had new information to share. With Tostig banished, Morcar was spending most of his time in York and leaving his deputy Osulf at Bamburgh. Malcolm felt that Northumbria was once again fair game for raiding and spoils. Although he had married Ingibiorg, he had not given up on the idea of making Margaret, Edgar Atheling's sister, his wife. Edgar was still young, but Malcolm still felt that he should have been the choice of the Witan, when King Edward died. He knew that he would have needed powerful allies if he was to stand up to threats from several directions. Malcolm still wanted to place Gospatric in Northumbria, as soon as possible.

"You might be needed to protect Margaret and Edgar. I cannot openly do that myself, but they are vulnerable with King Edward dead. Edward's lack of interest in acting like a king, trusting Harold to handle everything, resulted in Harold's power over the Witan," Malcolm stated.

"Do you think Harold would try to harm Edgar?" Gospatric asked.

"I believe he might. His family has some ties back to King Aethelred, and he used that in his claim, but his power was in the fact that he was running the country. I think that Margaret and Edgar's father was probably poisoned as soon as they entered England years ago, to eliminate him as the successor and I am concerned for Edgar."

"But surely Harold didn't arrange that," Gospatric protested.

"His sister Edith was already Edward's wife then, and we know what she can do. I'm quite sure she arranged the death of your uncle."

"I find it difficult to imagine women who are capable of that level of planning and intrigue," Gospatric confessed. "Perhaps I am naive."

"I believe so, Cousin, but you will learn. There are also women who can be trusted. I believe Tostig's wife is one of those."

"I certainly felt comfortable at her brother Baldwin's court and on our travels with her. The family seems to have a history of protecting banished people. Did you know that Tostig met Judith and married her during the Godwinson family's banishment?"

"I did hear of this, and it must have softened the blow of banishment to have made that connection. I have felt it was a matter of love, and not expediency, however."

"That seems true. Have you heard from Tostig?"

"Yes, and he is very bitter about Harold's support for the rebellion. I'm afraid he would do anything to eliminate Harold as king," Malcolm stated.

"He would then still support the plan of putting Edgar on the throne?"

"I think so, but he is concerned about Edgar's youth and lack of leadership qualities, as am I."

"He was very young when he was taken from Hungary and brought to England. He lost his father but continued to live at Edward's court, where he might not have been welcome," Gospatric commented, thinking of his own losses.

"This is true, but Margaret has proven to be the strong one. If Edward had approved my marriage to her, when Tostig and I went to court a few years ago, we could have groomed Edgar in Scotland and built the support of the north of England for him."

"Now, what is it you want of me, Sire, with Harold in place and Morcar as earl?"

"We wait to see what Tostig has planned and for opportunities to respond. Be prepared to move quickly if I send word to you. Raise those children and have more sons. We will need them to manage the large territory we will hold going forward. And how is your brother Maldred? Could you count on him if we needed to get Edgar and his family out of England?"

"I'm uncertain of his political alliances. My mother has arranged much of his life for him, and he is now on the coast, northeast of York."

"And your mother, how does she fare?"

"She continues to disapprove of my life choices, and she believes she could make better ones for me, but she mellows a bit with each new grandchild. I am grateful that Maldred is accepting of her patronage. She is, without question, my grandfather's daughter!"

"Yes, I am sure Uchtred the Bold, as he was known, was a powerful character, but he died about the time she was born. She did grow up at Bamburgh, and that family was rife with revenge and murder. I suppose she learned survival skills. We will use her if you think she is helpful. And what of your other little brother, Waltheof, now Earl of Northampton and Huntington?"

"I hear little from him, but he must be in favour with Harold."

"Or Harold is using him. Waltheof is known for his physical strength and his character, but not for his strategic thinking. As Siward's son, he does still have friends in the north."

"Should he not be the next Earl of Northumbria, Sire, if things were to change?"

"He was not the choice of the thanes, nor was Osulf."

"Then, why should they accept me as their leader? I don't understand."

"You are known as a strong leader of all of Cumbria. They trust you."

"Even though I was in Rome with Tostig?"

"I have heard they believed that Tostig took you with him because of his fear that you could overrun his territory. They may have supported you in that challenge if you had not been removed from the scene. It was a dangerous time for Tostig."

Gospatric kept his thoughts to himself, the fact that Malcolm sent him with Tostig, and said, "And so, you raided Northumbria to keep them in line?"

"Yea, we had agreed that I would quell any rebellion by keeping the thanes busy until you both returned." And if we didn't, thought Gospatric, you would have taken as much territory as possible.

With these final comments Gospatric was dismissed, and he left the following morning on the journey back to Aspatria and the family he loved. Leaving at first light with his two companions, he hoped they could cover the seventy-five miles before darkness fell. He feared that the peaceful times would soon be over and his promise to support Malcolm would take him away from his wife and children once again.

South Queensferry, Scotland
March 2017

Robert had insisted that Mr Wakefield, his housekeeper's husband and gardener for the estate, drive Helen and Samuel to the airport to pick up their rental car. Later, they drove first to Dalmeny Church and spent more than an hour writing down details of everything they saw that was not listed in the pamphlets they had. Helen held up the tapestry on the wall that was referred to in the church information, and Samuel tried to capture the inscription on his phone, then he held it while Helen drew a replica of the mostly erased letters and symbols. Helen sketched the patterns from the gravestones in the church floor and did the same with the skull and crossbones of the gravestones outside. A woman from across the street had opened the door for them and they returned the key, asking if she had any other information about the church. She did have a copy of an article about some excavation work where a skeleton of a man who rode extensively on horseback was buried beside a woman, probably his wife, in the same grave. The article conjectured that he was a knight, and the dating was eleventh century. They made some notes and thanked her for helping them. When they got to the car Samuel said, "Do we dare drive into the castle grounds and check out the fountain?"

"I don't feel very comfortable doing that. What about buying some groceries, taking them to my place, and having lunch? Then you could try to call and see if that is possible."

"Groceries, lunch, yes, phone call, I don't know…"

"You can say that you are a history professor from the States, a Dundas descendant, and you read about the fountain and the Dundas Keep and wonder if you could look at both."

"It might be worth a try. Let's go," he said as he got into the driver's seat. "Lead me to the grocery store."

Helen and Samuel unloaded the groceries, leaving the ones for his place in the car. Helen cut slices of bread and put out the meat and cheese, while Samuel sliced onions and tomatoes. The division of tasks happened easily, and they had a quiet smile between them, bringing the food to the table where Helen had placed plates and silverware. Samuel went back for glasses of water, and they began their lunch. Helen broke the silence after a few minutes.

"I know a little about your wife's illness, but not how it fits in with Sarah's return home from Scotland and Juliana's birth."

"We had been living together for a few years when Sarah left on her trip that summer. I had a permanent teaching position for the fall and Helen was working night shifts at the same hospital where I met her. I knew that she was fine with having the boys around while Sarah was in Scotland, trusting I'd make sure to take them on an adventure every morning so she could sleep. When Sarah returned from Scotland, seeming like her old self, I felt relieved of a lot of burdens. I suggested to Helen that it was time to get married and start thinking about our own family. I guess she had been waiting for me to propose."

Helen was taken aback when he said his wife's name, although she had always known it was the same as hers.

"It's strange now saying her name to you," he said, and then continued. "We had a simple ceremony at the registry office and a party at Will and Sarah's. I had the money from the sale of my mom's house, and we used it for a down payment on a duplex in South Minneapolis. We decided we could start there and use it as a rental property until we knew where we wanted to live later. She didn't want to work when our children were young, so we weren't going to rush into having a family until I was settled in a job that I liked, that also paid enough to take care of us. I suppose I regret that decision, putting off having a child…"

"Even if you had to do it as a single parent?"

"Yes, but you never know how you will react. When Juliana was born, I was excited about having a little baby around again. The boys were more interested in being with their friends and I was missing being involved in their lives. Soon, it was clear that Sarah and Will didn't need me in the same way they had in the past. Sarah had an easy pregnancy and birth. She loved caring for a baby again, without her emotional problems dominating her life, and Will was thrilled with having a little girl. It took me some time to recognise my loss. We still had all three of the kids with us occasionally, but it wasn't the same. When Juliana was about a year old, I started talking about starting a family. I didn't have tenure yet, but I liked my position and I felt we could manage on one salary in another year. Helen liked her job and just wasn't ready to think about having a baby..." Sam hesitated and got up to get another glass of water. Helen could feel that the difficult part was coming next and remained silent.

Sam sat down again and continued. "I poured myself into my teaching job, worked during the summers at camps and stopped pressing about a family. My wife was a couple of years older than me, and I was thirty. She wanted to go slow, seeing a doctor, going to another form of birth control for a while. It was the next fall before she was referred to an obstetrician. That doctor found a cyst and more time passed while it was checked out, then it was malignant and there was an operation. I was still hopeful and convinced we had been lucky to find the cancer early. Then the nightmare began. They found the cancer had spread and recommended aggressive treatment. There was radiation and chemo, good days and bad, hope and defeat. The process went on for several months of denial. During hopeful times, I mentioned adoption since a pregnancy was no longer an option. She wasn't comfortable with that idea and, I guess, she was more realistic than I was. I'm not sure what is worse, losing someone quickly, like my mother, or the slow process of losing a bit of them every month, then every week, until the last day..." Sam wasn't crying, but he sat staring into space, as if he were reliving those last moments with his wife.

"I'm so sorry. I shouldn't have brought it up," Helen reached out and touched his hand. He turned his hand over hers and held it.

"No, I'm glad you did. I haven't talked about it for a long time. If we had been parents, I would have had some reason to keep going, a reason to get up in the morning, to cook a meal, to plan a trip. I just wallowed for months, lost interest in my job and then quit at the end of the year. Finally, Will and Sarah sat me down and confronted me, as we had done with Sarah when she was depressed. It worked. I saw a counsellor, got into a grief group, and made some positive decisions. I rented the lower-level apartment we were living in and moved upstairs and applied to a doctoral program. I spent more time with Sarah and Will and the kids and came back to life. Substitute teaching paid my expenses, and I was too busy writing my dissertation to feel sorry for myself. Gradually I recovered from depression and my passion for life returned. What I didn't find was another relationship, and I never had a child, which I do regret. When Will died I had another loss, but I re-gained my family. They were all dependent on me in new ways. Now Sarah is dying, and I am the only one left to be a parent to my nephews and Juliana, and potentially a grandparent to their children."

"How did you react when you found out about Robert being Juliana's father?"

"First, I couldn't believe it. When Sarah presented the evidence to me, I think I was jealous. This stranger had what I didn't. He had a daughter, even if he didn't know about it…he had one."

"And now?" she asked. "What do you feel?"

"I like Robert and I feel sorry for him, because I'm afraid that Juliana won't want to meet him."

"Why do you think that? Is she like her mother? Sarah sounds quite determined when she decides something."

"No, she's not like Sarah. She's more like my mother…a free spirit. It's about Will. You know how some adopted kids want to find out about biological parents and others think it would be too hurtful to their adoptive parents. Even though Will has been dead for four years, I think that Juliana will feel that it would be a betrayal to acknowledge another father."

"Would she not be enticed by the manor house, the money, Scotland?"

"I don't think so. I hope you can help me think this through, so I'm ready for her reaction," Sam paused. "Let me make that call to Dundas and then I should be able to check into my place."

"I'll clear the dishes while you call." Sam was back in minutes, helping her. "I had to leave a message with the wedding centre staff at Dundas. I didn't say what I wanted, hoping they will return my call to find out."

Sam found the keys for his cottage and was pleasantly surprised by its location close to the water. They put his groceries away and decided to walk to the marina.

"Do you know the name of Robert's sailboat?" Sam asked. "It must be here."

"No. I don't think he has ever mentioned the name. Did he talk to you about it?"

"No, but my sister mentioned something about being on his boat. I wish she had written a journal about her time here, like my mother did. I don't think we will know the whole story from either Sarah or Robert."

"Maybe that's okay. It is their personal drama. Not everyone is willing to share…"

"What about you? I have exposed my soul to you, but I don't know anything about your relationship and why it ended."

"Not remarkably interesting. We met at the university, got married after graduation, bought a house with a picket fence, had 2.3 kids. That's a boy and a girl and one miscarriage, and we didn't live happily ever after."

"That sounds cynical."

"Flippant, I guess. We were quite different souls. We had similar social concerns and political views, but different family systems. As the years passed, those everyday issues became more obvious. I felt unfulfilled and I think he felt trapped. He married again recently, and I hope he is more contented. I just feel free to be me again and make some new life choices. There's not a lot of animosity between us, but I am not looking forward to weddings and family events with him and his new wife."

"No relationships on the horizon?"

"None. I've been much more involved in trying to find out who I am, separate from wife, mother, and librarian, and what I want for the rest of my life."

They had reached the marina and realised they would never find Robert's boat among the myriad of sailboats, both in and out of the water. The little cafe was open, and they stopped for a coffee. Sitting together again, Sam continued his questioning.

"Have you arrived at any conclusions so far…about what to do with the rest of your life?"

"I'm not sure. I know I'm loving the research work we have been doing, and I clearly am not missing being a librarian. I know I can't stay here for more than six months, so I must think about whether I want to go back to living in Minnesota or try out some new location. The problem is that I don't have any other place that I think I would like. I love the Seattle area, but it's overcast a lot of the time and the traffic is horrendous. Mountains make me feel closed in and the plains and deserts are not my thing. I love being by water, but that requires more money than I have. I like the changing seasons and I would hate living in a place with hot weather, so the whole south of the country is out. It's an odd feeling, not knowing where I'll be just a few months from now."

"When are you returning?"

"July, I guess. I have a sister who will be thrilled to have me back. I can stay with her and her husband until I make some decisions."

"My tenants are leaving in July. You could rent my downstairs apartment. It's not on water, but it is close to Lake of the Isles."

"What's it like? I will need a place, because I won't be able to handle living with my sister for too long."

"It's a typical stucco duplex, with wood floors and natural woodwork, small kitchen, and a dining room and living room opening into each other, not very large. It has two bedrooms about the same size, and a small bathroom between them with a tub and shower. Not much grass, mostly driveway to a garage that can hold a car and a half or two compacts."

"Sounds all right, but I'm an open window sort of person and I wonder how safe I would feel on the main floor. It's something women think about when you live alone."

"Foolish of me, I never would have thought of that. Here is a silly idea. I've been looking at other places to buy and then thinking I don't really want more grass to mow and a longer driveway to shovel. I've been toying with the idea of living on both levels. Then I think about wanting to travel more, so why have more space and no one to keep track of the house. We could house share and you could have an upstairs bedroom," Sam said, then saw the expression on her face. "Sorry, I can see I'm getting carried away."

"Yes, but I'm right with you. I was just thinking it would be great to have an option. How much would it be?"

"Oh, the current tenants pay $800, but that includes their heat. There is only one furnace, but the rest of the utilities have separate meters. Mine runs about $50 a month, but if that's too much, we could work something out…"

"That would hardly be fair, but I would have to go back to work at the library to afford that kind of rent. I'm glad you brought this up. It's forcing a little reality thinking on my part. I took a leave of absence with the expectation that I would return to my position in July. Right now, I'm thinking that it would be smart to do that, rent your apartment, and then I would be free to think about what's next. If I am busy trying to find a place to live and find another job in a hurry, I won't be able to focus on what I really want to do."

"But what if you know what's next by the time you go back. Isn't that possible?"

"Not likely, because I'm not going to waste a minute of my time in Scotland researching graduate school programs, making applications or looking for alternative positions in my field."

"So, it's settled then? What colour shall I paint your bedroom?" Sam looked at her and laughed. "Just kidding. Take your time. Let me know after supper," he said, still chuckling.

"Seriously, I will sleep on it and see what I think in the morning, but it just feels right. Do I have the downstairs living room and kitchen and the upstairs bedrooms and you the reverse?"

"Well, there is an advantage upstairs, but I suggest we share the sun porch on the second level and there are a couple of attic rooms."

"This sounds better and better. What about a grill outside? Do you allow that, Mr Landlord?"

"In the garage, ready for the summer season, along with a basic, but comfortable, table and chair set for outdoor eating on the lower porch."

"Any closet space?"

"Small closets in the bedrooms, just enough for a man who wears mostly jeans and t-shirts. Could be a problem…"

"Not to worry, I got rid of most of my clothes when I left. If I can put suitcases and off-season clothes in the attic, I should be fine. This is fun, could you draw me a floor plan."

"Let's walk back to my place and I'll do it before dinner," Sam said, as he pulled out some pounds and put them on the table.

"This is so great. We can have a beer and look at the Firth of Forth, then go to my place to cook those lamb chops." Helen got up and followed him out the door. "I have to tell you that if the Scots would let me live here for longer than six months, your place would hardly compete with Queensferry."

"Lucky for me that they'll kick you out then."

After dinner, they began studying the Dalmeny Church booklet they had picked up, as well as their notes.

"They must have been very religious," Helen stated. "This church has a lot of the characteristics of Dunfermline and Durham Cathedral, and we have read that they gave a lot of property to the church."

"Historically they were a part of the early Celtic Church and opposed to Roman rule. They fought to keep their faith, which was much closer to early Christianity. Are you religious, I mean do you belong to a church?"

"Not really. Why do you ask?"

"I guess I don't want to offend you. I have some strong opinions about what is happening in Christianity. It is not unlike the struggle that happened in

Gospatric's time," he added and continued. "It's a reversal. By the late eleventh century the Roman Church had suppressed the Celtic Church which was much more egalitarian. Women held high positions, priests could marry, and there was a deep respect for the natural environment. Now the mainline faith groups are being undermined by evangelistic Christians, with some of them having hidden agendas for power and control. The progressive congregations are very social justice oriented, so they are often feeding the hungry, visiting prisons, fighting for human rights and supportive of women and gay clergy."

"And the evangelicals are the opposite?"

"I'm not putting them all in that box. It is difficult to name the category, but by their rhetoric you will know them."

"I suppose that is why I have stayed away from the organised church. I hear so much that has nothing to do with the teachings of Jesus that I embraced as a young person. We should have progressed to eliminating world hunger, releasing the prisoners, welcoming immigrants, and addressing the immense gap between the obscenely wealthy and the rest of the population."

"Oh my god, you're a socialist." Sam laughed as he said it.

"Whatever. I'm just a realist. Our current political situation isn't sustainable, but here I can escape from it. Sometimes I think I should try to get a job working to change all of it, but I am entirely unqualified."

"You could write," he said, with enthusiasm.

"I've thought about that, but I don't know if anyone would take me seriously. Where are you with the religion thing?"

"About the same place. My mother was a 'new ager' and I really identified with her thinking until she died. At that point, I didn't have any belief system. My wife was not religious and then she blamed God when she was going to die. I realised she had a kind of faith background where God was created in the image of man. I knew I couldn't comprehend that image. God, if there is such a thing, is a much broader concept. My master's thesis work led me to study all the groups that had been persecuted by the Church in the past. Millions have been killed in the name of Christianity. Muslims, Cathars, Templars, Huguenots, healers, and so-called witches were killed in incredible numbers because they couldn't buy into the dogma and doctrines created by men for their own power and control." He stopped and looked away, feeling like he had just gotten on his soapbox without wanting to do so.

"And now you find the same thing is happening. It certainly seems so when you see how women and people with different sexual orientations are being treated," Helen exclaimed, not at all bothered by his exposition.

"Thanks for listening. We should get back to looking at the booklet. It seems to have the Gospatric line wrong, doesn't it?" Sam asked, secretly pleased that he and Helen seemed to be agreeing about religious thinking.

"Yes, you are right. They have Waldeve's son, Gospatric, as the apparent owner of Inverkeithing, Dalmeny and Dundas. We know that he was Waldeve's illegitimate son and that he was given the area around Bolton, in Cumbria. Waldeve's son Alan and his two daughters also had land in Cumbria."

"Look, they show the son of that Gospatric from Bolton, another Waldeve, granting the land to Helias, son of Huctred," Sam read, "so, the error continues."

The next morning Sam picked up Helen and they found their way to the Forth Bridge and on northwards towards Perth. An hour later they saw the exit to Dunkeld. They turned left into the town and drove to the far end where Andrew had described a car park. The town was small, but charming. As they walked down the main street, they noticed several places to stop on their way back, including a sign for fresh salmon, a unique store with interesting Scottish food, and the pub Robert suggested for lunch. Turning the corner towards the abbey, they wandered through a couple of shops, and Helen bought a gift for Kit. She told Sam about their trip to Ireland and how they had left her husband's sister with the cooking of Thanksgiving dinner.

"Does everyone have someone like that in their family? My mother's sister and her husband were the same type, but they insisted on Thanksgiving at their house. I didn't mind because they were rich and had a big television to watch the game on, but Sarah hated every minute of it. She was stuck with our aunt Karen, in the kitchen preparing the food, making the pies, and then cleaning up. I must admit I wasn't much help."

"Are they in Minneapolis?"

"Both have died, they were older than my mom. Getting together stopped after the twins were born. That Thanksgiving Karen insisted on planning a memorial service for my mother. Sarah finally agreed but would have nothing to do with it. After the service, we all went to Karen and Jim's house. It was clear that the whole thing was for Karen's friends, and it turned into a cocktail party with photos of Karen and my mom all over the entry. Sarah got so angry that she walked out. Will followed her and I left as soon as I could. We all embarrassed

Aunt Karen so much she was unable to invite us to anything else. I had just started dating Helen and I took her to the memorial service and then to Karen's. She thought we were all very rude, but it was difficult for her to understand how phony it all was and how painful for Sarah. She was hospitalised again that night."

"Now, I've brought up a bad memory again." All conversation ceased as they entered the grounds of the Dunkeld Abbey. The beauty of the scene was overpowering. Ancient trees formed a canopy over the fresh new spring grass, leading to the wide flowing river. The peaceful scenery was in direct contrast to the unease Helen felt inside her. They walked forward to the crumbling ruins of the abbey, past the church, finding no way into the surrounding grounds because of construction work, but there was a door into a small entry with several old stones. After reading the inscriptions, Sam spoke.

"Let's see if the church is open."

"Sam, I'm feeling an overwhelming sense of sorrow. It's so beautiful here, but I don't know what is happening. I'm going to sit by the river for a few minutes, alone."

"I'll check out the church," he said, brushing her shoulder with a tender touch. Sam found the church door open and walked in. He read the list of past clergymen on the wall, going back in time, although not far enough for their search. The tiny museum had some artifacts from an earlier period, but no information that was helpful. He wanted to give Helen space, so he sat in a pew, in the stillness, staring at the walls surrounding him.

As Helen watched the river rushing in front of her, she felt the tears begin to slowly run down her cheeks. Shutting her eyes, she heard a faint sound of men yelling and swords clashing in the rumble of the moving water. The sadness and sense of sorrow increased, and she began to sob without trying to hold back what was inside her. It lasted only a few minutes and then she was struck with a feeling of total loss and despair. When Samuel sat beside her and put his arm around her, she realised she was shivering. She leaned against him wondering if he felt any of the same kind of pain. After a few minutes, they rose together and left the area around the abbey.

Sam and Helen ordered their lunch at the pub that was recommended and didn't return to their feelings about their experience. Helen was clearly interested in changing the subject, as least for the time they were in a public place. She was unsure whether her emotions might overcome her again.

"I'm still curious about the relationship of Tostig, Gospatric and Malcolm."

"What are you thinking about?" Sam asked.

"We know there is a record of King Malcolm going to King Edward with Tostig and that they became blood brothers. We believe that Gospatric went to Rome in 1061, with Tostig and Archbishop Ealdred. Then, some historical records report that Malcolm came as far south as Durham and then into Cumberland while they were in Rome, but Tostig did not retaliate. So, did Gospatric go to Rome with Malcolm's support, as a part of planning for the future? Or was Tostig keeping him in line, not wanting to leave his territory vulnerable to a play by Malcolm and Gospatric to take over Northumbria?"

Sam was quiet for a moment and then spoke. "I think the planning for the future when Edward died makes the most sense. Tostig was asked to go to Rome by his brother Harold, to gain favour with Pope Nicholas. There had also been issues of Rome being unhappy with appointments in Glasgow and wanting all the power to emanate from Canterbury and not York. All of Scotland was suspect because of its loyalty to the Celtic Church over the Roman Order. The journey would seem like an opportunity to influence the Pope on several counts. Tostig and Harold would not have known that Pope Nicholas would go out of his way to snub them and take power from Bishop Ealdred, for what seemed like a technicality. In the end, after the robbery on the road out of Rome, Nicholas gives in and acknowledges Ealdred as Archbishop of York. Since the Pope dies not that long after Tostig's party leaves, it was a stroke of luck that Ealdred ever got the pallium."

"And the supposed invasion of Malcolm while they were gone?" Helen asked, as their food was placed in front of them. "How do you see that fitting into this scenario?"

"If neither Gospatric nor Tostig was upset about Malcolm's activity in their territory, he may have been making a pass through to make sure no local thane was out of line. The *English Chronicles* were, it seems, always portraying the Scots in a bad light and trying to lessen the harshness of the English kings. There may have been less raiding and taking of booty than reported. Malcolm would not have known if Tostig and Gospatric were safe. Their trip must have taken at least three months. If something happened to them, I'm sure that Malcolm wanted to be able to hold onto Cumbria and take as much of Northumbria as he could."

"Makes more sense to me than any other explanation," Helen agreed. She stopped, about to put a forkful of food into her mouth and set it down. "Sam, what if Gospatric's Writ was done before he left for Rome? If he knew he was going to be gone for months, that perhaps he would be killed, he would have wanted to protect his son's right to that territory. He would have trusted Thorfinn to ensure the safety of his son, particularly if Dolphin was Thorfinn's grandson."

"If the Writ came after Siward's death, and we know it might have, that could be the case. We haven't seen that date as a possibility because most historians don't even acknowledge that Gospatric was in Allerdale."

"I'm not sure, but I think the documents from Aspatria that Andrew showed us had the date 1050 listed for the Writ, but that doesn't seem logical," Helen stated. "The other date might have been 1067 when Gospatric left Aspatria for Bamburgh, knowing that he was unlikely to be present in Cumbria over the coming years. I guess we will never be able to prove it, anyway. Every piece of information we have leads to another question." She began eating again, after her momentary excitement.

"We do know a lot, Helen, and applying the logic of the four of us, we are likely to arrive at more constructive conclusions than those who don't even understand the different Gospatrics in the drama."

"I suppose. Let's check out that neat store across the street and then search for some salmon for tonight, before we leave here."

"How about dinner at my place tonight? I want to hear what you felt at Dunkeld, if you think you could share what you experienced."

"I'd like to tell you. I think I'll be able to talk about it later."

After dinner, Sam asked Helen about her reactions in Dunkeld. She asked for another glass of wine and then tried to explain what she was experiencing.

"I can't say it was sadness, like when you hear that someone is ill or has died. It was an overwhelming sense of devastation. I could feel the grief and loss of a hundred souls. I just don't know any other way to explain it. Did you feel anything?"

"No, but I don't think I'm as sensitive to what might have happened in the past as you are. My mother was like you and I'm afraid her death made me even more reluctant about letting in those kinds of feelings. Have you had this happen before?"

"Nothing like this has ever happened to me, but I haven't been in a place with this much historical angst before. There was the fire that burned Dunkeld in 1027, as well as the battle in 1045, where Maldred and Crinan and so many others were killed. Are you worried that I am like your mother?"

"No, but it's scary to think that someone might get caught up with something powerful from the past and not be able to escape from it."

"Is that what happened to her?"

"It's difficult to explain. I was busy with work and my university classes, and I didn't see any changes in her. Then when I read her diary after her death, I began to wonder if she was able to hide what she was experiencing, or if I just wasn't paying attention. Now I worry about Juliana, because she is so much more like my mother than Sarah is."

"I must ask. Do you think it is a mental illness?"

"No, but I understand the question. My mother was having reactions that might be classified as hallucinations, but they were real in some mystical way. She wondered if she was sensing energy in the old Dundas Keep, a ghost of sorts. She also thought it might be genetic memory, triggered by being in a place where her ancestor had a difficult experience."

"Or a past life memory? Did she wonder about that?"

"Yes, and that seems the most feasible to me, but why was she so susceptible to that when most of us are not?"

"Maybe openness, maybe multiple triggers, like a person and a place..." Helen stopped talking and then felt very tired. "I think I should go home. I suddenly feel exhausted."

"We have a big day tomorrow, Rosslyn Chapel, Temple and Arniston House. I'll drive you home."

"I think I prefer to walk and clear my head. Why don't you come for breakfast about eight and then we can be off by nine?"

"Are you sure...if you're tired, it's a long walk up that hill?"

"I'll be fine, but just bring that bag with my groceries with you in the morning or we won't have any bacon and eggs."

Helen kept trying to relax and let sleep overcome her, but it didn't work. She was physically tired, and she wanted to sleep, but her mind wouldn't stop. She kept thinking of Sam's questions and his thoughts about his mother and his niece. Was it a form of mental illness to be so tuned into a long distant past? She certainly had felt a little crazy when she was overwhelmed by the sensation of absolute grief, like she had never felt before. It worried her a bit, that they were going to three places where there could be a recurrence of her experience.

Helen need not have worried. Rosslyn Chapel had queues waiting to get in and the cafe was packed with people. Helen and Sam looked at each other and left. They walked to the village for a quiet coffee and then drove to the park below the chapel and walked up the steep path to Roslin Castle. Looking down in all directions from the top of the walls caused uninvited vertigo.

"How did they ever build places like these...on the tops of soaring rock formations?" Sam asked.

"I suppose it was natural to pick the highest ground in an area."

"And then have only one way to get in, a way you could defend. Are you ready to go back down and have our picnic lunch?"

"I think I'll need to eat in the car. I'm chilled. I'm not sure if it's from the wind or the terrorising effect of the elevation when you gaze over the edge."

"I'd like to come back sometime, especially if we could find a way to get into the chapel without hundreds of other tourists," Sam added.

As they approached the remains of the Knights Templar site an hour later, they were taken aback by the beauty of the area. Driving down a steep hill off the main road, Sam edged his way to the side and parked the car. The actual ruin had a metal fence around it, but it didn't stop Helen. She pulled the bars apart where there was a wider space between two parts of the fence and slipped inside. Sam followed, with a bit more trouble getting through. He supposed that the fence was to limit the liability if someone was hit by a falling stone from the twelfth century skeleton of the ancient Templar structure. He reminded Helen that King David had welcomed the Templars to Scotland in the 1100s. "When the King of France and the Pope ordered the arrest of all of the Templars, Scotland was a natural place for those who managed to escape from France to seek refuge."

"You and Robert know a lot about the Templars, don't you?" Helen commented.

"Yes, but I know about them intellectually, from studying their history and potential survival. I sense that Robert's knowledge is much deeper. I wonder about his involvement with a secret society that might still have a connection to that history..."

They were both silent for a few moments while they stared at the few broken gravestones left and at the sky above through the empty spaces. It seemed the whole place would collapse within a few years.

"Look, here is a Dundas gravestone," Helen said, calling Sam. "Why would someone be buried here? I suppose they must be from the Arniston branch since they lived close by."

"I'll put this name on my phone and we can check it out. Henry Dundas—1866–1940."

"We should try to get back out of here, so we don't miss our tour of Arniston House," she said, as she headed towards the fence where they came in. Sam spread the metal poles for her and then pulled himself through between them.

"Let's just sit on the bench over there for a few minutes. We are only fifteen minutes from Arniston now," Sam said, as he led her across the grass.

"Any weird feelings here?" Sam asked, as they sat down.

"No, nothing like Dunkeld, but I am curious about the connections of the Templars to the Dundas family, if there is one, and what you were saying about Robert."

"I think we will find a connection, if we dig for it, and Robert knows what it is. I'm not sure if he will tell us, but I want to push him a bit. He wants Juliana here for some reason, beyond his paternal relationship. It has something to do with his secret society."

"You think it is a Templar organisation?" Helen declared.

"There are some different Templar groups. One is a part of the Catholic Church, and they want the Templars exonerated from the charge of being heretics. There is another one that is here, in France and in the US. It has a lot of ex-military people; they supposedly do a lot of charity work, like the Masons, and they have some standing in the United Nations on the question of Israel," Sam stated, emphasising the last part of his sentence.

"Standing in the United Nations—how crazy is that? What position do they take?"

"I'm not sure. They say there are no secret initiations. They accept women. You need to be nominated by a member, to be considered. I suspect that they recruit people with money, but they deny it."

"You think Robert's a member? Is that what you really think?" Helen demanded.

"Somehow, no. I feel like he is a part of something else, but I can't really tell you why. I know a couple of the people in the US who are a part of the group, and they have very conservative values, and I don't see Robert that way."

"You know someone?" Helen asked, with suspicion in her voice.

"When I was researching a lot of this for my thesis, I was introduced to someone in the group. I was able to interview him, but he was careful. He was trying to find out if I was the kind of person that the organisation was interested in having as a member. He asked me more questions than I asked him. One question was whether I had considered visiting Israel. He had some ability to provide funds for certain individuals to be a part of a study group."

"What did you say?" Helen was concerned now about how Sam had handled the invitation.

"I left the door open, claimed that I had too many commitments at the time. Frankly, I was a little scared. I thought if I went along with him, I might not find it easy to reject an invitation without some repercussion. I was torn between joining and investigating and running the other way."

"Something intuitive, perhaps," she teased. "A little gut reaction, maybe?"

"Even shivers up the spine, from a couple of comments," Sam responded, as he ran a hand up her back. She was surprised, but his physical touch made her tingle a bit. She reached over and gave him a squeeze around his waist.

"Let's go Sherlock. Time for our next adventure."

"At your service, Dr Watson," he answered, as he stood and pulled her up from the bench. They walked arm in arm to the car and then the spell was broken.

Arniston House failed to produce any added information, as the family knew less about their Dundas family history than Helen and Sam did. They decided to eat dinner in Queensferry when they returned. Tired from the day, neither of them wanted to cook a meal. They found a table at the far end of the restaurant, where it was quiet, and both ordered a pasta dish and some wine.

"We seem to have similar tastes in food and wine."

"It will make sharing an apartment easier," Sam stated, with a smile.

"You mean I must share meals with you, as well as living space?"

"Absolutely, and you'll also be expected to get the groceries, cook, of course, and clean the bathroom."

"Does that imply that you are not capable of doing those chores?"

"I am an exceptionally good cook, I think, and enjoy shopping for fresh food. The bathroom, not so much, so best we each clean one."

"My sentiment exactly. We should be able to share the responsibility for chores quite equally. I don't think we should share the plans for living together with Andrew and Robert tomorrow night, do you?"

"They might get the wrong idea, but what if they decide to write us letters?"

"No one writes letters!"

"I think Robert would send information by mail. I could even see him sending a hand-written letter with real ink," Sam added.

"Still, we have months to tell them, so what should we focus on when we see them?"

The plates of pasta were set in front of them before Sam had a chance to answer, and they began eating and pouring more wine.

"As a history buff, I'd like to talk about Gospatric and 1066," Sam said as he wound some pasta onto his spoon. "I know more about the invasion by Harald Hardrada and King Harold's defeat than most people, but not as much about the Godwinson family as we do now."

"Not being a student of history, I only knew that 1066 was the Norman Conquest. And now, not only are we wrapped around Tostig, his anger at his brother, his part in the invasion and his death, but so much more."

"Don't forget Judith, Tostig's wife. I suppose that she was still in Flanders when he died at Stamford Bridge. I wonder how long it was before she knew about his death."

"And how long before King Malcolm knew and relayed that information to Gospatric?"

"I'll look it up on my phone…find out how many miles between Stamford Bridge and Edinburgh," Sam said, as he pulled out his phone. "It's about 200 miles. I suspect that Malcolm would have arranged for a rider to get him the information about the outcome."

"How far can a horse and rider go, I wonder?"

"I have it here because I've looked it up before. There are lots of conditions listed, but a good horse can do a hundred miles or more in a day. That means that in two days or less Malcolm would have known the outcome. He may even have been waiting farther south and been able to alert Gospatric quite quickly. If Harald Hardrada had won, they would have put their plan in place, at once."

"Of course, William would have been waiting to face the victor, so perhaps nothing would have been different in terms of outcome."

Sam put down the phone and began to finish his meal. Helen was finished and spoke about the dinner the next night. "If you took us through the events by the month, after King Edward's death in January, then we could try to speculate about where Malcolm and Gospatric were during the major events."

"We could work on a chart with the months and the characters and try to place them in their respective places. We should do that tomorrow. I'm tired of driving around, but is there somewhere else you want to go before we give up the car?"

"Just Dundas, and we could still do that if they call you. I'm ready for a low-key day, as well, and I think I'm ready for a hot bath and an early night."

"Agreed, let's get you home and we'll re-group in the morning. My place for breakfast?"

"Yes, I'll walk down, unless it is raining."

England
The Years 1066 and 1067

King Edward died on the 5th of January and Harold wasted no time in having himself crowned as king on the 6th of January, the same day as the burial. Although some members of the Witan had promoted Edgar Atheling as Edward's successor, Harold won out. He knew he had many enemies and he tried to anticipate where the attacks would take place. William of Normandy had his own problems to deal with and had no great fleet of ships. The first plausible danger was to come from Harald Hardrada, and King Harold left for York in the spring to join Edwin and Morcar in heading off an invasion. He had married their sister Edith as a way of gaining their support.

Harold's brother Tostig had joined with the invading force of Hardrada. They were delayed and landed later than expected, giving King Harold time to get ready for the attack. Tostig was killed on the 25th of September, as was Hardrada, in the battle at Stamford Bridge, just northeast of York. King Harold took a small force and started back south, knowing that William had landed on the south coast. He left his troops to rest, counting on them to follow shortly after him. Most of his force in the South had been released to return to their farms for harvest and they had to be reassembled to face William at Hastings. King Harold's forces fought valiantly, matching William's men, but Morcar and Edwin and the reinforcements from the North did not arrive in time to aid them. On October 14th, King Harold was surrounded by William's knights and hacked to death. His brothers Leowine and Gyrth were also killed. Now four of the surviving sons of the Godwinson family were dead within three weeks.

King Malcolm requested Gospatric's presence as soon as possible and, once again, he set out hoping to return before the storms of November made travelling difficult. Gospatric selected two of his men to accompany him and they left at first light. By nightfall, he sat in Malcolm's private quarters at Edinburgh Castle, having been served both food and drink. As Gospatric ate, Malcolm shared his thoughts.

"With the loss of Tostig and Hardrada, and now King Harold, we face a new dilemma. The Duke of Normandy is a powerful and dangerous man. William has already proved his ruthlessness by laying waste to everything around Hastings. He will push his way to the throne, with no one strong enough to stop him. I suspect that Morcar and Edwin will attempt to prove their support by claiming their delay in reaching Hastings in time to aid King Harold was deliberate."

"They have survived then, and what about Waltheof? Is he alive?" Gospatric asked with concern.

"Yes, but he will have to swear allegiance to William, and I fear for Edgar Atheling. The Witan met and chose him as successor as soon as they heard that King Harold was dead. William will want to eliminate him, one way or another."

"With no army, won't he succumb to William's forces and swear his fealty as well?"

"That will be the advice, and I believe he will do so. If he survives in the first few months, because William perceives him as a mere boy with no support, we must find a way to get him and his family to safety."

"But how, Sire?"

"I am in contact with Bishop Ealdred, and he has communicated with Edgar asking him to request a return to Hungary for his family, as soon as possible. Once safely out of the sight of William's forces, their ship will head north along the coast until we can bring them ashore in Northumbria."

"And how should I assist with the plan?" Gospatric asked, now finishing his meal.

Malcolm poured more wine for them and continued. "I want you to meet Edgar and the family in Northumbria. They must trust whoever greets them and feel confident that the greeting party will get them to safety. Margaret knows of you and the relationship to her through your mother. We may still be able to place you at Bamburgh, if Morcar is needed somewhere else or if he is eliminated by William, and that will be the most secure site for protecting them."

"Would not William choose Waltheof?"

"I don't believe he will trust Waltheof's connections with Denmark. He will keep him close in Northampton and Huntington, where he can keep an eye on him."

"This, then, is why you have kept me out of the conflict, for which I have been grateful."

"Yea, Gospatric. You have kept a steady hand on all of Cumbria and we will try to hold that territory, and gain Northumbria. As Edgar matures, we may yet see the day when he is King of England and Margaret my queen."

"And how do we proceed, Sire?" Gospatric was feeling a little dizzy from the wine and the warmth of the fire, after his intense ride to Scotland.

"We wait to see the outcome. To stop the killing and burning there will most certainly be acceptance of William, but little peace. Once we see how William moves ahead, we can strategise. I think he will be too busy to think about Scotland or Cumbria, while he is gaining control of the South, but he must deal with Northumbria."

"What would you have me do, while we wait?"

"We will prepare a request. You will list your family connections to Northumbria, as the grandson of Uchtred the Bold, your mother's relationship to the throne of England through King Athelred, your position as Lord of Allerdale, ruling all of Cumbria, and then ask to be named Earl of Northumbria."

"Why would he do this, rather than choosing one of his own Norman lords?"

"He knows of Tostig's history and the refusal of the thanes to accept him. Tostig went to William in his search for someone to take on Harold, and I am sure he would have shared the reason for his hatred of his brother for not supporting him in his fight to keep Northumbria. William will know Northumbria needs a strong leader, acceptable to the northern thanes and the local people. He'll maintain control of York, in another way through someone he deems loyal to him."

"What if we send the request and it is refused?"

"He has used all his resources to build ships for the invasion and fortresses when he landed. He must pay his forces and he will be desperate for funds."

"I have little to offer."

"I have all you need to make it worth his while. You prepare your justification for the earldom, and I will give you the resources. And tell me now, how is that growing family of yours?"

"A third daughter, Octreda…"

"Only two sons and now three daughters. We need more sons to cover Cumbria, but we can marry those girls to some powerful men." He laughed, making Gospatric feel uncomfortable about his cousin's ability to control not just him but his family.

"You think far ahead, Sire," he answered, hoping his fear of Malcolm's power over him was not obvious.

"Yea, and so should you, Cousin. I count on your loyalty, like no other. Ingibiorg is to have a third babe next year, but she is not young like your wife. I have sons to succeed me, but we must continue to work to free Edgar and Margaret from William's clutches so we may someday see peace in our land. In a few years, your son Dolphin can take his position and later Waltheof. But there is much to accomplish in the coming years. I know you worry about your family, but you must know that I will protect your children, whatever happens."

"Thank you, Sire. I hope I can serve you well."

The weather was mild for late October, as Gospatric and his men left the next morning for their journey back to Aspatria. They could have taken two days to ride back, but they proceeded ahead to take advantage of the lovely weather. Athelreda would be relieved upon their return, especially when she learned that there were no demands at present to go on a mission for King Malcolm. She could never forget that her father had died serving Malcolm in his struggle against Macbeth. Athelreda's brother Edmund had returned to their father's land in Edlingham and would be supportive, if Gospatric needed him, but he did not think he would share his assignment with his wife. There was little chance that he would ever be the Earl of Northumbria. Morcar would convince William to leave him as earl. There was much to fear if the Normans dominated the country. There were many Normans who had been invited to England during the reign of King Edward, but they had integrated into society gradually, often marrying Anglo-Saxon women in families with no male heirs. Gospatric could see that this could become a major thrust for William—marry his knights and followers to women in England, thus assuming the inheritance of their lands. Malcolm was suggesting something similar for his little daughters. Gospatric knew most of the Cumbrian families and he hoped he could give his daughters a choice about who they might marry and grant them land as a part of their betrothals.

Gospatric was so lost in thought, that he was hardly aware that they were nearing Carlisle, and now only a few miles from the coast and the warmth of his home and family. Athelreda had been a good wife, a willing bedding partner and a loving mother to his children, including Dolphin. He still thought of Dolphin's mother as his true love, and he could never give his heart totally to another.

Dolphin was his special child, so like his mother in looks and nature…a constant reminder of his loss, regardless of his happiness. It was time to put aside his thoughts, decide what he would share about the meeting, and get on with his life, until the next demand from Malcolm.

William had marched to London and quickly had himself crowned King on Christmas Day. In the spring, Gospatric learned that William was leaving for Normandy and taking several earls with him. Waltheof had sent him a letter at the end of February, assuring Gospatric that he was safe and would be travelling as a guest of the king and not as a hostage. He added that Edgar and others were leaving with him. Waltheof had a final message, written in Runes at the end of the letter, as if it was a blessing. Although Gospatric had not learned to read the Runes, Dolphin was quickly able to interpret the message as 'sister in danger.' The mention of Edgar, just before the end of the letter, helped Gospatric to decipher the message. Neither Gospatric nor Waltheof had a sister, and he was certain that the Runes referred to Edgar's sister. He needed to tell Malcolm and he set out at once for Scotland.

Malcolm was loud and angry as he talked with Gospatric. Gospatric feared what was coming next.

"He has taken Edwin and Morcar, Bishop Ealdred and Bishop Stigand to Normandy with him, as well as Edgar, Waltheof, Merleswein, and other thanes he doesn't trust."

"Do you believe they are hostages, not guests? Was that what Waltheof was really saying in his message?"

"Most certainly. In his absence, many families are sending their daughters to convents for protection. They have learned that, upon their return, Edwin and Morcar will escort the Normans to find brides and land. This will happen all over the country, assuring both wealth, loyalty, and a payment for Norman services to William. Waltheof's letter, I agree, relates to the danger of Margaret being forced into a marriage with a high-ranking Norman."

"What can we do?"

"Again, we wait with readiness. It is now imperative that we have a plan to get Edgar and Margaret to safety as soon as Edgar is brought back. I trust Bishop Ealdred and Waltheof with this plan, but not Edwin and Morcar. They may help with a move against William at York, but I prefer to keep this close. We will have Edgar ask to return to Hungary with his family as soon as he can. Hopefully, he can be convincing."

"How long do you think William will keep them all in Normandy?"

"That is the difficulty. We will not know. If he waits too long, the seas will be rough and dangerous for Edgar to travel when he returns, but it could justify landing on the coast. It must be far enough north to escape from William's forces."

"Would it not be better to get them to safety in Flanders? Judith would be certain to assist, would she not?" Gospatric asked, understanding the geography a bit from his trip to Rome.

"This is wise thinking. We will consider that action. I'll send a messenger to Baldwin's court, without disclosing the total plan, only the need to get Edgar and his family out of England. Now once again we wait but, in the meantime, we are prepared. The Danes are restless. If they do not strike this summer, they will certainly be back next year, and we shall be ready to assist them."

"Would England choose a Danish king over a Norman one?"

"The Northumbrians would, I believe, and Harold's family is preparing their own invasion in the South. All of this will be helpful to us, if we remain vigilant and ready to move when the opportunity arises."

"I'm not sure of Maldred's position, as I have said in the past, but he is near the coast and may be of assistance if we need a landing place further south."

"It might serve as a temporary site, but I think we must get them as far as possible, first to the River Wear, then to the River Aln. From there they can reach Bamburgh, if it is in our hands, or make the longer journey into Scotland."

"I'm still concerned, Sire, that Waltheof should take his birthright in Northumbria, not I."

"There is much trouble in Northumbria. Osulf will not tolerate Copsi, who King William left in charge, and he will have some support of the other thanes, even if they are not involved."

"Involved in what—do you think he will move against Copsi?"

"Of course, he will. Copsi is not strong and Osulf has some rights as Uchtred's descendant. He has been waiting to make a move for the earldom and now he will take it any way he can."

"But if he takes over, he could have a greater claim than either Waltheof or myself, Sire."

"William will not accept that interference with his choice. He will arrange a way to remove him. We will have Waltheof ask for his place in Northumbria, but William will want to keep him close, knowing his powerful connection to the Danes. The Danes would consider Waltheof's position as Earl of Northumbria as an invitation to invade and retake England from the North. There are rumours that your young cousin has fallen under the spell of Judith, William's niece. If he is lucky, Waltheof will get more than his father's southern estates. Does that make you more comfortable with the title of earl?"

Gospatric frowned, then spoke. "It does, but I would now be afraid for Waltheof—that he might find himself tied to William and I would lose him."

"Do not fear for him or yourself. He is as loyal to you as he has ever been since you became his 'big brother' at Bamburgh. He will be pleased to know you are the earl and will support our efforts."

"You speak as if you have met with him and know his mind," Gospatric said, looking directly at Malcolm.

"Trust, Gospatric, that I have ways to learn what is happening. Waltheof will surely contact you as soon as he is able to do so, and we will then make our move. He has been confirmed in his possession of Northamptonshire and Huntington and he knows this is the way for William to control him. Waltheof is a leader who is powerful and respected. William wants him as near as possible and has chosen to put his niece in his path, as a further way of ensuring Waltheof's connection to him. He may play at not allowing a marriage between Judith and Waltheof, while plotting to do exactly that."

"How can you be so sure of this, Sire?"

"Because, Cousin, I would do the same."

South Queensferry, Scotland
March 2017

Sam and Helen walked to the restaurant where Robert had arranged for a private room for their dinner party. They brought along some charts they had prepared, which made the events of 1066 and the questions about the location of certain characters very clear. After ordering drinks and asking for a break before dinner, they reviewed the charts and added information that helped them with their research.

"I think we all agree that Malcolm and Gospatric were on the sidelines, during Harald Hardrada's invasion," Robert said. "And it is likely they did not show their hand as William was crowned."

"It must have been very painful, as they waited for news, not knowing what would happen to Edgar and his family. We have no idea how long it took for information to reach them," Helen stated.

"I think Malcolm would have been as close to York as he dared to be, when Tostig and Hardrada's forces invaded."

"That's true, Andrew. We know that Harold had married Edith, Edwin and Morcar's sister, to gain their support. Morcar would have been near York, with most of his forces with him. Perhaps Malcolm was close by, waiting to support Tostig and Hardrada if they succeeded in defeating Harold."

Sam continued. "Malcolm would surely have a spy close at hand to relay the outcome to him."

"Gospatric would have been waiting for Malcolm's communication, ready to take over Northumbria if that was ordered by Malcolm," Robert continued. "Let's speculate. We know that by Easter, William feels secure enough to leave for Normandy, taking Edwin, Morcar, Edgar, Waltheof, Merleswein, and the two bishops with him. Edwin and Morcar had supported Harold, Edgar had rights to the throne and both Waltheof and Merleswein had a great deal of territory.

William must have felt threatened by the men he took to France. He treated them well, we know, but had them under his control."

"He couldn't have prevented some private conversations and perhaps planning," Helen posed, loving the way in which the four of them could play out the events.

"The plotting started, but certainly Edwin and Morcar played along with William for a couple of years," Andrew added. "Waltheof might have been a part of the planning to get Edgar and Margaret out of William's clutches, and safely to Northumbria or Scotland."

"Since Gospatric and Waltheof were working together in the plot to put Edgar on the throne, by the summer of 1068, perhaps there was a line of communication between them much earlier."

"You are right, Helen. Malcolm would have wanted to use the close relationship that Gospatric and Waltheof had as children in any way he could. He would know that Gospatric had feelings of loyalty to Waltheof and would be conflicted about taking over as Earl of Northumbria. And now we should probably order our dinners, before it gets too late. It is sad to think this is our last chance to work together. It has been so helpful."

They all nodded in agreement and picked up their menus, feeling the impact of the last statement.

As they left the restaurant after dinner, Robert spoke first. "Let's all read as much as possible about the events while King William is in Normandy, his decision to name Gospatric as Earl of Northumbria when he returned and the subsequent plots to overthrow him as king." Robert turned to Samuel and put his arms around him. "Hopefully, you will be back with us with good news in a few short weeks, and we can continue our work together. We are a good team, I think," he added as he drew all of them close in an unexpected hug before leaving with Andrew.

"That was rather out of character," Helen said, as they walked back towards Sam's flat.

"Yes, but we have seen a lot of changes in him over a brief time…at least I have."

"You are responsible for that. He has changed since you arrived."

"I think it is finding out that he is a father, rather than my presence, that has brought out something different in his behaviour, but I am worried how Juliana's response will affect him."

"You really believe she'll reject him, don't you?"

"She is a young woman who lost her father to an early death and is now losing her mother in a similar way. She is preparing to handle the dying process, but not shocking information that changes the very nature of her family as she has known it. I think her response to the information won't allow her to see her parents as human beings with frailties. She will feel deceived by us all, even though I have only known for a few short weeks that Robert is her father..."

"Don't you think you can help her, especially since you know Robert?"

"I wish you could be there with me," he said, as they reached his door. He leaned down and kissed her and then seemed shocked by his own behaviour. He turned and unlocked the door, letting her walk in before him.

They both tried to speak at the same time.

"You first," Sam invited.

"I'm not ready for this, Sam, but I want to be with you tonight."

"I understand. It is happening too fast, and it may be the magic of the moment, of the excitement of what we are doing together."

"Let's blame Gospatric. I just might be falling out of love with him and..."

"Let's have a coffee and talk. Then later, I'll drive you home if that's what you want...unless you have already made up your mind."

"I'd like to stay with you," she whispered.

England
The Year 1067

Several months had passed since Gospatric's meeting with Malcolm, and there had been little news from Normandy. Waltheof wrote occasionally and had emphasised his desire to remain in the South on his father's land, if he was granted permission by William. He praised William for his kind treatment of those he had brought with him. One letter confirmed Waltheof's obsession with Judith, and his hope that William would approve of his betrothal to her. Once again there was a final greeting in Runes and Dolphin interpreted them as 'Preparation is needed.' In October, a letter alerted Gospatric to action. Waltheof wrote that plans were being made to leave for England before the storms of November.

Osulf had killed Copsi, King William's appointee, as Malcolm predicted and placed himself as Earl of Northumbria. Now, before William returned with his hostages, Osulf had been killed by robbers. King William would be concerned about how to deal with Northumbria. He had trouble in Kent, with the sons of Harold threatening a rebellion, and the Welsh were also rebelling. Waltheof invited Gospatric to visit London upon his return, to meet Judith at court, and he assured him that the king would welcome him. Edgar was especially eager to meet the Cumbrian leader who was known as Waltheof's 'big brother.' The Runes at the end were interpreted as 'the Time is Now.' Dolphin asked what it meant and wanted to know why he couldn't also go to court to meet the king. Gospatric went to Athelreda and shared the letter. He told her only a little of Malcolm's plan—that Malcolm wished him to ask to be named the earl of Northumbria. He would assure William that he could manage the thanes and the robbers, and he would pay a large sum for the privilege of being named earl to replace Osulf.

"How can you pay him and make such promises? And what of our lives here in Aspatria?"

"Nothing may come of it, my love, but I must go to King Malcolm now and speak with him of Waltheof's invitation. Malcolm has promised to provide whatever gold is required."

"And if King William says yes, what then? Do you intend to move us to Bamburgh Castle? Is this about getting it back after all these years?"

"I have not had time to think on this, wife," he answered with some irritation. He only knew he had to leave soon and didn't know if he would return before going to meet Waltheof. The winter storms were imminent across the hills, and it would be best to head south, perhaps reaching his mother and brother, to await the arrival of the ships from Normandy. "I must prepare to leave, and I cannot tell you that I will immediately return. I will take my finest clothing for the visit to court. I beg you to understand this is not for me, but for all of us, that I do what Malcolm wants. I will send a messenger if I'm to go south immediately."

"I'll have your clothes made ready," she retorted, as she turned away from him in anger. He knew she would soften by nightfall, as they said their goodbyes through their lovemaking. He was right, as they reached out for each other that night. He tried to be tender, but they both felt the fear of pending separation and loss, and it made them desperate to have each other. He held her in his arms as she fell asleep, but none would come to him. He knew this was the moment his life would no longer be his own, and he wondered how he could protect this woman and his children from the coming events. More difficult than leaving Athelreda was the problem of Dolphin begging to go with him and the absolute necessity of saying no to his son.

He stoked the fire in the room and crept downstairs, leaving his wife asleep. His men were waiting, getting the packs and food ready to take outside. They ate some warm gruel that had cooked overnight and set out into the frosty morning just before sunrise. Two men rode with Gospatric, and one was to be released to return to Aspatria to alert Athelreda and Thorfinn of their intentions. On the road to Carlisle, they were intercepted by soldiers sent by King Malcolm. Malcolm's instructions were to bring Gospatric to Northumbria, where he was currently assessing the situation around the Tyne Estuary. He had been raiding in the area, as there was no earl in charge any longer and he wanted to make his presence known to the people. The party reached Malcolm by nightfall, and the king and

Gospatric were left alone, while the others arranged for food and drink to be brought into the manor house of one of the local thanes.

"I am pleased that you have heard from Waltheof," Malcolm said, with enthusiasm. "It means that the plans have materialised, as we had hoped. We are unsure of when they will land and I suggest you visit your brother, who is nearby."

"That was my thought, also, and might I ask him if he is prepared to shelter Edgar and his family if it is necessary?"

"It is a risk, but it is my understanding that he did not support either Harold or William and was able to stay out of harm's way. You might first try to see what position he will take as William returns. Morcar has surely been in touch with him or will be as soon as they land in England."

"And Morcar and Edwin, are they to be trusted?"

"I believe they are but will appear loyal to William until we have our plans in place. They will bring the Normans north to York. Waltheof will take his position in Huntington and Northamptonshire, and Merleswein will return to Lincoln. I believe Waltheof has the ear of William because of Judith, and you should be able to make a personal request to William for the earldom. He is in a weak position right now, and Morcar and Edwin will also lend their voice to the need for a strong leader in the North. They will keep control of York, but they will accept you at Bamburgh Castle."

"What about Edgar and his family? How should I proceed?"

"You must meet with Edgar and arrange a way to move his family away from London. It is possible that Waltheof can bring them to Northampton to meet with you, but he must not take that risk unless William has already agreed to let them return to Hungary. We will arrange passage for the family to sail up the coast and land before the worst winter storm hits."

"I will see my brother tomorrow and learn of his leanings. How will I hear from you?"

"I must return to Scotland as soon as possible, and from now on your contact will be Waltheof."

Malcolm's men returned and the conversation was over. Gospatric wanted more guidance, more assurance, and more discussion of the options if any part of the plan failed, but there were no further opportunities for questions. Food and ale were served, but he was barely able to finish his meal before the need for sleep overcame him. He retired to his quarters, feeling alone and fearful, but with a certain sense of excitement. They might stop King William from taking over the country and he might play a part in making that a reality. He fell onto the bed, having only pulled off his boots, and did not wake until morning.

Gospatric had sent his companion Erik ahead to his brother at Winlaton, to announce his arrival. Although he wanted to see his mother, he hoped she wouldn't be there immediately, as he wanted private time with Maldred.

Unfortunately, that was not to happen. His mother was at Maldred's manor to meet him. Although she had refused to acknowledge his first marriage, she had met Dolphin, but not Waltheof and his girls. She had approved of his marriage to Athelreda but was not willing to travel to Cumbria to visit the family. It would have been possible for her, as she was still a very able woman. She chose to dote on Maldred's young sons, Ulkil, Uchtred and Robert, but she wanted to hear news of Gospatric's children and was asking why he had come alone without the family. He was not prepared for that question and did not have a good explanation, but she accepted his excuse of the difficulty of travel with such young children. He did not mention that Dolphin had begged to join him in this visit.

Finally, Ealdgyth left with the boys and Maldred's wife, and the brothers were alone sitting close to the open fire conversing.

"You are doing well, brother, with a family and a fine manor house. You escaped the fighting, I presume." Gospatric hoped to gain a perspective on Maldred's feelings about William of Normandy.

"I did, by taking no sides in the struggles. By rights, it should have been Edgar on the throne. He was the choice of the Witan. It is unfortunate that he is so young and not known by many of the nobles in the country."

"Nor by the thanes of Northumbria, but they would support him against William."

"I think only if you and King Malcolm would do so. You have both been quiet, perhaps awaiting a better time?" Maldred looked at Gospatric, himself searching for confirmation of his brother's position. "I understand that William is returning to England with his guests," Maldred added with a heavy emphasis on the word 'guests.'

"That is why I am here—to meet with Waltheof and to see what can be done about Edgar," Gospatric confessed, hoping he had made the right decision to trust his brother.

"William thinks him a minor threat, although the stirrings of the Godwinson family and the Welsh must make him nervous. He knows that Edgar was the chosen heir by the Witan, despite William's claims. I would say it is likely that Edgar will have a premature death, as his father did, and there are rumours of marrying Margaret and her devout sister to returning Norman lords."

"Would you help get Edgar and his family out of William's clutches?" Gospatric watched Maldred carefully to see what his response would be to the question. He sensed it was the one he had hoped for but was still cautious.

"I would, of course, if it were possible. I am not sure you know who you are dealing with in the usurper. He is ruthless. He burned everything around Hastings that he did not want and left the people to starve. He has no intention of ruling by winning the hearts of the English. He will rule by force and intimidation!"

"There is a plan afoot. I don't know all of it, but I am here to help with its execution. I'm grateful I can depend on you. We haven't had much contact in the years since we left Bamburgh."

Maldred's wife and Ealdgyth returned to the room and ended their conversation, but later they whispered to each other by the fire, discussing possible scenarios. The plan was for Gospatric to meet Waltheof and Bishop Ealdred when they landed at Dover, riding back to London with them.

"I hope to have an audience with William and ask him for the Earldom of Northumbria. If it works, I'll then try to take Edgar and his family north to Waltheof's manor in Northamptonshire. We will travel on from there as quickly as possible, while William is occupied with his return and his problems elsewhere."

"Godspeed, brother. This could be the first step in overcoming the power of this king, before he does any more damage."

Riding from Dover with the royal party gave Gospatric and Waltheof a few minutes of conversation. Waltheof had prepared William for Gospatric's request for Northumbria. He was to emphasise his success in ruling Cumbria, his connection to the House of Bamburgh, his ability to control the northern nobles and his generous resources. There was no real audience. William was feeling the urgency of getting his family to London, and in a quick meeting he granted the northern part of Northumbria to Gospatric for a large amount of gold. He acknowledged that he was placing trust in the recommendations of Waltheof, Morcar and Edwin, as well as the bishop, and asked for fealty to him. Gospatric complied, saying a silent appeal for forgiveness for his blatant lie. He was ordered to ride north, with Morcar and Edwin, accompanied by the Norman knights and soldiers that were going to York. Morcar and some of his men would escort Gospatric, to ensure that there was no trouble, leaving the Normans in York with Edwin and Bishop Ealdred. The Normans would begin building a castle for their occupation, taking what they needed and wanted from the people living in York, including food and women.

Waltheof had spoken to William about Edgar's desire to return to Hungary with his family. William had agreed that Edgar could leave, but his family would remain, potentially to wed Margaret and Christina to Norman lords. Waltheof assured him that Edgar would never leave without his mother and sisters. The sisters had left Romney Abbey and were now with their mother Agatha at Wilton Abbey, where she wished them to take the veil. Edgar wanted to return them all to the safety of Hungary, where they yearned to go. Since the sisters had no resources and no titles, Waltheof persuaded William they were not desirable marriage alliances for his fine Norman knights. He left the encounter with permission for Edgar to bring his family to Waltheof in Northampton, and Waltheof would ensure that they were put on a ship on the coast, on their way to Rotterdam. William was sceptical about whether they would leave so late in the year. Waltheof explained that allowing them to leave would mean that William would not have to worry about Edgar being a focus of a rebellion. If they were lost at sea, he could not be blamed. This last argument settled the issue and Waltheof, like Gospatric, said a silent prayer of forgiveness for his deception. William was distracted by his troubles from the factions that were invading his southern shores. He was relieved to have Gospatric taking over the recalcitrant thanes, settling the issues brewing in Northumbria, and to accept Waltheof's offer to get Edgar out of the way.

The strategy had succeeded, and now the conspirators had to quickly get Edgar's family to safety. The revised plan was for Gospatric to proceed to Bamburgh Castle, while Edgar and Waltheof went to Wilton Abbey to move the family to Northampton. They planned to make the trip in one day, and rest before proceeding to Crowland Abbey, near Peterborough, where Merleswein would take them to a ship on the coast. Maldred would greet them if they made it to the landing on the Tyne. When they heard that the time was right, and the weather reasonable, they would sail to the mouth of the River Aln, where Gospatric would meet them, taking them north to Bamburgh Castle. Stories would be told about their ship being washed ashore in a storm, thus keeping blame from

Waltheof, if William should learn that they were still in the country. Waltheof, Gospatric and Edgar had a quick moment in which to confirm their plans, wishing each a safe journey. Judith was close by, and Gospatric was worried that she was trying to listen to their final whisperings. Gospatric could see the appeal William's niece had for Waltheof, but he was not comfortable with her. Some deep instinct suggested that she was a part of William's plan to control Waltheof and thus not to be trusted.

The plan proceeded with little drama; the family of Edgar was eager to return to their homeland and confident in Edgar and his friend Waltheof. The travel was demanding, but Margaret and Christina were relieved to be free of life at the abbey and rode confidently next to Edgar. He did not intend on deceiving them indefinitely, but he had agreed with Waltheof that they could not take a chance that someone might betray them if they revealed their intention to remain in England. The ship's captain was instructed to act as if he intended to cross the sea to the continent.

Once they arrived in Northampton at Waltheof's manor, they rested a day before proceeding to Crowland Abbey, making the remainder of the land journey more manageable. They had few possessions, but thinking of their return to Hungary, his mother wished to have everything with them, including the few servants who had survived in her service. The sea journey was challenging, but they were reassured when they were met by Maldred, Gospatric's brother and a cousin to the family. Merleswein had taken them from Crowland to the ship and sailed with them.

It was Margaret who first asked the question about why Merleswein was sailing north with them. At first, she accepted that he was assuring their safety partway, before they made the sea crossing. She knew her brother well and guessed that he was holding back information. He swore her to secrecy and confessed the plan to make their way north, as a part of King Malcolm's decision to support him for the English throne. Margaret had a mixed reaction knowing that it was her brother's right to be the king of England, but she knew her mother yearned to go back to Hungary. Edgar had been the choice of the Witan at the time of Harold's death at Hastings, but she was concerned about William's power to not only ignore the Witan, but to execute all of them for treason.

Margaret asked what King Malcolm, who had a reputation for breaking promises, wanted in return. She remembered well that he had appeared before her mother five or six years earlier, asking for a blessing of his betrothal to

Margaret. King Edward had approved of the alliance if Agatha agreed. Her mother had flatly refused, saying she was much too young to marry. Malcolm made an impression on her then: his large stature, his boldness in approaching her mother and his scoffing when Agatha said she wanted her daughters to take holy vows. Margaret had little experience outside of her family home and the Church. This unusual man frightened her, but also intrigued her. Although he was from a wild land in the North, he spoke French and English more fluently than her mother. Now he was plotting with others to overcome William, Duke of Normandy, and place Edgar in his rightful position. Her brother was not strong, neither physically, nor emotionally. He suffered from losing his father so young, having just arrived in a foreign country where he did not speak the language. He was more interested in art and music than in warfare, but with the King of Scots behind him, and Waltheof and Merleswein, who held large territories in England, she could see the possibilities.

Gospatric arrived at Bamburgh Castle and was greeted by those who had remained after Osulf's death. They had waited with trepidation for William to choose a new earl and were relieved to be welcoming Gospatric. It was quickly known that after his father's death he had grown up at Bamburgh Castle, with Earl Siward, and was the well-respected Lord of Allerdale. He was related to the House of Bamburgh, but also to the ancient family of his grandfather Crinan. Most of those in service had a connection to him, but Gospatric knew there would be a spy for William in the group that accompanied him north. He would have to be incredibly careful not to expose their plans. He gave orders for spaces to be set up for his wife and children and guests, without exposing the possibility of Edgar's arrival with his family.

When they reached York, Gospatric had sent Erik to Aspatria to tell Athelreda that he would remain at Bamburgh Castle now that he was the earl. He suggested that the journey for her and the children would be too difficult this late in the season, and that she should wait until spring, when the castle would be more settled. He reminded her of Bamburgh's position on the wild, windy sea coast and tried to make a case for her to stay in Cumbria. As much as he missed her and the children, he didn't want them to be embroiled in the intrigue that was about to commence. He missed Dolphin more than the others. He always had a special place in his heart for him, from the early years when they had spent so much time together. Erik was to take a message to Thorfinn, as well, explaining the situation and asking him to manage Cumbria for him. It was Gospatric's decision to assign responsibility for the area, for it was unlikely that he would be able to return any time soon. He included a document for Thorfinn, to ensure the support of all men in the territory for him.

Erik arrived at Bamburgh shortly after Gospatric's party. He said that Athelreda, who always had a strong will, would not listen to Gospatric's advice to remain in Aspatria. She immediately ordered the household to pack and journey to Bamburgh to be with Gospatric, the new Earl of Northumbria. Thorfinn had advised her to avoid the Cheviot Hills and follow the Roman wall to the coast. She said she would travel to her brother Edmund, in Edlingham, and ask him to accompany her north to Bamburgh. Gospatric was not totally surprised, but now he had to prepare for his family as well as Edgar's family. The news from Maldred said he was busy with guests, who would soon set sail across the sea, and Gospatric knew this was his notice to prepare for their arrival.

Gospatric set about making the castle ready for the influx of both family and guests, without disclosing any expectations of who might be arriving. There were few women in the castle to work on making the space comfortable. He gave orders to ready as many rooms as they could manage, hoping that Athelreda would bring bedding and suitable items from Aspatria. He did not believe she would encounter many problems at this time of year, but there were bandits roaming the forests. He hoped that Thorfinn had insisted on her taking a large escort of men to protect her and the children. Dolphin would be excited about the adventure and the prospect of being at Bamburgh Castle, but Waltheof and his three little sisters would be subjected to the long journey in the cold. Four babes in five years and Athelreda seemed to thrive on motherhood and the running of a household. He wondered how she would handle this huge draughty castle. Gospatric knew it well from the years he had spent with Siward and his family. He had been younger than Dolphin when he and Maldred saw Bamburgh for the first time. They had never seen anything like this huge fortress, close to the sea. Waltheof was still a babe in his mother's arms the day they arrived, and now he was a part of an effort to defeat William and put Edgar on the throne of England.

There was a great flurry as one of the men came to warn him—a raiding party coming along the coast from the North. Looking out from the tower, he could see the leader, a familiar sight on his great black horse. He was not flying any banners, but Gospatric knew it was Malcolm. The king arrived bringing items for the castle, as well as animals. Giving orders to unload, he took Gospatric aside while his men brought in the large containers of food and household items.

"I believe you will need some things to make your guests feel at home, Cousin," he whispered.

"Athelreda comes with the children, against my good advice, Sire." Gospatric apologised, knowing the need for secrecy regarding the royal guests.

"Well, that is not a problem. She will be surprised, as all of us. We will ride south shortly to wait for the ship," he said quietly, but then boomed out so all could hear, "I want you to ride south with me for a raid at Alnwick. It will establish you as the earl but let us eat first." He grabbed Gospatric with an affectionate slap on the back and proceeded to order his men to get the women cooking the food they brought.

Later Gospatric tried to express his fear about his wife and children being in Northumbria, considering what they were planning. Malcolm was dismissive.

"It is all the better for our deception. We will move the women and children to Scotland at the appropriate time, but now let them enjoy this beautiful place by the sea."

"I always loved walking the beaches and watching the giant waves rolling in, but I'm not so sure it is a good place for my family in the dead of winter, with the raging storms from the North." He turned to Malcolm and spoke with some distress in his voice. "Why are you here, Sire? Did you not trust that I could carry out my mission?"

"Not at all, Gospatric. I wish only to know our guests are safely ashore and then I will continue my raid in your territory for a brief time before heading back to Scotland. I would have a word with Edgar and you about our support from Edwin and Morcar."

"Would you also want to meet Princess Margaret, Sire?" Gospatric asked, with a lighter tone.

"Yes, I do wish to see her. At my last encounter, I observed a young woman who tried to act shyly, but who displayed a great curiosity and intelligence. I expect to find her pleasing in my sight but upset by her situation. If there is no rough weather on the journey, the captain is to say that his ship has a problem that prevents him from making the crossing to Rotterdam. They will then be delivered into your hands to ride to the nearest place to shelter them, Bamburgh Castle."

"Do you believe they will be so easily deceived, with us there with extra horses and ready to receive them?"

"We will have been raiding the area, so we have gained these handsome mounts. I will give them extra men to assist their party with taking their possessions here. It is not our problem if they are not fooled; we will play our part well. Edgar can handle their questions and reveal what he likes."

The ship came into the mouth of the River Aln heading for shore the next afternoon, while they were close by. The king, rather than raiding, was assuring the common folk of his pleasure that his cousin, a true Scot, and a descendant of the ancient House of Bamburgh, was now earl, and warning them to support him if they wanted peace. The raiding party rode down to the shore to meet the ship, as it landed. Edgar exited first, with relief in his eyes, as he saw Gospatric there to greet him and bring him to King Malcolm. Gospatric then helped the women onto the shore, while his men assisted the rest of the party to unload their possessions. He brought Agatha, Christina and Margaret forward to meet the king, who just happened to be in the area with the new earl. Gospatric observed both Malcolm and Margaret, seeing just the slightest spark on her part and wholehearted approval from him. He knew that Ingibiorg was still alive, but not well, after losing her third child in a difficult birth. She was not young like Athelreda, and already had two grown sons left behind in Orkney. He did not wish her ill, nor want her young boys to be motherless, but he hoped she would pass on soon, for her own sake and for Malcolm's.

Bamburgh Castle
The Year 1068

After Malcolm had spoken with Edgar that day at Alnwick, he rode off to finish his journey through Gospatric's land, warning the people to support their new earl. Gospatric led the party along the seacoast to Bamburgh Castle. They could see the large fortress from a great distance, and it clearly impressed his guests. Although they were used to splendid buildings, they expected little in this wild territory. Relieved to be on land rather than the water, the party entered the castle walls in less than two hours. Edgar had informed Gospatric that Margaret knew their plans, but he was not yet confiding in Christina or his mother, who now believed they might wait until spring to travel to Hungary. Thankfully, Athelreda and the children arrived later that day, accompanied by her brother Edmund. Dolphin had ridden ahead with a small escort, and he threw himself into Gospatric's arms, proudly announcing their safe arrival. After much scurrying to find space for everyone, the household gathered in the great hall warmed by a roaring fire, enjoying food and wine. It was several hours before the children were settled and Athelreda was alone with Gospatric. She scolded him for his message to stay in Aspatria for the winter. She then confessed that she already knew she was with child again and not about to be left alone, while he enjoyed his new role as earl.

 At the end of June, Athelreda gave birth to a healthy baby girl. This time she was surrounded by women, who also cared for the other children, and the running of the castle. Margaret and Christina had immediately bonded with Athelreda, and Agatha mothered all three of them as they cared for the family. Dolphin spent more of his time with Gospatric and was followed around by seven-year-old Waltheof, who wanted little attention from the women, except for food. Ethelreda, Gunhild, and Octreda, who were five-and-a-half, four and two, were thriving with the female attention. Athelreda had plenty of time to rest and nurse the new babe named Matilda. It was a lovely summer, and the children were frequently on the beach, enjoying the magical finds that were thrown ashore by the waves.

King Malcolm had made several visits to Bamburgh and there had been occasions when Merlewein and Waltheof had joined with Edgar, Gospatric and the king to plan their next moves. They brought news of the other conspirators, Edwin and Morcar. Between them, they covered a large territory, and with the help of those in Wales, Hereward in Ely, and the sons of Harold Godwinson, they felt they could plan a rebellion from all directions. They always hosted a large banquet for the king and his guests, and Margaret and Edgar were placed on either side of Malcolm. He had made it clear to Edgar and the others—the plan required the betrothal of Margaret to him, as soon as possible. He would do what he needed to ensure he was free to marry, even if it required putting aside Ingibiorg. He had already removed her from Dunfermline to an abbey and she was not well. At their last meeting, Malcolm had suggested that they take the two families to Scotland, propose the marriage ceremony, and leave Gospatric's family with Margaret and her sister and mother. He had observed the closeness of the women and felt they would not be opposed to the decision. Margaret would need help with settling into her new role, as future queen, and would want the companionship she had enjoyed over the past months. Gospatric was not opposed to the plan, for he knew that the coming months could mean danger for those plotting against King William. Although Bamburgh was impregnable, in terms of invasion by land or sea, he did not want to defend his family or force them into a frightening situation. Edgar was more hesitant. His sister was still claiming that she and Christina wanted to become nuns. His mother Agatha also opposed the marriage and continued to believe they would return to Hungary. Gospatric had watched Margaret from across the dining table, as she spoke to Malcolm on several occasions, and he felt the spark was smouldering into a low-burning fire. He asked Athelreda for her opinion, as a woman and as a friend of Margaret. She maintained that Margaret had never shared a secret thought about Malcolm, but she agreed with Gospatric—there were certain signs of attraction. Malcolm arrived again in late summer. The rebellion was now planned and Edwin and Morcar would lead it in the South, with the help of Waltheof and Merlewein.

"We must move the women and children to Dunfermline now," Malcolm stated with his usual authority to Gospatric and Edgar. "I have arranged for a ship from Berwick to take them to the Forth. You can send some trusted men to accompany them, and I will meet them when they arrive. Gospatric, you and Edgar need to lead our Northumbrian forces towards York, to meet Waltheof and Merlewein as they move north. Edwin and Morcar and the others are ready to make a move across all of Mercia, and the Danish fleet is rumoured to be heading for our coast. Edgar, you must tell your mother and sisters that you have agreed to the marriage, and they should travel to Scotland to prepare for the ceremony."

"They will ask about Ingibiorg, Sire. What should I answer?"

"That it is not their concern. It will be handled before they arrive," he answered, leaving no room for protest. Gospatric shuddered a bit at Malcolm's response, but perhaps it was because he was now going into battle for the first time.

"I will alert the thanes that we must muster our forces for the day after tomorrow. We can ride hard and then rest before the attack." Gospatric tried to sound confident, but he was not. He remembered Maldred's words, 'you do not know who you are dealing with in the usurper—he is ruthless.' He shuddered again at the audacity of taking on the man now known as William the Bastard, for reasons other than his illegitimate birth.

The arrangements were made quickly, and Gospatric faced Athelreda that night in their private quarters, where questions could be asked.

"How is Margaret? How is she reacting to her brother's decision?" he asked with some trepidation.

"Brother's decision, no. I say Malcolm's order, is it not?" Athelreda spoke too loudly.

"Hush, wife, the walls have ears. Answer me, how does she fare?"

"She accepts her fate and tries to deal with her mother's rage and Christina's grumbling. She can see Edgar's position, and she looks forward to having her own bairns. She is such a good mother to our little ones. I am grateful to go with her, but I know you are not telling me about the danger for you and Edgar. All this secrecy. I suspect there has been a plan all along."

"Yea, my love, and I cannot tell you all of it, but when you have left, we ride to meet others to rebel against the tyranny of the Normans," he whispered. "I would have you safely in Scotland, for there is no guarantee of our success."

"You are afraid, then, of what might happen to you?" Athelreda reached for him, and he encircled her in his arms.

"I will return to you and the children, wherever you are," he promised.

South Queensferry, Scotland
April 2017

Helen had continued to work on their research and had learned much more about Gospatric's Writ. She had been in the library a few times and had dinner with Andrew only once, although they shared thoughts often on the phone. He did ask if she had heard from Samuel, but his queries were more about the news Robert was waiting for, rather than an interest in her contact with Sam. She hadn't talked with Sam, but they did exchange emails. He was busy with his final term of the university schedule and spending all his free time with Sarah and the family. She had rallied a bit and there was some thought that the chemotherapy treatments might be working, but he was not hopeful. Robert had asked if they could plan another weekend together, to share any new findings, and they had agreed on the following Friday. Robert would pick her up in the afternoon, and Andrew would come after work. She found she was not looking forward to the time together without Sam, and she wasn't sure why she felt that so strongly. She would spend the rest of the week trying to put her notes and thoughts in order.

When Robert arrived on Friday afternoon, he seemed subdued. As she got into the car, he immediately asked her about Samuel.

"Have you heard from Samuel?"

"Not for a few days. He said he was busy with his lectures and seeing students, and then spending every evening and weekend with the family. Did he tell you that Sarah is in remission?"

"No, perhaps that is why he is silent. He wouldn't have any news if she has maintained her decision to not tell Juliana until the last moments of her life. It is selfish to not help her deal with the truth. What do you think?" He glanced over at Helen as he entered the main road into Edinburgh.

"It is understandable. You may not have chosen to do it that way and I may not have, if we were in similar circumstances, but none of us knows what it is really like to be facing a certain death."

With that Robert sank into silence and Helen followed suit. Their communication seemed strained when they arrived. Helen said she needed a rest before dinner and headed up the stairs to her usual room. She wanted to wait until Andrew arrived before they started any sharing, and she didn't want to talk more about Sam and Sarah.

They met in the library at six, shortly after Andrew knocked to say he was next door, and Robert had suggested gathering for drinks before dinner. Helen did look forward to having this cocktail hour before dinner, and then wine with their meal. It eased the anxiety and awkwardness of this gathering without Sam for the first time.

"Has either of you had any major finds since we have been apart for a few weeks? I presume you have seen each other." They were settled into their favourite spots around the fire. The weather was still quite cold during the evenings and early mornings but had improved.

Helen spoke first. "I have given a lot of thought to the Writ that Gospatric wrote and changed my mind about it. When it was confirmed that he would be staying at Bamburgh Castle, Gospatric would have been concerned about his family and the future of Cumbria. The conspiracy to move against William was already shaping up, as well as plans to get Edgar's family to safety. That would mean leaving Allerdale without his leadership for months or longer."

"You think it was in 1067 then?" Andrew asked.

"It is a definite possibility, and it seems logical. Thorfinn was well established in the area. He had a manor at Ravensworth and several other properties. He was certainly to be trusted by Gospatric and Malcolm. What do you think, Robert?"

"Interesting, because I read some vague reference to Waltheof being the first to witness the Writ, but I didn't think there were any witnesses, so I looked at it again. There was no witnessing in any usual way. My memory of reading writs and charters was that there were no witnesses to writs. They were royal documents and had a Royal Seal on them."

"Does that mean it wasn't really a writ, after all? I don't remember any discussion of any Royal Seal," Helen queried.

"The interesting fact is that the practice changed with the Normans," Robert commented. "Writs started to be used more freely for other purposes."

"That would fit with your theory, Helen, that it happened in 1067," Andrew concluded.

"That does support the later date," Helen agreed. "The other interesting piece for me is the listing of names. The familiar ones were Waltheof, Gamel and Kenneth. Wygande and Wyberth did not bring up anything in a search but could have been lesser-known thanes. The Williann that is interpreted by some as a name does not start with a 'W' in an early reproduction of the original. It has the word as *pillann* and I found the phrase '*by(n) spa pillann*' translated as 'in like manner' and that would make sense if referring to the earlier names."

"Helen, can you share that information with Samuel, so he keeps up to date with any new thoughts we have?" Robert asked.

"Yes, of course. I'll try to keep some notes of what we discuss this weekend and copy him."

"I think dinner is ready," Robert announced, as Mrs Wakefield peeked in from the doorway.

England
The Year 1068

They rode south, as soon as the women and their escort left for Berwick. The most difficult moment for Gospatric was saying goodbye to Dolphin, who was sure he was old enough to join in the fight. He stomped off, angry at everyone who assured him he was needed to be the strong one to protect his brother and sisters. If they returned from this struggle, successful or not, Gospatric needed to talk with him about the true costs of fighting. He had never shared his own painful story of losing his uncle, then his father and grandfather. That was a mistake, he thought. Dolphin was old enough now to understand the complexity of wanting justice, not just revenge, and wanting peace and finding yourself at war.

When they reached York with a large force, they were able to surround the garrison and set it afire. Gospatric sent his men throughout the city to take prisoners of the Normans who were in drinking establishments or harassing local people. They felt confident in their success, not knowing that their fellow conspirators were being defeated in the South. William's forces had marched against the rebellion, building a castle at Warwick where Morcar and Edwin had been forced to surrender. They marched on, building castles at Nottingham, Lincoln, Cambridge, and Huntington. Merleswein, Waltheof and Turgot had managed to escape and rode to York to warn Gospatric and Edgar's forces. Knowing the strength of the army coming at them, they abandoned York and made their way to Durham, and on to Bamburgh, to tell their supporters what had happened and to warn them of forces moving against them. The rumour of the Danes' arrival was just that. William's forces took over York and built a castle, his last outpost. Fearing that he might continue to send troops north, those left at Bamburgh made the journey to Malcolm's court at Dunfermline.

Athelreda and the children were with Margaret, Christina and Agatha, waiting to greet Gospatric, Edgar and the others as they rode into the courtyard. Although they already knew the sad news of their defeat there was a grateful feeling that the men had returned safely, with no great loss of life. They waited to hear the outcome across the country, before planning their next moves. The news came that Gospatric had been removed as earl, and Morcar and Edwin had sworn fealty to King William. The positive news was that York was the last castle built, and the Normans had marched no farther. A new earl was to be appointed by William.

Although losing the opportunity to take back England, they had escaped William's wrath and the planning for another assault began. If they could re-take York, they could reverse the process and force William back south. As the men plotted, the women prepared for the wedding of Malcolm and Margaret. There was now no question about the necessity of the marriage to cement the support of Scotland in placing Edgar on the throne of England. William had been forced to return from Normandy late the previous year to deal with the rebellions of the surviving Godwinson family and the Welsh, and this year he had faced down their rebellion. Most of the Anglo-Saxon nobles and the Northumbrian thanes were prepared to continue plotting a way to defeat William, and the Danes were eager to exploit his unpopularity with his subjects.

The marriage was a simple Celtic ceremony performed by Bishop Fothad. Margaret did not seem unhappy and there was a great feast to celebrate the union of the ancient family of Dunkeld with the Anglo-Saxon line. No one spoke about Ingibiorg, and what happened to her was only a matter of whispered rumours. Later, after the festivities, Gospatric and Athelreda were finally alone.

"Margaret seems quite content with these events, is she not?" Gospatric asked.

"Yea, she is. When we arrived on the ship and Malcolm was there to greet us, I knew she favoured him. He spent much time with her during those days we waited to hear if you and Edgar and the others had succeeded or were dead." She looked at him then, with a questioning he could not avoid.

"You wish to know what we are planning, do you not?" Gospatric asked, knowing her mind.

"Yes, I have a right to know. You constantly conspire in secret with Malcolm and the others. It is my future and the children's lives that are being determined without my knowledge."

"You are right, my love, for I will soon have to leave you once more to return to Bamburgh, and I do not want you and our children to journey with us. There is no other choice at this moment," he said, with an authority he rarely expressed with her.

"But a new Earl of Northumbria will be appointed, and surely, he will make his way to Bamburgh soon, will he not? So why should you travel there now?"

"We know William has returned to Normandy once more, believing that his new earl can keep the thanes in line. No doubt he will send a large force with him. I suspect he will not make it to Bamburgh, but if he does, I will be forewarned. I will return here to you; do not fear."

"I did love Bamburgh, but I do not wish us to be there if it means danger. Can you not give up this fight to defeat the king and put Edgar on the throne?"

"It is not my choice. I committed to this cause long ago and will continue if Malcolm requires me to do so."

"I love Margaret and hope that Edgar and Malcolm can achieve peace for our children, but not if it means losing you." He enfolded her in his arms, kissing her neck and then her breasts. She melted under his touch, hoping that Matilda would not wake to be nursed.

After the New Year's celebrations, and just before leaving for Bamburgh with the men who had come north with him, Gospatric took Dolphin aside to reason with him. His eldest was, once again, insisting that he should be allowed to go back to Bamburgh.

"Listen to me, my son. We may be back soon having learned that the new earl is marching north with a large force to protect him, but we may not. If we are not back soon, it is because we plan to make another effort to overcome King William and help Edgar to be the King of England. That will mean a battle, or many battles. I do not wish you to lose your life in that struggle."

"But what about you, Father? What if you are killed, and Uncle Waltheof and Prince Edgar?"

"That is possible, but we have made wise decisions. We do not want to fight, Dolphin. We want justice. We believe William should not have declared himself king. We believe we will have some outside support against him this time, as well as more support from the people in the South who have suffered because of him. He is not our king. He leaves for Normandy as soon as he suppresses a rebellion. Perhaps this time he will tire of trying to conquer the English and go home permanently and leave us in peace."

"I still don't see why I can't ride to Bamburgh with you. I could stay there and protect the castle while you go to York."

"King Malcolm would be proud of you suggesting that, but he has other plans for you. As soon as the weather warms, he wants you to spend time with Thorfinn in Cumbria."

"I thought we wouldn't go back to our home there again, but I would like to see grandfather." Dolphin now sounded more like the child he was, rather than a boy trying to be a man.

"King Malcolm wishes for you to be made the Lord of Carlisle, as soon as you are old enough to assume the title, and that means learning about the land and knowing the people whom you will serve."

"Wouldn't they have to serve me, if I am the lord?" Dolphin was warming to the idea.

"No, Dolphin. A good leader serves the people, protects them, and helps them to prosper. We have much more to speak about, but there is little time left. You must pay attention to your grandfather Thorfinn and watch how he leads the people."

"Waltheof says Thorfinn is not really his grandfather, just mine, but he wants him to be his," Dolphin stated, being a confused child again.

"Because my father died, and Athelreda's father died, Thorfinn is a grandfather to you all." Gospatric answered his underlying question, which always led to difficult explanations. Dolphin knew that his mother had died, and that Athelreda was the mother of his brother and sisters, but Dolphin seemed satisfied with his response.

"Will I have to wear grand clothes if I am a lord? I don't think I will like that," he said, with the innocence of a boy not yet thirteen, but growing up quickly.

"Not to worry about your clothes just yet, my son." Gospatric put his arm around Dolphin. "Let's find your mother, for I must be saying my farewell."

Edinburgh, Scotland
April 2017

Robert, Andrew and Helen had gotten little more done that evening. They had enjoyed a lovely meal with too many glasses of wine and then a nightcap in the library. They promised each other they would work more seriously on Saturday. Andrew came prepared to talk about the rebellions against William the next morning.

"There was a lot going on with the Godwinson family and the Welsh in 1067 and that was why William returned to England. By that time, he had some faith in Morcar and Edwin, as well as Waltheof and Merleswein, and they represented a large amount of territory north of the Thames, all the way to Lincoln. By placing Gospatric at Bamburgh in the North, with Morcar still having the southern portion of Northumbria, he probably felt he had the capacity to suppress any other rebellions. Then in the summer of 1068, a major conspiracy was unfolding, most likely planned during the time some of our characters were in Normandy together."

"I hope you can straighten out the dates. I found so many conflicting stories about these rebellions, the Danes' arrival and leaving. Exactly what happened and when?"

"I know what you mean Helen," Robert said, "I have written down everything I could find in a timeline. There is so much confusion by someone placing things in the wrong year. One source said the Danes brought 300 ships into the Humber between August and September 1068, and that is part of the problem. It happened in 1069, but there was a rebellion in 1068, where Morcar and Edwin were forced to surrender in Warwick, and they were the leaders in the South. Since William's forces went on to build castles in Cambridge, Huntington and Lincoln, we can conclude that Waltheof, Merleswein and Turgot all fled north, where Gospatric and Edgar would have been trying to overcome the garrison at York. It seems that all escaped before William's forces arrived and built another castle at York."

"This is such an amazing feat, to put up castles that fast," Andrew noted. "It was this activity that made his invasion a success."

"I read somewhere that he came to Hastings with these castles ready to assemble." Helen chuckled. "His own do-it-yourself flat pack castle. I can't imagine that he had a pack of ten with him."

"No one has really explained it, but maybe he brought more materials every time he returned from Normandy. He certainly constructed at least five on that march. What do you think happened next, Andrew?"

"Well, I speculate that if the conspirators all fled to Scotland, they continued to plot their next move. What we know is that Gospatric was removed as earl, Morcar and Edwin swore fealty to William, and the king returned to France once again. Before he left, he named Robert Cumin as the earl to replace Gospatric. It is possible that Gospatric and some of the others had already returned to Bamburgh and Durham. They knew that York was the last outpost with a garrison of Williams's soldiers, and that William had sailed back to Normandy. Robert Cumin rode north to take his position as earl, and is slain while entering Durham, along with his large force. Gospatric might have orchestrated this, but there were plenty of Northumbrian lords who would have gladly done the deed."

"Yes, and William never accuses Gospatric of being a part of it until 1072, when he charges him with the killing of Cumin and the slaughter in York," Robert added.

"After the attack on Cumin at Durham, there was another threat to William, as the same men rode south to attack York," Andrew continued. "William rushed back to stop the attack and then had another castle built at York to protect his garrison. I just find it difficult to understand how all this communication worked so well and so fast with no internet and cell phones. You think it would have been weeks between knowledge of an event and the response. What do you think, Helen?"

"I agree. I know there were spies everywhere to keep kings informed, but they still had to ride horses and take ships to reach their audience with news. I must remind myself that Britain is the size of Minnesota, and the English Channel is only a few miles wide at Calais."

"Yes, not as large a territory as we might think and horse and riders could cover long stretches quite quickly," Andrew added and continued.

"In any event, there were now two castles at York. I think Waltheof, Merleswein, and Turgot would have remained in the north because they couldn't return safely to their lands. They would have been planning the next rebellion, with the knowledge that the Danish fleet was on its way. The King of Denmark was sending 240 ships, with three of his sons and his brother, to support the rebellion. They might have been relatives of Waltheof and his father Siward, and certainly there was an important communication line between Scotland and Denmark."

"Before we go on with this, Helen can you shed any light on the marriage of Malcolm and Margaret?" Robert interrupted. "If we have some idea about the timing of the actual ceremony, we can discuss all this during lunch."

"Like the rebellions, but even more controversial, are the various dates of the wedding. We have some early historians and later sources claiming 1068, 1069, 1070, and the *Chronicle of Melrose* has an inserted folio which states, 'In the year 1067, the glorious Queen Margaret was married to Malcolm.' Then Fordun quotes a lost work of Turgot, who says they were married in 1070." Helen took a deep breath and continued, "and that document also has the fantasy tale of meeting first at St Margaret's Hope when Edgar's ship was blown ashore on its way to Hungary. Since we know a lot more about when and where Edgar was in the earlier rebellions, I can't accept any of that as gospel truth. There are documents that say they met earlier at Wearmouth, and several other romantic tales. The *1291 Chronicle of Tewkesbury* implies the marriage took place in 1068, and I would bet on that date before others. There was a modern assessment written in 2000, using a lot of old church documents, that says the most likely date was 1068. It lists the births of the children of Margaret and Malcolm, with their first son Edward born in 1069, when Margaret was 24 and Malcolm was 38. There is some evidence that Ingibiorg, Malcolm's first wife, was still alive when Margaret married Malcolm. Given the move to make Margaret a saint, any irregularities would have to be covered up, so we will never know. I'm going to try to find the person who wrote that 2000 document, who is from Scotland, and I am also reading a book with another more recent look at the situation."

"With that conundrum, let's have our lunch," Robert announced as a bell rang in the hallway.

Northumbria
The Year 1069

When the party reached Bamburgh, they learned that King William had appointed Robert of Comines, a foreign-born mercenary, as the new Earl of Northumbria. Some of the men left for Durham to join others who were awaiting the arrival of the new earl. When Earl Robert Comines reached Durham with a force of seven hundred soldiers for his protection, they were besieged by a large force and slaughtered.

When the news from Durham reached Gospatric and Edgar, they regrouped once more, now with the knowledge that King Svein of Denmark was ready to send a large force under the command of his brother, Asbjorn. The fleet was expected to reach the Humber in late summer and the conspirators were ready to join them. Merleswein and Turgot would lead the forces south to organise an attack on the castle at Lincoln, and Gospatric and Waltheof planned to take York, with the help of the Danish soldiers, and then ride south with them to join the fight. There had been much planning, with a meeting with Malcolm in Scotland. Malcolm decided it was best to keep Edgar safe in Bamburgh. If the Danes continued south to take London, they might not choose to put Edgar on the throne. One of the sons of Svein might be expecting to be crowned, but no one could predict the outcome. The meeting had given Gospatric an opportunity to see Athelreda and the children. She was not insisting on coming to Bamburgh, because Margaret was carrying her first child and needed her. She was worried about young Waltheof, if his big brother Dolphin left him to be with Thorfinn. They made the decision to send both boys to their grandfather in the spring. The king approved and repeated his plans to have Gospatric's daughters marry Cumbrians. The exception was Ethelreda, whom he had chosen to be the wife of Duncan, his first son with Ingibiorg. Duncan and his brother Donald were similar ages to Gospatric's younger children, and they all spent their days together in the care of the women who were teaching them to read and write. Waltheof always wanted to be with Dolphin, who didn't seem to mind watching over him. Malcolm had decided they should plan to declare Waltheof the Lord of Allerdale. Athelreda scoffed at these ideas, especially about her daughters, but Gospatric had come to accept Malcolm's vision for the future of their children.

In August the men rode south, confident of Danish support joining the thanes and their men near York. When Gospatric had returned to Bamburgh earlier in the year, he had been welcomed back by the Northumbrians, who were ready to fight against William. When their large force met the Danes at Stamford Bridge, they split into two regiments, one to attack the castle on the other side of the river, and the main force to enter the garrison at York. The Danes had their ships on the Ouse where it met the River Trent, putting them in an excellent position to move into Lincolnshire next.

Their large force overcame the Norman garrison, burning the castles and killing most of the Normans whom Morcar and Edwin had brought with them in 1067. The city was freed from Norman control, but the people had already experienced great hardship, with the soldiers taking whatever they wanted from households. Fields had been planted and hope was renewed, as they began to harvest food. The Danes marched on to take Lincoln with Merleswein and Turgot leading them and a large contingent of Northumbrians.

Gospatric and Waltheof had not been hurt. The weakened Normans were easily overcome by the large force and the people's support for the rebellion. They left the thanes from the area to help those in York and returned north, leaving protective forces as they went. Once they had ensured that Durham was secure, they rode on to Bamburgh to tell Edgar of their success.

Their plan had worked this time, with rebellions in Wales and the West Country requiring William to take large numbers of his forces across the Pennines and into Wales, and then south to overcome the opposition. They feared he would come back north with his full force, but winter was coming. The Danes had returned to their ships with food and booty, promising to fight to take London in the spring. They were all hopeful they would force William to retreat now that he had been driven from Lincolnshire and Yorkshire. Gospatric felt it was safe to have the family return to Bamburgh and to be together again. Margaret's first child, a son named Edward, was born in July, and Athelreda felt she could leave Margaret. Thorfinn brought Dolphin and Waltheof and his family to Bamburgh. They had a great reunion and celebration for a few days, before Thorfinn and his family returned to Cumbria, leaving the boys at Bamburgh. It was a joyful time, with only an occasional sense of underlying anxiety. Waltheof had lost his lands with little hope of recovery until the Danes defeated William. War was difficult in winter when troops needed shelter and food to handle the unpredictable weather. It was unlikely there would be any more fighting until spring. Gospatric talked with Waltheof about taking over as Earl of Northumbria, while he returned to Cumbria, but Waltheof was not interested.

"I don't need to be an earl. I would be in a monastery now if I hadn't met Judith."

"Not much hope of wedding and bedding her now, my friend. We'll be lucky to stay alive if William wins back Northumbria."

"Do you think that is possible, that he won't give up?"

"We've heard from Merleswein," Gospatric answered. "William has suppressed Wales and the West Country again, so it is possible. We can only hope that your Danish relatives keep their determination to take London."

"King Svein would do that, but I am not sure about his brother or his sons. I don't think we can count on them. I think I should take some forces south to Durham, just in case."

"Drink up, little brother. We must enjoy what we have now—a little bit of peace and some time together before you leave."

Edinburgh, Scotland
April 2017

Andrew started the conversation in the afternoon with a question about the sources who mention Gospatric's lack of loyalty to the Scottish effort.

"That's nonsense about Gospatric changing sides," Robert stated. "Any of the historians who know of his history with Edgar's family, with the rebellions, and the family relationship and protection Malcolm provided to him, should understand the closeness of the two cousins. When he returns from Flanders, he is given responsibility for Dunbar and most of Lothian, and then Gospatric's family receives all those lands in Cumbria, resulting in them covering the entire area."

"*The Chronicle of Carlisle* is an example," Andrew said. "They have Malcolm ravaging Cumbria and Northumbria in 1070, according to Palgrave. We know that Dolphin is named Lord of Carlisle about the same time. It just doesn't make sense."

"I read somewhere," Helen inserted, "that the *English Chronicles* tried to place the blame for the devastation of Northumbria on Malcolm, rather than King William. I wonder if the *Chronicle of Carlisle* was done after William's son took over there."

"We could check that out," Robert said, "but I think, once again, we know more than the early historians."

The three of them spent more time reading different documents that each had identified as important. Helen had prepared a chart of the ages of the children in Gospatric's and Malcolm's families as the years progressed through the crisis. She started with Dolphin, adding Malcolm's sons with Ingibiorg, then Waltheof and the four girls, followed by the children of Malcolm and Margaret and lastly the younger Gospatric.

"I can't claim it to be accurate, but it is as close as I can get with the information in records and common sense about what was happening at the time. I needed to see how old the children were, as the rebellions happen and Bamburgh is lost, regained, and lost again."

"And where do we think Gospatric's wife and children were when he left for Flanders with Edgar in 1072?" Andrew asked.

"It makes sense to me that his wife and younger children were in Scotland with Margaret. We know the relationships must have been close, and Margaret was known to have many children around her. Since the men fled to Scotland during the different rebellions, it only makes sense that the women went with them, or more likely were safely removed with the children, when it was dangerous."

"I must find the reference about Dolphin being Lord of Carlisle in 1070. How old do you have him by then?" Andrew asked.

"If we are correct that he was born shortly after Gospatric arrived in Aspatria, then he is still only about fourteen," Helen answered.

"That's old enough in that time period," Robert stated. "Girls were often married by that age, and the boys were off fighting battles. Let me look for that reference. It's time to have a rest. We can come together for drinks at six, and I will try to have the information for us."

When they gathered again in the library for drinks before dinner, Robert was waiting to read what he had found. Andrew poured a scotch for himself and Helen, and they sat beside Robert.

"It is in a strange document by R.S Ferguson, FSA regarding *Alston in the Diocese of Durham, and in the County of Cumbria, read at that place, on July 10th, 1884.* 'In the middle of the eleventh century both Cumbria and Strathclyde were in the hands of Malcolm Canmore, but about 1070, Gospatric, Earl of Northumberland, severed the district of Carlisle, or all Cumbria south of the Solway, from Malcolm's dominions, and handed it over to Dolphin, his son.' On the next page he refers to it as dismemberment."

"Gospatric wouldn't have severed it," Andrew asked, "without the blessing of Malcolm, right?"

"Agreed. I wonder if it is some old legal term, but it gives us a date for Dolphin to be named the Lord of Carlisle, even if he didn't take that position in a formal way."

"Perhaps he did," Helen speculated. "If we think of the position of Gospatric in 1070, giving his fealty to William, in desperation, and perhaps having to pay some financial penalty to be reinstated as earl, wouldn't Malcolm want to start securing Cumbria?"

"But does a fourteen-year-old boy as Lord of Carlisle do that?" Andrew asked.

"We have to think like they did in the eleventh century," Robert said, with a sense of excitement. "They have lost another battle for the throne of England, but they still have what is later known as Northumberland and there was no invasion of Cumbria. Why not try to solidify as much territory as possible? Malcolm had strong men to support Dolphin. Thorfinn was presumably still there and Gospatric was the Lord of Allerdale as well as the Earl of Northumbria."

"Before we leave, Andrew, we must finish that look at the rebellions tomorrow. It's such a terrible time, the way it ends. I can only imagine how the men fighting for Edgar felt when the people were being killed and their homes and crops destroyed."

"Yes, I'll continue in the morning, and I also want to talk about the contradictions about how much of a leader Edgar was in this story. I want to hear your opinions."

"That's the dinner bell," Robert announced, as they set aside their papers and finished their drinks.

England
December 1069

The next few weeks were quiet at the castle, except for the voices of little children. The girls spent time with their mother and the other women in the household, Dolphin and Waltheof with their father. They were missing the companionship of other children, but happy to be together as a family again. The boys shared stories of their time with Thorfinn and organised games, where they were the lords of Carlisle and Allerdale, and their little sisters were their subjects. Athelreda was pregnant again and due to have their bairn in the new year before the fighting would resume.

As Gospatric walked along the shore, he stared at the quiet sea. It is the calm before a storm, he thought. He felt with dread the pending threat of William's wrath. It was like the dark clouds building on the horizon, filled with the power to crash into Bamburgh with a force that couldn't be stopped. He shuddered, decided it was the rising wind making him shiver, and returned to the warmth of his home to prepare for the imminent storm.

King William's soldiers had recovered from their battle to overcome the rebellion in the West and now marched towards Lincoln. Without the support of the large Danish force, Lincoln Castle was taken over once more. Turgot was captured and imprisoned, but Merleswein and a few others escaped. They headed north along the Roman Road, riding without a stop. They warned others as they continued heading to the Trent, where the Danish ships were moored by the River Ouse. They were aboard the lead ship, planning a way to counter William at York, when his forces arrived. William met with Asbjorn and negotiated a promise that the Danes would leave as soon as possible, in return for a generous sum of gold and the right to plunder the coast as they left. When William's forces retreated, Merleswein challenged Asbjorn about his decision. He scoffed at

Merlswein's concerns, assuring him he had no intention of complying with the bribe.

As Merleswein and his followers were preparing to head north to warn York of an attack, they saw smoke rising from the north shore, for as far as they could see. Looking south, they saw the same. The soldiers were burning everything as they left the area but were also going east along both sides of the estuary starting fires. The Danes scrambled to find any food they could save, as Merleswein and his party rode north, surveying the damage. The homes and the stored crops were burning, and people were trying to save whatever they could. Many lay dead on the ground. Merleswein now understood William's plan to make sure the Danes had no resources in the spring. Starving men cannot fight. As they rode behind the path of destruction, they could see smoke rising from York. They kept to the east of York, riding hard. Merleswein sent two men to warn Maldred at East Riding and continued north into Durham to meet Waltheof and his forces. They knew there was no hope of resisting the large force coming towards them, and they learned from fleeing peasants that all of Yorkshire was being set on fire. Whatever William did not need to feed his soldiers was burned, leaving the people with no food for the winter.

King William stayed at York for Christmas, in a city with no castles. York Minster had been nearly destroyed by his own soldiers. His forces killed everyone in their path, and he encouraged their wrath, sending them into the countryside to gather whatever they wanted and to destroy everything else. After Christmas, William forces continued north, killing and burning as he went. He made camp on the north side of the River Tees, preparing to enter Durham.

Christmas had been a sombre event at Bamburgh. Gospatric and the men had ridden south to support the force at Durham. The family simply waited for any news, with fear for themselves, as well as those who had left for the battle. Even the children were quiet and spent more time together with Athelreda, asking questions she could not answer.

Edinburgh, Scotland
April 2017

Sunday arrived with its large Scottish breakfast, including black pudding, haggis, sausage, bacon, tomato, mushrooms, and eggs. Helen had learned to like black pudding and haggis, having resisted even tasting it when she first arrived in Scotland. Now she simply refused to think about what might be in the mixtures. Their plan was to work all morning, then go out for Sunday lunch. Robert had suggested driving to Dunbar and later dropping off Andrew at Musselburgh on the way back, after seeing the ruins of the castle on the coast. They would also drive by another old fortification, most likely built by Gospatric.

Andrew began taking them through his earlier information. "Before we diverted our attention to the marriage and other items, I was summarising what had happened with the early attempted revolt after the death of Robert Cumin. We were going on to the Danish fleet arriving in the Humber Estuary, which was documented by several sources as late August or early September. According to the *Anglo-Saxon Chronicle,* the leaders of the Northumbrian revolt, who had fled to Scotland the previous year, now returned, 'riding and marching with an immense host, rejoicing exceedingly.' Together with the Danes, they took York, burned the castles, and killed most of the Normans at the garrison."

"We presume," Helen added, "the leaders included Edgar, Gospatric, Merleswein, Turgot, and Waltheof. You must read multiple sources to get all their names. You don't see them together. I am unsure about Turgot. He is supposedly present for Malcolm and Margaret's wedding; he is later imprisoned in Lincoln Castle, and then he escapes to Norway, returning in 1074."

"What's our timetable? What's your best guess, Andrew?" Robert asked.

"The ships landed no later than the 8th of September, so presumably they sacked York shortly after that date. They were in the estuary where the Trent meets the Ouse, if one of the sources is correct. The Ouse put them in a great position to attack Lincoln next. The information we have is that King William marched his forces north but then had to send troops back to Wales and south to the West Country to suppress other rebellions, burning the Welsh Marches as he left. There is a source that says he was forced to cross the Pennines from Yorkshire to suppress the rebellion directly."

"Perhaps this is when he decides on his strategy to destroy the land," Robert commented. "His submission of England was in question, and he needed a new plan."

"His attacks were so vicious!" Helen exclaimed. "He and his men were clearly taking revenge on the population. It's like Nazi Germany—kill the local people to devastate the leaders."

"We'll get to that thought," Robert interrupted. "Go on, Andrew."

"The next thing we know is that William is back in Yorkshire in December and finds the Danes have returned to their ships, leaving York with a much smaller force. He can't attack their ships, but he manages to bribe their leaders to leave in the spring. I'm not sure how that happens. To ensure they do leave, he has his soldiers burn everything around the estuary, so they have no way to get supplies. Next, we know that William is at York for Christmas."

"Where would he stay? The castles had been burned; his own soldiers had ransacked the Minster during the spring…"

Robert answered Helen. "That is a good question, and this is the start of the revenge. You kill anyone left in York, you take their food supply, their animals, their houses and use them. When you are done with them, you burn everything to the ground. You send your soldiers out into the countryside to do the same."

"It does seem like the plan," Andrew confirmed. "When they leave York, they burn everything behind them all the way to Durham and they end up camping on the banks of the Tees in January 1070. It is there that Waltheof surrenders and pays homage to William. Gospatric and Edgar, if he was at Durham, and others like Merleswein, must have escaped to Bamburgh Castle. There is a record indicating that Gospatric made his peace with William by proxy, with promised gold."

Helen wondered about William. "Does the king decide to go no farther because of the problems of camping out in the winter? Was he worried his troops would start defecting as food was getting scarce? Was he afraid he could lose a battle trying to capture Gospatric, knowing the impossible task of assaulting Bamburgh Castle?"

"Knowing what happens in the next two years, perhaps he is biding his time," Robert answered. "All of what you are asking was probably true. He had devastated Yorkshire, from south of York to Durham. They also went north of Durham where many had hidden in the hills, with their livestock and whatever they could carry. We must assume that Gospatric and Merleswein were able to warn those north of Durham to run for their lives with everything they could take. This would have forced William to stop, as he was faced with the continuing need to feed his troops."

"He was back in Winchester for Easter, the records say," Andrew continued. "The Danish fleet was starving by spring, accepted the bribe and left. Some records say that King Svein came to the area and was angry when he found his forces unable to fight the battle to take London. I agree…William probably felt he had done enough damage to the North to keep them quiet for a while, while he could re-group for the future."

"When you read the records now," Helen stated, "and find Yorkshire was empty for two decades, with perhaps 100,000 people and 150,000 animals fewer in the region after the land was 'wasted' by his forces, you can only imagine what the leaders must have felt."

"Yes, Helen…back to your point comparing it with what the Nazis would do in a village. This was wide-spread genocide," Robert continued. "All the arguments about this being ordinary warfare and acceptable behaviour have been re-examined and found wanting. William's troops killed men, women and children and left the rest to die of starvation. Waltheof would have been relieved to have his fealty to William accepted, his lands restored, and William's niece Judith in marriage, but he must have felt responsible for the treatment of the people. Likely this was the moment of acceptance of defeat of their cause."

Andrew continued. "The chronicles record that Edgar, Merleswein, Bishop Aegelwine, Siward Barn and many others fled to Scotland. The last two, however, joined Edwin, Morcar, and Hereward at Ely in 1071 for another rebellion. Hereward disappeared or was killed, the Bishop and Morcar were imprisoned, and Edwin was slain trying to escape to Scotland."

Helen spoke up, with an urgent plea. "Let's stop there, please, and try to digest all of this before we go on."

Robert responded. "Yes, I think we must reflect on what was going on for Gospatric, as he dealt with this defeat, the horror of what they had brought upon the people and what it meant for him and his family, as well as Edgar and Malcolm's hopes for the future."

Northumbria
The Year 1070

Waltheof insisted that Gospatric and Merleswein ride back to Bamburgh to protect Edgar and Gospatric's family. To avoid further bloodshed, he would surrender Durham to William and swear fealty to him. He was sure that Gospatric should do the same, but from the protection of Bamburgh Castle. They knew no one would survive much longer without food and protection from the elements.

"What if his men slay you before you can even swear fealty to him," Gospatric argued, not wanting to leave him to face the wrath of William.

"That won't happen. I know the king. He will want to ride triumphantly into Durham and have all his men, and any of our forces, witness my begging forgiveness on my knees."

"How can you do this?" Gospatric asked. "I cannot."

"It is the only way to stop the carnage. You must do it, but by proxy. He knows you are the leader, not Edgar, and he knows Malcolm is behind us. Leave me with your sworn promise to be his loyal servant. Ask for your earldom to be returned and promise to pay his price. Do it now and ride before it is too late. Your family needs you, and we need peace, even if it is not the peace we desired. We can only hope William stays out of the North now that he has made it uninhabitable. Help save the people you can. The survivors will be starving before spring comes."

They prepared the document, shared the plan with the others and embraced one another. A few minutes later, Gospatric mounted his steed and rode out of Durham, with Merleswein, Siward Barn, Bishop Aegelwine, and other northern thanes. They spread out to warn the villages as far as they could, asking them to pass the word to take their families and animals into the hills. It was now the dead of winter and travel wouldn't be easy, but they hoped their warning would help some to escape before the Norman soldiers began foraging for food and animals, burning anything left behind. Some asked to follow them, and they agreed to take them, knowing they would soon be left with nothing.

At Bamburgh Castle, Dolphin had been going to the tower every day, watching for any sign of horses coming from the south. He remembered the story about the night Siward returned to Aspatria without Gospatric's father. He willed his father to return and would not listen to any other possibility. A previous runner had told Edgar that York had been taken and William was marching on Durham with a large force. Malcolm had sent an escort party from Edinburgh Castle, to accompany Edgar, Athelreda and the children to Dunfermline. She felt unable to travel, being late in her pregnancy, and wanted to wait for Gospatric. Edgar and others left reluctantly without her.

It was a warmer afternoon without any wind, and his little brother had begged to go to the tower with Dolphin. Waltheof was the first to see the riders coming up the coast. When they were certain it was Gospatric, they rushed down to tell their mother. Preparations were made for food and the household was in the courtyard as the men rode in. Athelreda could tell from Gospatric's face…the news was not good.

"Are we to leave immediately?" she asked, as he dismounted and took her in his arms.

"Where is Edgar? I must speak with him."

"King Malcolm sent an escort to take him to Edinburgh Castle. He wanted us to leave as well, but I just couldn't." She touched her swollen belly. "I needed to wait for you." The children had crowded around them. "Dolphin promised us you would return and has been watching for you every day."

"I saw you first, I did," Waltheof cried out.

"Good, son. Well done, both of you," he added and nodded to Dolphin, who stood a little apart with teary eyes. "We all need food and drink. Let us go into the warmth." He walked to Merleswein to tell him Edgar was already safely removed to Edinburgh and there was no rush to go on to Scotland. They all walked into the castle, defeated but alive. His greatest fear was for Waltheof in Durham, facing William the Bastard without him.

In privacy later, Gospatric confided his fear to Athelreda. He did not know if Waltheof would survive and whether William would continue north or take his troops back south. He cried as he described what had happened to the people, their stores of grain burnt to the ground, their animals slaughtered, their food stolen, and their shelters torched.

"Some who were escaping told us the soldiers were riding through, grabbing what they wanted and taking the sword to anyone in their path," he said, still hardly able to speak.

"What about the people north of Durham?"

"We were ahead of the soldiers and stayed on the coast. We sent someone west at each juncture to pass the warning to take everything they could, especially their cattle and sheep, and find a hiding place."

"It's too cold for them to stay in the hills for long."

"Yes, but it's better than being cut down and seeing your children die in front of you. Some may be able to return, but it is not likely they can survive without the grain they had stored."

"We must find a way to help them. What about those who followed you here?"

"I said they could join us, but we could not guarantee their safety. We will know shortly what happened in Durham and whether we shall all leave for Scotland. I gave my fealty to William by proxy. It is doubtful it will be accepted."

Edinburgh, Scotland
April 2017

As they gathered for their last time together before going east to Dunbar, Andrew made an announcement. "Easter was April 10th in 1070, and we know William was celebrating his victory in Winchester by then. That means he didn't stay long camping on the Tees. He probably left after Gospatric and Waltheof swore loyalty to him, and he must have taken Waltheof back with him to Lincoln or Northamptonshire."

"Did you find that on your phone?" Robert asked, not able to use the technology himself.

"Yes, it came up with dates for Easter for a complete range of years," Andrew stated. "Part of Northumbria was saved from burning, but anyone who survived in Yorkshire might have headed north, when William left for the South."

"I've been reading the early comments about William's action, and they are all pretty damning," Helen commented. "Here is one from William of Jumieges describing how the King 'massacred almost the whole population, from very young to the old and grey.' He was probably bragging for William. Even the *Anglo-Saxon Chronicle* says that he went to Yorkshire in 1069 and 'ruined it completely.' You would think that all the conspirators would have given up after the devastation, but they didn't."

"No, and it seems foolish for Morcar and Edwin to have joined Hereford in Ely, when they had seen what happened when they didn't have the Danes to help them fight William's strong force. There is a difference in dates about their rebellion, some saying 1071 and others 1072. It was more likely it was in 1071, and then in 1072 William decided to eliminate Edgar Atheling as a threat, and arrest Gospatric. It does not seem that Edgar was active after the defeat in 1070, but William perhaps feared that he was still a rallying point for rebellion. William had Waltheof under his control and that would have given him some assurance that the Danes would not be planning another invasion."

"Back to the subject of Edgar," Helen intervened. "Was he really a leader or a figurehead for Malcolm?"

Robert answered her question, "I believe the sources that list him as the leader have not studied their history. He was young, not necessarily a fighter, not a powerful figure physically…"

"Probably gay," Andrew stated, surprising Helen.

"I wondered about that, but there isn't any evidence that I saw, nor any intimations…" Helen challenged. "Did you find any?"

"No, but he never married, was not known to have any lovers or illegitimate children. He may have been too busy for a relationship, but even after he settled in France, he didn't have a known lover. He did have a close friendship with Robert of Normandy, King William's oldest son."

"What do you think, Robert?" Helen asked.

"I see him having a different kind of strength. He endured a great deal. He had a sense of duty, given his father gave his life for the succession of the Anglo-Saxon royal line. We see him later with Robert of Normandy, as a negotiator, and that may have been his real talent. The times required a strong leadership figure, not a young soul who wanted peace for his country and his family."

"There were some leaders around," Helen posed. "Edwin and Morcar had designs on the throne and both Waltheof and Gospatric appear to be leaders, although some people characterise Waltheof as naive and easily led by others. I don't picture him that way. Perhaps, like his father, he was a physically strong person, with a soft heart and a trusting nature."

"I love it," Andrew said. "You always help us see the feminine side of our characters. How do you see Gospatric handling this defeat?"

"I suppose I always see him as doing Malcolm's bidding and wanting to create peace for his family. I don't see him as loving the fight, but as a survivor—or just lucky. I think he would have been devastated by what William did to the people of Yorkshire and feeling responsible for it even if the common folk wanted to be free from the king's tyranny. He must have asked himself if it was worth it."

"Let's get on our way to Dunbar and we can talk more over lunch. I so value this time together although, as both of you know, I would wish to have Samuel with us. Helen, you must let him know how much we have missed his company."

Bamburgh Castle, Northumbria
The Year 1070

There was a daily expectation of a message from Durham, and they didn't have to wait long for the news. Two messengers arrived within hours of each other. One was from Waltheof, saying he was returning to London with the king, asserting his absolute loyalty to William and gratefulness for the return of his lands. He expressed his sorrow that Gospatric would not attend his wedding to William's niece, Judith. The king had been told that Gospatric's oath of fealty by proxy was necessary because of his need to return to Bamburgh for the imminent birth of his child and he expected Athelreda had safely delivered their bairn. They would begin marching south when Gospatric kept his oath to deliver his payment to William. The ending, in Runes as usual, translated by Dolphin, was 'A Tie That Binds.'

"He states most of what we need to know, Dolphin," Gospatric explained, as other men listened. "William and his men will leave their encampment outside of Durham when I deliver on my promise. Waltheof is to be forgiven and placed back as the earl of his lands. He is marrying Judith immediately, and says he used the birth of your baby brother as justification for me to swear my oath by proxy."

"Am I to have a second brother, at last, and not another sister?" Dolphin asked, as it was his most immediate concern.

"So says your mother, but we shall see in a few days. We shall be happy, whether brother or sister, if your mother and the bairn are safe."

Merleswein then spoke, "Waltheof is clever with words, but we know not of your status to keep Bamburgh."

"Although he must always write knowing William might see his messages, I think he would have tried to warn us if a threat was pressing. We must wait for a message from the king or a warning from Durham."

Within hours a royal messenger was asking permission to enter the castle and Merleswein and Gospatric went to receive him. His title as earl was safe for the moment, with the order to send the messenger back with the promised gold. There was considerable risk, if the man chose to not return to William, or if he was robbed on his way. Gospatric decided to send two soldiers with the messenger, to ensure his payment reached the king. Merleswein suggested another plan. He wanted to be the one to go and find a trusted contact among the soldiers to stop at Lincoln Castle on their way south, to assess Turgot's situation. Gospatric convinced Merleswein that it was too dangerous for him to be seen, and they chose two lesser known but trusted thanes, with extra bargaining funds for Turgot's release and escape on a ship. There was little gold left in the coffers, but they would be safe for the immediate future, if William accepted his payment and returned to London.

Athelreda insisted on sending a messenger to Dunfermline, to ask Margaret to plead with Malcolm to come south and take the starving people to Scotland. Her idea was that each Scottish family could support another person or a family if they had some means. This could help with the extra work of the household and the planting in the spring. Many would choose servitude, or even slavery, over watching their loved ones slowly die. She had already sent some of the wandering people to the monastery at Lindisfarne, after feeding and giving them shelter for the night. She made sure they had an escort, to get them safely across to the island at low tide and to the welcome arms of the monks. She asked Margaret to provide space for others in the community at Coldingham Priory, and any other religious houses where food was grown and shelter available. Margaret responded with a message that Malcolm would bring his men south quickly to lead the people north, as she had suggested. Gospatric said he would send his men to as many of the villages as possible with hopeful news, ensuring them this was a different kind of raid by Malcolm. Satisfied that she had done all she could, Athelreda went into confinement for the birth. She was not as confident as she usually was before delivery and it worried Gospatric. He tried to cover his anxiety with teasing her about Dolphin saying it needed to be a boy, since the boys were falling behind in numbers. When she couldn't respond, except to say that only a boy would be giving her this kind of trouble, he left her with the women, assuring her he would carry out her wishes to help the people who had no homes or food. It gave him something to occupy his mind, organising his men to ride out with food and ale for those they could find, and bringing the news that Malcolm's forces would arrive soon to escort any who wished to go to Scotland. They would be taken to families in Lothian to be their loyal servants until better times. Gospatric intended to ride to meet Malcolm, to help his men locate where people might be sheltering from the cold. The few who had survived the carnage from York to Durham had struggled to find any standing shelter and source of food. Often, they were taking a chance of being killed themselves by William's soldiers, who were foraging before marching south. Some had made it to Hexham, Edlingham and Alnwick, and a few as far as Bamburgh, telling of the horrors left behind. Edmund, Athelreda's brother, had taken in many, saving what animals they could for food for the rest of the winter. They all prayed for an early spring.

Gospatric found King Malcolm at Old Melrose where there were people trying to shelter in the ruins. They sent them north with some of the soldiers who helped by taking a child or woman on their horses. They spoke for only a few minutes before moving on.

"And the Queen, how is she?" Gospatric asked, hoping to hear positive news.

"Aye, she is fine, and pregnant again with another son, so she declares. And Athelreda?"

"She is about to deliver the bairn, and not so easily as in the past. She claims it is a boy who is giving her more discomfort, but I am concerned for her."

"She'll be fine, and you must name this one Gospatric for he will take your place as earl someday."

"Do you truly believe William will leave us in peace, Sire?"

"No, I fear not. He will bide his time. If he keeps Morcar and Edwin under control, he might feel he can take over the rest of the country now that he has Waltheof tied to him."

"What of the Bishop and Siward Barn? Are they content to stay in Scotland?"

"No, they are not settling. They want to try again, but we are witnessing the power of William to wipe out the people's ability to survive in the future. Even I can see there is no point in fighting if we are all to die. I think Edgar's desire to be king is a distant hope. We will be fortunate to keep you at Bamburgh and to hold on to Cumbria. Is Dolphin ready to take his place as Lord of Carlisle?"

"He believes he is, and he does mature every day. I am choosing to have him involved when we receive news or make decisions, to help him understand his future responsibilities. He is riding now with Merleswein to help the people on the coast north of us to find shelter on the Holy Island and at the Priory in Coldingham and St Abbs."

"Let us hope our brothers and sisters of the faith are welcoming and generous," the king said, with a doubting tone. "We must ride on, but as soon as the summer comes let us make our plan to give Dolphin his honour. Now you must ride south to Bamburgh to see if a son is born."

"Yea, Sire. I will alert the people east of here if you are continuing south."

"Take some of my soldiers with you," he said, as he motioned to one of his men nearby. "Hugh will go with you, so they can lead the people north who want to leave. Take care, Cousin, and God be with you."

"And you, Sire," Gospatric nodded, as he turned to ride with Hugh and a few others back east towards Bamburgh.

When he arrived at the castle, there was a flurry of activity. More homeless families had arrived and there was soup being brought to them at the table. Small children were shivering and weeping. Gospatric strode to the fire, putting on a few more great logs. Turning to his little girls, he asked Waltheof to take them to find something for the little children, to make them feel welcome as well as anything they had to warm them. He told the soldiers to prepare places for the families to rest after they ate. Hugh and a few of his men were still with Gospatric, planning to have a hot meal. They talked with the people, telling them of their option to travel to Scotland, to stay with families who would employ them and provide food and shelter. It would be best for this group to move on now, to make room for others who might still arrive. Soon, there would be no one left alive to journey north. There was no one in Yorkshire to bury the dead, their guests said. The bodies were left with the burned animals, to be picked apart by wild creatures and the birds. He was overwhelmed by his part in causing this pain, when he heard a cry from above, a bairn's cry. Gospatric rushed from the room to find Athelreda. She held the babe to her breast, but he could see that she was weak and tired. He reached for the tiny bundle and looked down at his son.

"It's a boy, as I promised," she whispered, barely able to speak. She slipped away into sleep, and Gospatric let the women tend to her, as he stared at the bairn in his arms, who seemed bigger than any of the others he had held.

"Welcome, my little Gospatric," he whispered, as he kissed the top of his forehead.

"They are asking for you below, my lord," one of the women spoke gently, easing the babe from his arms. He looked at Athelreda with dread, but she appeared to be sleeping without distress. He had that terrible sense that she should not have any more bairns…she wasn't young anymore. Although Dolphin would soon leave for Cumbria, there were still six children who needed a mother. His future was uncertain, his survival unknown. The man who had ravaged the countryside in revenge in the last few months might not leave them in peace. William's vengeance might extend to Gospatric, but hopefully not to his family. He went to see what his men wanted, praying that Athelreda would be awake when he returned to her side.

East Lothian, Scotland
April 2017

They continued their discussion over lunch in North Berwick. Robert had taken the ring road around Edinburgh heading east to Dunbar. There was a fierce wind blowing, and they quickly walked to overlook the rock ruins of Dunbar Castle with the waves smashing over them, before heading back along the coast past Tantallon Castle. Settled in a quiet restaurant, where most of the patrons had already eaten, they made a quick order from the menu, before starting their conversation.

"I looked at this book I am reading, as we were driving out to Dunbar," Helen confided. "When William died in 1087, Robert was made the Duke of Normandy, although his father wanted to disinherit him. Edgar Atheling joined him and was given lands in Normandy by Robert. Later when Robert had a feud with his brother, William Rufus, he was forced to take his gift back. Edgar returned to Scotland, but then worked with Robert in negotiations between Rufus and Malcolm. The author implies that Robert and Edgar were good friends and Rufus did not approve of the relationship, perhaps because of Edgar's long abandoned claim to the English throne."

"Or he disapproved for other reasons," Andrew commented. "I suspect they met early on. Wasn't Robert in Flanders when Edgar was exiled?"

"I believe you are right," Robert confirmed, "and that was one of the times he was rebelling against his father, and friendly with Malcolm. But, of course, there was a lot going on between Flanders and Normandy. William married Count Baldwin's niece Matilda, and Tostig married her aunt Judith, I believe."

"There's another major story here," Helen said, as their food was set before them. "I think we will have to leave Edgar to other historians, but it is fascinating seeing him weave in and out of our story."

They ate in silence for a few minutes, hungry after not having eaten for several hours. When Andrew finished quickly, he took a drink of his wine and returned to the earlier conversation about the next insurrection.

"*The Early Sources of Scottish History* have Siward Barn and Bishop Aegelwine leaving Scotland to join Hereward and Earls Edwin and Morcar in an insurrection in Ely. This is where the years of 1071 and 1072 are listed, but there is a line that states, 'after their surrender, William led his forces north to Scotland' as if it happened immediately, which I doubt. I'd say 1071 makes sense. It is agreed that Morcar was taken prisoner and transported to France. William freed him shortly before his death, but Rufus took Morcar prisoner again and he is believed to have died in prison. Edwin's presence at Ely is not confirmed, but it does make sense that he had joined the rebellion when his land was given to Alan Rufus in 1071. There seems to be agreement that he was betrayed, captured and killed fleeing to Scotland that year. The bishop was also captured and died soon afterwards in prison."

"What do we think Gospatric was doing during this period of time?" Helen asked. "We know he retained his earldom in early 1070, after giving his oath by proxy, and there is the time from early 1070 until 1072, when presumably he stays at Bamburgh. I think his family would have been with him, if not from before the attack on York in September of 1069, certainly in 1070."

"We won't ever know," Robert answered, "but I would agree. Once assured of his position as earl, with Waltheof in an important position in William's court, he might have been resigned to their defeat, and grateful to be alive with his family."

When the three of them left North Berwick, they drove along the coast and Robert pointed out another site where Gospatric probably had built another tower.

"I believe that once Gospatric was given Dunbar and so much territory in Lothian, he would have been building towers to watch for any activity on the Forth. That, of course, implies he was still alive."

"Would that have included the old Keep at Dundas?" Helen asked.

"I believe so. You can see for miles from the top of the Keep and a torch light from there could have warned people all along the Forth that there were ships moving in, as well as any troops coming from the West."

They stopped to drop off Andrew at Musselburgh and continued along the water around the north side of Edinburgh. Helen was content to see the scenery, not having travelled the road before. She was posing a question in her mind, but she wanted to be careful how she asked it. Finally, she just tried to explore the question she had.

"Robert, you said there was no representation of the Dundas family in your secret group. Why do you think that is?" He did not answer right away, as he negotiated the turns into South Queensferry, and she was afraid she had overstepped her bounds. Finally, he spoke as he pulled up in front of her flat.

"All I can imagine is that it was lost in some generation. The family was connected to the Crinan line, and the oral history was passed from father to sons, or daughters, if there were no sons. That is our assumption, but we could be wrong. Duncan and Maldred should have known the story, and then Malcolm, Donald, Gospatric, and his brother Maldred would have been told. Of course, their fathers died when they were all young. Maldred's line becomes dominated by marriage into rich families in England, losing his identification with the Dunkeld family. The Dunbar line is consistent, and they are represented, but it should have been the same with Dundas. They were as prolific as the Dunbar family but spread out more, including your ancestors' move to Ireland and on to North America."

"Wouldn't Juliana, as your daughter and with Dundas heritage, have rights from two families?"

"Correct, but there was still a break in passing on of the information in the Dundas line. If we could find the break, we might also find some written evidence that was hidden for some reason. If that is true, there would have been some clues to finding it."

"And you believe Juliana might be able to identify these clues…isn't that a stretch?"

"It is, and if it wasn't for the experience of her grandmother Mary, I would say impossible."

"Have you studied the Dundas family, as it breaks from the Cumbrian and Dunbar line?" she asked.

"I have had what you have seen on paper—hereditary charts. I have no sense of who the people really are, like we have with Gospatric. Our work together has been a completely different process. Our characters seem real to me, and you have helped to make it so. I want you to know this. Gospatric lives inside of me. Does that sound strange?"

"No, he's in my dreams and sometimes he seems to be answering my questions. Would you like to come in for tea?" Again, he was silent, seeming detached from the space.

"Sorry, I drifted away for a minute. No, I must be going. I have said too much already."

As she got out of the car, he jumped out and took her bag, always the gentleman. As he left her at the door, he spoke.

"Perhaps when Samuel is back, I can share more of what I know." With that statement, he turned and walked back to the car, leaving her wondering what would have been passed down from generation to generation, that was so important it must be kept secret.

Northumbria
The Years 1071 and 1072

Dolphin had travelled to Cumbria with Gospatric in late summer, to take his place as Lord of Carlisle. Although his baby brother Gospatric was only a few months old when he left, the babe was already attached to his two older brothers. The girls wanted to hold him, but they soon lost interest, whereas the boys were happy to provide entertainment, and they were rewarded by smiles and laughter. Dolphin was less interested in being the Lord of Carlisle since little Gospatric's birth, and it was a painful separation the day he and his father left to meet the king in Carlisle. Waltheof had promised he would take care of their little brother, as Dolphin had cared for him. Dolphin was holding back his tears, as he promised both of his brothers that he would always be there for them.

 The group at Bamburgh had received periodic news from the South that year. Gospatric's payment of gold had reached William safely and William had stayed in England and celebrated Easter in Winchester, before leaving once again for Normandy. Turgot had escaped, with a bribe to his jailers, and stowed away on a boat at Grimsby travelling to Norway. Merleswein spent time at Bamburgh, and in Dunfermline with Malcolm. Bishop Aegelwine and Siward Barn had headed south to join others planning another rebellion. Hereward's brother had been killed by the Normans and his head placed on a spike for all to witness. Hereford had retaliated by killing several Normans, putting their heads on spikes, and then escaping to the island of Ely. Siward and the Bishop joined Hereward, and when Edwin's land was given to Alan Rufus, he and Morcar also went to Ely to plan another attack. William was in Normandy, leaving his half-brother, Odo, and FitzOsbern in charge of the country. Hereward, they learned, was betrayed by the monks, and William's forces were able to march onto the island of Ely by building a causeway. Morcar and Aegelwine were prisoners and Edwin was fleeing to Scotland when he was betrayed by his own men and killed by his pursuers. It was unknown if Hereward had died or escaped. No one had heard from him.

When William returned to England to suppress the rebellion, Bishop Aegelwine was imprisoned, and William appointed Walcher as the new Bishop of Durham rather than waiting for the Pope to make a choice. Walcher had been a priest in Liege but had spent time in Normandy. William sent a message to Bamburgh demanding that Gospatric escort the new bishop to Durham, and there was great concern for this plan. It was possible it was a plot to take Gospatric prisoner, but he had no choice, having pledged his allegiance to the king. He travelled to York to meet Walcher, wondering about the people's acceptance of the first non-English bishop appointed to Durham. By bringing him to Durham, he was indicating acceptance of the appointment, which is exactly what William wanted, he thought. He took a party of thanes with him in case it was a trap.

When Gospatric's party arrived in York, he was surprised to find both his brother Maldred and Waltheof with Bishop Walcher. Maldred was there on another mission. He wanted the bishop, who would now be the secular leader as well as the spiritual leader in Durham, to acknowledge the ownership of land in Thornley for his mother, Ealdgyth. Since she was, of course, also Gospatric's mother, it seemed an opportune time to ask for this favour. The favour was granted but there was no time for Gospatric to have private time with Maldred and Waltheof.

When Gospatric had delivered Bishop Walcher to his post safely, he rode back with his men to Bamburgh Castle. He was greeted with great relief by the family. There was a general unease that permeated their thinking, but Gospatric learned that William had returned to Normandy and the household began to relax and enjoy the last of the summer weather. Since being in Old Melrose with Malcolm, Gospatric had considered restoring the old ruins. He told Athelreda that the area might be a more suitable place to spend the harsh winters when the northern storms made it difficult to keep Bamburgh Castle warm. He had men building a small tower on a backwater of the Tweed, near Old Melrose, conveniently concealed in a heavily wooded area. He told those few who knew of it, that it would provide a place for workers when they began the restoration of the ancient abbey. His true motivation was his lingering feeling about William's need for revenge and the possibility of needing a place to hide. Although the king seemed to have genuinely accepted Waltheof's plea for forgiveness, he had never had the opportunity to humiliate Gospatric publicly, in the same way. Now, so many of those who had conspired to remove William as king had been killed in battle or imprisoned. Merleswein was only free because he had relinquished his fight for his rights and settled in Scotland. Merleswein knew that William had granted much of his land to Ralph Paynel, the Sheriff of Yorkshire, and fighting for its return would mean prison or worse.

Gospatric did not share his fears with the family, and they had many happy months with the children growing up. Athelreda continued to have the babe to her breast, believing this might prevent another bairn. They all made a trip to visit Dolphin in the summer, with the opportunity to stay at Aspatria, visiting among the people with the children. Waltheof was now a young man of ten and eager to see his future home, as Lord of Allerdale. The girls were all charming the villagers, Ethelreda, eight, Gunhild, six, Octreda, four, and Matilda, three. Gospatric had his young son, with the shortened name of Patric, on his horse in front of him when he rode around the countryside.

It was difficult to leave Dolphin again, but Gospatric could see how much he had matured in the past two years. He was still devoted to his two younger brothers, doting on little Patric and spending time with Waltheof, filling his head with his future responsibilities as Lord of Allerdale. Thorfinn had aged a bit but was still fit and raising a young family. Gospatric tried to thank him for his ongoing work, while waiting for Gospatric to return or Waltheof to grow up.

"I hope Dolphin is of help to you, and not a burden, my friend," Gospatric said, trying to express his feelings.

"Aye, he is an immense joy to us and a quick learner. He observes whatever I am doing and tries to do the same."

"Excellent, for I admonished him to do so."

"Sometimes it is quite humorous—when he tries to treat my wife as I do," he laughed. "Do you trust the king to leave you as earl?"

"I trust him not at all. He can be vicious and vindictive. What has saved us is his desire to spend his time in Normandy. Odo and FitzOsbern have enough to occupy them running the country for William, without riding north to bother us."

"And what of the new bishop? I can't think the people find him acceptable, being a foreigner."

"He is a learned person, not a particularly good administrator I hear, but he has been tolerated. No one cares much that he wasn't named by the Pope, and he is not a Norman, and that helps. Waltheof seems to approve of him, but then he must do so. Perhaps he appeals to the monkish side of Waltheof."

"How is he—now married to William's niece and does he have children?"

"A daughter, yes, and another child on the way. He adores her and names her Matilda, like our little one. We'd best be on our way, now, but I hope we can visit again before the snow comes."

"And let us hope it will be in peaceful times, my son." Thorfinn had been like a father to Gospatric, since he lost Siward and had come to Aspatria. He knew that Dolphin would do well with Thorfinn's attention, but he missed the closeness with his oldest son.

They rode back to Bamburgh stopping at Melrose for a long rest before proceeding. It was not far past mid-summer, and it was still light until late evening. The children loved riding fast during the first part of their journey, Patric with his father, and Matilda with her mother. Waltheof was proud to take Ethelreda, and their two companions had Gunhild and Octreda riding with them. Gospatric led them to a place by the river and they ate the food that had been prepared for them and watched the flowing water. When they had rested and the horses were refreshed, they carried on arriving back at the castle as the light was disappearing. Little Patric travelled the last miles cuddled across his mother's breast and Matilda happily rode with her father. Little did they know that the next time they made this journey, it would be in vastly different circumstances.

South Queensferry, Scotland
May 2017

It was six hours earlier in Minneapolis. Helen thought that Sam might be back home on a Sunday afternoon, and she decided to call him before going to bed, hoping he would be able to talk for a few minutes. He answered quickly.

"Helen, I was just about to try to reach you. How was the weekend?"

"Not the same without you. Robert wanted me to tell you that as well. He really missed having you with us."

"How about you?"

"Missing you goes without saying. How are things with your sister and the family?"

"Stable, that's why I'm at home. I needed some time alone and time to talk to you."

"It's been difficult not hearing from you, except for our quick emails. I'm supposed to tell you about our conversations and conclusions, but that can wait until I record my notes for all of us. We talked a lot about the rebellions and the damage done to the whole of Yorkshire and north of Durham, as well. He really was a Bastard! It was genocide."

"Aren't you a bit harsh, considering the times?"

"Not really. Even Robert feels the carnage was way beyond what was acceptable in the eleventh century."

"Did you get to his invasion of Scotland and Edgar's banishment in 1072?"

"No, but I've been thinking about William's decision to take on Malcolm. He must have finally felt powerful enough to do it."

"I was reading some of the material you were covering, just to be with you in my mind, and found that he had literally wiped-out Edwin and Morcar, Hereward and several of the others, like Bishop Aegelwine and Siward Barn; and he had Waltheof under his thumb. It probably gave him the confidence to make a move to eliminate his final threats—Edgar and Gospatric and, of course, Malcolm."

"And William must have been angry at Gospatric for hiding out at Bamburgh and swearing his loyalty from a safe distance. William was probably a Scorpio, holding a desire for revenge for months and years. Whoops, you're not a Scorpio, are you?"

"No, I'm a Taurus. I guess you haven't asked me that question."

"Ah, steady, grounded, but can be stubborn."

"And you?"

"A real mess, on the cusp of Leo and Virgo. I told Kit that I spent my life until recently being a Virgo, and now I am living my Leo side."

"And which do you prefer?"

"I'm really enjoying the Leo, wild and adventurous nature, but my Virgo side worries about what comes next, the job, the housing, the funds to do what I want to do."

"Have you decided what you want to do? With the rest of your life or in July?"

"A few clues, I think. I love the research—that's a Virgo activity. I'd like to write a novel—that would be more like a Leo." Helen hesitated. "Or are you wondering if I am still interested in sharing your house?"

"All of the above," he answered, not wanting to commit to what he was feeling.

"I'm seriously thinking it is a good option if it's still available. I miss you," she blurted out, not meaning to reveal any personal feelings over the phone.

"That is a relief, because I feel the same, but I know I haven't acted like I do. I have been so wrapped up with the end of the semester and the family."

"I understand. I knew you would be and you're facing a lot of uncertainty."

"Yes, I want to book a ticket to come back to Scotland, but I don't think I can, not knowing how Sarah will be. If I think about coming at the end of May, am I expecting she is going to die by then or…?"

"Why not buy a ticket with no penalty for changing it? It will cost more, but it's better than not having one."

"Good idea. I'll see what's available. I've been looking, but it's been a waste of time. I also must think about whether to rent a car, which I don't want to drive from London. I think I should fly into Glasgow or Edinburgh and pick up the car. I need to figure out where to stay." He stopped, hoping to hear an invitation from Helen.

"Let's think about a plan to see some other places, and you can stay in my humble apartment or in Robert's grand manor house—your choice."

"No choice there, I'm a humble sort of person. You have cheered me up. I'll start thinking of places we might go, and you can do the same and we can compare notes. When is your ticket back to Minnesota? Maybe we can fly back together."

"I'll check on it for sure and send you an email. I flew into London and then on to Edinburgh airport. I haven't looked at my return date since I arrived."

"It's a plan. We can talk again, maybe on the weekend."

"Great, and I will start working on those notes and thinking about some places we can visit. Bye for now."

Helen signed off without saying any more about what was on her mind. It was not the time to discuss her confusion about her feelings for Sam, her desire to stay in Scotland or her plans to share a house with him and go back to work. She could see a temporary plan, but she knew she couldn't remain at the library, back in the old rut. Part of her was afraid the relationship with Sam, living with him and going to work at her old job, would trap her and keep her from a new path. On the other hand, she didn't have a vision for the future. What did she want to do? Where did she want to live? Since there were no answers, she returned to the dilemma about Gospatric and his family. What happened when they were forced to leave Bamburgh and flee from William?

Northumbria
The Year 1072

It was quiet for a few months, without much news from Malcolm, Maldred or Waltheof. As September approached, Gospatric began to think they might be safe for another year, but once before they had counted on William not coming north in the autumn to be trapped with soldiers to feed as winter neared. Maldred had moved his family closer to Durham near his mother at Thornley. Waltheof had a second daughter, and he found no disappointment in not having sons. Queen Margaret had delivered yet another son and there now was Edward, Edmund, and Ethelred, all with Anglo-Saxon names, destined to be kings of England, as well as Scotland. Gospatric and Athelreda were grateful that she was not with child and the family was enjoying the mild weather by the sea. Despite this, Gospatric had an uneasy feeling—a sense that life was about to change. A messenger arrived in early September with a letter from Waltheof. He brought the man into the castle to rest and eat while he found a quiet place to read the news. At once, he knew how serious the situation was, and tried to understand how to respond. The words turned quickly into fearful images and the need for action. Young Waltheof came into the room, as he was re-reading the letter. Waltheof stood quietly, as if he knew there was trouble. As Gospatric looked up, he noticed his son's look of apprehension.

"I need your brother's help to read these Runes, but there isn't time…"

"He was teaching me to read them. I could try." Gospatric handed the letter to him and Waltheof stared at it. Athelreda came to hear what the message said, but she quickly realised that something was wrong and remained silent.

"Perhaps, I can't read them for they make no sense."

"What do you think it means?"

"Well, the first one stands for true or truth and the next means the opposite."

"You are right, Waltheof! It's a way for your uncle to send us a hidden message. Go now and find your sisters and bring them to the hall and alert anyone you meet to do the same. I must talk with your mother." Waltheof looked at his mother and she nodded to him.

"What is it that he says to you, what hidden message?"

"William's forces are marching north to Scotland and William is coming with his fleet to enter the Forth and the Tay. The forces will split at the hills and half will march towards Carlisle and on to Falkirk, then to Dunfermline."

"He's invading Scotland. My God, what do we do?" she cried out.

"It is worse than that. Waltheof is to bring his forces to bear on Bamburgh and fight to take the castle from me. I have been charged with the murder of Robert Comines and the conspiracy to kill William's forces at York. Waltheof is named the new earl and he must take me prisoner or fight me until one of us is dead," he told her, as he stared at the letter.

"But this is the Waltheof you love like a brother, that our son is named after, how can this be?"

"William has found a way to take revenge on both of us. He knows I would not leave Bamburgh and it would take him months to starve us out, but he has cleverly thought of a way to make it happen. He counts on my surrender, rather than a battle with Waltheof. The Runes read truth and the opposite. It is Waltheof's way of saying that the information is true, but his agreement to this is not. Come, we must make haste. We have no choice but to leave immediately."

Gospatric left the messenger waiting. He knew that he had to be careful in his response, for as Waltheof knew well, there were spies everywhere and William would see his answer. He went first to Merleswein, sharing his immediate plans and sending him to warn Malcolm, who may have had a message as well. Next, he sent two riders to reach Thorfinn and Dolphin, to advise them to head for Aspatria as fast as possible. A plan was forming in his head. The family had to get as far west as possible, but not run into the forces marching towards Carlisle. They could send out scouts to see when it was safe to reach Aspatria. They needed a hiding place, to wait out the marching soldiers. He had asked the messenger where he had ridden from and he said York, so the forces could be in Durham by now. They would be ready for their final assault north, with those going to Carlisle already heading west around the other side of the hills. Gospatric made an announcement to all who were assembled.

"We will take a small band with us, but many of you can remain here. Waltheof won't harm you, nor will he allow others to do so. I suspect, if he finds us absent and the castle surrendered to him, he will stay on and send most of the troops towards Edinburgh. They intend to surround Malcolm and force him to fight or surrender, swear fealty, and banish Edgar from English soil forever."

"And what of you, Sire?" asked one of the men before him.

"I am to be taken prisoner or killed. I will first get my family and those with us to safety, and then I must disappear. You may spread the word that I am riding north to warn King Malcolm. We leave within the hour. I need scouts to escort our messenger south towards Durham and to discern how distant the forces are. We will head west, taking as much food as we can carry and warm clothes. Prepare to have the children ride with others and assemble as fast as possible."

Still struggling with how to write the return message, Gospatric called Waltheof to him. "I need two Runes that mean something like 'Leaving and Acceptance' or a similar concept. Can you try to write them for me?"

"I think I can do those," Waltheof answered, eager to help. When he had made the symbols, Gospatric copied them at the end of his letter. The letter acknowledged Waltheof's right to the earldom through his father Siward, challenged him to come to Bamburgh to exercise his rights, and asked for his considerate treatment of the family, servants and soldiers should Gospatric be slain. He knew Waltheof would understand the Runes, as he did, to mean that he would leave and avoid a fight and the second Rune meaning acceptance of his message, as well as of the situation. The messenger was sent off with an escort to watch for evidence of William's forces, and they prepared to leave. Gospatric's calculations from Waltheof's message was that the soldiers marching to Falkirk would head west from York, while Waltheof's troops would stop at Durham to rest before moving forward against Bamburgh. His plan was to go directly west to Melrose, the same route they had taken to Aspatria. They would seek to find shelter in the tower by the backwater of the river, prepared to disappear into the forest if necessary. He knew William's forces would not come through the hills with their heavy mail and would avoid crossing any streams. The scouts he sent out would find out when the soldiers were past Carlisle, and then they could try to reach Aspatria. He hoped that Thorfinn and Dolphin would be there, safely escaping the soldiers marching through Carlisle. Gospatric planned to leave them at that point, travelling back to the tower at Melrose, where he could hide until he learned what was happening. Merleswein knew of his plan and would try to reach him as soon as it was safe.

They needed to shelter for only one night, before the scouts reported that the large army was already marching north out of Carlisle, heading for Falkirk to attack Dunfermline from there. They started out cautiously with the scouts out ahead of them.

Thorfinn was at Aspatria with Dolphin at his side welcoming them as they arrived. They all greeted each other with great relief and were taken into the hall to rest and eat. The little girls thought they were on a great adventure, but both Waltheof and Dolphin knew the seriousness of their flight and the impact of an invasion of Scotland. They could do nothing but wait to hear the results. Athelreda knew that Gospatric would have to leave them and find a way to hide and potentially leave the country. He left her with the children to talk with Thorfinn privately.

"Where will you hide, my son? I suspect that William will stop at nothing to find you. Too many have been betrayed by people they trusted for a bit of gold," Thorfinn said, with concern for his safety.

"I will go to a remote location near the river Tweed, close to Old Melrose, where I have been building a tower. Merleswein is the only man who knows of this, other than you, and he will come to find me with the news and any plans."

"I will watch over your family. Trust they will be safe. We will pack food for you, and we have a fresh horse. Your steed might be recognised, and a less impressive mount is more in keeping with a travelling clergyman," he said, as he handed him a monk's robe.

"Thank you, and please give my horse to Dolphin, and he can give his to Waltheof. I'm afraid I will have no need of such a steed for a long time."

"You will know best once we see what happens in Scotland," Thorfinn assured him. "I think Malcolm will have no choice, but to bend a knee to the Bastard and we won't know what that means for any of us for some time."

"I think I must eat something and say goodbye to the children and Athelreda, then I will rest for a few hours."

"I would trust no one with your plan. When you are ready to leave, the steed will be in the barn ready to ride, with a bed roll and provisions. I will place this monk's habit in the pack. I suggest you not put it on until you are alone in the woods."

"You have thought of everything, my friend. I can never thank you enough for all you have done for us," Gospatric whispered, trying to keep his emotions under control. "If we do not meet again, know that I love you as I loved Siward."

"You will return, my son. We have much to accomplish yet. Malcolm will protect you if he can," Thorfinn whispered, fighting back his tears.

After a full meal and drinks, Gospatric called the children and Athelreda to his side and tried to explain why he had to leave them. Matilda began to cry, and he picked her up. Little Patric stood between his brothers.

"You must all be very brave, and I will come back as soon as I can. Until then, Thorfinn will take care of you and Waltheof can begin practicing being the Lord of Allerdale." He handed Matilda to her mother and whispered to Athelreda, "I'm going to rest in the barn, so I can slip away without anyone noticing." He turned to the boys and gave them a special message, "You are now in charge of the family, but you must listen to your grandfather and to King Malcolm, if he asks you to do anything for him."

He left immediately, moving quietly to the barn, finding the horse waiting for him. He recognised him as almost identical to the horse Gunhilda had been riding when he met her, white with some mottled grey and a grey streak down his head. He spoke quietly to him, like an old friend, and found a place to lie in the hay. He woke a few hours later, starting his journey in the dark. At dawn he stopped for a drink and changed into the monk's robe, before heading northeast towards his destination.

He reached Old Melrose before nightfall and carefully surveyed the area to make sure no one was nearby. Then he slipped into the woods and walked his horse to the water to drink. He sat there for a few minutes watching the stream moving slowly over the rocks. The water was quite low from the warm summer without much rain. He would be able to bathe in the river if he felt the need. Now he took the pack from the horse and led him to the tower. It was still rough inside, and he didn't want any reactions to wild creatures in the woods. He hoped the horse would warn him of any human activity. He was not sure who was the most tired, the horse or him. He had a few bites of the food from the pack and a drink of water from the stream and then opened the bedroll and laid it in the corner. There was hay in the tower and the horse munched a little before settling down. Gospatric lay down covering himself with his robe and fell into a deep state of dreaming.

He woke when the horse, who he now called Greyson, stood up and rustled around. He looked carefully for any signs of life before leading Greyson out. He let him graze, while he began his day. He knew he had to find food. Exploration of the double pack Thorfinn had placed on the back of the horse produced a small hatchet, some fishing line, and hooks. He looked for a long branch, cut it and used his knife to create a pole to catch fish, then collected small brush, sticks and bigger bits of wood from fallen trees. He did not want to call attention to his location, so he found a secluded spot close to the water where the bank would hide the fire. He would build only small fires, when necessary. He had bread, a hunk of cheese, and dried meat to last for a few days. He searched for berries and other wild items he knew could be eaten. This busy work kept him from thinking about the children and whether they would be safe in Aspatria. It had been a good growing season and the land would produce what they needed for the coming winter. He didn't think the soldiers would veer west off their path on their way back to York. He prayed they would not burn the crops again, as they had two years earlier. When he was done with all his preparations, he mounted Greyson and moved slowly along the backwater to the ruined abbey of Old Melrose on the River Tweed. It was the land of St Cuthbert, and it would one day be restored to its former glory, he thought. He gathered some more berries and plants that were growing wild from the years when the abbey had been occupied long ago. As the days passed, he wished he could live in this peaceful place with his family. He might not ever see them again, or it might be many years if it meant waiting for William to die. The days went by without knowing how much time had passed.

He had finally caught another fish and cooked it along with mushrooms and wild weeds. He was losing weight but feeling healthy in his solitude. He could not survive here during the winter, but he didn't want to risk trying to get back to Aspatria yet, putting the family in danger. He felt like he was living the life of a solitary monk and perhaps it was time to start praying.

While Gospatric was eating his dinner, Greyson started to neigh, and he immediately jumped up, grabbing his hatchet from beside him. He crept from the trees to a position behind the tower and watched for signs of anyone entering the area. He could hear some movement in the woods, and it did not sound like a deer. He gradually could see some brown cloth, and then realised it was a monk or someone in a monk's robe. He pulled up the hood of his robe and moved out of hiding. The man coming forward threw off his hood and Gospatric saw Merleswein. In great relief, he dropped the hatchet and pulled down his hood.

"I didn't believe I would find you here my friend," Merleswein said, as he dropped the reins of his horse and came forward. With arms around his friend, Gospatric could hardly speak.

"I was giving up hope and wondering what to do next. The nights are chilly, and the food is getting scarce. Come sit by my small fire. I may have a bite to share." Gospatric's voice rasped, and he realised he hadn't spoken aloud for days.

"I have some food. Let me get it and some wine," Merleswein said, as he brought his horse to the water to drink and got out the supplies he had brought.

They ate bread and cheese and drank the wine in silence for a few minutes, before Gospatric asked the important questions.

"There really was no choice, and difficult as it was Malcolm saw this. Some wanted to fight, but we knew from Waltheof's message that we were being surrounded, and Malcolm asked us to stand down. He sent a message of submission to William, and they met at Abernethy. William had ships in the Forth, but he also had sailed into the Tay. Malcolm agreed to bend his knee and swore fealty to William."

"It must have been devastating for him. What about Margaret and the children?"

"We had moved the family to Edinburgh Castle, not knowing what the soldiers would do at Dunfermline. As it was, the message of surrender reached them at Falkirk, and they remained there awaiting orders."

"What of Edgar? What was the demand?"

"Hostages, and William demanded Malcolm's son, taking Duncan with him along with others. Banishment for Edgar and it is of this we must speak."

"Has Edgar sailed and to where?" Gospatric asked, hoping to accompany him. "Did William banish me, as well?"

"No, he wants you in prison in Normandy like Morcar, or maybe worse. You are an outlaw and whoever finds you will be rewarded. Edgar has not left, and Malcolm believes you should go together. He thinks you should sail to Flanders and go to Robert, Baldwin's brother, who is now Count. He thinks you would be welcomed by Tostig's wife."

"I last heard that Judith was in Denmark, but I presume her brother Robert would help us."

"Malcolm has arranged a ship from Berwick to take Edgar to Flanders, and a poor monk will accompany him, as well as his companion, Eldred. It is clear we already had the same idea…no one will expect an earl in monk's robes. No one can know who you are. William has left spies to ensure that Edgar leaves the country, because Malcolm refused to put him on a ship until William's fleet had sailed south."

"What is the plan, my friend? Will you join us, as well, presuming I can get safely to Berwick and aboard?"

"We will leave on the morrow for Berwick, just two monks travelling. We will avoid Norham, and any other villages and arrive at the harbour in the dark. The ship was to sail in two days if I did not find you here. This was our only chance to get you out of the country, and if you weren't at our meeting place there was nothing more we could do. I'm to get you aboard and return to Edinburgh Castle."

"Thank you for listening to my plan and probable location. I wasn't sure how clear it was since you hadn't been here."

"Malcolm remembered being at Old Melrose with you two years ago, and he pointed out the best route for me to take. I was sceptical about finding you alive."

"Have you had any news of my family…of Thorfinn?"

"Yes, after William's troops marched past Carlisle on their way back to York, Thorfinn sent a messenger to say that everyone was safe and back in position. We assumed that meant Dolphin had returned to Carlisle. Malcolm intends to officially recognise young Waltheof as the Lord of Allerdale, making it clear that you are no longer around."

"That eases the burden for me, as I leave…to know they are safe…at least for now. I wonder what William's next move might be?"

"Malcolm believes he is going to return to Normandy with the hostages, including Duncan, and parade them around like he did with the other thanes after he was crowned. He thinks William now feels that he has suppressed all the rebellions and potential threats, except you of course."

"Does Malcolm think I must stay away permanently?"

"I don't think so. Who can know his mind? He has another plan to consolidate what we control in Lothian and Cumbria. We could cover much territory with Waltheof's support in Northumbria, but he must be very careful. I think the king has plans for you, but Edgar is another matter. Malcolm knows he can no longer support Edgar in a bid for the throne."

"William has been known to visit Baldwin's court since there is a family relationship between his wife Matilda, Baldwin, and Judith. I might not be safe in Flanders, but I have no other alternatives."

"Malcolm wants you to settle Edgar and then return. He needs to always concern himself with Moray and the thane's dissatisfaction leaves him little time for Lothian. He also knows the people and the thanes respect you. That is what scares William, I think."

"I haven't seen Judith for several years and it has been six years since Tostig was killed. I wouldn't be surprised if she is remarried."

"But she still would remember you and, in any event, Baldwin's court is known for taking in banished nobles. Think of their response to the Godwinson family."

"Yes, did you know that Tostig met Judith when his family was banished, and they stayed with Baldwin and Judith's family?"

"I heard that story and that they were apparently attracted to each other…not a politically arranged union. Now, my fellow monk, where do we rest our weary bodies for this last night together?"

"Come and see my humble tower house. You might want to escape here yourself sometime."

The ride the next day was uneventful, and they said their farewells outside of the city in case this was their last private moment. They tied the horses near the wharf and made their way to find the ship. Gospatric asked Merleswein if he could take care of Greyson and he agreed to take him back to Scotland to await Gospatric's return. When they found the ship, they watched from a distance to see what was happening on the deck, but it all seemed quiet. Merleswein stopped a young lad, giving him a message to bring to the captain, in return for some food. He returned shortly with a request for the monks to come aboard. They moved cautiously to the gangway and quickly onto the ship, hoping they were not being watched. A large man wearing a captain's hat escorted them into a small room and asked, "Which one of you is the monk accompanying my guest? I was only paid for one." Gospatric stepped forward and nodded to Merleswein to leave. The captain introduced himself to Gospatric, known now as Brother Roger, and led him to a stateroom, where he knocked on the door. When it opened Gospatric saw familiar faces, young Eldred, and Edgar sitting on a bunk. The captain inquired, "May we now set sail for Flanders?"

Edgar stood and answered, "Surely, we can leave immediately." As the captain left and started shouting orders, Edgar embraced Gospatric with tears in his eyes.

"I did not trust Merleswein to find you and bring you in time. Thank God you are here. Is Merleswein gone?"

"Yes and plans to ride as far as Coldingham and stay the night." The three of them sat and drank mead poured by Eldred, who had volunteered to accompany Edgar to Flanders. They spoke a bit about the plan when they landed.

The trip was not difficult for Gospatric, but Edgar suffered a bit from seasickness. He was also worried about the reception they would receive, but Gospatric was confident that Judith would welcome them. He had also met many of those at court when they stayed with Baldwin on their way to Rome, and on their return. He could remember meeting Baldwin's brother Robert and was surprised that Baldwin's son had not succeeded him. Gospatric had donned his regular clothes and packed the monk's robe away in case it was needed again. Now they would pose as three noblemen on an adventure together, wishing to reach Ghent. He thought constantly about the children. He knew they would be safe and protected by Thorfinn and Malcolm, but he no longer knew when he would see them again, if ever. He had to make the best of this present time, but he had no future. Merleswein had said Malcolm had plans for him when he returned. If William continued to search for him, he would need to hide to survive. The threat of imprisonment and death would be a constant possibility and how could he protect his family, if he could not ensure his own safety?

When they landed the next evening, the captain told them to remain on board until the ship was unloaded. They were eager to find a place to stay if there was no straightforward way to go on. While watching the men unload the cargo, they saw a well-dressed young man speaking to the captain on the shore. Suspicious of what was occurring, they slipped back out of sight, wondering if they had been betrayed by the ship's captain. Now that he had his payment, he might have exposed their identity to someone in Flanders for a bit of gold. Looking out from their hiding place, which offered no protection, Gospatric saw the captain and the young man coming aboard. The captain came ahead and called out to Edgar.

"There is a young man to greet you from Count Robert's court. He has brought a horse for you," he shouted. The young man handed Edgar a letter, with a Royal Seal, and they sighed with relief at the introduction of Reginald, who would bring them to Ghent. He had been watching for their landing for two days and was himself relieved to see the three of them. He had only one extra horse, but they were great steeds, and each could carry two men for the short distance up the river. They set out immediately, reaching Ghent in good time.

When they arrived in the courtyard, Count Robert came out to greet them, introducing himself to Edgar and Eldred and welcoming Gospatric. When asked about his sister Judith, Robert said she was in Bavaria, but she had left a message for Gospatric. Later when they were settled in lavish apartments and well fed, Robert explained why Judith was no longer at his court.

"She has just given birth to a son. She was remarried last year to Welf, the Duke of Bavaria. She is no longer young, but having babes again," Robert noted. "Her husband desired her from the first time he saw her and divorced his wife. He wanted children, but she has, as you probably know, two grown sons."

"I remember them, Skuli and Ketil. When I was here last, they were just small like my own children are now. What has happened to them?"

"When Tostig and Harald Hardrada were killed, the survivors got back to their ships and left for Denmark and the boys went with them. They were then about fourteen and sixteen and old enough to fight. Thank God they survived, for Judith was already devastated by the loss of Tostig. She left as soon as she could to look for her sons, finding them in Denmark. They were relieved to see her, but gradually made their own way in life, and she returned here to Flanders."

"How difficult it must have been for her…to hear the terrible news of Tostig's defeat. The Danes came again later to help us overcome King William and we were also defeated."

"William the Bastard is not someone to oppose, my friend. I suspect you and Edgar have learned this lesson well."

"Yes, and now there is a price on my head and Edgar is banished from his home and family. I am concerned that Matilda and perhaps William might learn of my presence here and decide to make a visit…"

"There is no love lost between us. Matilda is our niece, but she chose to marry a dangerous man. They genuinely love one another, but her choice was a difficult one for us. After you have had some time to rest, Judith has asked for you to visit her. It would be best for you to travel soon, while the weather is still mild. You could remain in Bavaria, if you would feel safer, but I can assure you that William will not harm you here. None know who you are other than a friend of Tostig, and we will leave it that way. You are a Scottish noble who supported

Edgar as the rightful heir to the throne of England and now, like Eldred, you are to be with him as his future is determined."

"I would very much like to see Judith again. Your sister is a remarkable woman. I have never met anyone with such a breadth of knowledge."

"And so many books. Most of her library is still here. She hasn't had time to move it. If we can arrange for your escorts to take part of her collection, it would please her."

Gospatric left for Ravensburg in early October, and Edgar and Eldred decided to join the travelling party. They considered it to be an adventure, but Gospatric had made the trip to Rome with Tostig and knew it was not an easy journey. He discouraged them from coming, but they had nothing meaningful to do and it was clear there would be no plans to return to Scotland soon, if at all. Gospatric found the trip quite different to the one he had made with Tostig. They could move at their own pace and admire the landscape as they made their way into Bavaria. They enjoyed the hospitality of the villages they stayed in on the way, all arranged by Robert and Judith. They were treated like royalty when they arrived, and Judith was eager to speak with Gospatric. She was still a beautiful woman and she seemed pleased with motherhood. After settling in, he went to her private quarters to see her alone.

"Gospatric, it is so good to see you, but I wish it was not in these difficult circumstances." She motioned for him to sit beside her by the open fire, as she placed the babe in the cradle. "Tell me about your family—you had but one child when we met, and you had lost your young wife at your son's birth."

"Being with you and Tostig on that journey changed my life. I didn't believe I would ever find anyone to replace Gunhilda, but I believe you had something to do with sitting me next to Athelreda and her brother, when we returned to Bamburgh Castle that summer."

"I believe I did, and I heard that you married her shortly afterwards. Are you happy you did?"

"Yea, I am, but it is not a good time for either of us. I've left her alone with two boys, one only a babe, and four little girls. Dolphin is now the Lord of Carlisle, but he is barely a young man," he answered with distress. "But I want to hear about you. What happened when you heard about the defeat at Stamford Bridge?"

"Tosti had already been absent for a long time, both physically but also emotionally," she said, using her affectionate name for her husband. "Once he was banished by his brother and King Edward, who had always favoured him, he was consumed by anger. At first, Baldwin offered him a position and he seemed to be settling in, but revenge for what happened consumed him. He even went to William to offer him support to invade England, and he finally found Harald Hardrada to be his partner in the invasion. I hardly saw him in all those months and in the end, he took our sons with him."

"Robert told me they survived the battle and were taken back to Norway and on to Denmark."

"We had argued about taking them into danger. They were boys, not yet men, but they wanted to go with him. My final words were, 'You will die regretting this decision' and I could not forgive myself for saying it. I had to search for them, but my little sons were all grown up and didn't need a mother anymore."

"They were relieved to see you, weren't they? Can you imagine what they had experienced in those months? Anyone would change in the circumstances," he said, trying to comfort her.

"I know, but I finally left. The Danes were not my people, and I had no place. It was a rough environment, with little respect for women. I came back to Flanders and had the opportunity to serve the church and build my library. Baldwin was kind to me, and it is through him that I first met Welf. Then he died and there was trouble, with Robert taking over in a struggle with our nephew."

"He seems a good man, but I must say I am surprised to see you with a babe. Your brother is as well."

"Welf was married before and had no heirs. When he was made Count of Bavaria, he wanted to have children. I knew he was in love with me, but I didn't believe he would divorce his wife. I would have taken him as a young lover, but he would not hear of it. He wanted to marry me and have sons, like so many men."

"And you did as you were expected," he teased.

"I was as surprised as anyone. I warned him I might not be able to have any more children at my age, but here I am. Frankly, I am enjoying it more than I did before. Our lives were chaotic, and Tosti was filled with ambition. I adored him from the moment I met him, but our needs change as we grow older. Do you find that to be so?"

"I think I have always needed to have a home for my children and a peaceful place to live, probably because of all the changes and losses when I was young.

I thought I might achieve that until the upheaval began after King Edward's death."

"Were you there at the battles? Tosti defeated Morcar and Edwin, didn't he? Before Harold brought his force against them…"

"I wasn't there, Judith. Malcolm had me standing by, waiting to see what would happen. Morcar and Edwin were never to be trusted because they always wanted to do things their way, not to support others. I heard that Harold stopped the battle and proposed peace to Tostig, but he rejected the offer. We had been planning many things with Tostig, but he did lose his way when Harold forced him to leave the country. Harold would have given him his own lands when you returned, but he couldn't risk the northerners turning against King Edward. The thanes would have started a civil war if their demands that he be banished hadn't happened. I don't think Harold had much choice. You know he married Edith, Morcar and Edwin's sister, to gain their support."

"And he gave up the woman he loved, the mother of his children."

"I couldn't understand why he didn't marry Edith Swanneck. He left her and then lost his crown and his life. It was such a waste."

"And what is there for you now, Gospatric? Are you done with fighting William?"

"Even Malcolm is done, and Edgar may be relieved. I have no choice. I seem to have no future, and no way to provide for my family."

"Will not your cousin Malcolm help you? My brother said his understanding with Malcolm is to protect you, while he plans for Edgar's future. He thinks William will not bother much with Scotland now that Malcolm has been forced to swear fealty to him and submit hostages, including his son Duncan."

"I believe he will try to protect me and will provide for my family. He has always said I can rely on him, but right now it is difficult to see any way forward."

"Do not despair, my good friend. You could always bring your family here and build a life with us," she said, reaching out to touch his hand.

"Thank you, Judith, but as you found in Denmark, we need the place we call home and I know where my heart lies."

He left the room when her son woke to be nursed, relieved that she had an attentive young husband to satisfy her needs and care for her. So far away from all that he loved, he would have been tempted to look to her for solace.

South Queensferry, Scotland
May 2017

Sam had called to say he had booked his ticket for two days after the end of term—time to get his grading finished and pack. So far, Sarah was in remission, and she was encouraging him to travel. He had purchased an open return just in case things changed. Although he had a car scheduled for pick-up at the airport, Helen would take a cab to meet him. They decided they would pay the extra money for two drivers and an automatic vehicle.

Sam and Helen were discussing what happened to Gospatric's family when William marched into Scotland, and how they managed to get out of Bamburgh Castle in time. Without any conclusions, they thought perhaps the family had headed back to Aspatria. Gospatric, some sources said, had left for Flanders with Edgar—how, they didn't know. Helen reminded Sam that Gospatric had been at Baldwin's court in Flanders when he went to Rome with Tostig, and Judith had travelled with them. It made sense that they would go to Baldwin, since he was known to offer hospitality to banished nobles. On a whim, Helen looked up Judith of Flanders and found she was the aunt of William's wife Matilda. She was talking again with Sam, on the phone, telling him what she had found.

"After Tostig's death Judith ended up in Denmark, probably because her two sons were with their father during the battles. They went back to Norway or Denmark with Harald Hardrada's surviving force. Later Judith met and married Welf, the Count of Bavaria, and moved to Ravensburg, southeast of Stuttgart. She donated an impressive collection of books and gifts to the nearby Weingarten Abbey, but the strangest thing was that she had three children with Welf, and she was at least thirty-eight when she married him."

"And she had grown children by then, right?"

"Yes, they were probably sixteen and eighteen or older. Isn't that amazing—she survived three more births?"

"Are you suggesting we could consider having children, at our advanced ages?" Sam teased, hoping she heard the joke in his voice.

"I'm quite beyond that. I'm afraid you will have to find a younger woman, quite a bit younger."

"I prefer the company of women my own age, thank you, preferably yours." She ignored his comment and went on.

"We won't ever know if Gospatric saw Judith again, or if he and Edgar stayed at Ghent."

"The questions remain—how did Gospatric know about the invading force and why did he leave Bamburgh without a fight, when it was almost impossible to attack it with any success?" Sam queried. "It could take months to starve the occupants, so perhaps he didn't want to put his family or his men through that ordeal."

"Or the people through more devastation…burning of homes and crops, before winter, as William had done in Yorkshire just two years earlier."

"What's the agenda for our weekend after I arrive?" Sam asked, wanting to spend more time with Helen but also excited about the gathering.

"We are going to look at the sources that say Gospatric came back in 1072 or 1073 and was given Dunbar and other lands in Lothian. It's difficult to understand how that could happen without William sending some soldiers to arrest him."

"Agreed, but even more mysterious is that brief passage from Roger de Hoveden, that shortly after receiving Malcolm's gift, he became ill, summoned Aldwin and Turgot from Melrose, confessed his sins, died and was buried in the porch of the church in Ubbanford, called Norham now."

"Robert is planning to drive us to Norham on Sunday morning and have a pub lunch."

"We have all read the Hoveden passage so many times, but now we will have the time to really examine it together," Sam said, before ending their conversation with plans for meeting at the airport.

Less than two weeks later Helen waited in the car rental area, as agreed. The plane from London was on time, so all Sam needed to do was pick up his luggage and make his way to her location. She was a little early, so she started to search through Nigel Tranter's book, *Margaret the Queen*, for the passages about Gospatric. She was sure he placed Gospatric as a spy for Malcolm posing as a monk, after his return to Scotland. Tranter was a historian of some repute, so he may have had some historical information or may have just made up the story. It would be fun to speculate on whether Gospatric died about 1074 or whether he needed to die to end the search for him. Helen was reading the passage she was looking for when she became aware of someone in front of her.

"Sam, you're here," she exclaimed as she dropped the book and stood to receive his hug.

"I am, and a bit early," He kept holding her but backed away to look into her eyes. "I have been waiting for this moment."

She didn't answer, but reached up to kiss him, before she spoke. "Let's get this car rented and get you home for a rest. You must be exhausted."

When they reached her apartment, Helen made breakfast for them and encouraged Sam to use the bedroom for a nap. He was asleep in minutes. She hadn't decided what came next and was glad they had a couple of days to figure it out before the weekend with Robert and Andrew. When Sam woke, he asked about taking a shower, and whether she wanted to go out for dinner. He was acting like a guest and that made her uncomfortable.

"I thought we could cook dinner together here tonight. With jet lag, you will want an early night, and I bought lamb chops and new potatoes." It had the effect she wanted, as he moved to her side, and put his arms around her.

"That sounds perfect, all of it." He kissed her before going off to the bathroom. She sighed with relief, knowing he would settle into the routine they had started to establish before he left.

After sharing the cooking and salad making, they enjoyed a candlelight dinner. They were having a second glass of wine, when he brought up the subject of his sister.

"I didn't want to tell you on the phone, but I had an argument with Sarah before I left."

"That must have been difficult. About what? Did it get worked out or is it hanging over you?"

"Let's move to the couch and I'll tell you about it. It's important for us and for the weekend," he said, as he took their wine glasses to the coffee table. Helen picked up the plates and took them to the sink and then sat beside him.

"This sounds serious."

"The argument started when I said I didn't want to leave for Scotland without her permission to tell Juliana about Robert, should anything happen suddenly. I begged her to reconsider her insistence on waiting to the last hours of her life to share the information. She absolutely refused, and she was already angry at me for asking her for our mother's diary. She said she had destroyed the diary and I said she was lying. She admitted she had it but wouldn't tell me where it was."

"What is her problem? She was your mother too and Juliana's grandmother. I presume you wanted to share it with her."

"Yes, but that wasn't the immediate issue. I told her about you. Sarah said I didn't have the right to take it with me, to have you read it." He stopped waiting for her reaction.

"Did you want me to read it? How did Sarah know that? I'm confused."

"This is the difficult part. I said it was important to me for you to know about my mother. I insisted I had as much right to the diary as she did…more because she never wanted to read it."

"Difficult, because you had to take on your sister when she is dying?"

"No, difficult to tell you that I told her we were planning on living together and I wanted to share my life with you," he blurted out. "She asked if I was thinking of getting married again after all this time and I said it was a possibility." He looked away, not sure of the reaction Helen would have.

"If that's a proposal, it's a very strange one, so I'll consider it a warning of something coming sometime in the future." She was trying to lighten the mood.

"And I'll consider that a warning to delay any thoughts like that until well into the future."

"Well into the future might be a little too distant," she heard herself saying, and wondered where that statement came from.

He reached over to her then and she went into his arms, responding to his long kiss that brought back the sensations from their last night together before he flew to Minneapolis. She hadn't intended to make love. She just wanted to stay with him for the night. It had started out that way but finished with some gentle and then passionate lovemaking during the middle of the night. When she opened her eyes again and looked into his, she asked the question, "So, did you bring the diary?"

"Yes, do you want to see it now or wait until morning…"

"I'll definitely wait until morning."

Flanders
The Year 1073

Gospatric, Edgar, Eldred and their companions had returned from Ravensburg, after spending time with Judith and her family. They were treated well by Robert, but the weeks weighed heavily on Gospatric. After the Christmas holiday season, he spent most of his time alone, avoiding discussions about William. He was done with invasions and death. He just wanted to get back to his family, to see his children. Robert Curthose, King William's oldest son, was spending time in Flanders and he was talking with Edgar and the Count about a rebellion against his father. He hated his father and was sure of support from the King of France to remove William as Duke of Normandy and organise another effort to end his reign in England. It renewed Edgar's hopes of being king and his interest was understandable. The two Roberts were negotiating for Edgar to be granted a castle and a small tract of land just outside of Normandy by King Phillip. This would set the stage for a later invasion. Edgar was upset about Gospatric's lack of enthusiasm for the plans. Gospatric tried to explain his feelings about his family, and his need to return to them. He could not risk imprisonment or death in another attempt to end William's control over England. He finally just stopped meeting with them. Count Robert had written to King Malcolm, to tell him of the arrangements for Edgar. He asked whether it was safe for the monk who accompanied Edgar to return, since he did not wish to move on with Edgar. He indicated that William was occupied with problems in Normandy, and not likely to be bothering with Scotland soon. Gospatric was grateful to him for the communication, but not hopeful. His depression was growing with little to do and without the companionship he had enjoyed earlier.

Within the month, the Count called him in to read a communication from King Malcolm. Malcolm thanked Robert for providing hospitality for his guests and approved the plan to settle his brother-in-law Edgar in France. Then he added that a sailing ship with goods from Scotland was on its way to the area and would be able to pick up Brother Roger, a favourite of his wife, for attendance at the baptism of their child. Gospatric was relieved and planned immediately with the Count to meet the ship when it arrived. Robert suggested that he should start acting more like a monk, as he prepared to leave, and invited him to visit a nearby monastery. Gospatric agreed. He had some final time with Edgar, Eldred and Robert Curthose, advising them to proceed with great caution in any moves against William. He sent a letter to Judith saying his farewells and wishing her a peaceful life. She sent a message back, which arrived before he left, saying she was with child again and hoped this one would be as gratifying as her first.

While Gospatric was sailing back, now always wearing his monk's robe and acting the part, he wondered how long it would be before he could see Athelreda and his children. What did Malcolm have in mind for him? How could he pretend to be a monk and live at Aspatria with them? The unknowns made the journey more difficult, and he began to try the meditative prayer he had observed while visiting the monastery. He found it had the right result and enabled him to enjoy the wind and the waves and worry less about the future.

The ship sailed into the Firth of Forth, a thrilling sight for a man who had not been sure he would ever see his country again. Although he had spent so many years in Cumbria and Northumbria, he identified with Scotland as his true home. He agreed with Malcolm—all of Cumbria and Northumbria should be part of Scotland. He breathed deeply and absorbed the landscape on both sides of the Forth, and the islands, and then saw they were apparently turning to the north side to land. He grabbed his small bag of clothing, left the bed-roll behind, and packed the gifts Robert had sent with him for Margaret and Malcolm and for his family. Back on the deck, he looked at the landing area with disbelief. Standing on the shore with Athelreda were the children, all waving to him. Dolphin was there as well, as tall as Merleswein, who was beside him with Greyson. He choked back the tears for a few minutes, and then just let them come. He was home, his family was safe, and nothing else mattered now. He leapt to the shore and was surrounded by his children. He picked up little Patric whose first question was, "Why are you dressed like that?"

"It's a long story, my son, and you will hear it many times," He put Patric on Greyson, as Merleswein gave him the reins and said, "Welcome back, my friend." They all mounted their horses and headed north to Dunfermline, where Queen Margaret and King Malcolm were waiting to greet him.

After hours of celebration, eating and drinking, with Athelreda at Gospatric's side and surrounded by his children, Malcolm asked to see him alone. They left the hall for a small chamber where a warm fire welcomed them.

"William left shortly after he accepted my homage. He shows little interest in our land, once conquered."

"I understand from the Count that he has as much opposition in Normandy as he had from us, and more on the way."

"I hope Edgar does not become an active part of another rebellion, but he is making his own decisions now. I have my own opposition as well. The thanes in Moray are forever causing trouble."

"Are they not grateful for peace, Sire, at any price?"

"It is their claim that I lived too long in the South and have abandoned my northern heritage by taking an Anglo-Saxon wife and naming our children after kings of England. But we were married by a Culdee bishop and have supported the old ways. We continue to honour St Cuthbert, as is required by our ancestors."

"Having a mother from the Northumbrian line leaves me in the same position, but I yearn to have a united country living in peace."

"This is what we must speak about. I have placed Merleswein in Fife, along with others and I need you to handle the area from Dunbar across Lothian. You are known and supported. Walcher is in control in Durham and north to Bamburgh, but he is not trusted by most of the thanes. I need you but I cannot give you a title without alerting William to your presence. It's not necessary to be disguised as a monk, but I did not want your return to be obvious. If we do this quietly, we can yet have the land we wish, with Waltheof as the Earl of Northumbria. If William has trouble in Normandy and is forced to stay there, we may have another opportunity to take the country from him and, of course, he may die or be killed. His son Robert, as you now know, is not in favour, but as the oldest should succeed him."

"He truly hates his father and doesn't hold much affection for his younger brothers either," Gospatric added, remembering the conversations they had in Flanders. "Am I not to return to Aspatria with my family, Sire?"

"After the baptism of Edgar, you should travel back with them and assess how things are being managed in Allerdale. I have heard no unwelcome news, and Thorfinn will be happy to see you once more. Then, as the weather warms, I want you to spend your time in a more strategic position, where you can reach the East coastal areas easily. I have arranged for building work on the tower near Old Melrose. It should shortly be adequate for your family if they wish to join you. We need to have young Waltheof start taking responsibility for his position as soon as you think he is ready. If he is half as talented as Dolphin, Allerdale will be safe in his hands and we will look for the future husbands of your three girls, as well as wives for Dolphin and Waltheof, among the families in Cumbria."

"And what of the fourth?" Gospatric asked, thinking Malcolm had lost count.

"Although Duncan is in Normandy with William, I am hoping to negotiate his return and arrange his marriage to Ethelreda. She asked me where he was and why he was not here to meet her when she arrived. I think they will be a good match."

"Do you have other plans I should know about, Cousin?" Gospatric said, with concern about his life and his children being controlled by Malcolm.

"Many plans, but some can wait. At present, we hope there is no longer a threat from Norway or Denmark, nor from William, but we need to protect our lands from invasion with fortresses along the Forth. I do not intend on losing Lothian or Cumbria. Now return to the celebration and take that wife to bed. Like Margaret, she seems to thrive on having bairns. We are lucky men. I now have healthy sons to succeed me, and perhaps one to be a king of England."

Gospatric left and joined the group below in the great hall. He hoped that he had not offended Malcolm by his question, but he had that uneasy feeling in the pit of his stomach, disturbing his sense of joy and relief of being with his family again. Athelreda showed him their sleeping space with a private alcove for the two of them. There was a place for all the children to stay together. The girls were happy to be sharing with their big brothers Dolphin and Waltheof and were content to be taken off to bed for the night. Margaret and Malcolm had retired to their quarters, and Merleswein and Athelreda were sitting by the open fire next to Gospatric. They wanted to know what Malcolm had shared with him. When he got to the part about the tower house, Merleswein added his thoughts.

"You will love it, Athelreda. It is in a beautiful peaceful place on a backwater of the river, where the children can fish and swim."

"I think I would miss Aspatria, now that we have settled there again."

"It was only months ago that you and I sheltered there, my friend. It would take a great deal to ready it for my family," Gospatric stated, sensing Athelreda's concern.

"You might find it quite changed. Malcolm sent me back to organise further work with the local men and they made much progress before winter set in."

"Could we take that route back, so I might see it?" Athelreda asked, preferring to know what the tower was like before decisions were made to move her family again. "The children are still young to make the trip in one day and the weather is unpredictable."

"We could," Gospatric assured her. "What would we need to stay and keep warm for the night Merleswein?"

"Let us talk with Malcolm. Since he wishes you to consider the area around Old Melrose as your base, we could take some carts ahead of you and begin to set up the household at the tower for your comfort."

Athelreda was not impressed with the tower, although it looked better when they had taken in the furnishings the men had brought. The children thought it was a wonderful place to hide and Gospatric was inclined to agree with them as he saw the difficulties of getting through the forest to the tower. It was for this reason he was not upset when Athelreda told him she did not wish to move the children, having finally settled at Aspatria. She scolded him for not being aware of the frightening events they had experienced when forced to leave Bamburgh, taking only what could be carried. He would have to travel, if that is what Malcolm demanded, but she would remain at Aspatria. She seemed surprised when he agreed with her. They left early the next day for Carlisle, hoping to stay with Dolphin for a night and reach home the following day. Once the family was resettled, Gospatric would leave and spend a few weeks visiting families in the area, taking his son along with him. Waltheof was not officially the Lord of Allerdale, but Malcolm wanted the people to know that he would be in the future. Gospatric felt the best way to do this was to ride out together and visit every family and village they could, to talk about the spring planting and assure them of their support. He tried to confide the need to be discreet about his return from Flanders. He and Waltheof also talked about the young boys they were meeting, who could grow up to be suitable husbands of the girls in the family. When they returned Waltheof teased his sisters, telling them he had found their future husbands. He did not know how true it would be. With disappointment Gospatric watched his little son run to Waltheof, rather than his father. He wanted to change what was happening, but he knew he would soon be leaving to spend time with Dolphin, then Thorfinn, and moving east across the country into Lothian. He would need to see Malcolm and tell him of Athelreda's decision to remain in Aspatria and his willingness to be the constant traveller as his cousin required.

Edinburgh, Scotland
June 2017

Helen and Sam were planning to drive to Robert's home, intending to assemble all the information they had on Gospatric's return to Scotland to take to the gathering. They had worked on very little since the day of Sam's arrival and hadn't been anywhere except to walk to the marina and through the cobbled streets of South Queensferry. Primarily they had concentrated on their own relationship, where it was going and how it affected their immediate plans and the future. Their talk was marked by intense discussions about life and death, as Helen read his mother's diary the morning after Sam's arrival. He handed it to her after breakfast, suggesting he would clean up the kitchen from the morning, and the dinner dishes from the night before. She was in tears from the beginning, reading what Mary had written about their goodbyes at the airport. Knowing that her instinctive reaction had become fact was heart-breaking. As the entries unfolded, Helen was pulled along into the strange occurrences Mary was experiencing. It felt like someone from the past was conspiring to capture her mind and her body. Dreams were one thing, but this was more. She found she had to speak to Sam before she went on reading.

"Sam, I just read the part where she walks back into the other room and sees the black ribbon in the book from the library and it opens at Coldingham Priory. That is scary. What did you think when you read it?"

"You must realise I was so young, and we had just picked up my mother's things from the airport. My sister was a mess. She screamed at me to get rid of everything and then locked herself in the bedroom. I remember getting a beer and just reading the diary straight through. It was like reading a novel, an unfinished one. I knew the ending came at St Abbs by Coldingham but there were no details. Only Sarah and Robert know what happened next and she's not talking. When you have finished, we can discuss whether I question Robert about what happened. He was supposedly a witness. If we are going to Norham, we could go to Coldingham and to the beach…" He stopped and started to cry. "Sorry, it's so long ago, but I still feel it at unexpected moments."

She took him in her arms and cried with him, not knowing why. "Do you think it will help to see where she disappeared?"

"I really don't know, but I feel I should see it now that I'm here and face the consequences."

"Let me finish and we'll talk about it."

There were little moments of relief when Sam's mother would describe time with Robert, or when she was struggling with her feelings about him. This was a much younger Robert, not the man they knew, a man who might have had a permanent relationship with Mary. This would have changed all the events that followed, including her own life. If one thing had changed in the subsequent days recorded in the diary, the outcome would have been different. As Mary turned away from the relationship with Robert to the pending arrival of an old love, Helen felt the inevitable trap of the past closing in on Mary. Then the diary ended, without any further record of the events that followed in the next few hours. She found Sam in the bedroom getting the last of his clothes unpacked and sorted to take for the weekend.

"Sam, how much of what happened in the next few hours of her life do you know?" she asked, holding the diary in her hands with the last entry open. "She's waiting for a phone call…"

"Not much. The police thought she disappeared at St Abbs, where she had been with Robert a few weeks earlier. Robert claimed she called and left messages that she needed to go there. He didn't get those messages until he arrived at his jewellery store. A car belonging to the owner of Dundas Castle was found on the cliff overlooking the beach, with my mother's purse inside. Somehow Robert was there, but Sarah refused to tell me what he knew. I do know she wouldn't trust him with Juliana, if she felt he had been responsible in any way for our mother's death."

"And the man she was waiting for…the one she was convinced had been her twin in another life…"

"We had never met him, but he wasn't heard from again and we didn't have a name. You must understand…the hours and days after the call from Scotland and getting her luggage from the airport were a blur, with Sarah nearly dying and then unable to function. Will and I were trying to take care of two babies and

Sarah, and cope with my mother's death. By the time there was any normality in our lives, all concern for details was gone."

"I do understand, but is it important to bring it out now? I'm curious, but it is up to you whether this is something you want to confront Robert with, at this time."

"I think I do. I want to ask him if he will share what he knows with me. I think he owes me that, however much it hurts. I won't ask about Sarah. I just want to hear what he knows about the last hours of my mother's life, and I want you to know."

"What about Andrew? He has nothing to do with this," she commented.

"I don't know. Let's see what happens. I don't mind if he is there when it is discussed."

They dropped the subject of the diary but continued to talk about what life would be like as they prepared to make a home together in Sam's duplex, when his tenants left in July. It wasn't a difficult conversation, but it did bring up subjects they needed to discuss. Helen had her two children to think about, and Sam had none, but he was like a parent to Matt, Jake, and Juliana. They each had separate resources and possessions. They had no experience with the subject matter of cohabiting, but there was a lot of humour in their discussions. Helen shared her concerns about not knowing what she wanted to do in her work life. Sam's response was brilliant and now he was adding to it.

"I've been thinking about our discussion, and I want you to know I can afford to keep us in food and fun for a few years, if you decide to work on a master's degree. You wouldn't have to work while going to graduate school."

"I think I might want to get a master's in history. I would have all the research done to cover most of the eleventh century in England and Scotland. Is that a possible thesis topic?" she asked, laughing at the idea.

"Could be a little broad! You could look at the Conqueror from a new perspective. I don't remember anyone writing in detail about all the rebellions surfacing throughout his reign."

"How about William, a war criminal? I'd probably have to take a couple of years of history undergraduate courses before I even started."

"I don't know. Maybe not. What would you do with a history degree?"

"Teach; but most of the history teachers I had were track, football, or basketball coaches. That was why they were so bad at teaching."

"If you do decide to get a master's and teach, we would have time off together and we could come to Scotland."

"For a vacation? For a week or two?" she asked.

"No, I was just thinking…we could spend our summers here, rent a cottage and cover various parts of the country."

"Now I know why I am going to say yes, when you ask me," she said, as she hugged him. The marriage idea had become a joke between them, a way to talk less seriously about a commitment that went further than moving in together.

"We'd better be going, or we will miss drinks before dinner, your favourite part of the weekend," Sam teased. "On the way, we can talk about what we are going to tell Robert and Andrew about us."

"Do you mean when we ask for one room instead of two?"

"Oh, I hadn't even thought of that. It's one way to tell them, I suppose," Sam said, chuckling.

"Not to worry—I called Robert yesterday and suggested that Mrs Wakefield only had to arrange one room for us."

"What if we break up on the weekend?"

"Well, I picked my room, since it is bigger, so I would just throw you out and you would have to fend for yourself."

"On that note, let's go."

Traffic was heavy in both directions, and Helen navigated while Sam watched the road. She kept thinking about how much had happened between them and that she hadn't shared any of it with Kit. She didn't really want to but knew she should tell her something to prepare for her return. When they arrived, Andrew and Robert were having sherry in the library. Neither of them seemed uncomfortable, just welcoming of Sam. When they had their drinks, Sam shared his news.

"Let me tell you that Sarah is in remission. Not knowing how long-term her situation is, she gave me permission to tell Juliana about you, if something should happen suddenly before I get back to Minnesota."

"I am grateful for you convincing her, but it is sad that she is unable to tell her while she is still well enough to deal with the questions Juliana will have."

"No movement on that score. She was angry when I insisted on bringing my mother's diary with me to share with Helen."

"You have it here?" Robert asked, with surprise.

"Not here, but at Helen's. She read it this week. Did you ever read it?" Helen was uncomfortable. Sam was trying to start the discussion about his mother's death.

"I did. Your sister shared it with me, before she left. We can talk about it later," he said, dismissing the topic. "I'd like us to decide on what we can accomplish tonight and what we want to cover tomorrow. Since we will be going to Norham on Sunday, it doesn't leave us much time to get to the main question—did Gospatric die in 1074 and is he buried at Norham?"

"I brought my shovel," Andrew chimed in.

"I thought of that myself," Helen said, chuckling. "Do we have enough evidence to get the body exhumed?"

"Here's what I found out," Andrew continued, "and Robert probably knows this. The church was there way back, re-built in 830 by Ecgfrith, the Bishop of Lindisfarne, but burned down in 1136 by David I. The old ninth century church was probably set in the clump of yew trees, so I figure we start digging there. The only problem is that the old church might have been by the preaching cross in the village green."

Robert chimed in, "And Ceowulf was also buried in the porch of the church, so it really is unfortunate we can't dig the area up and see how many bodies we have."

"Personally, I would settle for our individual reactions to whether there is any truth in the story of Gospatric's death and burial at Norham," Sam said, trying to bring them back to the point. Robert welcomed the opportunity to take charge.

"Right, Samuel, and I heard the dinner bell, so let's read the text of his return to Scotland and the great Simeon's words about his 'death' which have been passed down through history, when we return from dinner."

When they came back to the library after dinner, the conversation continued. They had discussed how little anyone knew of Gospatric's return to Scotland. Robert summarised their lively dinner discussion to get them started again. "We have all agreed we know little about Gospatric's return, so most of what we have discussed is speculation. The limited records say he returned from Flanders and received Dunbar and adjacent lands in Lothian from King Malcolm. He is accounted the first Earl of Dunbar, although he did not hold that title. Roger de Hoveden wrote: *'not long after this, being reduced to extreme infirmity, he sent for Aldwin and Turgot, the monks who at this time were living at Melrose, in poverty and contrition in spirit for the sake of Christ, ended his life with a full confession of his sins, and great lamentations and penitence at Ubbanford, which is also called Norham, and was buried in the porch of the church there.'* We could pick the language apart. For example, who is living in poverty? It must be the monks, as Gospatric had just been given the most productive land in Scotland to manage."

"Ended his life," Andrew dramatised, "with confession, lamentations, and penitence. Does this sound like our Gospatric?"

"And he does this at Norham, so he can be buried in the porch like Ceowulf, king and monk," Sam said. "It is all too overdone to be true, so what do we really think?"

Robert started. "We must look at Aldwin and Turgot and what they were doing in the ruins of Old Melrose. We know Turgot was from Lincolnshire, that at some point he was imprisoned as a part of one of the rebellions. He escaped and ended up in Norway serving the king."

"That's a lot, right there," Helen commented. "One source said he was at the marriage ceremony of Margaret and Malcolm in 1070, but I don't think that fits with the story. Turgot was involved in the rebellions, and he could have been at the ceremony if it were earlier, when the conspirators escaped to Scotland in 1068. He was clearly tied into the family, and when he returns from Norway, he goes to Bishop Walcher. Walcher would have been handling Durham and Bamburgh for Waltheof, but was he trusted by Malcolm?"

"Some think he might have met Waltheof in Normandy and been close to the conspirators and others think he might have been involved in setting Waltheof up," Robert answered and turned to Andrew who was trying to speak.

"But why does Walcher send Turgot to Aldwin and why do the two of them go to Old Melrose? It must tie into this meeting with Gospatric, and his dramatic death and burial."

"I'm going to pose a theory for the three of you to dissect," Robert declared. "Turgot has been in Norway, learning about building cathedrals. He learns there is a new plot brewing for the Danes to invade England again, while William is pre-occupied with Normandy. What does he do? He needs to tell the conspirators, who are still alive, about the plan and that means some contact with Malcolm. Walcher sends him to Aldwin at Jarrow, maybe because he has professed a desire to become a monk, and they proceed to Old Melrose. Perhaps they meet Malcolm and Gospatric there. With the knowledge that another invasion is possible, they know that when William learns of it he will return, gather his forces, and potentially finish off those involved in the conspiracy. He'll look first to any who have participated in the past. So, they determine it is best to have Gospatric dead and buried, with enough drama to create a viable story to send back to Durham. What do you think?"

They discussed the possibility of Robert's proposition and produced no other alternatives. They would go to Norham on Sunday, but thought it was unlikely they would sense that Gospatric was buried there. They felt it was quite likely Gospatric began to dress as a monk after his 'death,' to ensure he was not identified.

The Border Lands, Scotland
The Year 1074

Gospatric spent many months travelling from Aspatria, across the border and north to Dunbar. He always stopped at the tower near Old Melrose. He wondered if he would ever be able to build a large hall nearby, where Athelreda would be willing to move with the children. She was pregnant and not happy about it. Although there had been no trouble, he could not assure her that William wouldn't send out a party of soldiers to find him. By now rumours may have reached him in Normandy, telling him about Gospatric's position of authority in Lothian and Dunbar.

Whenever Gospatric circled the area, he would ride back west from the fortress at Dunbar, where many of his men were located, to meet with Malcolm. He had to cross the Forth, but it was always good to see Margaret, who was pregnant again and surrounded by her children. When he saw the king, he saw the concern on his face, and Malcolm led him to a private place to talk.

"It is good to see you, Cousin. I was about to send a message to you to come. We have a new problem."

"What is it, Sire? Has something happened to Merleswein or Waltheof?"

"No, it is Turgot. He has returned from Norway and gone directly to Durham. Bishop Walcher sent him to Aldwin at Jarrow. Turgot sent news that there is talk of another invasion from the Danes, with the intention to take the crown from William."

"Surely not," Gospatric gasped. "He was not here to watch Northumbria burn and the people starve."

"And he did not witness my humiliation in bending my knee to the Bastard. I am not asking you to participate. Turgot could be arrested, and you as well if any news has reached William. Turgot may become a monk, or pose as one, until this is over. Aldwin and Turgot are at Old Melrose apparently thinking of reviving the abbey."

"I have been fortunate that William has been preoccupied with his challenges in Normandy, but I cannot rest easy."

"That is the point. If there is a rebellion, or even a hint of one which reaches the king, he'll set about suppressing it and may return to take charge himself. I have heard that the Earl of Hereford wishes to marry William FitzOsbern's daughter Emma. Apparently, William is refusing to allow the marriage."

"Why would he do that? FitzOsbern is his trusted man, handling part of the country."

"He has died, and his son is now earl and perhaps the king doesn't feel as secure as we might imagine. William might be threatened by the alliance of the two families."

"What are you suggesting we can do?"

"I need you in place, where you are, but I fear for your safety. I am going to suggest a drastic measure. Our only path is to assure William you are dead. He has no doubt heard from some spy that you are serving me in Scotland. I want us to arrange your death with Aldwin and Turgot, and then I will send someone back south with the news. You, like Turgot, can undertake a death of sorts, by giving up your title and privileges for the simple life of a monk."

"Do you think it will work? It was one thing to pose as a monk to leave the country, but to be a different person would be difficult. What about my family and those who know me well? They could not be fooled."

"No need to worry about it. You can tell them the reasons. It will primarily keep William's forces from coming north to find you. You can still travel the area, but you must not reveal where you are going next. No one should be aware of your place near the Tweed. Think about it, and we will meet again to make our decisions. Perhaps William will be defeated or give up his crown. We may yet be free of him."

"I think I will rest and consider how this might work, Sire."

When they met next, they agreed on a strategy. Malcolm sent a message to Turgot and Aldwin at Old Melrose that said they would be contacted by someone who needed their services for his confession before ending his ordinary life. The last sentence was an admonition to follow the orders of the visitor, as if he were the king himself.

Gospatric left the next day, bidding Margaret and her family goodbye. He took with him all he would need to assume the role of a monk. He would shave off his beard and cut his hair to assume the tonsure style of a monk. He had continued to ride Greyson, to avoid someone spotting his great steed, now in Dolphin's care. He took supplies for the monks and little for himself. He intended to travel soon to alert his family of his change in status and the intent of King Malcolm to officially name Waltheof the Lord of Allerdale, after acknowledging Gospatric's death. At thirteen, Waltheof was a tall, handsome lad, well-liked by the thanes. He had spent much time with them over the years and learned a great deal from his father, brother, and grandfather. He was no longer the naive childish boy, but a young man ready to serve and accept responsibility. Sometimes Gospatric wished both he and Dolphin were his little sons again, but he was grateful for their maturity and sense of duty to their family and to the people.

When he neared Old Melrose, he rode to the hill overlooking the river and could see the monks below. There was a sadness inside of him, a sense of loss, but at the same time he felt free. He thought of Maldred and Waltheof. Would they believe he had died, and mourn his passing? Would he ever be able to see them again?

He rode the short distance and entered the ruins of Old Melrose. Someday, it would be a beautiful place to stay, but right now it was not an easy situation, even for monks used to poverty. He had brought both food and ale for the monks. Turgot came forward to greet him, recognising him at once. Gospatric slipped down from Greyson and hugged his old friend. He gave the reins of his horse to Aldwin and told him about the supplies.

Later, Turgot and Aldwin sat with Gospatric, enjoying the ale, bread, and cheese. Turgot spoke quietly.

"The message from the king came yesterday, and we are prepared to do your bidding as soon as you wish."

"I would like to be with you tonight and leave for Norham in the morning. I want a ceremony to make it more real to me. I assume you understand the importance of both secrecy and appropriate sharing of information. I believe you may have something of the same problem yourself, Turgot, and I see you have taken on the physical appearance of a monk. Have you gone further?"

"I am preparing for that event when we return to Jarrow. I feel it is my calling, but it may not be yours."

"Perhaps not, but I am done with war. We fought for a peaceful future and our efforts ended in destruction and death. The quiet life of a monk becomes more appealing as the years go by."

"I understand, my friend. And now tell us what we shall do on the morrow."

Gospatric explained what he wanted to happen. Aldwin and Turgot were to take him to his final resting place at Norham. He was dying and wanted to be buried in the porch of the church, beside the saint he admired, both king and monk, Ceowulf. When there, he only wished for Aldwin to hear his confession, to cut his hair and shave his head in the Roman style tonsure, and to take his clothes to distribute to the poor. There were other items identified with Gospatric to be given away strategically. He would don his monk's clothes and boots and accept their acknowledgment of his death as earl and rebirth as a new man, a humble monk. They would disturb the earth around the porch and then leave Gospatric to disappear, while they returned to Old Melrose. Gospatric asked them to deliver a message to Durham lamenting the loss of Earl Gospatric. He would complete the transformation in the following days. This would be an emotional experience for him, and he needed the time to gradually take on a new persona to fit with his character. He would be Brother Patrick and his young son could now be Gospatric, the future Earl of Dunbar and Lothian, as Malcolm had promised.

When he left the tower, he rode first to see Thorfinn and Dolphin. He did not want them to hear of his death in some other way. It would also help to have their opinion of whether his disguise would work, and how it should be handled in the family. He wasn't looking forward to explaining to Athelreda. Dolphin came running out when he saw Greyson without his father. It took him a minute to realise who he was looking at, as Gospatric greeted him.

"Let's go inside so I can explain." He had already stopped to see Thorfinn, who reacted much the same. When he had told him of the pending problem and the plan, Thorfinn was relieved. It was more difficult for Dolphin to accept.

"Surely, Father, this will only be for a short while, and then you can be the Earl of Dunbar, as Malcolm wishes."

"We shall see, Dolphin. If William is not defeated, his sons will succeed him when he dies. I don't believe he will name Robert, even if he is the eldest. He is not favoured by William."

"Can he name some other son? Is that possible?"

"We know him well enough to see that he can and will. That is why, Dolphin, I want you to be prepared to be the head of this family. Waltheof will help and he will be named the Lord of Allerdale by Malcolm soon, but he and young Gospatric and your sisters will need you. Can you do that for me?"

"I can, but I don't wish to do so. You are a great lord, and the people love you. You would be their Earl of Northumbria if William hadn't taken your title away. I can't bear to think of you as a lowly monk, living an unknown life…"

"I have already lived more than many ever do, and I am grateful for this, and for all my children. You must not worry about me, but I'm not a monk yet, my son. In time perhaps, but for now I am still a man in monk's clothing. I will stay the night so we may talk and then I must be off to Aspatria."

"Mother is not going to be happy about this."

"She has not been happy for a while. I had hoped to see the day we could live as a family near Old Melrose and your brothers and sisters would be able to grow up in peaceful times, but it is not to be."

Dolphin was right about Athelreda, but it was much worse than Gospatric expected. She had miscarried the babe that morning and the entire household was frantic. It did not help that Gospatric was not recognisable when he rode in on Greyson. As soon as Waltheof saw it was his father, he took him at once to see Athelreda. She turned away from him. The tiny babe was still in the room, and he had to deal with burying her. He gave the orders and ignored the pleas to wait for the priest. He didn't need a Roman priest telling him his daughter would go to hell. The old ways of his people did not believe that an innocent child who died would have everlasting punishment. The family had to fit into the Roman Church, but they would have their own ceremony and not wait for the priest.

It was a difficult burial as the tiny bundle was put into the earth. His children hadn't faced this kind of death and they clung to him, weeping. He understood that they sensed a greater loss still coming and the transformation of father to monk was unsettling. When a local Culdee priest said his final words, Gospatric sent the children off with Waltheof to pick flowers for the little grave, and he went to Athelreda. She was awake, sitting up and staring into space. He sat quietly by her side for a few minutes, waiting to see if she would speak. Finally, he could wait no longer.

"It is done. We have buried her, naming her Juliana, and the children are gathering flowers."

"I didn't want another child. Now God has punished me."

"No, Athelreda. Many women lose their babes. It is nature's way, not God's punishment."

"But I didn't want it. I don't want any more children, and I don't want to go through this again. Why are you dressed like this?"

He explained the reason for his garb, Malcolm's concern for his safety, and the plan to grant Allerdale to Waltheof.

"So, we are still not safe. I can't live like this. Now you come dressed as a monk again. You will leave, and I will not know when and if you will return…"

"It may not be for long. It is just until this rebellion defeats William or is suppressed by him. He may not even come to England. He cares nothing for our country."

"But still your loyalty to Malcolm is more important than your family."

"I took an oath. Think what he has given to our children, Athelreda, and their future."

"And what did he take from this family…and what will he require of the children, as they grow older?" She turned away from him, as she spoke, "I can be your wife no longer. You are a stranger to me."

Cumbria and Lothian
The Year 1076

Gospatric had continued to cover the large territory of Lothian and Cumbria, where he spent most of his time. His son, Waltheof, was the Lord of Allerdale, as promised by Malcolm. Gospatric learned that the promised rebellion had been suppressed. The Danes failed to appear in time to aid the Earl of Hereford and his brother-in-law, the newly wed Earl of East Anglia. Roger FitzOsbern was imprisoned, and Ralph had escaped. The Danes had finally arrived, ransacked what little was left of York and sailed again. There were rumours that Waltheof had been involved in the plot but had gone to Normandy to warn the king. As far as Gospatric knew, he remained in Normandy with William. He desperately wanted to see Waltheof and Maldred. He missed them and Merleswein. He had no one to talk to, as he had when they were all working together to put Edgar on the throne. Malcolm was the king and, although he was a cousin, Gospatric's relationship had always been one of service, not friendship. Without the closeness with Athelreda, he felt very much alone.

He circled back to Aspatria as often as possible and spent Christmas with the family. There was no change in Athelreda, but she continued to mother the children and manage the household. She treated Gospatric as a visiting monk, and he had given up trying to change her mind. He slept in separate quarters with Waltheof and little Gospatric, and the girls slept with Athelreda.

Early in the new year, after Twelfth Night, he left with Dolphin for Carlisle, and continued north and then east to Edinburgh Castle to meet with Malcolm. Once again, he could see the concern on Malcolm's face as soon as he entered the great hall, still decorated from the season. Malcolm dismissed others around him and bade Gospatric to sit, ordering food and wine to be brought to him.

"We have just heard. William brought Waltheof back with him from Normandy when he learned that the Danish fleet was back again. He accused him of supporting the rebellion at a trial a few weeks ago. Lanfranc claimed he was innocent, but when Judith testified against him William put him in prison. He's at Winchester and William hasn't pronounced his sentence."

"Why would Judith testify against him? He is the father of her little daughters. My God. How do we get him released?"

"You can do nothing. I'm trying to find out exactly where he is, because he was moved to a secret location. I'm concerned about William's need for revenge."

"He's killed many people and imprisoned others, but he has never executed anyone. I cannot believe William will dare to harm him and Judith…I never trusted her…"

"William may banish him or send him to a monastery. Waltheof wasn't directly involved, and he warned the king of the plot. We must hope that he plans to release him."

"Do you think it is impossible for me to go to Winchester to see him, as a monk of course?" Gospatric asked.

"It would be asking for the same treatment or worse. We were right to announce your death."

"Will you try to free him by force, Sire?"

"I don't think it possible. He will be well-guarded. William suspects someone will try to release him, or he wouldn't have moved him. Now what is your news?"

"Not much has changed. Young Waltheof handles his position with care. He admires Dolphin and asks him many questions. Little Gospatric follows him everywhere and the girls still favour their mother's company. I find I have no children anymore. It is as if my monk's robes have caused them to forget I am their father."

"And Athelreda? Margaret asks of her often."

"She is the same. I am dead to her. I think it would have happened anyway. She was afraid of losing another child and wouldn't have lain with me again. She believes God punished her with the death of the babe, because she wanted no more children."

"And your needs, how do they get met? You are yet a young man."

"And a monk, in all but the vows of the Church. Have you heard anything of Maldred? It has been six years since we met."

"I have heard that his wife has died, leaving him with three sons. He still has lands where you visited with him, but also near Durham."

"I am sorry to hear she has died. Perhaps I could try to meet him in Durham, at one of the monasteries."

"I would not take the risk now, with William in the country. We must see how he treats Waltheof. If Lanfranc cannot convince William of his innocence, I don't think we can do anything to change his mind."

"Do you wish me to continue on to Dunbar tomorrow?"

"It's important for your men to know you are still close if William decides to do more than buy off the Danes again. If his men don't have any trouble heading off the invaders, he may send his soldiers into Durham and north to Bamburgh."

"There is nothing left for them to burn. Surely, they wouldn't stay long in the winter knowing there is no food for them."

"He might order his men to march north of York and kill a few more people who have returned, just to make sure we understand his power."

"God save us from the brute!" Gospatric exclaimed, with a shudder.

"Where is our God in the face of a man like William, who professes to be a devout Christian?" Malcolm shouted. "He pretends to have faith, by building churches where he won battles."

"Judith knows her niece Matilda is a committed Christian and she tries to influence William, but he continues to destroy our country."

"Take heart, Cousin. His son Robert is plotting against him. Many in Normandy will join Robert. William is bound to leave again by spring. If he is kept busy defending his Norman territories, we may be able to take control south to Durham. Now you must go and see Margaret and the children. My sons always ask about you and your children. Perhaps we should have left the women together at Dunfermline, on a permanent basis. I still believe we will see the day that Duncan is released and can be wed to Ethelreda."

Lothian, Scotland
June 2017

The following morning, they began to examine the next attempt to move against William. Robert began again to offer his perspective.

"Although we don't have any evidence of the involvement of Malcolm or Gospatric, we need to look at what happens to Waltheof. He has been Earl of Northumbria since 1072, when Gospatric was forced to leave Bamburgh and flee to Flanders. Gospatric returns in 1073, is said to be dead in 1074, and the next rebellion is organised in 1075. There are some who think Waltheof fell into the rebellion by attending the wedding of Ralph, the Earl of East Anglia. William refused to sanction the marriage of Ralph to William FitzOsbern's daughter, and FitzOsbern's son Roger joined in the rebellion. By coercing Waltheof into the plan, they would gain support from a great deal of territory in the South, and they probably thought they would have support from the North, with Waltheof as the Earl of Northumbria and previously in league with Malcolm and Gospatric." Robert took a deep breath and went on.

"Waltheof's confession to the archbishop is evidence of his lack of enthusiasm for another rebellion. Archbishop Lanfranc advised him to go to Normandy and beg forgiveness from William, which meant warning him of the plot. William keeps Waltheof with him until he returns to England and then imprisons him."

Sam asked a question. "What happened to the others? I've only heard about Waltheof, and the rebellion being suppressed by William's forces."

"I just read about it," Andrew answered. "Ralph escaped to get help from the Danes, leaving his new wife to defend Norwich Castle. The rebellion didn't amount to much, although William heard of the threat and blamed the involvement of the Danes on Waltheof's connection with them. Ralph and his wife Emma escaped to Brittany where he had land and later died on a Crusade to Palestine with Robert Curthose. Roger was imprisoned and not released until William the Conqueror died."

"Think about it," Sam suggested, "William's friend FitzOsbern, who has been running the country for him, has children who are part of the conspiracy, and they are friends with William's son Robert. Later, William arrests his own half-brother Odo, who has also been handling England for him alongside FitzOsbern. He has all those betrayals, but the one he seems to despise the most is Waltheof."

Helen had been silent, but now spoke. "And he was family, married to William's niece and she implicates him. Did she want to get rid of him? By then they had three small daughters, so why testify against him? Did she want his property for her own? It is possible she was a pawn in the marriage and never wanted to be Waltheof's wife?"

"She may have thought her uncle would release him or let him enter a monastery," Andrew said. "Lanfranc insisted on Waltheof's innocence, so many thought he would be forgiven. He had already been imprisoned for some time, and it is clear there was a lot of support for him. He was well loved, so William made sure no one knew where he was." Helen spoke softly in response to Andrew's statement. "I don't know how long it would have taken Gospatric to learn of Waltheof's situation, but I can imagine the pain it would have caused. I suppose no one connects him to Waltheof in the same way we do, but he must have been like a younger brother to Gospatric. I wonder if Waltheof had heard the rumours of Gospatric's death. And did he know that Judith had testified against him?"

"What I find interesting," Sam said, "is that Waltheof's daughter Matilda becomes the wife of an older Norman, when her mother refuses to marry him, and later marries David, the youngest son of Malcolm. We see Matilda, then called Maud, become Queen of Scotland. She has children with her first husband, is quite a bit older than David, but also has four children with him."

"Another story, and an interesting one," Robert suggested. "Let's have our lunch and I'll tell you about my plans for tomorrow."

During lunch Robert talked about the route to Norham. He wanted to take the A68 to Earlston, then cut across to Norham. He told them they could be in Earlston in less than an hour, have morning coffee and get to Norham in about forty minutes. He wanted them to see the extent of Gospatric's territory. From there, he planned to cut across to Berwick and have lunch at Coldingham, which was only a half hour away. On the map he showed them the distance, which appeared immense, but they knew he had made the trip many times and would drive quite fast. When he mentioned Coldingham, Sam took the opportunity to ask about St Abbs. Robert did not appear surprised. Helen thought he had secretly wanted Sam to ask about St Abbs, and Andrew was unaware of the reason, and questioned Sam. Sam explained that it was where his mother had drowned, and he wanted to see the location since they would be so close.

Later, over their pre-dinner drinks, Robert asked Helen about their plans for travel now that Sam was here.

"We're planning to spend at least a week in Cumbria. Andrew, we'll take the information you provided us about Gospatric's daughters receiving land when they married and drive the area. It should be a beautiful time in the Lake District, so not all work. We have rented a cottage on the Solway Coast for a week. It is just west of Aspatria, in Allonby, and it will be a holiday, as well as research."

"Don't leave out the lands Waltheof gave to his children and to the Church," Andrew said. "There are also more St Cuthbert connections all over the territory. If Gospatric was dead, I wonder where his younger children were living? His youngest son is thought to be born about 1070. Given he was leading an army in 1138, it is unlikely he was born any earlier than that year. His sisters were a little older, maybe six to ten in 1074."

"I remember reading that Malcolm marched to Durham in 1079," Robert said, bringing them back to the subject, "and it was thought that Gospatric might have been with him. The author, as I recall, said it could have been Gospatric's son, which was an uneducated speculation, since he was a child."

Helen intervened with a connected thought.

"I didn't think of it before, but we know from the information gathered about Edgar, that William's son was rebelling against him in 1079, with his mother's funding. Robert Curthose attacked his father and brother in Flanders in that year. With William dealing with problems on the continent, Malcolm may have been testing the waters a bit, and Bishop Walcher didn't oppose him. It was one of the reasons the thanes were angry at Walcher. It was Walcher's deputies who killed Ligulf, who was a highly regarded thane. That brutal murder brought the wrath of the Northumbrian thanes down on Walcher. Does anyone remember that reference to Maldred marrying Ligulf's widow?" Helen asked.

"I vaguely remember it," Andrew said, "so let me look for it. We need to fit Maldred into our timeline somehow."

"I think we should stop here," Robert suggested, "and each of us can do more work on Maldred before we meet again. I would like to plan a time when we could all go to Durham together. We can cover some of Maldred's territory on the visit. I will take care of all the arrangements for three nights at a hotel. The primary reason for this visit is to ask the Cathedral staff to show us the stone with the inscription of *Gospatricus Comes*, which is noted in the Dundas material."

"The translation does make it clear that it is Gospatric the Earl. I am looking forward to seeing it," Sam stated. If all goes well, Helen and I are booked to return on the same flight, leaving Edinburgh the 25th of July."

"We'll be back from Cumbria the first week of July, so any time after that would work for us," Helen added.

"Andrew, up to you," Robert replied. "The rest of us are more flexible. Do you have any days off during the week? I think it would be our best chance of having the staff help us."

"I have my vacation scheduled for the second week in July. I can work my plans around Durham, so ask when they will see us at the Cathedral. Didn't we try that once before, Robert?"

"Yes, but I didn't push them, so they failed to get back to me with a date. They did say the stone was found in the crypt as we thought. I know Samuel wants to have a conversation with me, so I need to rest before we talk."

"Robert, I'm fine with the others listening. In fact, I'd like Helen to be with me, and Andrew if he is interested. It should help all of us tomorrow when we go to St Abbs." Sam looked at Helen and Andrew, who both nodded their heads.

"So be it. Please do not have any high expectations. I have little to add to what you know."

Robert returned to the library and poured drinks before dinner. He hadn't left much time for discussion, but perhaps he was right, he didn't have much to add.

"I will tell you what I know. It is what I told the police and shared with your sister. When I got to my business that morning, I had some phone messages from Mary, saying she needed my car to drive to St Abbs. I tried to call her back, but there was no answer, so I locked the shop and drove to Dundas. I saw a car leaving the drive as I was coming close, and it might have been Mary. Not being sure, I drove down the long drive and knocked on the door. Lady Jane said that Mary had asked to use her car because she urgently needed to go to the coast. I went back to my car and tried to decide if I should follow her. I started driving, still unclear if it was the best thing to do, when I heard a radio announcement about a deserted sailboat found off the coast near St Abbs Harbour." Robert paused and then went on. "Mary had told me that her friend was sailing into the Firth of Forth to see her. She believed there would be a reconciliation. It was her way of ending our relationship, and making it clear this man was someone for whom she cared deeply." Robert stopped again. When he went on, it was obvious the past was present for him. "I drove as quickly as I could and thought I could catch up to her, since I knew I'd drive faster than she would. I thought she would take the same route we had taken together, and I took the ring road, where I could make better time. She was at least fifteen minutes ahead of me." Robert stopped to take a drink, and the three of them did the same. No one wanted to interrupt with questions. After a few minutes he started again, but his voice was quivering.

"When I reached the area, I drove first to the harbour, thinking she might have gone there. When I couldn't see her, I drove back up the hill and into the village. When I came to the first street, I saw Lady Jane's car. Relieved, I parked behind it and found Mary was not there. I ran to the edge of the cliff and that is when I saw her. She was in the water, and I can't remember much more. I was screaming and trying to run down the slippery wooden stairs. I saw the waves rolling over her and when I reached the bottom I fell. I was screaming for help, and someone must have called the police because they arrived. They sent some men into the water, but they couldn't find her. I told them what I knew, and they arranged to follow me back to Queensferry, driving Lady Jane's car to verify my story. For a while I checked with them to see if they had found her body, but they never did, and I stopped calling."

"What about the sailboat?" Sam asked, hoping he had the information about his mother's friend.

"I didn't see any information about the incident. I presumed you would have figured out who the man was."

"Sarah and I hadn't met him," Sam explained. "He was a friend from work, and we weren't paying attention to what was going on with him. The diary clearly said she felt he was connected to a past life somehow."

"Was there anything else that happened?" Helen queried, feeling he was not disclosing everything. The dinner bell rang, and Robert took the opportunity to end the conversation. The subject didn't surface again.

The next morning, they set out early after a proper Scottish breakfast, prepared by Mrs Wakefield and delivered to the table by Mr Wakefield. Sam and Helen had talked about how much they fit the stereotype of the long-serving staff of a manor house in a changing world. At one time there would have been more property and cottages, now sold off to pay taxes. Families would have lived on the land, taking care of the walled garden, and managing the wildlife for food and sport. There would have been a butler, a footman, and house maids, as well as kitchen staff. Now only the couple were left, kept on by Robert for his comfort, but more to provide a home for the Wakefields, who had served the family well for many years.

The road to Earlston, after they left the ring road, was a lovely country drive across the Cheviot Hills. Helen was fascinated as they drove through Earlston and the surrounding area.

"Gospatric's son had a manor at Earlston in later times," Robert said. "And I think Gospatric may have had a place close to Old Melrose where we are stopping for tea." In a few minutes they parked next to a meadow with a river flowing near-by and entered a tea shop.

As they sipped their delicious tea, Robert told them about the history of the area, the early development of the ancient abbey and its decline. They had driven by ruins of Melrose Abbey in town, before their journey to Old Melrose.

"When Gospatric was meeting with Turgot and Aldwin, the ancient abbey here at Old Melrose had been long abandoned. It would have provided little shelter for the monks, and there were no plans to revive it. When the abbey was renewed, it was built in Melrose leaving the old abbey site to continue its decay."

"And you think Gospatric had a hiding place near here?" Helen asked.

"Yes, he must have had during the challenging times when William's forces might have been looking for him. There is a ruin of an ancient tower house on some private property near here. It is on the backwater of the river, and I have imagined the tower being his secret hiding place surrounded by forest and overgrown weeds."

"Like in Sleeping Beauty," Helen said, as she pictured the site Robert described.

When they returned to the car, Robert drove the short distance north and east on small winding roads, into the village of Norham, locating the large, impressive church. The minister was there to show them around. He didn't know anything much about the Gospatric story, but there was a small plaque indicating his burial. The minister left them in the circle of yew trees, where they believed the old church had stood, and went off for his Sunday lunch. The four of them remained in the circle, feeling the energy. Andrew spoke first, "Does anyone feel any connection to Gospatric?" They shook their heads.

"What a relief," Andrew joked. "I don't need to start digging." With that statement, they left the trees and went back to the car, heading east to the coast and the tiny village of Coldingham. They stopped at the one small restaurant on the main road through the village. It had a special Sunday lunch menu and Robert had made a reservation. There was still no discussion of St Abbs, their next stop. After lunch they walked through the Coldingham Priory grounds, where there were excavations taking place. Some stones with skulls and crossbones, like those at Dalmeny Church, had been propped against a wall. They had read that the bones of a nun had been found, having been sealed up alive in some dark past. Suddenly they were startled by the organ playing inside the church. They knew it would be someone practicing, but it was still unsettling. Robert led them back to the car, aware of the time passing. He drove first to the beach at the bottom of the hill and asked Sam if he wanted to approach from the cove or drive to the top of the cliff. Sam said the cliff, and they set out on a drive around the headland and back towards the village at the top of the cliff. Robert parked in a place that seemed like his description of where he had found Mary's car. He led them towards a gate that opened onto a path. A short distance away, there was a long wooden staircase going down to the beach. From the top, the vista opened on a circular cove, with a beautiful sandy beach. The waves were rolling in but seemed harmless in the afternoon sunshine. Children jumped in them, with their dog playing alongside them. As they started down the stairs, one at a time, Helen could imagine a scene of much higher waves crashing into the shore, with storm clouds threatening in the sky. She wondered what Sam was experiencing, as he led the way. Robert was behind and she became aware that he had stopped. She went back to him.

"What is it, Robert?"

"I can't go any further. It was happening again," he whispered, looking pale and sick.

"What was happening? Tell me."

"I saw her from here and she was in a nun's habit and then she was gone. When I looked down, I had a large cross around my neck and a black hassock on, and then I don't remember anything more." Andrew had come back up the staircase and she asked him to stay with Robert, while she went down the rest of the stairs to run across the beach to Sam.

There was no discussion as they returned to the car and drove back along the coast road towards Edinburgh. At one point, Robert pulled into a tea shop that was serving and opened the car doors for them.

"I think we need to talk a bit before we drop off Andrew," he declared.

When they were settled with their pots of tea and biscuits, he shared his experience on the stairs and his thoughts. "The only explanation I can find for what happened to me on that staircase is that I knew Mary in another life. We had some strong connection to that place, and we were repeating an earlier scene."

"Is that why you want to see Juliana?" Sam asked. "Do you think you will have a similar experience? I don't mean a tragedy, but a memory."

"I want to meet her because she is my daughter. That is the most important reason, but of course I suspect there could be a similar connection of some kind which could be explored."

"But you have implied a deeper need," Helen challenged, "a connection to a secret group, not currently represented by the descendants of Dundas, and the potential for her to join the group, right?"

"I have said I am not at liberty to tell you about the group, so I must assure you…she is my first concern and the addition to the inner circle is secondary. I will say this…to allay your fears…we are looking for documents that would help the world see the commonality of all faiths, rather than their differences. Too many wars have been fought based on religious fanaticism and we have been searching for the key to changing this. It is not like the current Knights Templars, here and in the US, who are doing the opposite—trying to prove Christianity as the only true way forward. I must not say anymore, and I beg you not to talk about this anywhere outside of this circle."

Sam got up and paid the bill and they proceeded to get back in the car. There was silence on the way to the house, with just goodbyes to Andrew when they left him in Musselburgh. Little conversation occurred when Sam and Helen picked up their car at Robert's. Their baggage was already in the car, and Robert, who looked exhausted, wished them success on their journey to Cumbria. They continued their drive to the apartment in silence, watching together to make sure they didn't miss any turns on the way into South Queensferry.

Cumbria
The Year 1076

It had been a long winter, and Gospatric travelled less, faced with the deep snow in the hills. Athelreda was frequently ill, and the children needed his attention again. Before the spring arrived, she had stopped eating and drinking, and they knew she would not survive many more days. The priest came to hear her confession, but she would not speak with him. She still believed that God had punished her for not wanting a child, and she was sure He would go on punishing her after death. Gospatric sent the priest away and called on one of the Culdee monks to try to comfort her. The children each came to say their farewells, including Dolphin. They had sent a messenger to tell him of the situation, asking him to alert Thorfinn. Gospatric was the last to see Athelreda and went to her with the Culdee monk, asking him to quietly assure her of God's goodness. The monk spoke of a loving God, who would gently take her to the afterlife, where she would be welcomed by those who had passed before her. His gentle manner calmed her, and she died with Gospatric holding her hand, as he had in their marriage ceremony. Her brother Edmund arrived shortly after her death, and he helped Dolphin and Thorfinn dig a grave, while Gospatric and Waltheof stayed with the children until it was ready. Edmund carried Athelreda, wrapped in a beautiful cloth and placed her close to where her tiny daughter was buried. There were no flowers to pick but each child threw in a bit of soil, as the men covered the area, and then they found a stone to put next to the two graves. The monk said a few words and then they returned to the hall. It would be many days before the voices of the girls were heard laughing again. Edmund stayed a while to help support Gospatric, when Thorfinn and Dolphin left. Edmund was little Gospatric's godfather, and he promised to take care of him, if anything happened to his father. Gospatric was relieved to know this. He was sad to see him leave, as the weather improved. Edmund agreed to see Maldred, as soon as possible, to let him know what was happening. They shared their concern for Waltheof, who had not been released from prison.

Gospatric did not return to Old Melrose until May. After Easter, when the roads were clear of mud from the melting snow, he and his son Waltheof visited all the communities in Allerdale to check on planting and any flooding damage. He stayed a few days with Dolphin and then some days with Thorfinn. He knew he must travel to see Malcolm, but he waited a while after arriving at the tower. He felt he had not had time to mourn Athelreda's death, because there was so much to do, helping the children find new ways to be together without their mother. The months she was ill had been devoted to her care and concern for her recovery, but after her death they needed to change how they managed the household. Ethelreda took charge of many of the duties, as she had already been doing, and the others helped her. It was little Gospatric who suffered the most, being so young. Waltheof was good with him, but he now had responsibilities that made it impossible for him to always take his little brother along. Gospatric had suggested to Dolphin that he might have young Gospatric spend time with him and with Thorfinn's family.

Alone at the tower, Gospatric allowed himself to let the full impact of the last difficult years take over his emotions—from the painful escape of the family from Bamburgh, his time in Flanders, his hopeful return to Aspatria. He went on to relive the estrangement from Athelreda, the death of the babe and now her death. Rather than thinking of the events, he experienced the emotions of each, some known and some hidden even from himself. At times he sobbed without being able to stop, much as he had aboard the ship with Tostig, when he had lost Gunhilda and left Dolphin behind for months. He did not want to see the king under these circumstances, with his feelings so raw. He might lash out at Malcolm as the reason for his pain and loss. None of the attempts they had made to achieve a peaceful future had made any difference. It had all been a waste, with death happening all around them. After a few days of no sustenance and little rest, he collapsed into a deep sleep. He awoke refreshed and hungry, and set out for Dunfermline, where he would have a warm meal and wine to renew his spirits.

The king was north when he arrived, and he spent some time with Margaret and the children. When her sister Christine left with the boys, Gospatric was finally alone with her, and the queen shared news she did not want to deliver.

"I have not wanted to share this," she began, "but I can wait no longer. We learned a few days ago that Waltheof was condemned to death for consenting to the conspiracy and not resisting or publicly denouncing the conspirators against the king."

"How can this be happening?" Gospatric shouted. "He was innocent, he warned William, the Archbishop defended him! What is Malcolm going to do?"

"He can do nothing, Gospatric. He has ridden off to tell others, but he is devastated. I know him, and he would move mountains if he could do anything to save him."

"Perhaps William is just being dramatic. Now he might let him enter a monastery. He surely is not going to execute his niece's husband when he has not ever executed a noble man in all these years."

"I hope you are correct, my friend, but he is an unpredictable and vengeful man. He has faced threat after threat since he crowned himself king and he is opposed by many in Normandy, including his son Robert. This may be his message to the rest of us. I am grateful he believes you dead, and you must remain so."

"William has not left England now for months. We must wonder if he has determined he cannot rule from Normandy and trust our country to his followers, like FitzOsbern."

"This might be so; and now I must return to the children. Will you wait here for Malcolm's return?"

"I think I will travel to see Merleswein and I'll return here before I go on to Dunbar. Pray for a miracle, Margaret."

When he arrived at Merleswein's hall in Fife, he had to remind himself that he was a lowly monk, calling on a thane. He asked the soldier who greeted him to announce that a monk wished to see him. It worked, and Merleswein was quickly at his side, guiding him to the great hall and asking for food and wine to be brought to them.

"So, have you done the deed, taken your vows?"

"No, but I may do so. I must tell you that Athelreda died late this winter…"

"Having a babe? Do you have another son?"

"No, she lost one earlier and wouldn't forgive herself for not wanting that child, a little girl."

"You are fortunate to have the healthy children you have. How are they?"

"Dolphin is a fine young man and has assumed his responsibilities as Lord of Carlisle and young Waltheof is doing the same as Lord of Allerdale. The girls are young ladies now and running the household and little Gospatric is trying to manage without a mother."

"Perhaps he has too much mothering with four sisters to supervise him."

"You may be right," Gospatric said, chuckling. "I am hoping he is staying with Dolphin and then Thorfinn for a few weeks, while I am away. Have you heard the news of Waltheof's execution?"

"Yea, and it is unbelievable, but this king has always been erratic and vengeful. You cannot order the slaughtering of thousands of the people whom you were crowned to serve and be a sane person. I pray he will change his mind and want to be seen as a forgiving sovereign."

"I'm not sure I can bear another loss, so soon. It has brought me back to my father and grandfather's deaths. I am thinking of riding to Dunkeld to see where they died."

"I would not, my friend. It is not a good time. There is much unrest everywhere. Remain with me for a few days. Rest and converse with me, then go about the king's business as before. We have suffered under the reign of William. We can only hope to be rid of him and wait upon that day."

"I forget how much you lost…all your lands everywhere across England. How do you manage to not brood?"

"I did not lose my life and I am grateful to King Malcolm for what I have. My family is safe."

"You are right, of course. We are both alive, and our children and their children will perhaps live in a better world. I will stay and eat and drink. You will cheer me, but I don't know how I will deal with Waltheof's death."

"Let us pray that the Bastard changes his mind. Now come to my table and enjoy."

When Gospatric left a few days later, he did feel better and stopped only briefly at Dunfermline to find that Malcolm was still away. After a visit to the garrison at Dunbar, he headed south to visit Coldingham and St Abbs, before heading west back to Old Melrose. Those who knew him well recognised him, but others accepted him as Brother Patrick. He gathered supplies, as he went, to ensure he could stay some time at the tower.

Gospatric led Greyson through the woods and reached his hideaway with relief. He built a fire without fear and sat by the water in the long evening hours, thinking of Waltheof. He did not believe in Athelreda's punishing God, but he wasn't sure what he did believe. Like his ancestors, he felt closest to the divine in nature, in the trees and sitting by the calm water. He tried to pray, but he struggled with the words. He tried to reach Waltheof in his mind, remembering every moment, from when he first saw him at his mother's breast, to the last time they were together in Durham. He had grown up to be a large man, like his father, and he reminded Gospatric of Siward in so many ways. He was strong and overpowering, yet soft and gentle. His daughters would not even remember him, as they grew up with Judith, who had betrayed him. Why, of all of them, did he have to suffer? The fire was burning down when he left the shore. He entered the tower and collapsed on the straw bed, still trying to reach out to his 'little brother.' At dawn he woke with a sense of fear and the words 'deliver us from evil' running through his mind. Then, without warning, a sharp pain like a cruel wind cut across his body, and he fell to the ground. He knew at once…it was over. No prayers would save Waltheof now. He fell back into a disturbed sleep, filled with darkness and grief.

Gospatric heard the official news of Waltheof's execution several weeks later, when a message came from Malcolm. It said that the executioner ended his life by the sword at dawn on the 31st of May, while Waltheof's recited the Lord's Prayer. He was buried in Winchester, but Judith begged to remove his body to Crowland Abby and that was done. Malcolm wrote that William had left the country, refusing his request to release Duncan. He ended with a request for Gospatric to visit, hoping that with trouble brewing in Normandy, they would see little of the king. Gospatric had been mourning for so long, he felt no more pain from the message, but it did serve to confirm his experience when he was at the tower. He knew he had been contacted by Waltheof, as he passed into whatever awaited him. He believed now that there was some form of life after death and a way to communicate from the beyond with those left behind.

He found himself tired of posing as a monk and had let his hair grow back. There seemed no point to continue the charade. When he met with Malcolm a few weeks later, the king agreed. He needed Gospatric as a strong leader at Dunbar and across Lothian. With a respected representative of the king, there would be little trouble, and disputes would be settled with authority. Malcolm felt it was best to make no announcements, but to have Gospatric act as earl in every way. Malcolm wished to give him a great white stallion to acknowledge his position. He wanted to refuse the gift but knew it would be a mistake. He would take Greyson back with him, to give to his young son, as another step of turning over his position. They talked of the need to identify potential husbands for his daughters. Gospatric was able to tell him of several Cumbrian thanes with sons who would be looking to marry in the coming years. Malcolm wished him to speak to Ethelreda about her betrothal to Duncan. He felt he could not force her into a marriage agreement that might not be fulfilled now that William had refused to release Duncan as his hostage. It would be her choice whether she wished to wait for Duncan or choose another, as husbands were proposed for her younger sisters. Gospatric was relieved by this change. Malcolm now had four sons, and no daughters, but Margaret was pregnant once more and hoping for a girl. She had proven to be an ideal wife to the king, moderating his fighting instincts and his distaste for the Roman Church. Like Gospatric, Malcolm was more comfortable with the Culdee monks, and he relied on Bishop Fothad. Before Gospatric left they discussed the political situation which was unfolding. The King of France was known to be considering an invasion of Normandy. William had taken many of his soldiers back to Normandy with him, making everyone feel more secure in England. Walcher had paid William a considerable sum to take Waltheof's place as earl, as well as continuing as the Prince Bishop of Durham. Malcolm expressed his suspicion that Walcher had exploited the execution for his own benefit, gaining both secular and spiritual power over the population of Northumbria.

Allerdale, Cumbria
June 2017

Helen and Sam decided to take the ring road around Edinburgh and head south on the A7. They would stop in a village for coffee and then reach Carlisle by lunchtime, where they could buy food for the week. The first day they would locate their cottage, settle in, and walk around Allonby. The cottage was larger than they needed, but reasonable in price, and they would use the big bedroom for sleeping and the two smaller ones for clothes and their maps and information about Gospatric's children.

They had left behind the diary, the scene at St Abbs and the emotions of Robert's disclosure. They would spend the week driving through the villages, venturing into the Lake District, and seeing the lands Gospatric's daughters received as they married. Since Gospatric's son Waltheof, who was the grantee of land and manors, named two of his girls after his sisters and had an illegitimate son named Gospatric, they had to be careful to keep everyone straight.

The village had one main street, and it was easy to find the right cottage. It had no real view of the sea except through the kitchen window, but they could walk along the shore in two minutes. When the groceries were put away and they were settled, they left to explore the area by foot. It was a lovely day, and the sea was tempting them to enter. For some reason, it had not occurred to them they would be able to swim in the sea. They found a place to have dinner later in the week, the village shop for food, and an antique store that would be open the next day. After cooking a meal, they studied their maps and picked out the route to follow for Gunhild's land. Helen looked at the transfers of land and Sam checked the map for the villages.

"The lands and the manor of Seaton, Camerton, Flimby and Greysouthen went to Orme, son of Ketel, when he married Gunhild, the sister of Waltheof."

"Here is Seaton and the others. They are south of Maryport."

"So that is one daughter. We can follow the line and they had a Gospatric, just to complicate matters. Orme was the Lord of Wokingham and later his son got Ireby from Alan, Waltheof's son. Got that?"

"High Ireby is east of Maryport. Who's next?"

"It goes on and on, with the next generations, but they take the name Curwen, in a later marriage, and that name keeps going into the sixteenth century."

"Go back to Alan's sister for a minute, because she is also a Gunhild, and we need to get this straight," Sam stated.

"Okay, here it is. She marries Uchtred, son of Fergus, Lord of Galloway, and they get Torpenhow which is south-east of Aspatria, and her sister Octreda marries Ranulf de Lindsay and gets Blennerhasset in that same area."

"Now what about the other daughters, the sisters of Waltheof? We have Gunhild and we need Octreda and Matilda."

"Octreda, the sister of Waltheof, marries a Waldeve, son of Gillemin and they have the area around Broughton and Riverton. Can you find it?" Helen asked.

"It is here, just west of Cockermouth."

"Matilda married a Dolphin, son of Aylward, and they had Applewaite, Crosby, Langrigg, and Brigham."

"Applewaite is just north of Keswick and there is a stone circle called Castlerigg close by. We should go there and see the circle."

"The last daughter, Ethelreda, married Duncan, King Malcolm's son, and that probably didn't happen until after her sisters were married. Duncan was not released until the Conqueror died in 1087, and then he doesn't seem to have rushed back to England or Scotland. We know Duncan became king in 1094 and was assassinated six months later. He and Ethelreda had a son, William FitzDuncan, and he enters this picture as well. He becomes the Lord of Allerdale, when Waltheof's son Alan dies. Alan's son is also named Waltheof, and he died young, leaving Alan without an heir."

"How can we keep this straight?" Sam queried. "Isn't he known as the Boy of Egremont, which is near St Bees, south of Whitehaven, so they must have had that territory as well?"

"Not sure, perhaps that was William FitzDuncan's son who also died young. We haven't touched on Alan's illegitimate brother named Gospatric. He received Bolton in the forest and Bassenthwaite outside of the forest from his father. At least Waltheof took care of his illegitimate son."

"I'm having to look at three maps to find even one or two of the names," Sam said, struggling to find the towns, sometimes spelled differently. "Here is Bassenthwaite, also north of Keswick. That is a perfect route to take and come back through Cockermouth."

"The moral of this story is that they covered most of the territory, and if we could look at the manors and the lines they were drawing, they probably had most of the land and then gave the rest to the Church," Helen concluded.

"Am I remembering that the Dalmeny Church had this Gospatric, son of Waltheof, owning land by Queensferry? Do you have that book along?"

"Yes, here is the chart in the Dalmeny book and the Gospatric block is yellow, not white like the other names, and it says he 'apparently owned' Inverkeithing, Dalmeny, and Dundas and was the probable founder of Dalmeny Church."

"Apparently not! Let's try to figure out another Gospatric, son of a Waltheof or Waldeve, who it might be," Sam commented.

"This might be a potential clue; King Malcolm the fourth sent a letter to a Gospatric at Dundas Castle, regarding the Forth Ferry, and Malcolm reigned from 1153 to 1165."

"We know that a Waldeve, son of a Gospatric confirmed Dundas to Helias, son of Huctred. 'Confirmed' is the important word. I think that happened when Huctred died, so which Gospatric has a son, Waldeve, at that time?" Sam asked.

"Gospatric II inherits Dunbar and all of Lothian, when his father dies, date unknown. He has a Gospatric III, who continues the Dunbar line. It makes sense for his second son in that generation to inherit some of the land in Lothian, most likely Dundas. His name is Waldeve, and he gives up his name, becomes a priest named Adam, and could have given the land to his brother Huctred and confirmed it to Helias when Huctred died. He was alive in 1154, in fact until 1179. Perhaps he had a son named Gosptric before he took vows later."

"Let's quit for tonight. I'm ready for a wee dram and bed," Sam declared.

Later, as they sat up in bed still talking, Helen brought up St Abbs. "We haven't talked about how you felt when we were at the beach with Robert and Andrew. I didn't ask because I thought you should choose the time to share your feelings…"

"I haven't been avoiding it, exactly, but it hasn't seemed like the right time. All I can say is it brought back the feeling I had when I got back from the airport with my mother's suitcase. It was the night I read the diary and it seemed then like the past had come full circle, and my mother was with her lover once again. It was as if she had been floating out to sea to meet him, as she had once before in another life. When Robert said they had never found the body of either my mother or the man on the sailboat, it just reinforced that feeling. Does that sound bizarre?"

"No, but doesn't it scare you to know she got trapped in another life and it swept her away from the one she had, where she was your mother?"

"I don't think it does, but it has occurred to me that Juliana could be pulled into some occult activity with Robert."

"Do you think she could? Is that likely, with her personality?"

"My mother was on one side of the spectrum and Sarah on the other. One accepted and the other rejected the possibility of past lives. I think Juliana would be in the middle of that spectrum. She studied psychology and was particularly interested in near death and past life regression experiences. She became a journalist interviewing and writing stories about people who had experienced psychic phenomena."

"And you're wondering why she has taken that path, right?" Helen asked, hoping he would keep talking.

"Yes, I suppose I am, more than ever. And the interesting thing is…she knows absolutely nothing about her grandmother."

"I can't understand how that could happen, and why she wouldn't be curious. I would be, and I just see her wanting to know who your mother was, what was she like, how she died?"

"I told you. It was a closed subject for Sarah, and Juliana was very perceptive. She stopped asking questions when she was young, sensing it was not an acceptable topic."

"Didn't she ever ask you or her father?"

"Not Will, as far as I know. She asked me once when she saw a picture of my mother in an album. I told her it was her grandmother, but she had died young and that she had drowned. It satisfied her."

"Where did Sarah keep the diary hidden and what about other photographs? Is there an attic or some storage place?"

"There is an attic, but I can't see Juliana going up there and snooping around. The diary was in an old trunk of my mother's…"

"That's it then. I would bet she did snoop around, like many kids, and looked in the trunk. You might find out the truth about that soon. Perhaps she did it when she was quite young and forgot about it, but it's still in her subconscious," Helen posed.

"The boys never asked, and I can't see them going in the attic in search of anything except a piece of sports equipment."

"Of course, they wouldn't. Girls are much more prone to find answers, more likely to have questions."

"Are you saying the male species lacks some important qualities? Should I worry about this?" Sam asked, laughing.

"You can ask Juliana; she probably knows from her psychology work. Men can compartmentalise and it can be helpful, but less so in some circumstances. They listen to the drummer and miss the melody," Helen challenged.

"On that note, I believe it's time to sleep." He leaned over, kissed her, and turned out the light on his side of the bed. She turned out her light and snuggled down beside him. There would be another day to talk about this, in fact there would be many more days.

They left after breakfast on a pleasant day. They took secondary roads, getting lost a few times, but finding their way to Torpenhow, then east to Ireby and south from there to Bassenthwaite. This was the territory of Gospatric, the son of Waltheof, and grandson of Gospatric the Earl. From there they took the main road towards Applewaite, then into Keswick for coffee. Sam got instructions to the Castlerigg Stone Circle. When they parked on the hill and walked across to the stones, they were alone. It was rare to be anywhere near these ancient standing stones without tourists. Although the stones were not large, it was a sizable circle and left them with a feeling of awe and curiosity.

"How about going on to Appleby for some food?" Helen asked. "It's not many miles but will probably take a bit of time."

"Sure, we have nothing but time." That was an understatement, as they wound their way through the twisting and turning roads. They stopped at Appleby Castle and found tea was being served. They decided to join the group, filling up with delicious sandwiches, scones, and cakes. When they went on a tour later, they found that the castle had Gospatric connections, which they decided to check out later. After a quick stop in town for a few items, they retraced their route. Every other way seemed too far to drive.

When they woke up the next morning, it was a dull and drizzly day. They decided to have a leisurely start with a breakfast of eggs and bacon, and then just go to Aspatria to check out the library and the church. The drive the day before had been interesting and beautiful, but very tiring. They realised it was difficult to estimate driving time based on miles, when they were travelling on narrow, twisting roads. They started first at the library, a two-room space filled with important information. They were able to make copies of pages in a book for later reading. They couldn't help sharing some of the interesting facts. Helen read from the book, *Aspatria: A Cumbrian Town*. "Listen to this. A surgeon named Riggs decided to excavate some land, called Beacon Hill in 1789. About 8 feet down, he found a burial chamber, probably very old, with a skeleton of a man who he measured at over seven feet tall. The bones disintegrated, but the sword, dagger, a gold buckle, a part of a shield, and a helmet of tenth century Viking design were sent to the British Museum."

"Do you suppose they would be able to find the items now?" Sam asked, chuckling.

"I doubt it. Also, the feet were missing, and they didn't know if they cut them off to stuff him into the grave or because of some ritual."

"Maybe we should try to order this book. It is filled with history and confirms a lot of what we found in our other sources," Sam declared.

"How about using it for my master's thesis…maybe I can write it on the lost history of Cumbria." Sam ignored her ongoing joke about her history degree.

"We need to go to the church. It's dedicated to St Kentigern, and we have run across him before."

"Here, look, I found this in *The Medieval Fortified Buildings of Cumbria*," exclaimed Helen with excitement. "Aspatria Castle, standing on some high ground one kilometre west of the city, built by Earl Gospatric, who died sometime after 1092."

"I wish we knew why they say that date. What else?" Sam asked.

"It is currently a modern house called Castlemont."

"Let's drive there after we see the church. There's not a lot more in town," Sam said, with equal enthusiasm.

When they drove up the hill later, having found the church locked and no one to open it, they found the house had a Bed and Breakfast sign.

"Let's knock on the door and inquire about staying," Helen said, directing Sam into the driveway. When they got out of the car, a man came to greet them. He was very friendly and showed them around his garden and then invited them in to see the house. When the tour was over, his wife invited them for tea. They felt a little guilty and confessed they were staying in a cottage in Allonby and researching the history of the area. The couple had no knowledge of any castle ruins below their property but said they would love to hear if Sam and Helen found any evidence. They left with some new friends and plans to return the next summer.

Back at the cottage, they read some more interesting information. "There were five manors in the Parish of Aspatria," Helen read. "The Parish got its name from Gospatric, Earl of Dunbar, father of Waltheof. There were several manors: Aspatria, Hayton, Outerby, Alwandby, and Brayton."

"That's the area that Waltheof would have had, then Alan, followed by William FitzDuncan and his descendants," Sam commented. "His youngest daughter, it says, inherited the land, and then her sisters, but there were no males in the family and that line died out. The Lucys and the Morvilles were involved at that point and then parcels of land were given to many people in the area, and to the Church."

"And that is the line from Malcolm's son Duncan, with Ingibiorg, and Gospatric's daughter Ethelreda, so we know where that one ended," Helen added.

"We don't have time to follow the others, but we are probably distantly related to half the population of Cumbria. If we are just two of thousands, imagine it. We are just one small part of the Dundas line and the one rarely mentioned, because they left for Ireland."

"To say Gospatric was a survivor is an understatement," Helen said, emphasising survivor.

"Here is that bit about the Gospatric who gave up the keys of the castle at Appleby. He was the son of Orme and Gunhild and named for his great-grandfather."

"We also keep encountering the family giving land to Holme Cultram, and it certainly became important to both Henrys," Helen noted. "One was the King of England, the Conqueror's youngest son, and the other Henry was the son of David I of Scotland."

"Henry of England and David I were brothers-in-law, because Henry married David's older sister, when he became king of England. That's another whole story," Sam added. "The daughter of that marriage is named as the successor to the throne but is challenged by Stephen. King David takes an oath to support his sister's daughter and drags Gospatric and probably Waltheof, the two sons of our Gospatric, into the Battle of the Standard in 1138, where they both die. David and his son Henry narrowly escape to Carlisle, but hundreds of Scots and Cumbrians died in that useless battle."

"You really do know a lot about English history," Helen commented. "I think I'll have you write my thesis."

"Until we started this, I knew a lot of facts and some of the players at different times in history. Now they are integrating into a whole picture, and we find them wound around our ancestors. Just look at Gospatric, whose childhood is devastated by Macbeth and whose adult life is dominated by William the Conqueror, as well as King Malcolm."

"History isn't written that way, is it? It rarely includes women, unless they were as powerful and devious as men. It doesn't remember the children, unless they died mysteriously in the Tower of London, and it gives little mention to the farmers and labourers who kept the country fed and cared for in other ways. I guess it's not much different from our situation today when you think about it."

"So, let's go for a walk on the beach," Sam suggested, "and stop thinking about it for a while."

"Great idea."

"Grab the rain jackets, just in case," he said. "By the way, have you told your sister about our plans?"

Cumbria and Northumbria
The Years 1080–1085

Disaster had struck again. Ligulf had been murdered by two of Walcher's counsellors and the Northumbrian thanes were demanding justice. Their anger would not be quelled. Walcher agreed to meet them at Gateshead. He foolishly took Leofwine and Gilbert, the organisers of the killing of Ligulf, with him. Walcher lost control of the situation and was slain in front of the church where he had been secluded with his friends and supporters. He had sent the murderers out to their death, but it was not enough. Some thanes were angry because Malcolm had marched an army through Northumberland to Durham, and Walcher had not stopped him. Malcolm knew that Robert Curthose was working against William in France, with the financial help of his mother. Robert had attacked his father, leaving him with a significant leg injury, and attacked his brother Rufus. Father and son had fled back to Normandy. Malcolm decided to test the possibility that the king was too weakened by trouble in Normandy to react to what might be happening in Northumbria. Malcolm was angry that William had refused to release his son Duncan, for seven long years. He had not challenged William's authority for all that time, but then had done so by riding into Durham. Gospatric rode with him, no longer posing as a monk. Malcolm wanted him by his side, because Gospatric was still well-known and respected in the area. When William heard of Walcher's death and Malcolm's invasion, he sent Odo north with a large force to lay waste once again to Northumbria. Now, it was likely that William would return to England. He needed to appoint a new Earl of Northumbria and a bishop. Whoever it was, they would not be on friendly terms with the King of Scotland. Gospatric felt at risk again, with the very real possibility that William would hear that he was alive, having joined Malcolm in the raid on Durham.

Dolphin was to be married in the next month, followed by Gunhild's marriage to Orme, the son of Ketel. Waltheof, as the Lord of Allerdale would grant Orme and Gunhild lands at Seton, Camerton, Flimby and Greysouthen, as they had planned with the king. The betrothal of Octreda to Waltheof, the son of Gilmyn, was arranged with lands going to them at the time of their marriage, and the same was done for Matilda when she married Dolphin, the son of Aylward. Ethelreda was determined to wait for Duncan's release and return from Normandy. She remembered her childhood playmate, her best friend, although it had been more than seven years since he was taken away by William. Waltheof would continue to hold the rest of Allerdale, with the help of Dolphin and Thorfinn. He would divide the land between his children. He had already sired a son with a village girl, and he had assured her the child, who had been named Gospatric, would be cared for and given land when he grew up.

After the weddings, Gospatric would once again put on the monk's robes and spend most of his time between Aspatria and Carlisle. He would remain in the area, until they learned what William intended to do. It was not long before they had the answer. Gospatric left to hide in his forest retreat, which was totally overgrown. Robert had reconciled with his father and was marching north with an army to invade Scotland. Malcolm sent a message when it was over. Robert had done little damage but had reached Falkirk. He had negotiated a settlement with Malcolm and retreated to Newcastle, where he built another castle on William's orders. The immediate danger was past, but Gospatric had grown accustomed to his solitary life, foraging for food with Greyson his only companion. He had left his great white steed behind, and the life he had been living. When he was exploring the area, he had found a small mound covered by overgrowth. On closer examination, he was able to see that it appeared to be a tunnel. Unsure of its stability, he only entered the opening. It was too dark to explore without light, but it appeared to be a passageway under the water to the south side of the backwater. When the water level receded, he could take Greyson across and try to find the opening on the other side. It might prove advantageous if he needed to make a quick getaway, sending his horse galloping in another direction.

Once Robert left Newcastle and William appointed a new bishop of Durham, who also was the Earl of Northumbria, Gospatric was able to go about the land again, but still dressed as a monk. He had spent the winter primarily in Aspatria, taking no chances with any delegations from William's court or from Durham.

As the months passed, and spring melted into summer, there had been no outside activity crossing into Lothian. Gradually a sense of security set in again and Gospatric abandoned his monk's tonsure and grew his beard once more. Robert was still reconciled with his father, but he sent messages to Malcolm through Edgar. Robert and Edgar had become close friends, spending quite a bit of time together, sometimes plotting against Roberts's father and brother. In 1083 Malcolm learned that King William's wife Matilda had died, and it now seemed unlikely that William would travel to England. Malcolm told Gospatric that he had asked Edgar and Robert to plead for the release of Duncan, so that he might return to marry Ethelreda. They were not successful, and Malcolm named his eldest son, Edward, as the presumptive heir to his throne. Ethelreda was freed from her commitment to wed Duncan but refused to entertain any other marriage proposals. Other than young Gospatric, Ethelreda was the only unmarried child and she continued to live in Aspatria caring for her younger brother. The rest had taken their places in Cumbrian society along with Waltheof's children, covering the entire territory with manors.

When Gospatric travelled to Edinburgh that summer, Malcolm and Gospatric met to discuss the future of Lothian. Malcolm was getting older, less willing to go to war or raid other lands, but still wanting to find a way to regain Northumbria. He felt that William's death was imminent and wanted to be prepared to move quickly, as the succession was determined. He had learned that Robert's reconciliation with his father had ended after his mother's death. Robert was building support to take the crown of England. His younger brothers could have Normandy, if he were able to establish his right to inherit England. Malcolm asked Gospatric to once again be visible in all of Lothian and particularly with the garrison at Dunbar. Gospatric was ready to return to his role, and it was not important for him to have the title of the Earl of Dunbar. He was still known to his men as the Earl, although he had been the leader of Northumbria for such a short time. They agreed that it was time for the young Gospatric to become known, for he would succeed his father with the responsibility for the area. Gospatric built a manor house near Old Melrose, and kept his hideaway a secret, except from his son. Ethelreda was not happy about her little brother leaving Aspatria to be with their father, but young Gospatric was very excited. He had watched his elder brothers Dolphin and Waltheof take over their positions as Lord of Carlisle and Lord of Allerdale at an early age, with the help of Thorfinn and their father. He was now fifteen and ready to do the same in Lothian. He loved his sister, but he had spent as much time with Dolphin and Waltheof as possible. He now considered himself a man, while Ethelreda still saw him as her baby brother. Gospatric hoped that the separation from her motherly role to her brother would change Ethelreda's mind about waiting to marry Duncan. It was a tearful parting, but father and son rode off with a sense of relief, heading first for a visit with Dolphin and then Thorfinn, before travelling east to see King Malcolm and Queen Margaret.

Allerdale, Cumbria
July 2017

Helen and Sam were still enjoying Cumbria, giving less time to the family charts and more to being tourists. They travelled a bit more, spending a day driving deeper into the Lake District, just for pleasure and sightseeing. They took a picnic lunch and drove to the far south in the morning, returning by an alternative route in the afternoon. The weather was perfect, with intermittent sunshine and clouds.

"It's a magical place, isn't it, even though it isn't much different from northern Minnesota?" Helen commented, as they left the area for the main road back.

"I suppose the lakes and vegetation are similar, but I see northern Minnesota dominated by the culture of fishing and hunting, as well as camping and boating. Here it is more about the ancient landscape itself and imagining what it must have been like in Gospatric's time."

"Pretty remote, I would guess, and not easy to get around during the winter or the rainy season."

"Right, and in northern Minnesota the quiet of the winter is replaced by racing snowmobiles," Sam declared with a bit of cynicism.

"Don't like snowmobiles?"

"I don't like a lot of noise when I am in the wilderness. Frankly, I don't even like listening to lawn mowers in the city."

"Does that mean that you don't mow your grass and your neighbours are not happy?"

"Not really, but what it does mean is that I am supporting our neighbourhood transition from groomed grass, that requires fertilisers, watering, and mowing, to a more sustainable way of using our green space."

"I'm relieved to hear this. I have always rejected the idea of living in the suburbs, where you must listen to noise constantly as people continue to mow every blade of grass."

They remained quiet for a while, watching the scenery as they returned to South Queensferry on an alternate route. They both felt pleased that they had learned a lot more about each other on this trip, and what they had discovered was additional compatibility.

Sam and Helen had only a couple of days before they would join Robert and Andrew on the trip to Durham. They decided to try to see Dundas Castle by saying they would like to explore having a small wedding and made an appointment for a viewing on Monday. They had picked the following summer as their choice for their wedding but told the woman meeting with them about their flexibility regarding timing. It would be a family wedding with a few guests from the US and a few from Scotland, including Lord Hamilton. They decided to drop Robert's name, to help legitimise their intention to explore the option of Dundas. The more they had discussed the possibility before they reached the Castle, the more real the idea became. They had the guest list outlined and thought they might even be able to handle the expense if the guests all paid for their rooms for the night. They had been shocked that the fee for usage was not only expensive, but did not include the rooms or food, just the exclusive use of the property for the event. Margo, their guide, gave them a brochure and the rate sheet and then proceeded to take them through the manor house, built in the early 1800s. They began upstairs with the bedrooms and en-suite baths for guests and the master suite for the bride and groom. Then Margo took them through the public rooms downstairs, where the guests could have drinks before dinner. As they entered the library, Sam thought about his mother's description of her first visit, with stacks of books on the floors, dust billowing out of furniture and Lady Jane's invitation to tea. They had disclosed to Margo that they both had ancient Dundas ancestry and that is how they had learned about the wedding venue. Sam had not mentioned his mother or his sister and their connection to the castle, so long ago. It was easy to see that the entire manor had been restored and redecorated to a remarkably high standard. They left the manor through a side door that led across a small courtyard to the iron gate of the ancient tower, called a keep. Relieved at the level of preservation of the entry, they continued to be pleased by the authentic renovation. Lighting, toilets, and safety features were discreetly placed, not destroying the sense of the twelfth century. The wedding dinner could be served in the Stag Room, with a large open fireplace, and the wedding in the room Sam's mother had described as having a wall of green velvet-looking moss in the sunlight. They asked to see the rest of the tower and were led to a spiral staircase, with a quick look into the rooms off the stairs. Sam and Helen met each other's gaze, as they recognised the room where Sam's mother had become ill. Helen had agreed that she wanted, if possible, to walk into the space to see if she felt anything unusual. They both stepped inside the low-ceiled room with a small fireplace and windows close to the floor. They left to follow Margo, their eyes meeting as she continued up the staircase, spiralling to a small door leading to the roof. As they looked in all directions, they could see east to Edinburgh and the widening of the Firth of Forth towards the sea, north overlooking South Queensferry to the bridges and the hills, west towards the narrowing of the water towards Falkirk, and south to the lowlands heading into Lothian.

"A very strategic site for a tower, isn't it?" Sam commented, but their guide ignored him and led them to the door of the small circular opening and back down the spiral staircase. They hesitated again as they passed the room Sam's mother had described. In the wedding and dining areas, Helen could imagine the candlelight wedding followed by dinner and an evening in the manor house. Margo locked the gate as they exited and asked what they thought.

"It's perfect," Helen said, "but we will have to discuss the cost factors and the expense of getting our families here. I am concerned about how the dinner would be served."

"We can provide you with a list of those who have served food here, if you are interested."

"I think we will discuss this with our friends and family and get back to you with any other questions," Sam answered, now anxious to leave. "Is it all right for us to drive out the other entrance?"

"Yes, of course." She put out her hand to shake theirs and suggested they walk around the stable area back to their car. She was probably relieved to get rid of them, having figured out that they were not prime customers for an expensive event.

"Maybe we could win the lottery or ask Robert to pay the basic charge?" Helen said, when they were around the other side of the building.

"You're not serious?" Sam asked.

"About Robert, no, but it would be wonderful to have an event here. I wish they allowed a dinner in the old keep, just for the experience."

They drove by the tower on their way out the back drive, down the hill and past the farm. "This is where my mother talked to the farmer, and he told her about a passageway from the farm to the priory next to the Forth."

"They wouldn't have put in a tunnel if there hadn't been a threat. Can you imagine how much work it would be to build it?" Helen reflected.

"We don't have much time before we leave for Robert's and then on to Durham," Sam commented. "Is there anything we should prepare for that meeting?"

"I think that we will try to discuss the major events taking place up to Malcolm's death and beyond. We can't determine a year of death for Gospatric, so it could be anytime, even into the 1100s. He could have been with Malcolm in 1093 and died in the surprise attack, but it is unlikely. Our most likely scenario would be that he went to Durham and became a monk, and that accounts for his stone sarcophagus being found in the monks' burial grounds."

"I think we will all agree on that," Sam declared. "Maybe he had grown so weary of the senseless killing and fighting for the throne and became a monk after Malcolm's death."

"That makes sense to me. He must have been heartbroken to see Malcolm's brother, Donald Bane, take over before Duncan ever had a chance to be named king. Duncan must have been back in the country and married to Gospatric's daughter by the early 1090s. Margaret and Malcolm's daughters, Matilda and Mary, would have been at Romsey with their aunt Christine. I have never read anything about where Edgar, Edmund, Ethelred, Alexander, and David went, have you?"

"We would have to study their later movements and surmise what happened. It is possible that Edgar stayed with Donald Bane, as a prisoner, but they work together later. Ethelred goes into the Church, so he may have already been in a monastery. David was in England when he was still very young. I doubt that Gospatric could have protected them."

"Perhaps Gospatric was around to offer some protection to Duncan and his daughter. They may have gone to Cumbria to be with Alan, until Duncan was called to the throne in 1094. Then when he was murdered six months later, Ethelreda would have needed to take her son William FitzDuncan to safety. I think she went to Alan, Waltheof's son, because he later leaves his territory to young William, since his oldest son had died. That might have been the final blow for Gospatric—a brutal murder of another King Duncan…"

They had reached the house and were sitting in the car finishing the conversation. With a sense of the terrible drama reverberating through Scotland and their ancestral family, during that period and going forward, they sighed and went into the house.

By the time they left for Robert's two days later, Helen and Sam had tried to outline the events recorded in various sources during the years after Walcher's death and Robert's march into Scotland. The list grew, as they perused various sources, planning to pass out the information at the gathering.

"Enough!" Helen shouted. "I can't handle this unemotional listing of facts. Let's wait with the rest. We know a lot of it without any references to these early sources of Scottish history, which are written by anyone but the Scots."

Lothian and Cumbria
The Year 1087

Young Gospatric was now as tall as his father, and he rode his stallion with an air of authority and self-assurance. He was sixteen and had enjoyed the guidance and companionship of his father for two years, as they covered the areas of Dunbar, the border lands, and the rest of Lothian. They were doing Malcolm's bidding, keeping the border safe by settling disputes and having towers built to protect Scotland from unexpected invasion from North or South. They lived together in a hall built near Old Melrose and frequently went to visit the growing family, who would all gather in Aspatria. Ethelreda still maintained the castle and she was always grateful for the visits from family. She was twenty-six, still waiting for Duncan's return. He had recently written that King William was near death and had ordered the release of his brother Odo, Morcar and Wulfnoth, King Harold's young brother, who had been in custody since his childhood. He said there were others, but he had not been told of his own chance for freedom. Ethelreda was now hopeful that whatever happened next, Duncan would surely be released.

Gospatric was called to Malcolm's court shortly after the visit to Cumbria and his son rode with him. They knew it was likely that the announcement of King William's death meant it would be an event to be celebrated in all of Scotland. Gospatric rode with a sense of hope, and without the apprehension he usually felt when travelling to meet Malcolm. He and young Gospatric talked of a wedding for Duncan and Ethelreda, making the family complete.

"Next, the king will be trying to find a bride for you, my son. Do not be surprised if your future wife is present at dinner tonight."

"I'll pick my own wife, Father, as you did," he answered without hesitation.

"I've never told you that Tostig and Judith, characters you know from my stories, placed me next to your mother and your uncle when I visited Bamburgh on our return from Rome."

"My mother told me this, but that is not the same as forcing a man or woman to accept someone they would not choose, is it?"

"No, you are right. King Malcolm chose to betroth Duncan and Ethelreda, but he saw something between them I was not aware of when they were young. Margaret and your mother saw it, but most men are less aware of these types of things," Gospatric added.

"Well Father, I think I will be aware of any attempt to introduce me to young ladies at court. Matilda and Mary are safely away in a priory, so it will not be one of them. It must be difficult to find a person to love if you are always locked away with nuns, especially their fierce Aunt Christine."

"You remember Christine?" his father asked.

"Very well. We used to love spending time with Queen Margaret, but not with Christine…"

They had entered the steep hill leading up to the castle gate and the horses slowed to a trot. The gates opened for them, and they were greeted by friends. The courtyard was filled with excitement, celebrating the death of William the Bastard. Gospatric felt his loss of Waltheof at the hands of the executioner and the order of a merciless William. He knew it would press heavily on him during their celebration.

Gospatric awoke late the next day. It had been a long night of eating and drinking, more like drowning the sorrow of the years of pain King William caused than a celebration of his departure. He needed to dress quickly and partake of some porridge and bread before meeting with Malcolm in private. They already knew that it was William Rufus and not Robert, William's oldest son, who had been crowned King of England. When he was summoned to the king's private quarters, he heard the complete story.

"Robert and William Rufus have agreed to make each other heirs. Robert is the Duke of Normandy and Rufus the King of England."

"It is hardly an even distribution; and what of poor Henry?" Gospatric asked.

"Henry has been given funds to purchase land in England, which seems strange, but that is his choice. At nineteen, he has already ravaged a few English maidens and produced some illegitimate children. It's possible he and Robert will try to remove Rufus as King of England, and Rufus will be busy trying to secure his position."

"I understand from a letter Ethelreda received from Duncan that William released some hostages before his death, but what about your son, was he included?"

"He may have been released by Robert. I am not sure if he came with Rufus, but Morcar did. When they reached Winchester, Morcar and Wulfnoth were taken into custody. Rufus did release Ulf, King Harold's son, and may give Duncan and Ulf knighthoods."

"This is good news, Sire, is it not?" Gospatric asked, thinking of Ethelreda.

"It should be, but my son wants nothing to do with me or Scotland. His fifteen years of captivity in Normandy have convinced him to support Rufus. I do not know what to do. He either has no knowledge of my attempts to have him released, or he doesn't care," Malcolm confessed with obvious distress.

"What about his marriage to Ethelreda? He has been writing to her. I can't believe he is going to desert her now."

"She is our only hope. If she asks him to come to Aspatria, he may oblige."

"Would you accept a marriage ceremony performed there, rather than at Edinburgh Castle or Dunfermline?"

"We have no choice. He was close to your family, so being with them may ease his re-entry into our lives and our country."

"Need I worry about being present at a ceremony, as Ethelreda's father, given my position?"

"We have no idea what Robert or Edgar have shared with Rufus. He may know you are alive; he might believe you are a monk, and he might not care that his father wanted you dead or in prison. It is best to learn of his position before you plan to be at a marriage ceremony but let us first have Ethelreda plead to see Duncan as a starting point. I will try to reach Edgar and Robert on the subject. Edgar has been granted a castle and land in Normandy and he is now an advisor to our good Duke Robert of Normandy."

"That is interesting, but not surprising to me. Robert and Edgar became good friends while we were in Ghent together," Gospatric commented. "That was fifteen years ago, and their relationship is still strong, I gather."

"It is, but it may be threatening to Rufus. Time will tell. Now we should join the others in another night of celebration before you leave. The weather is still mild, but October can be unpredictable. Your young son is very impressive, like his brothers. I believe he will excel as the Earl of Dunbar one day. We must find him a good breeding wife, so he produces sons as we have done."

"Do you have someone in mind, Sire?" Gospatric asked with a chuckle. "I told him to expect to be sitting by a prospective bride."

"I'll ask Margaret. She usually has some ideas of that nature."

At the final celebration banquet, Gospatric sat next to Queen Margaret. She spoke of her sadness about missing Athelreda and Earl Waltheof while celebrating William's death but changed the subject when she observed Gospatric's distress.

"Thankfully, you and my brother are still alive. I wish that Edgar was here tonight, but he is safe with Duke Robert, at least for the moment. I am watching young Gospatric enjoy the company of the young woman I placed next to him."

"I see you are planning his future already," Gospatric announced. "I warned him this might be the case."

"He has forgotten your warning," Margaret retorted. "Look at the pleasure in his eyes as he speaks with her."

Edinburgh, Scotland
July 2017

Sam and Helen arrived just minutes before Andrew appeared and they all greeted each other warmly in the entryway. After suitcases were taken up to the rooms, and a few minutes of settling, they gathered in the library. Their spirits were high, as Robert told them of the plans for the trip to Durham. He was clearly the most excited about a confirmed meeting with the staff at Durham to see the stone sarcophagus with the words *Gospatricus Comes* across the lid.

They would leave in the morning, taking the A1 around the coast, then stopping for morning coffee at Bamburgh. Robert was a bit dramatic, saying they would have a few moments to walk to the beach around the impressive castle, where Gospatric had come as a small child. He intended to drive through village roads along the coast to Alnmouth for a seafood lunch, after which they would return to the A1 via the road from Alnmouth to Alnwick. Robert stopped to make his next point.

"We know that Malcolm was ambushed somewhere in that area on his return from meeting with King William Rufus. From there, we will make the drive around Newcastle to Durham and a small hotel in the city where we can enjoy drinks and dinner on the patio area and an early night."

As always, Robert had every detail planned. The following morning, they would have a half ten appointment at the Cathedral, beginning with a tour and ending in the crypt. Before any discussion began, Mrs Wakefield rang the dinner bell and they quickly finished their drinks and proceeded to the dining room for another excellent meal, complemented by the appropriate wines from the cellar.

After dinner, Sam passed around their brief list of the primary events from 1085–1093. Robert initiated the discussion.

"Most significant for us is the relief Gospatric and Malcolm must have had when the Conqueror died, even though they had to be concerned about what William Rufus would do in regard to Scotland."

"And there appeared to be a few years where Scotland was left alone," Sam added. "If Gospatric was alive, as we believe he was, he would have felt free of the oppression of William."

Helen spoke up, "Might I add that Gospatric's children would have been married and having children during this period. Ethelreda would have been the exception; they might have expected Duncan's release, since others were pardoned by William before his death, and they returned to England."

"Some were re-arrested by William Rufus. There is a question whether Robert released Duncan," Sam stated, "with some saying that Rufus released Harold's son and Duncan. Why does Duncan not return to Scotland?"

Andrew entered the conversation. "I think his time in Normandy, where he was treated well, must have left him feeling more loyalty to Robert and William Rufus, than to his father and Scotland."

"If he knew his father had named his half-brother as his successor," Sam said, "he was probably truly angry about being abandoned in favour of the sons of Margaret. Family relationships were no different in the eleventh century than they are now. There was jealousy and rejection, which often occurs where there are children of more than one partnership."

"But we do know he married Ethelreda, so somehow he returned to Cumbria and later to Scotland," Helen added.

"Let's go on for a moment," Robert interjected. "We know there is trouble in 1091, with Malcolm bringing forces into Northumbria and a peace between the kings negotiated by Robert and Edgar Atheling, both giving up something of value. Then William Rufus breaks that peace by marching an army into Cumbria and building a castle at Carlisle, removing Dolphin as lord. Think what that did to Gospatric and King Malcolm."

"When we were in Cumbria," Sam said, "there was only one person who acknowledged the relationship of children and grandchildren to Gospatric and the Dunkeld dynasty. Did the distancing start when the invasion took place and they needed to keep their property and positions safe?"

Robert answered. "It could have. William Rufus organised his march, built the castle, put a Norman in charge and left the area. Those in power had other demands and left the territory in the hands of Gospatric's family except for Dolphin."

"Did things settle down again?" Helen asked. "Malcolm laid the foundation stone at the new cathedral at Durham. Was it a public move that William Rufus approved of, or did he call Malcolm to a meeting in the autumn, accusing him of breaking the peace agreement? Some sources say that Rufus had broken the agreement, and Malcolm started the journey back to Scotland with no resolution."

"It seems pretty clear there was an ambush," Sam commented, "since he was already so far from London and heading north. The records differ and have him killed by Frenchmen, the Northumbrians, or the English. There is evidence that it was Geoffrey Gulevent along with Morel, a relation of the Earl Robert de Mowbray, who killed Malcolm but there were three thousand men killed that day. William Rufus imprisoned Robert de Mowbray for his actions."

"That would be a way to cover up his own participation, wouldn't it?" Helen asked, sceptical about the innocence of William Rufus.

Robert entered again with another theory. "As soon as Malcolm and his son Edward were dead, Donald Bane steps into the picture and declares himself king. He had the support of the Scots in the North, but did he have other support? If not, he certainly took advantage of the moment to take his brother's place."

"What I wonder," Helen questioned, "is where do the children go? Their father and brother are dead, Queen Margaret dies within hours of learning of the deaths of Malcolm and Edward, and then their uncle Donald Bane storms the castle and declares himself the king. There are tales of escape down the back wall of the castle with their mother's body, and recently a hidden staircase was found on the north face of the castle rock, but where would they go? Was Gospatric involved?"

"I'm afraid we shall never know, but we can continue to speculate on our trip," Robert declared, making it obvious they would need to end their conversation for the evening. They were all ready to do so, having eaten too much at dinner. Their drinks were finished, and they all left the library saying good night with plans for an early breakfast.

The next morning Andrew sat in front with Robert, and Sam and Helen happily took the rear seat. They had been on the A1 roadway before, but when they were around the city, they enjoyed the scenery. Helen had the map on her lap, to follow their progress. It was a bright day, and they could see the sea in the distance and the green hills leading to the water. Not long after the turn to Coldingham, Sam and Helen were in unfamiliar territory. Robert talked about the Holy Island of Lindisfarne, as they drove around Berwick-upon-Tweed.

"Another time we can make a pilgrimage to the island. As you recall there are some stories about Gospatric taking artifacts from Durham Cathedral. Others say he warned the monks to take their treasures and St Cuthbert's body to Lindisfarne, hoping that William's soldiers wouldn't go that far with their burning and looting as they did in 1070."

"It would take us years, I think," Helen offered, "to understand the importance of St Cuthbert to the Gospatric family and those before them."

"This is true Helen," Robert answered, "but we may need to do exactly that to find out how it is connected to the mystery for which I am seeking answers. On the other hand, it might only be about property and power. Whoever had the body of the Saint also had possession of his lands. It may explain the desire for Malcolm to lay the foundation stone at Durham Cathedral, even though it was not in Scotland. Was it a way to declare that the Scots would hold the area of the Cathedral, St Cuthbert's lands and everything north of Durham?"

Robert took the next exit, winding through the countryside, then pointing out Bamburgh Castle dominating the coastline in the distance. After morning coffee at a hotel, they drove to the car park across from the castle. From this position the massive structure was overpowering. It was not like any other castle Sam and Helen had ever seen.

"Bamburgh was rebuilt after Gospatric's time, but it would have been an imposing fortress for centuries," Robert declared. "We'll cross the road and walk along the north wall to the beach. Some of the structure is from the eleventh century. It was known as a place that couldn't be overcome in an attack."

They walked in silence, overwhelmed by the size of the stone walls looming straight up from the sand. Robert led them through the dunes to the sea. Looking behind them, they could see the unassailable castle wall facing the North Sea. Helen took off her shoes and waded into the waves, quite gentle in the summer breeze. She could see Gospatric and his brother coming here and running along this beach. Robert interrupted her reverie.

"When there is a storm from the northeast, with a powerful wind, the waves crash against the castle walls and anyone standing here would be pulled out to sea."

Another image invaded Helen's mind and she shivered in the warm sun. Sam saw her reaction and reached for her hand to steady her as she came out of the waves to the sandy shore. They all continued with their own thoughts on the way back to the car, glancing up at the dominating castle walls.

Robert drove through small villages close to the coast with confidence at each turn. Helen and Sam could not locate where they were on the map and gave up, just enjoying the scenery. The car windows were open, and it was a lovely day to be travelling. Robert entered Alnmouth and parked by a very ordinary-looking building. When they entered the restaurant, they were on the estuary of the River Aln and they had a view of the sea from their table. Robert suggested they share a fish platter which was quickly agreed. When the waiter left, Robert addressed them with more emotion than he usually revealed.

"Remember that this estuary is where Edgar Atheling landed with Margaret, Christine and his mother, met by Gospatric and perhaps Malcolm. Twenty-six years later, in the same season, Malcolm and his oldest son with Margaret are ambushed and slaughtered along with most of their army. We will drive the road to Alnwick slowly after lunch and I will be interested if any of us feel any sense of the ambush."

Later, they looked across the fields for any sign of the site of the battle, but no one spoke up. As they drove into Alnwick Robert asked for comments, but there was no response until Helen spoke.

"There was just a sense of sadness in me on the entire drive. I can't say it was as powerful as my reaction when I was at Dunkeld, where Crinan and Maldred were killed, but there was a similarity."

Sam spoke after her, saying, "I suspect they were surrounded with the sea on the east side, forces coming from the north and the men from the west circling behind them to prevent a retreat to the south. It would have to be carefully timed to succeed, so I suspect there were traitors in their own party."

"That might be the connection to Donald Bane," Andrew stated. "Think about it. If Donald had people loyal to him in Malcolm's forces, they could be the ones who coordinated the timing of the ambush, sending ahead information about their location and approximate arrival near Alnmouth."

"Not something we can prove, but I think we have identified a reasonable theory," Robert added.

"Can we talk about how Gospatric would have heard about the attack and Malcolm's death, when we gather this evening?" Helen asked. "I want to think through his response together."

"Yes, certainly," Robert answered for the rest of them.

They arrived in Durham before five and easily located the hotel without one missed turn. They decided to rest for a while and meet at six for drinks before ordering dinner.

It was a warm evening in the shelter of the enclosed patio. When they were settled with their drinks, Andrew spoke first.

"Helen, I have been thinking about your question. I think someone who escaped the battle would have ridden directly to Edinburgh Castle, but another soldier would have found Gospatric. No doubt he contributed some men for the venture to meet with William Rufus."

"I agree," Helen confirmed. "When I think how close Gospatric was to the family, to Margaret and to her children, I believe he would have headed straight for the castle to help her deal with the tragedy. Would Donald have already arrived with his own forces, or did that happen after a few days?"

"We don't know, of course," Robert answered, "but we can surmise that he was there quickly and that he had some powerful men with him."

Sam spoke then. "I'm going to suggest a possibility. We know the daughters were with their aunt Christine in a priory. I think Ethelred, who was designated for a church life, had already gone north to the monastery at Dunkeld for his studies. He was about twenty-one and surely would have been there for some time. Since Alexander is later attached to the North, my guess is that he was taken to Ethelred for protection. Edmund might have taken his mother's body to Dunfermline, but he is later working with Donald Bane. It is possible he returned to Edinburgh, although it would have been a dangerous position. That leaves Edgar, about twenty, and David, only nine, who needed assistance and it seems likely that Gospatric and his family would have made sure they were safe."

"I think that is as good a guess as possible," Robert concluded. "Malcolm's two sons with his first wife were Donald, who may have died in 1080, and Duncan, the hostage, who had been released when William died. He had not returned to Scotland, so he was not an immediate threat."

"Certainly, David ends up in England," Andrew said, "but he could have remained with the Gospatric clan for some time. By 1100, when his sister marries

Henry and becomes Queen of England, he would have been given land and support."

"I think," Helen added, "that David and Alan, Waltheof's son and Gospatric's grandson, become close friends later. I suspect they were around the same age."

"We can try to check on that in the Cumbrian records," Robert said, "but we do know that our second Gospatric was often witnessing documents for David, in a prominent signing position."

"That would affirm the likelihood that the Gospatric family supported Malcolm's children," Helen asserted. "David would have lost father, mother, and oldest brother in one week, then his uncle and brother Edmund take charge. He has his sisters and Edgar, but David is still in his early twenties when Edgar dies. Ethelred and Alexander are removed from his life, but Gospatric's family would have been there for him."

"Again, Helen brings in the personal side of the family," Sam declared. "I think it is time to order our dinner."

The conversation turned to their next day's adventure and speculation of what they would see and feel at the Cathedral. They were all tired from the drive and left for their rooms just before nine.

Lothian
The Years 1088–1093

The first years after William's death had been quiet. Malcolm and his men were disappointed when Robert Curthose became Duke of Normandy and William Rufus King of England. William's youngest son, Henry, was simply given funds to purchase land in England. Queen Margaret's brother Edgar was given land in Normandy and became one of Robert's advisors. Although Rufus was king, Malcolm felt that there might be peace in Scotland, and Edgar seemed to be in a strong position.

The agreement of the brothers, who had named each other as heirs, did not last. Robert and Edgar began an attempt to overthrow Rufus by the end of the next year. The attempt failed and Rufus forced Robert to end Edgar's possession of property in Normandy, and Edgar returned to Scotland. Gospatric was called to meet with Malcolm and Edgar, fearing the worst once again.

Malcolm shouted and blustered, more for drama than for sincere concern for Edgar's future. "He cannot treat you like you are a common noble. You should be in his place right now."

"Perhaps I should be grateful to be alive, Sire," Edgar said, looking to Gospatric for support.

"He is right, Sire. We know little of his nature, but if it is akin to his father's, we must be careful."

"I shall declare war and invade Northumbria!" Malcolm shouted. "It is time to take our territory back. We shall organise our armies to march south before the autumn winds blow."

"He is not absent from England like his father, and he will muster his forces against you," Edgar stated. "And Gospatric, you must hide once more. If he sees you leading your men, it will rekindle his father's desire to see you dead or imprisoned for the remainder of your life."

"Your son can lead your forces," Malcolm retorted, sending shivers down Gospatric's back. He had been able to protect his family from war, but now it would start again.

Later Gospatric met with Edgar and together they went to Margaret, pleading with her to reason with Malcolm. She agreed with them that there was no need for war, but she didn't seem confident that she could restrain Malcolm.

Gospatric's son left with the men from Dunbar and joined with others moving into Northumbria. Gospatric waited near Berwick for any news. They heard that, before getting far into the territory of England, Malcolm's forces learned that William Rufus was marching north with his large army. Edgar had ridden ahead with a party of his men to meet with Robert Curthose, who now represented his brother in negotiations. Gospatric prayed that his son was not with Edgar, but he surely was.

The hours passed slowly as Gospatric tried to visit with the thanes who had stayed behind. Everyone was uneasy and it was difficult to conduct any business. When a rider came galloping into Berwick, the word went out and the thanes assembled for the news. With relief they heard that Edgar and Robert had negotiated a peace agreement. Malcolm would swear fealty to Rufus, twelve towns would be restored to Malcolm, and Edgar would be reconciled with William Rufus. War had been averted and the troops were able to return home for the harvest. Gospatric waited near Berwick until he saw the Dunbar banner and then rode out to greet his youngest son, who was only twenty-one years old, but already a leader of men. He was proud of young Gospatric but felt the slightest tinge of remorse about his own situation, and his inability to lead the men who had served him so well for so long.

There was a quiet time again and Gospatric travelled to Aspatria for the marriage of Ethelreda and Duncan before the winter months made travel impossible. It was a grand family affair for the Gospatric clan, as the growing family gathered to celebrate Ethelreda's happiness in marrying her childhood friend. Malcolm did not attend the wedding, and Duncan was relieved. He had not seen his father since his return from Normandy and seemed content with life in Cumbria. Gospatric knew that some of the thanes had other ideas. Malcolm's sons with Margaret were still young and immature compared with Duncan, who had spent so much time in Normandy, and with William Rufus in England. They felt he had a greater capacity to stand up to Rufus and keep the peace than Malcolm's son Edward. Even some of the Northern thanes appeared to value his

Celtic background. Malcolm's aging was noticeable to the thanes, inclining them to think about his death and the succession.

Gospatric returned to his home for the winter and hoped that they had averted another war. But within months, Robert Curthose accused his brother of not holding to their agreement and left for Normandy, taking Edgar back with him. Then later in the year William Rufus marched his army north through Cumbria to Carlisle. Dolphin was removed as lord, and William's forces built a castle. He put a Norman lord in charge, following in his father's footsteps. Hope for peaceful times were over. Dolphin came to Lothian with his family and those who had loyally served him. Shortly thereafter, Dolphin and Gospatric travelled to see King Malcolm, who had several ideas about where to place Dolphin until he was able to reverse the situation. Once again Malcolm was talking invasion and war.

"First we must take back Durham and St Cuthbert's body." This time he was more strategic in his thinking. "I am planning to lay the foundation stone of the new cathedral at Durham with Prior Turgot and the bishop. This move is crucial to bring Northumbria into Scottish ownership, beginning with the kingdom of Durham." They all quietly waited for the Cathedral plans to develop. The foundation stone was laid on the 11th of August 1093, and it was a great occasion. The fact that King Malcolm of Scotland had been the one to place the stone on English soil was an affront to William Rufus. He demanded that King Malcolm meet with him in England, and plans were made to take a large force along with the king.

Once again Gospatric had to stand down. Margaret was ill and she begged Malcolm to stay, knowing how long he would be gone during his journey to London and back. Malcolm said he had no choice, but he would leave Gospatric with Margaret and the family. He also insisted that young Gospatric remain in his position at Dunbar but send some of his soldiers from the garrison to accompany him. Gospatric was relieved that his son wasn't travelling with the forces but found it difficult to stay behind himself. Only Margaret's relief that he was with her, eased his desire to be with Malcolm. His anxiety did not go away as he wondered if both Margaret and Malcolm had some sense of dread about this journey.

In a few weeks, Gospatric heard that the meeting with Rufus had been unsatisfactory and the forces were returning. A messenger had brought the news to the queen who was bedridden, with Gospatric or one of her sons constantly at her side. Gospatric talked with the messenger and learned that the forces planned to rest at Lincoln and Durham where they knew they had some support. They were expected to reach Scotland in a couple of days. Two days later a messenger came with news that Malcolm and Edward were leaving Durham in the morning on Monday, the thirteenth, and would reach Scotland by nightfall. It was November and the hours of daylight were short, and they were unlikely to make it to Edinburgh. They were taking the coastal path and would leave many of the men at Dunbar before travelling west to the castle. Malcolm had promised Margaret that he would have messengers keep her informed and he had kept his word.

Gospatric waited on Monday for further news from a messenger, hoping to hear that his men had safely reached Dunbar. Margaret was getting weaker every day, and she called for her youngest son David to be with her. Gospatric wasn't sure she would live through another night, and he had sent a message to Christina, asking if it was possible for her nieces to travel to Scotland. He was wishing that Malcolm had arranged to bring his daughters north with him, but no such plan had been made. Edmund was the first to greet the messenger, as he rode across the drawbridge into the castle grounds. Gospatric saw him shouting and doubling over and ran to meet him. Edmund could not speak, and Gospatric held him, asking the messenger to tell him the news.

"We were ambushed just after leaving Alnmouth. They came from all sides," he blurted out. "Two men attacked Malcolm and I am sure that Edward was also killed. A few of us escaped in the fighting to bring the message, but most of the men were being slaughtered. One of our soldiers went to Dunbar to tell your son, one to Berwick and another to Coldingham."

"Who did this?" Gospatric shouted, letting go of Edmund into his brother Edgar's arms.

"Someone said it was the earl himself and others said it was Geoffrey and Morel, but Robert de Mowbray was leading the attack from the North. They will say we were raiding, but we were trying to reach Scotland as fast as we could, knowing the queen was ill."

"Get this man some help!" Gospatric shouted to the men who now encircled them. "Edmund, we must go to your mother. Come, Edgar."

It was as if Margaret knew before the news arrived. "Malcolm is dead, isn't he, and my first-born?"

"Yes, Mother," Edmund answered quietly, "both slain in an ambush at Alnmouth, along with most of our men. What should I do now? Am I the king?"

Margaret turned away from them all and wept. Alexander joined Edmund and Edgar, and Gospatric took young David into his arms and held him.

"Is my mother going to die too?" David whispered. Gospatric thought of the night Siward had taken him and his brother from Aspatria, and his questions in the early morning hours when he knew his father and grandfather were dead. He did not want to lie to David or the other boys.

"I fear she will, my son. We must call for the priest to come and then we will all decide what to do now."

The sons of Malcolm sat with Gospatric around the fire in the great hall. Gospatric had said they must move quickly, to call the thanes together to determine who should be king, reminding them that his son-in-law Duncan was Malcolm's oldest son. Edward had been named as heir and was now dead, opening the subject of the rightful heir. Before they could continue, another messenger was brought into the hall. He reported that Donald Bane, Malcolm's younger brother was mustering a force to take over the castle and declare himself king.

"Would he dare to enter here with the Queen of Scotland near death and mourning the loss of her husband and eldest son?" Gospatric demanded. "Send a message to him to show respect to his nephews and his queen. He must not enter this castle while Queen Margaret is alive."

As Margaret slowly passed into another state, oblivious to the world, the sons of Margaret, without nine-year-old David, discussed their options with Gospatric. There was little time to contact Duncan and Gospatric's son Waltheof in Cumbria, but they sent messages to them. Then Gospatric sent messengers to his son at Dunbar Castle, and north to Merleswein and to Ethelred, who was at the monastery at Dunkeld. They also sent two men south, one to Christina and the other to Edgar Atheling. Edgar and Christina would need to arrange protection for David. Gospatric determined it was best to split their forces and send a group of soldiers to Dunfermline with Edmund, transporting Queen Margaret's body for burial. Edmund wanted to remain and negotiate with his uncle, but Gospatric advised him to leave and communicate by messenger with Donald Bane. Both Duncan and Edmund were in the most danger from their uncle. The advice to Duncan and Waltheof was to remain where they were until more was known about Donald Bane's success with the thanes. Alexander wanted to go north to the monastery at Dunkeld and believed he would be safe with his brother's protection. Gospatric agreed and hoped Merleswein could get to the castle in time to escort him. They were unsure where Donald would make his stand, but it sounded as if he already had men from the far north meeting at Falkirk to plan their move on the castle. Edgar and David would leave with Gospatric and he would take them to a secure place until further plans could be made, and the situation was clearer.

Margaret died in the early hours of Thursday, the sixteenth of November. The priest did what he could in terms of final words of comfort for the family. Gospatric watched as her loyal servants wrapped her body, now fragile and almost weightless, in a beautiful cloth. There was a secret staircase carved into the rock face on the north side of the castle down which Gospatric escorted Edmund, and the men travelling with him with Margaret's body, to horses arranged for them. The horses had slowly been taken to the area in the darkness, waiting for their riders. Next, Alexander left with Merleswein and others who wished to go north to Fife and beyond. Many would stay at the castle, knowing that Donald would need servants and soldiers to serve him. Gospatric left last, sealing up the secret staircase behind him. He had Edgar and the sleeping David, and they were accompanied by a small group of soldiers. As they reached the hills south of the castle in the dawn, they received a message from those who were left behind. The soldiers were marching towards Edinburgh with Donald Bane at the front with a Celtic cross on his banner. Donald, like Macbeth, would claim that he was the one who would maintain the Celtic heritage of Scotland, unlike the anglicised children of Malcolm. It was a winning lie that had worked well once before for an equally dangerous man who yearned for power. Both Macbeth and Donald had no family loyalty but only resentment for years of being less than their kin.

When Gospatric received messages assuring the safety of each group, he left for Cumbria to meet with Duncan. Although discussions were already underway to force Donald Bane out, a decision was made to build support and wait until spring to move on Edinburgh. Duncan would rally the support of both Edgar Atheling and King William Rufus, with whom he had spent so much time during his years as a hostage. Donald did what they expected of him; he tried to drive out any Normans and Anglo-Saxons who had come north in aid of Malcolm. There was also evidence that Donald had spies in Malcolm's forces, who may have revealed his location for the ambush. The anger that arose because of these actions built more support for Duncan.

Donald Bane was driven out of Edinburgh Castle in the spring, and Duncan was consecrated King of the Scots and Ethelreda his queen. It was a joyful day for Gospatric, but not without a sense of foreboding. Edmund was resentful of Duncan's position, knowing Duncan already had a son who could be named to succeed him. Many of the thanes were concerned that Edmund might decide to join forces with Donald, hoping to overthrow Duncan.

Gospatric tried to put aside his fear and lend as much support to his children as he could. He also spent time with Malcolm's sons when possible. Alexander was content to stay at the monastery in Dunkeld with Ethelred. Edgar and David had been taken south to England to see their aunt Christina and their sisters, and their uncle Edgar Atheling was helpful in assuring their safety until better times. Gospatric visited them in the late summer before travel became more difficult. At that point there was a feeling of some stability again in Scotland, but it was not to last.

While Ethelreda was bringing her children to visit their grandfather before the winter set in, Donald Bane and Edmund betrayed her husband, King Duncan. He was murdered on the twelfth of November, and Donald and Edmund took over, now ruling the country jointly. Knowing that her son was in danger, Gospatric took Ethelreda to his secret tower house and then back to Aspatria and Waltheof's protection as soon as he could. Like so many kings before him, Duncan's body was taken to Iona, and buried without his wife and children present.

Gospatric stayed in Cumbria for the Christmas festivities, but there was no joy in their celebration, just more sadness than Gospatric could bear. Ethelreda wept without ceasing for the husband she had waited to marry for so many years. She was inconsolable; he could do nothing but hold her children in his arms. The family felt once more the sadness of the past when Malcolm and Donald's father, King Duncan, was slain by Macbeth. Gospatric finally returned to the tower to be alone, although it was now deep winter, and he knew he should not stay without enough supplies to sustain him. Part of him was so tired of killing and sorrow that he was not sure he wanted to go on living. He had hoped that his children and grandchildren could live in peace, but once again tragedy had killed that dream. He thought about the monks at Durham and their peaceful lives of work and prayers and wondered.

Durham Cathedral
July 2017

Helen was getting impatient. Although she was interested in St Cuthbert's shrine, the memorial to the Scots who had died in a forced march to Durham in the winter, and the beauty of the architecture, she had come to see the stone sarcophagus of Gospatric. The viewing would be the culmination of all their work. Finally, the four of them were following two staff members to the crypt. One of the staff members unlocked the wooden arched door and warned about the low ceiling within; the other cautioned them about the flooring, as they slowly moved farther back through the dim space. They stopped and one of the staff uncovered a long stone, revealing *Gospatricus Comes.* Even Robert was silent, until he commented on the broken stone, which was cracked into two pieces.

"It was like that when we found it in here. We are not sure when it happened. The inscription is still quite clear, which makes it unlikely it is twelfth century. The original lid may have been replaced and it was probably protected during some period."

"It definitely was buried for a very long time," Robert said, countering their argument. "Our research leads us to believe that Gospatric came to Durham sometime in the 1100s, became a monk, and died here."

"Is it not more likely to be his son or a grandson who might have been the earl?"

"We can account for the year and place of their deaths," Robert added, "so not likely."

"Also, the cantor's book records Gospatric as an earl and monk, and no other Gospatric entered the monastery," Sam announced. Samuel had been introduced as a history professor from the United States. The staff also knew of Robert's background and extensive research of the Gospatric family.

"May we take photographs?" Helen asked. She wondered if this important stone would still be there for others since it had been disregarded for so long.

"We would prefer that you didn't. The lighting is not sufficient to capture the inscription fully. I am willing to set up lighting and take photographs for you."

"We would be very grateful," Robert declared, "and we want to thank you for giving us this opportunity."

With his comment, they took their last look and followed the staff out, with more expressions of thanks offered as they left. Helen wondered if they would ever see those photographs. It had taken Robert years to get them to search for the sarcophagus, and a couple more years to get this appointment. Would they complete the task, she wondered? She wished she had taken at least one cell phone photo for proof that the stone was in the crypt, as the literature from the Dundas records had said. They walked slowly through the streets and then decided to split up, meeting later for drinks and dinner. Durham was a beautiful city, and Sam and Helen wanted time to explore it fully, knowing they might not be able to return anytime soon.

They enjoyed a light lunch and then wandered through the winding streets on a downhill path back to the hotel. At three they stopped at a small coffeehouse, with plans to walk along the river after a snack. Sam connected to the Wi-Fi and found he had a message from his nephews. He read that the latest scan showed that their mother's cancer was spreading again, and she was experiencing quite a bit of pain. Sam immediately left Helen and found a quiet corner to call Minneapolis. Knowing his flight was within a few days, Sarah's children had all agreed that he should keep his current schedule. They planned to pick him up and take him immediately to the house. When Sam asked if anything had changed regarding Juliana, Matt confirmed that it hadn't. He agreed to pick up Sam and take him home first, before going to see Sarah. Sam said he would have another passenger with him and would send an email to explain, as soon as possible. He came back to the table and Helen knew the news was not positive.

"What is it, Sam? Is it Sarah?"

"Yes, the scan today confirmed that the cancer is progressing rapidly. Sarah was in pain, so she was already certain of the diagnosis," he answered.

"What should we do...tell Robert we need to leave to get you on the first flight?"

"The boys are confident that our flight date is not in question. I'll be there in time. The doctor said it was a matter of weeks, not days," he added, with a shaky voice.

"Are you sure? I can stay and finish the packing and closing of the apartment alone. It's not a problem," Helen implored.

"No, I agreed, and Matt will pick us up and take us to the apartment first. I told him that someone would be with me, but I'll send an email to them tonight," he explained. "After the argument with Sarah, I didn't get a chance to tell the boys and Juliana about you and our plans to live together. I was so rattled that evening. When she finally gave me my mother's diary, I left the house."

"I'm sorry I caused that grief," Helen whispered, taking his hand in hers. "I can go to my sister's when we land. In fact, she wants to pick me up. I think it would be better for everyone if we do this separately and you get to Sarah as quickly as possible."

"I don't like it, but you're right. It is not the way I planned our re-entry and the introduction to your new home," he stated, as he reached out to touch her hair.

"Do you still want to walk by the river or go back to our room?" she asked.

"I think I should go back and rest a bit before we meet. I feel very tired, just thinking ahead to the next few days and weeks."

They walked in silence hand in hand back to the hotel, and Sam fell into a restless sleep shortly after lying down on the bed. Sam had asked Helen to tell the others the news, so they could decide about changing the plans for the next day. Helen left the room and called Robert to tell him about Sarah. They agreed that it was best to leave in the morning and drive straight back to Edinburgh. He said he would talk with Andrew, who would also appreciate getting back earlier then they had planned.

Dinner was a solemn occasion. There was a little conversation about the experience in the crypt and what each of them had felt. Andrew said he was relieved to have seen the stone and that it had confirmed Gospatric's death at Durham for him. Robert agreed. Sam was worried about whether the stone would once again disappear into oblivion, even though it had such historical significance. He was determined to prove it was Gospatric's. Helen agreed but was the only one to express her emotional reaction as she looked at the stone.

"I can only say that I felt something inside of me. It was as if some entity was saying thank you for being here. Thank you for acknowledging that I was alive, and died in this place. The stone is all that is left of this man I have learned to respect, admire, and cherish as an incredibly special person. He is so real to me now, someone who experienced great losses, someone who had a family he loved, a survivor who is a part of all of us." She finished and realised she was crying, and she wasn't sure why. Was it for Sarah and Sam and his family? Was it for Sam's mother and Robert? Was it for Gospatric and all the other ancestors who were a part of her? Sam put an arm around her, and she leaned against him.

After dinner they all faced the fact that they would not be together after their return drive the next day. Andrew would be off on his holiday, Sam and Helen getting ready for their trip back to Minneapolis, and Robert would be waiting to hear about Juliana.

"Robert," Sam said, "you said you might share more information about the secret group. What do you expect to find? Is it something that will challenge Christian beliefs?"

"Not really, although the church is destroying itself without any help, with its quarrels about women and gay priests in this country and the 'crazy' right-wing thinking of the American churches. The early church in this country was based on principles we should recapture—respect for nature and all beings, equality of women and a deep spirituality. Can we deny that the world could use that kind of religious thinking?"

"No, but so much of the arguing and fighting inside of Christianity is about dogma, doctrine and interpretation of the Bible," Sam retorted. "It's not about what Jesus was trying to teach. I wish someone would uncover some valid early writing of scripture that would bring us back to the simplicity of his teaching."

"There will always be disagreements, particularly about the meaning of the resurrection, the organisation of the Church and the sacraments, but one of the most significant issues is the determination of the Christian Church to insist that it is the only route to salvation. What if salvation has been misinterpreted, what if the words of Jesus have been distorted, what if he did not die on the cross, making him superior to all others? What if Jesus was taken from the cross, his wounds treated and healed? There is evidence he was in India after the resurrection; others believe he travelled to Egypt and on to France with Mary Magdalene and his mother. We believe there is some knowledge that was passed down from generation to generation and then lost. The early church had different opinions about his divinity, reincarnation was a part of the belief system, and the gnostic beliefs were suppressed. What if, at some time in history, an important aspect of his life and death was written down and hidden away, as other early documents were. It could make a difference in bringing religions together."

"And you think Juliana can help you because of her interest in the esoteric?" Sam asked, with disbelief in his question.

"More than that, much more. She has links to the Celtic and Druidic past in her DNA from both sides of her ancestry. We know DNA carries memory. Maybe she can connect with these ancient people and tap their knowledge. Think what your mother was able to do."

"And look what happened to her. She was sucked into the past, with devastating consequences. Is that what you want for Juliana?" he challenged.

"Of course not. Your mother had no one to help her understand what was happening."

Helen and Andrew had been silent, listening to the points being made by Robert and Sam. Finally, Helen spoke up.

"Are you telling us that you believe that the man called Jesus might have been taken from the cross unconscious, but not dead, and healed of his wounds?" she asked, with incredulity in her voice. "It's not that I buy into the idea of him being God, but can that have physically happened?"

"There is the part about the sword in his side," Andrew said, "and blood came out indicating he was still alive. There's also the passage about bringing nearly a hundred pounds of aloe and myrrh to his burial site."

"How did I miss all of that? Wouldn't it have been to prepare his body for burial? Where did you find this?" Helen demanded.

"It's in John, at the end of Chapter 19," Andrew answered. "When I looked up burial practices for Jews in biblical times, it did not talk about any form of embalming, and you don't need a hundred pounds of healing oils to anoint a body."

Robert spoke up, interrupting them. "It does not matter whether he was saved or if he died and appeared as a spirit. The problem is the claim that Christianity trumps all other religions. It gets even worse when you think about Catholics claiming they have the only true faith, and now some of the evangelicals believe that if you don't accept their theory of the atonement, you will go to hell."

Sam pulled them back to the point, addressing Robert.

"I just want you to be clear that it will be difficult enough to convince my niece to see you, without the pressure of expecting a historical miracle from her."

"I understand, Sam. I would not even mention this, until we were able to build a relationship, but I am hoping she will be as curious about her ancestors as we are."

"Getting back to our ancestors," Helen said, "when do we think Gospatric came to Durham? Was he here a long time, as a monk, or did he come shortly before his death and take vows? Any opinions?"

"We can't verify anything more than we have," Robert said. "Gospatric is listed in the cantor's book as an earl and monk, along with other family members, to have prayers said for him and there is the stone sarcophagus with his name on it."

"But what do we think?" Helen asked. "If he died as late as 1115, in his seventies, did he come when his youngest son was ready to accept the responsibility as the Earl of Dunbar or Lothian?"

"His older sons, Dolphin and Waltheof, took on responsibility very young, out of necessity," Sam posed, "but they had more limited territory. If both the kings of Scotland and England depended on the Gospatric family to manage Dunbar, a large part of Lothian, and the border area, it may have been a divided responsibility. I see our Gospatric being the roving judge, to take care of the disputed issues in the border lands. We know this was the expectation of the descendants of the second Gospatric and his family for an extended period. That history started with Gospatric's assignment of duties from Malcolm."

"And the respect Gospatric had in Northumbria would have made that possible and necessary until there was a settled border," Helen added, smiling at Sam.

"Sadly, my friends," Robert declared, "we shall not ever know when he arrived at Durham and when he died. It is time for us to leave each other. We have a long drive ahead of us after breakfast."

The Tower, Ercildoune
The Year 1108

Gospatric was at his tower house, no longer an unknown hideaway. It had become a favourite fishing and swimming summer spot for the family, particularly the younger grandchildren. Today Gospatric was alone, having asked the family to give him the privacy he needed for an important decision. He was reflecting on all that had happened since Malcolm and Margaret had died. He remembered every detail of those terrible moments of getting the family out of the castle, knowing that Donald Bane was hovering outside the walls. He remembered thinking it could not get worse. When he and others had worked together to remove Donald from the throne and put Duncan in his place, they never thought that Donald would dare to have him killed six months later. Gospatric felt the pain of that moment and the next three years wash over him. Donald and Edmund reigned jointly, and Gospatric tried to assuage the grief and on-going sorrow of Ethelreda and the rest of the family. He supported Edgar's bid for the throne three years later, with the help of the Normans and the English, but was horrified by the blinding of Donald Bane. This event confirmed for him that Edgar shared his thoughts that Donald had been complicit in the attack on Malcolm, as well as Duncan. He had been relieved when Edgar banished his brother to a monastery, rather than blinding and imprisoning him. He continued to reflect on those next years when he and his family served King Edgar, as they had done with Malcolm. Gospatric had hoped that Robert Curthose would become king when Rufus died, but it was not to be. He and others had suspected Henry of killing his brother, while Robert was on his return journey from a pilgrimage to Rome. Henry had been hunting with Rufus in the New Forest when the accident happened. They had learned that he had immediately left, kidnapped Malcolm and Margaret's daughter Edith from Wilton Priory, taking her on to London. Within three days of the death of his brother, he was crowned king, with a Scottish princess as his bride. Robert and Edgar Atheling had returned too late to stop Henry. They had tried to bring an army to England to claim the crown based on the agreement Robert and Rufus had made when their father died. Robert lacked support and was defeated.

Gospatric knew Robert would not give up his fight for the throne, and would try to gather forces against Henry again, but he wouldn't help. His grandchildren were growing up and he wanted time with them. Even Gospatric, his youngest son, now had six sons and he saw them more frequently than the older grandchildren. He was closest to the second son, Waldeve, who reminded him of Waltheof. Waldeve was already talking about being a priest and giving up his lands to his youngest brothers, Huctred and Eilaf. He had overheard a discussion about whether there would be land available for the last two little brothers, with the eldest four - another Gospatric, Edward, Edgar and Waldeve - all having land designated for them. His son's wife Sybilla wanted a daughter, but continued to deliver healthy boys, year after year. He felt lucky to be alive and able to see the strength in his children's families. Even after all the strife in the country, his friends and family had survived and thrived. He had lost both Merleswein and Thorfinn, and the one positive thing in his life was his family.

He had not been able to protect Malcolm and Margaret's children from each other, and he worried about Edith, now called Queen Matilda. She was an extremely competent and intelligent woman and she had been a willing partner to Henry, but Henry's reputation for having mistresses was well-known. Henry already had several children with other women and he, like his father and brother, had a vicious streak. Many had felt his wrath. Robert was the only son of William the Bastard who had any sense of decency, but then perhaps he would have been the same if he had become King of England, Gospatric thought.

Gospatric had learned that Robert had failed in his last attempt to overpower his brother Henry and had been imprisoned at Devizes Castle. Edgar Atheling had been taken back to England, pardoned, and then released. His niece, Queen Matilda, had convinced King Henry to take this action. Normandy was now controlled by the English, and Gospatric hoped it would put an end to the fighting and to Henry's designs on more territory. If Matilda's son grew up to be king, perhaps Scotland could have a lasting peace.

King Edgar had died in early January the previous year and had wanted to have Alexander and David, his younger brothers, share the throne. Gospatric had supported that request, but Alexander had not honoured it. Again, Gospatric feared that two more sons of Margaret and Malcolm would fight each other for power, but David had accepted his position graciously and devoted himself to the Scottish territory south of the Firth of Forth. Gospatric's family had remained close to David, although he was younger than Gospatric's children. David and Waltheof's son Alan had become friends and spent time together. Gospatric was confident that David would be a king who could unite the interests of England and Scotland, and bring together the Cumbrians, Normans, Northumbrians, and Scots. He had his mother's reconciliatory nature and deep religious faith.

Gospatric had come to the tower alone because he had made a commitment to God. More than once in his times of hiding from the king's forces, he had asked God to spare him that he might live to protect his children. He desperately wanted to be there for his family and often thought about the loss of his own father and Malcolm's father. He and Malcolm had been blessed with the care that Siward had given them, but they still suffered. He did not want his children to experience that loss. He knew he had bargained with God, and he was not even sure what he believed. He had never accepted all the teachings of the Roman Church, but there was little left of the old ways of the Celtic monks. He felt the presence of the divine in nature, in birth and even in death. He no longer blamed God for the terrible things that happened because of men's greed and desire for power. He was not sure there was a hell or a heaven, maybe they were both here on earth. When he was in the monastery in Flanders, he had made his greatest promise. He begged God to bring him home safely to his family and his beloved country. If he should live to his seventieth year, he would take holy vows and become a monk, dedicating the rest of his days to the Church. The anniversary of his birth was coming in a few more weeks and he was here to spend the days and nights trying to reach a place in his mind where his soul could communicate with the holy spirit. He had pondered death so many times, wondering if he would be greeted by Gunhilda, Siward and Waltheof and his father. If a man had two or three wives who had died before them, would they all be there? What form would they take? Would his tiny daughter Juliana, buried at Aspatria, be a living babe? Would Athelreda be there and still be angry? Would Margaret and Malcolm ask him why he had not stopped their sons from fighting each other?

On his second night in some dream state, he concluded that you entered the energy of the heavens at death, that you joined with those who went before you in a spiritual meeting of souls. Perhaps later in time you returned to earth, entering a new-born body, with no memory of what went before, but with an opportunity to do things differently. Would you be punished in the new life for what you had done in the past? Would you meet those you loved and those you hated? Would you recognise them in some way? Every new thought resulted in new questions, as he pondered the meaning of life and death.

During the third night when he had consumed no food and had little to drink, he had a strange dream. Malcolm appeared to him, pointing to the foundation stone at Durham Cathedral; then Margaret appeared with the halo of a saint over her head, then Waltheof with the same kind of halo, and finally St Cuthbert held out his hand to him in silence. He woke with a start, wondering if he had heard something in the woods. His horse was silent, indicating there was no danger from outside. He tried to go back to the dream, asking the figures for words, for the answer to his questions, but he fell into a deep, restful sleep.

When he awoke in the morning, he felt refreshed and hungry. He ate the last of his provisions and decided to return to his home. His decision was made to travel to Durham, to ask to take his vows as a monk. He would want to be free to travel, to live in the woods and celebrate nature. When he died, he would be buried at Durham to keep the legacy of St Cuthbert alive. He hoped his family would live on, that his grandchildren and their children would seek peace rather than power. He wondered if his descendants would find his grave in the far distant future and be curious about the life of their ancestor called Gospatric.

Epilogue

Minneapolis, Minnesota

July 2017

Juliana sat on her mother's bed, staring at the box in front of her. She tried to steady herself, to keep the tears back. She had to face this. Matt and Jake were still her brothers. Sam was still her uncle. She was still the person she was earlier in the day, the same physical being she was before her mother told her—the same emotional entity before her mother died. And yet she wasn't. She was a different person, one who belonged to a man in Scotland she had never met, never heard about, didn't know existed. The others, her brothers and uncle, had known this. She was the only one that had not, until these last few hours. The papers in the box would tell her about her grandmother. She remembered seeing the box. She had found it once when she was a child exploring in the attic. Her mother had discovered her reading a poem that had fallen from a book that was on the top of the box. She had taken it from Juliana and sent her downstairs, yelling that she must never come up to the attic alone again. She remembered searching for the box one other time, when her mother was out. It had not been in the same place and the attic was filled with boxes. There was no way to go through them without leaving evidence and she had given up.

Now she opened the cover of the plain looking box with no markings and recognised the book inside. It was a journal, and she quickly went to the back and found the folded piece of paper with the poem she had been reading so many years ago. As she read, she could see the white sculptured figures hanging in an open area. She wondered if she had seen them some place. She was sure that she had but couldn't remember the location. Perhaps she had visualised them. She read the poem again.

The Trapeze Artists

We are like the sculpture of the trapeze artists we saw tonight in the square
Gracefully suspended now in time, moving towards each other
Never able to get within reach, looking, loving, with no hope of touching.
If the wires should break, would you catch me after all? Could you?
If we fell together into the net below, would we crush one another by our togetherness?
Do we need this time to be suspended, to understand ourselves, our needs and wants?
I do not need you. I can remain in this state forever. It is beautiful, graceful, safe, amusing.
But I do want you, yearn for you, to touch you, hold you, love you.
I want the suspension to stop sometime, to swing through space and catch your hands
At times to pass you gracefully, on my way through my own flight, but always to be within reach
As we live out the scenes of life, each completing our own acrobatic act
Supporting one another's choices, knowing and sensing they are right
But able to catch each other temporarily if they are wrong.
To fly freely to the conclusion, the finality of life
To land then, in the net, one by one
Bowing to the audience for our great performance and walking off the stage
Hand in hand to the Hereafter....

What did it mean? Who was it about? Had her mother written it? Was it about the man, her father? Juliana opened the journal and looked at the first entries. Dates in June were there, but there was no year to indicate when it had been written. The handwriting was familiar, but she didn't think it was her mother's. There were references to Sam and Sarah, so it had to have been written by her grandmother. No one talked about her. She had asked Jake and Matt about her, but they didn't know anything except that she had died the year they were born. Uncle Samuel wasn't helpful either. He said it was complicated and she should ask her mother to tell her about their mother's death. When she did ask her mother, there was a cold and icy silence followed by, "She died when your brothers were born. She was on a trip and never saw them." Juliana had protested, wanting more information.

"What was she like? I want to know about her…"

Her mother had fired back, "There is nothing to know, Juliana, and I don't want you to bring it up again. It's difficult for me to talk about her." She could see the pain in her mother's eyes, but more than that, she felt it in her own body. It was the first time she remembered being curious about how you could feel something that someone else was experiencing. It had led to her interest in psychology and psychic phenomena. She didn't have terms to name the things she felt, but she searched the library for books and gradually learned about different forms of psychic abilities. She read about them secretly, until she declared her major in college and authored papers on types of psychic phenomena which she already knew a lot about. A double major in psychology and journalism had led to a master's degree and work as a reporter and freelance journalist on issues even remotely related to psychic phenomena. She was paid for doing what she passionately wanted to explore, at a time when the field of research was growing every day.

Juliana closed the journal and took out a large envelope. Assuming this was some information about the mysterious man who was her father, and her mother's relationship with him, she pulled out the papers. Disappointed, she realised that all of them were genealogical charts going back in time. She threw everything back in the box and pushed it onto the floor. Then she curled up into a foetal position and sobbed, until she fell asleep, having been up all night at her mother's bedside.

Edinburgh, Scotland
August 2017

Robert faced them squarely, raising his voice ever so slightly, as he spoke, "You can't be serious. I have a right to pass on the legacy to Juliana."

"You have no evidence that she is your daughter!" Henry said, emphasising the 'no'. The other men sat back, letting Henry Douglas present the argument. He was a stout man, larger in stature than Robert, and his manner always implied authority.

"I've told you her mother had a DNA test, and her husband was not the father," Robert protested, tired of repeating himself.

"That does not prove that you are the father. It proves nothing at all," Henry continued. "Are we all agreed on this?" he said, as he looked at the other four men at the table. They each nodded, leaving Robert still on the defensive.

"Why would the woman write to me, telling me about her daughter…my daughter, if it wasn't true? She wanted nothing to do with me when she left. It was only because of her impending death that she had her brother make contact to see if I was even alive."

"You are a fool, Robert. You want to have a child so much that you will believe anything. This could be a swindle. You are not without resources, and it is quite easy for an American to gain knowledge about your assets and make this preposterous claim," Henry declared, intending to end the discussion. The others nodded like sheep and Robert knew he was losing his battle.

"I insist on permission to disclose the legacy to her, if I so choose after meeting her," he stated. "If you require a DNA test, it can be arranged," he added, as he stood to leave. He turned back, as he reached the panelled exit to the room, and challenged them, "Don't you see the implications? She has a connection to this from both sides of her family and she might just be the key. She has the right type of background. She has studied and written about paranormal activity."

"Nonsense, Robert. She's a journalist and she could use that skill to gain the information and write about it for the world. We cannot take that risk," Henry answered, attempting to end any further discussion, and making it clear to the others in the room that his conclusion was the correct one.

"We'll see," Robert shot back, as he pushed the button, opening the panel behind him. He crossed into the library. The men were meeting, as they usually did, in a dark oak-panelled room with elegantly carved chairs around a large round table. Once a member left the room, the others were not allowed to speak to each other and each in turn followed Robert out of the room.

As Robert left the front of the Georgian manor and got into his Rover, he realised how powerful Henry had become. Even the fact that they met at Henry's home most of the time now indicated the unbalanced situation. Henry had assumed the strongest position. He was the youngest member and had a male heir, which was important, despite the acceptance of women. He would have to address these problems before he could introduce Juliana to the group, but first he needed to patiently wait for the scenario of Sarah's death to play out and for Juliana to respond to the fact that he was her father.

Minneapolis, Minnesota
August 2017

Juliana drove from her apartment to her mother's house. She knew her uncle was still there sorting through papers and items that had to be dealt with as soon as possible after a death. The memorial service would be scheduled for the following week, as soon as all her mother's friends and relatives were notified and able to plan their travel if they chose to come. When she walked into the house, her uncle Samuel was sitting on the couch in the living room. Before he could offer her coffee, she challenged him.

"I've read the journal and looked at everything in the box, Samuel, and it tells me about your mother's trip to Scotland, but it doesn't answer the questions about how she died and there is nothing about Mom. What happened to her? And what's the importance of all this family history?" Juliana threw the packet and the journal on the table in front of Samuel.

"I can't add a lot to what you have. I hoped that Sarah had written her explanation of what went on in Scotland. I only found out about her relationship with the man called Robert a few months ago, when she asked me to find him."

"Well, what did she say? She must have told you how she ended up pregnant, how she got involved with this guy who is my biological father!"

"I'll tell you what I know, but it won't answer all the questions. I'm afraid you will have to go to Scotland for that…"

"In your dreams! Why should I want to meet this man and, frankly, why would he want to meet me after all this time?"

"He does want to meet you."

"How do you know? Have you talked to him?" Juliana hurled the questions at him, laden with suspicion and betrayal.

"Sit down, Juliana, and listen. I will explain what happened in these last few months, and everything I know about what went on in Scotland in 1990," Sam stated, with enough energy to force Juliana to a chair across from him.

"First, let me tell you this. Your mom and I received a call from Scotland and learned that our mother, your grandmother, had drowned off the eastern coast of Scotland in a place called St Abbs. We were in shock. The implication was that she had committed suicide."

"Oh my God, had she?" Juliana interrupted. "Her journal entries were getting very strange, and she was waiting for that guy named Mark to arrive…"

"Stay with me here. Your mother went into labour later that day, your father was in Alaska, and I was at work. It was a nightmare and your mom almost died. She survived, Jake and Matt were fine, Will arrived and we thought that we only had to face one crisis—struggling to figure out what happened in Scotland. But Sarah was physically recovering, but not emotionally…"

"Well, that happens to a lot of women after having a baby and she had a lot to deal with. I don't know why she wouldn't talk about this with me. Sometimes postpartum depression runs in families."

"It was worse than most. She was catatonic…unable to speak, to feed the twins. Nothing was reaching her, and Will agreed to a procedure to 'shock' her out of it."

Juliana sat up and leaned across the coffee table. "You're actually serious, aren't you?"

"We felt we had no choice and the treatment worked. She responded, but she was not the same sister I knew. This event we had been waiting for…the birth of your brothers…was not a happy one. Sarah would feed the boys, but she could do little else but sleep. Will and I picked up the rest…cooking, cleaning, and trying to be around as much as possible. Helen was there too, and we tried to support your mom, as much as possible." Juliana just stared at Samuel, wondering how all of this was a part of a past that was unknown to her.

Samuel continued, "For months Sarah would not discuss having a funeral. There was no body, and she believed our mother was alive. Finally, at Thanksgiving dinner at your aunt's house, she reluctantly agreed to a memorial service. It was planned for early December, followed by a reception at her sister's home. I am telling you all these details because they are relevant to what happens later. After the service, your mother left shortly after arriving at the house, thus angering your mother's sister and her husband…another story. Your mom stormed out, drove away on icy streets, and Will and I found her back at your grandmother's house. She had crashed the car into the corner of the garage, and she was curled up in the closet in a catatonic state again. This time the threat of the 'shock treatment' and some heavy drugs got her back to some sense of normality."

"This just doesn't sound like my mom. She just always seemed content and happy. No wonder she didn't want to talk about it. It must have been awful for her and for you and my dad," Juliana added, when Samuel paused for a moment.

"It was, but it got better. Helen and I got married, Sarah went back to work part-time. We had the boys quite a bit to give Will and your mom time alone. I think we all felt that we had finally reached some equilibrium. Sarah had experienced terrible nightmares in those first months, but they found some drugs that helped her to sleep. Then, as she was weaning herself off the medications, the nightmares started again. Your dad thought it was because she was asked to go to England on a school trip."

"What would that have to do with it? When was this?" Juliana asked, wanting to push the story ahead to hear what she needed to know—how did her mother get involved with a man named Robert?

"The boys were going to be six that summer. It was 1990, and your dad thought that Sarah wanted to go on the trip and then travel to Scotland, but she wouldn't admit it to herself. She had wanted me to go to find out about what happened, and I never did."

"Why not? Did they ever find out how she died? Weren't you curious?" Juliana demanded answers.

"I don't really know. I had two jobs, I was back in school, I had just met Helen and then there was the pressure of working and graduate school, getting a teaching job, marriage, helping Will with your mother…"

"All right, I get it. You were living your life." Juliana tried to soften her previous attack on her uncle, who was her favourite person in the world.

"There was more to it than that, Juliana. I picked up your grandmother's things from the airport when they were sent back from Scotland. Your mother went with me, and when we unpacked her suitcases, we found the journal. We found a couple of little bibs that our mom had bought for the boys. They said, 'my grandma went to Scotland and all she got me was this bib.' She read that and ran out of the room, wanting nothing to do with any of it. I read the journal that night and started to have some sense of what my mother was going through."

"But the journal doesn't explain how she died, does it? It doesn't say what happened to Mark. Did he come to meet her? What about Alex, the Scottish guy she was seeing? How did you answer those questions?" Juliana asked in a softer tone than previously.

"I knew there was a witness that saw her swept away into the waves. Her purse was found in the car at the top of the cliff. I don't know why, but I somehow felt that she had been caught in that past life she was describing in the journal. I tried to find Mark to let him know about the memorial service but had no luck. I just let it go and your mother didn't forgive me for that, and she couldn't forgive your dad for being away when she needed him. Will and I realised that she was still angry, not only at us but at your grandmother for committing suicide and breaking her promise to be home before the twins were born," Samuel explained, going back in his mind to that painful time.

"I guess she was justified in feeling that, but a counsellor could have helped."

"We tried and she went for a brief time and then rejected it. She said she was fine, and it really seemed like she was, but then your dad told me that she wasn't. Part of her seemed gone, and I think we both wondered if the treatment and the drugs had caused some permanent damage. We didn't talk about it, but we shared some guilt. Your dad insisted that I talk to Sarah about going on the school trip and spending time in Scotland. We countered all her objections, and Will was right that she really wanted to go and needed us to push her in that direction. She still hadn't even looked at the journal, but she wanted to take it with her."

"If only she had recorded what she felt going there like your mother did. I guess I should call her my grandmother, but since I didn't know her and never heard about her, I haven't ever thought much about having a grandmother. Now it seems she is an interesting character and I also have an extra father. It's a bit much to take in, Samuel."

"I know, dear, and there's more. Before I go on, I need to tell you something. When I went to Scotland this spring it was to meet Robert, to determine if he was worthy of you and only reveal your existence if my answer was positive. I had to see him in person to make that determination."

"And you met him, I presume," Juliana stated, now extremely interested in her uncle's opinion.

"I not only met him but also two other people. One was a librarian from Edinburgh named Andrew and the other was a librarian from Minneapolis named Helen." She looked at him with a quizzical expression. "I travelled to Scotland again, as you know. The four of us were working on the family history information together and we all became remarkably close…"

"How close?" she asked, with suspicion in her voice.

"Close enough for me to reveal your identity to Robert and," Sam hesitated, "close enough for me to fall in love."

"With Robert?" Juliana asked with a twinkle in her eye.

"No, with Helen. We flew back on the same flight, and we intend to live together. I need to tell you because she is coming here in a few minutes. We decided she should stay with her sister, and I would be with the family until your mother passed. She knows about the decision to not tell you until the end."

"Another person who knew about this before me. My brothers announce that I am to inherit the house, that I have special travel money to go to Scotland and to take a leave of absence from my job, and you tell me you have been playing house with my alleged father and his friends." Juliana sighed and sank into the chair, with her head in her hands. She looked up. "What more is there that I don't know?"

"When your mother left on her school trip, we weren't even sure she would go to Scotland. Then she came back a couple of weeks later. She was changed. She even came back a couple of days early. She was like the Sarah I grew up with. She was light-hearted and fun. She had energy and then she found out she was pregnant, and she was thrilled. Your dad and I were worried about the possibility of postpartum depression after your birth, but there was none. Whatever happened in Scotland transformed her and ended years of suppressed grief and anger."

"But didn't you want to know what had happened…why she had changed?" Juliana challenged, desperately wanting to know herself.

"Part of me did and part of me was just grateful. I was always a little afraid that the trip and reading the journal would throw her back into a worse state, and when it didn't, I was so relieved. Then she was pregnant, and your dad said that he felt like he had his wife back, the woman he had married. He asked no questions and needed no answers. We concluded that the trip had helped her resolve her despair about your grandmother's death."

"And you never asked?" Juliana queried, frustrated at the lack of information.

"Helen did, one night. Will was out with the boys and your mom had just told us about the pregnancy and how happy they were about it. Helen just came out with it and said, 'What did you find out in Scotland? The trip seems to have made such a difference for you.' That was the only time it came up."

"Well, what was her answer?" Juliana asked, leaning forward again with rapt attention.

"It went something like this, 'I met Alex, and he was the witness to her drowning. He had learned that Mark's sailboat had been lost at sea the day that our mother died. You were right, Sam. She was swept into another life, and we will never be able to explain how that happened, but it did. I want to forget it and get on with life.' And that is exactly what she did, so I didn't bring it up again," Samuel explained.

"So not a word about the man she had an affair with?"

"Not a word about it until a few months ago, when she knew she didn't have much time left. It was a confession and a request, not really an explanation. She said she had something important to tell me and I wasn't to ask questions, just carry out her dying wishes. She told me that while she was in Scotland, she met a man named Robert Hamilton and she had an unfortunate sexual relationship with him. When she learned that she was pregnant, she suspected he might be the father, but didn't really know. After Will died, she had his DNA compared with yours and it was not a match. The man, as far as she knew, had no children. She hadn't spoken to him since the day she left and had no correspondence with him. She gave me the address in Scotland he had lived at twenty-five years earlier and asked me to find out if he was still alive. If so, she wanted me to send him a letter, that she would write, telling him he had a daughter, or I could go to meet him under the pretence of family history."

"She hadn't made any contact for all those years and yet she wanted him to know that he had a daughter. I understand that she didn't want Dad to know, but if she knew four years ago, why not tell me?" Juliana's voice trailed off, as she pondered what was in her mother's mind during all this time.

"As far as I can figure out, it has something to do with the family charts she had in the box. He had agreed to not contact her if Sarah would promise to share the information about our family history with her children. She didn't tell you sooner, because she knew how much you loved your dad, and she was sure you would be angry with her. Once she knew she was likely to die soon, she still wanted to wait until the last minute to tell you. She couldn't bear to lose you in her final hours."

"She really didn't tell me…just said there was a box with some information for me and that you would share a secret she had kept from me all my life. She asked me to forgive her and begged me not to carry any anger or grief about her death, as she had done with her mother's death." Juliana's lip was quivering, a sure sign that the tears would start, but she didn't want to cry now. She wanted to understand what her mom wanted from her and why she should ever meet this man called Robert.

"Tell me how you found him and what happened next," she whispered. The doorbell rang and Sam stood and went to greet Helen. He introduced her to

Juliana and explained where they were in the story. Helen sat quietly beside Sam as he continued.

"He's from a prominent family, and I found him in the Edinburgh phone directory. He was alive and living at the same address. She wrote the letter, sealed it, and asked me to send it. I told her I had decided to contact him, asking about the family history charts, and would meet him in person. I wrote to him and included my contact information, and he invited me to stay with him and meet others working on the history of the Dundas ancestry."

"And that's when you went to Scotland," Juliana declared, "without a word to any of us? What happened next? You are writing to a stranger, he invites you to stay with you, and you meet two other strangers. This sounds like a fairy tale, Uncle Samuel," she said, with the first hint of a smile. "Tell on," she said, looking at Helen.

"After meeting Helen, I confessed my mission to her, and she advised me to be honest with Robert. I had already concluded I would give him the letter. I just didn't know how and when. When he read the letter, he asked if he could visit your mother and I said that she had explicitly told me that she wanted to only be with her immediate family during her final hours. He asked about you and I explained that you were not going to be told until Sarah was dying and then it would be up to you if you wished to meet him. He asked if he could contact you, send money for a ticket to Scotland or do anything else. I assured him I would let him know the answers, as the days progressed. He was very polite, concerned for all of us and anxious to talk with you." Samuel paused, giving Juliana time to take in what he had just disclosed.

"I was there, Juliana, when this happened," Helen added. "I would like to tell you how significant it was for Robert to find out he had a daughter. There was no hesitation in him. He wanted to see you."

"So, you think I should talk to him? What could I have to say to him? I'm interested in the family history. I could fantasise about Scotland, which has always been a place I wanted to visit, but seeing a biological father seems like a betrayal of my dad. Don't you think so, Samuel? Don't you think it would be wrong?" Juliana let the tears finally come. They were tears from years earlier when her dad had died and there were tears from holding her mother's hand for the last time. Now she was also crying for a lost grandmother she had never seen and somewhere inside her there were tears for a man who had never known he had a daughter…a man who had lost twenty-five years of her life.

"Juliana, Will was not only my brother-in-law, he was also my best friend. Thinking back, I believe he knew that something happened to Sarah in Scotland, but he was your father in every way he could be. Loving you as he did, he would take nothing away from your experience of life. He hated leaving you so soon and he would want you to have this other chance at having a father."

"How can you say that? Maybe I can meet Robert, even get to know him, but I will never, ever have another father!"

Trying to lighten the moment, Sam added, "He's a rich man with a manor house in Edinburgh and no other children."

"You're wicked," she said, as she threw a pillow at him and got up to find a tissue to blow her nose. When she sat down again, Juliana made her uncle a proposition. "I'll go to meet him, if you go with me."

"I will consider it. Helen and I would like to return to Scotland, depending on work schedules. We think it would be wonderful to travel with you, but there is one other thing you need to know," Samuel said, in a more serious tone.

"What else? I can hardly handle the last few days now."

"The Alex from the journal, the jewellery store owner from Queensferry, is our Robert Alexander Hamilton."

"What? You mean that my grandmother's lover, Alex, is also my mother's lover, Robert Hamilton! And this is the man that is my father. Oh no, I am not going to meet that man. No, no, no, not ever. Do Matt and Jake know about this?" Juliana asked, still wondering how this could be happening to their family.

"No, not that part. I found the information when I was searching for Robert for your mother. She probably knew I might find out, but I didn't tell her. I waited for her to explain, since she knew that I had read the journal, but she never did. Events were moving so fast, and I didn't want to upset her when she was so ill."

"Better to upset me…to have me learn about what a jerk this man is…a seducer of women."

"Don't you think your grandmother had some responsibility for her relationship with him, and your mother?" Helen speculated.

"Thinking about the journal, I think he must be a very charming man who could easily seduce women. He won't do that to me," Juliana stated. "If I decide to go to Scotland, that is," she added.

"He's over seventy now, Juliana. I think his seducing days are over, but he is very charming," Helen declared.

"And handsome, intelligent and rich," Sam added. "We can talk about travel plans when the memorial service is over and make some decisions."

Helen and Sam looked at each other, knowing Juliana had agreed to see Robert. As they got up from the couch, she came across to them and put out her arms to hug them. As she backed away from the hug, she asked a question.

"I must say that the charts have made me curious about our ancestor, Gospatric. Did you find out anything about him in your research?"

"Yes, we did," they answered in unison.

Appendix

Cast of the Charters

PRESENT TIME – MAJOR FICTIONAL CHARACTERS

HELEN – Librarian from Minneapolis, MN with family history connections to the Dundas Clan in Ireland and Scotland

ANDREW RAMSAY– Librarian at the National Library of Scotland, also connected to the Dundas Clan

ALEXANDER ROBERT HAMILTON – Scottish lord with connections to the Dundas Clan, with a previous relationship to the Mc Carthy family

SAMUEL Mc Carthy – University professor from Minneapolis, MN, brother of Sarah Mueller, son of Mary, and uncle to Luke, Matt and Juliana Mueller

PAST TIME – MAJOR HISTORICAL FIGURES

CRINAN—Lay Abbot of Dunkeld, Father of Duncan I. King of the Scots and Maldred, Lord of Allerdale, Married to Bethoc, daughter of King Malcolm II

MALDRED – Father of Gospatric and Maldred, husband of EADGYTH

EADGYTH (Edith), daughter of UCTRED, who ruled Northumbria until 1018, granddaughter of Athelred II and half-sister to a grandson of Uctred, also Gospatick who died in 1064

GOSPATRIC – Lord of Allerdale, Earl of Northumberland, holder of Dunbar and Lothian under Malcolm III, progenitor of the Dunbar,

Dundas, Hume, Arniston, Ormiston, Melville families, father of DOPHIN, WALTHEOF, ETHELREDA, OCTREDA, GUNHILD, AND GOSPATRIC II

SIWARD – Danish Earl of Northumbria until 1055, father of OSJBORsp, and WALTHEOF, uncle to Malcolm, Gospatric and Maldred, husband of ELFREDA (a granddaughter of UCTRED) and powerful ruler of Northumbria and Bamburgh

WALTHEOF – Young son of Siward and husband of JUDITH, niece of William the Conqueror, Earl of Northampton and later, Earl of Northumbria

MALCOLM III - King of Scots from 1058 to 1093, son of DUNCAN I, father of DUNCAN II and brother of DONALD BANE

MARGARET – Queen of Scots, wife of Malcolm II, mother of six sons and three daughters with King Malcolm.

EDWARD THE CONFESSOR – King of England from to 1066, husband of Edith, a sister to the Godwinson sons.

EDGAR ATHELING – The Anglo-Saxon young man designated to be the heir to the throne of Edward the confessor

THORFINN MAC THORE – Landowner in Cumbria of Nordic descent

HAROLD GODWINSON – Powerful Earl under King Edward, crowned king of England in 1066 and defeated by William the Conqueror that same year

TOSTIG – Younger brother of Harold, named Earl of Northumbria in 1055, banished in 1065

JUDITH OF FLANDERS – Wife of Tostig, niece of Baldwin of Flanders and aunt of Matilda, wife of the Conqueror

WILLIAM THE BASTARD (CONQUEROR) – Duke of Normandy who invades England and crowns himself King William I in 1066

MERLESWEIN – Large owner of English territory including the area around Lincoln

MORCAR – Landowner in England, named Earl of Northumbris in 1065, brother of EDWIN, Earl of Mercia

DOLPHIN – LORD OF CARLISLE, Oldest son of Gospatric and brother to WALTHEOF, ETHELREDA, OCTREDA, GUNHILD, MATILDA and GOSPATRIC II

WALCHER – Bishop of Durham, purchased Northumbria in 1076, killed in 1080

FICTIONAL CHARACTERS OF IMPORTANCE

GUNHILDA – First wife of Gospatric and mother of Dolphin, daughter of Thorfinn.

ATHELREDA – Second wife of Gospatric and mother of remaining children.
Historical relationship to a brother EDMUND, who had land at Edlngham.

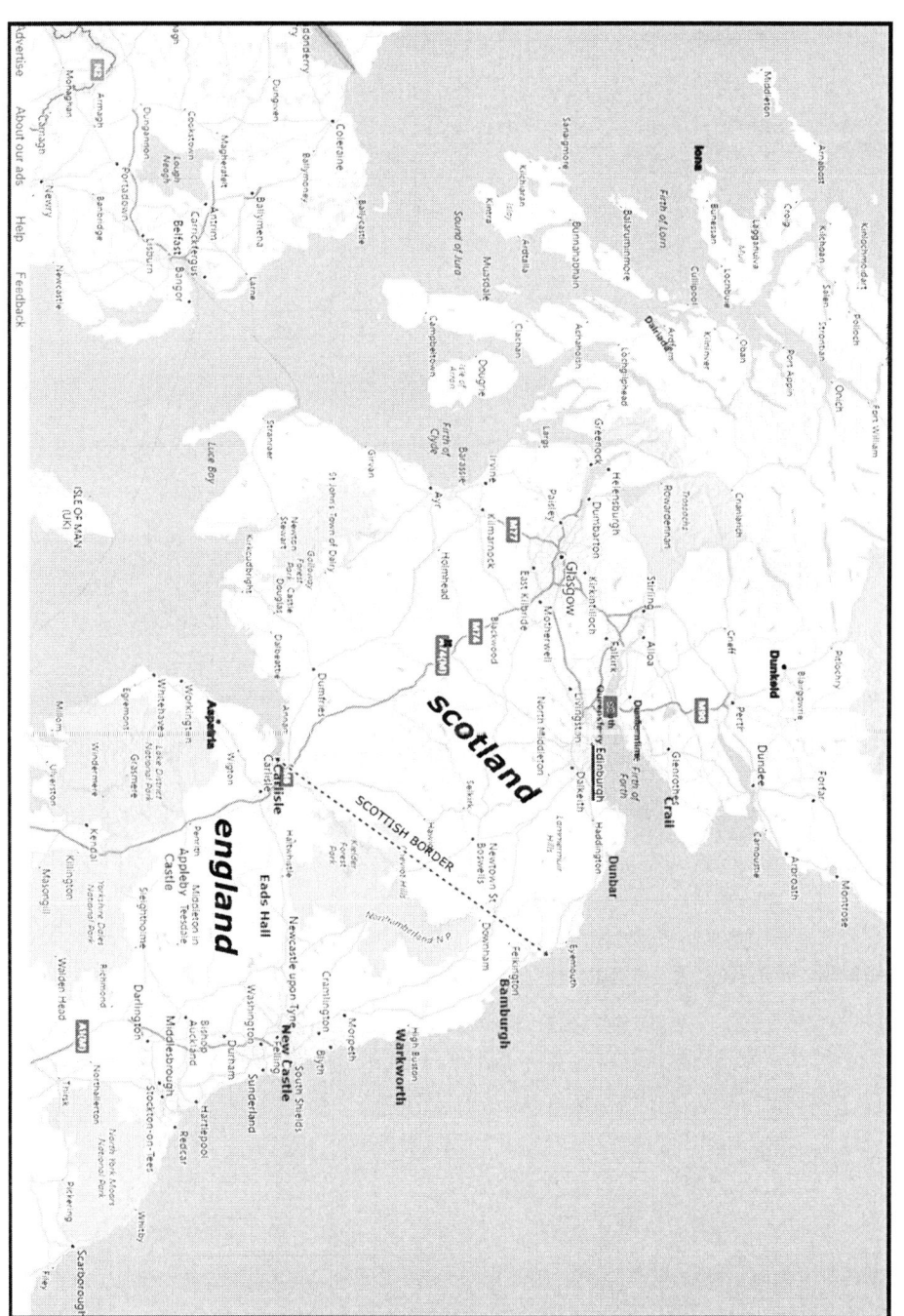

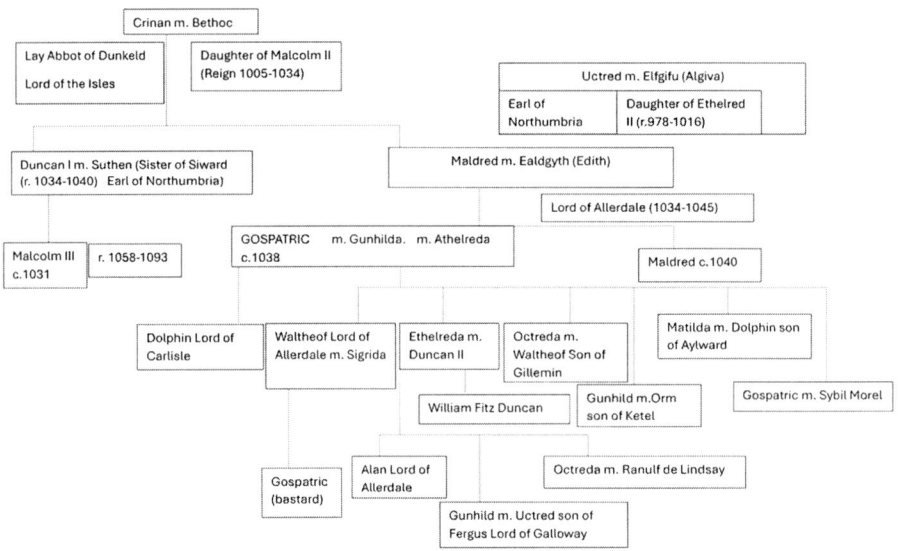

Chart 1 Relationship of GOSPATRIC to King Malcolm III

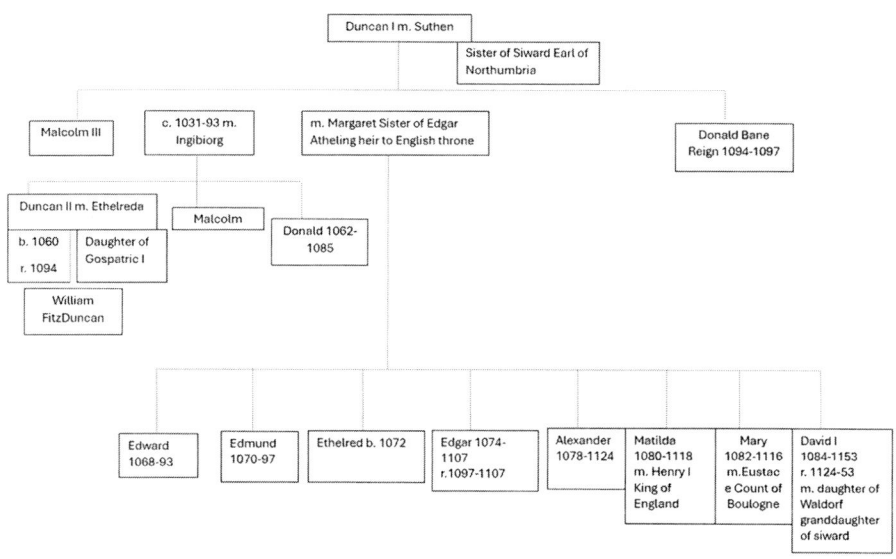

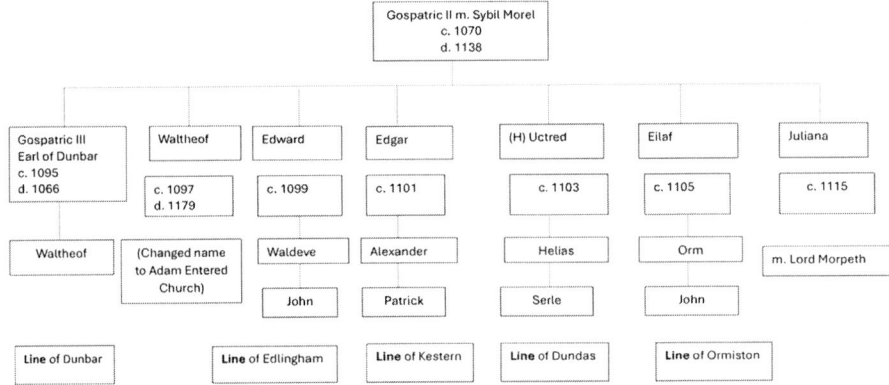

Chart 3

Family of Gospatric II